MISTR
MISTR

Also by E. R. Eddison

MISTRESS OF MISTRESSES

A VISION OF ZIMIAMVIA

by

E. R. Eddison

HarperCollins*Publishers*

HarperCollins*Publishers*
77-85 Fulham Palace Road
Hammersmith, London W6 8JB
www.harpercollins.co.uk

This edition 2014

1

978-0-00-757813-9

Typeset by Palimpsest Book Production Ltd, Falkirk, Stirlingshire

Printed and bound in Great Britain by
Clays Ltd, St Ives plc

MIX
Paper from
responsible sources
FSC™ C007454

Contents

FOREWORD

BY DOUGLAS E. WINTER

'Is this the dream? or was that?'

WORDS create worlds: storytelling is a kind of godhood, taking the imperfect day of language, moulding it in the writer's own image and, with skill, breathing it to life. The task is a formidable one, and it is little wonder that most fiction is content with reinventing reality, safely sculpting what is known. And why not? Stories are for the most part entertainment, ephemeral, meant only for the moment. Few novels strive for life beyond their covers; few hold us in their dominion for years, fewer still for lifetimes. The words and the worlds of E. R. Eddison, which I first discovered more than twenty years ago, still intrigue me, uplift me, haunt me, today. I know that I am not alone.

Eric Rücker Eddison (1882–1945) was a civil servant at the British Board of Trade, sometime Icelandic scholar, devotee of Homer and Sappho, and mountaineer. Although by all accounts a bowler-hatted and proper English gentleman, Eddison was an unmitigated dreamer who, in occasional spare hours over some thirty years, put his dreams to paper. In 1922, just before his fortieth birthday, a small collector's edition of *The Worm Ouroboros* was published; larger printings soon followed in both England and America, and a legend of sorts was born. The book was a dark and blood-red jewel of wonder, equal parts spectacle and fantasia, labyrinthine in its intrigue, outlandish in its violence. It was also Eddison's first novel.

After writing an adventure set in the Viking age, *Styrbiorn the Strong* (1926), and a translation of *Egil's Saga* (1930), Eddison devoted the remainder of his life to the *fantastique* in a series of novels set, for the most part, in Zimiamvia, the fabled paradise of *The Worm Ouroboros*. The Zimiamvian books were, in Eddison's words, 'written backwards', and thus published in reverse chronological order of events: *Mistress of Mistresses* (1935), *A Fish Dinner in Memison* (1941), and *The Mezentian Gate* (1958). (The final book was incomplete when Eddison died, but his notes were so thorough that his brother, Colin Eddison, and his friend George R. Hamilton were able to assemble the book for publication.) Although the books are known today as a trilogy, Eddison wrote them as an open-ended series; they may be read and enjoyed alone or in any sequence. Each is a metaphysical adventure, an intricate Chinese puzzle box whose twists and turns reveal ever-encircling vistas of delight and dread.

Eddison's four great fantasies are linked by the enigmatic character of Edward Lessingham – country gentleman, soldier, statesman, artist, writer, and lover, among other talents – and his Munchausen-like adventures in space . . . and time. Although he disappears after the early pages of *The Worm Ouroboros*, Lessingham is central to the books that follow. 'God knows,' he tells us, 'I have dreamed and waked and dreamed till I know not well which is dream and which is true.' One of the pleasures of reading Eddison is that we, too, are never certain. Perhaps Lessingham is a man of our world; perhaps he is a god; perhaps he is only a dream . . . or a dream within a dream. And perhaps, just perhaps, he is all of these things, and more.

In a transcendent moment of *The Worm Ouroboros*, the Demonlords Juss and Brandoch Daha, searching desperately for their lost comrade-in-arms, Goldry Bluzco, ascend to the dizzying heights of Koshtra Pivrarcha. There, in the distance, they see paradise. Lord Juss speaks:

'Thou and I, first of the children of men, now behold with living eyes the fabled land of Zimiamvia. Is that true, thinkest thou, which philosophers tell of that fortunate land: that no mortal foot may tread it, but the blessed souls do inhabit it of the dead that be departed, even they that were great upon earth and did great deeds when they were living, that scorned not earth and the delights and the glories thereof, and yet did justly and were not dastards nor yet oppressors?'

'Who knoweth?' answers Brandoch Daha. 'Who shall say he knoweth?'

If anyone knows, it is Edward Lessingham. In the Overture to *Mistress of Mistresses,* we learn that old age has claimed him, his final hours watched over by a mysterious lover. Lord Juss's question is repeated, and the reader – like Lessingham – is taken straightaway to Zimiamvia. This is neither the biblical paradise, nor that of classical mythology, but a mad poet's dream of Northern Europe during the Renaissance. Zimiamvia is an imperfect heaven – what other kind could exist without boredom for its residents? – a Machiavellian playground for men and gods, where mystery and menace, romance and revenge, swordplay and soldiering are the natural order of things.

Three kingdoms comprise this otherworld – known, from north to south, as Fingiswold, Rerek and Meszria – and all are ruled by the wise, firm hand of King Mezentius. In Zimiamvia, Lessingham lives on, his earthly self a duality. His namesake, Lord of Rerek, is his Apollonian half – the embodiment of reason, logic, science. Lord Lessingham is cut from the same cloth as the Demon heroes of *The Worm Ouroboros,* a demigod and bravo, a man of action and of honour with but a single stain: kinship, and thus loyalty in blood, to Horius Parry, the ambitious Vicar in Rerek. Parry, in turn, is the scheming serpent of this enigmatic Eden, a villain extraordinaire whose instinct for treachery and terror – and for surviving to scheme again another day – is worthy of the most diabolical of devils.

Lessingham's Dionysian qualities – magic, art, and madness

– are found in Duke Barganax, bastard son of King Mezentius and his mistress Amalie, the Duchess of Memison. Barganax takes counsel in the aged yet ageless Doctor Vandermast, a mysterious Merlin who is given to spouting Spinoza and minding his lovely shapeshifting nymphs, Anthea and Campaspe. 'My study,' says Vandermast [in *A Fish Dinner in Memison*], 'is now of the darkness rather which is hid in the secret heart of man: my office but only to understand, and to watch, and to wait.'

With the deaths of King Mezentius and his only legitimate son, Styllis – in which Parry's perpetually bloody hand is suspect – the crown descends to the beautiful and doomed Queen Antiope, with whom, inevitably, Lord Lessingham will fall in love. The struggle for power, by wile and war and witchery, enwraps Zimiamvia in a web of passion and violence that is tangled by strange shifts of time.

'Time,' Eddison tells us, 'is a curious business', and in Zimiamvia it grows more and more curious. 'Is this the dream?' his characters ask, 'or was that?' [*A Fish Dinner in Memison*]. These tales are not simply written backwards, they defy most novelistic notions of time. Eddison was exceptional in his embrace of the *fantastique*; in his fiction there are no logical imperatives, no concessions to cause and effect, only the elegant truths of the higher calling of myth. Characters traverse distances and decades in the blink of an eye; worlds take shape, spawn life, evolve through billions of years and are destroyed, all during a dinner of fish. These are dreams made flesh by a dreamer *extraordinaire*.

Ten years: ten million years: ten minutes. One and the same, says Eddison, and in Zimiamvia we journey beyond the pure heroic adventure of *The Worm Ouroboros* into an existential-romantic quest, a speculation on the nature of woman and man, Goddess and God, reality and dream: 'It was in that moment as if he looked through layer upon layer of dream, as though veil behind veil: the thinnest veil, natural present: the next, as if a dumb-show strangely presented by art magic' [*Mistress of Mistresses*]. Eddison's characters exist beyond time, beyond dimension, woven into a tapestry that circles and circles on itself, as abiding and eternal as its central image: the worm Ouroboros, that eateth its own tail.

'If we were Gods, able to make worlds and unmake 'em as we list, what world would we have?' [*A Fish Dinner in Memison*]. Here is the central dilemma of *Zimiamvia*: the nature and means of creation. Worlds within worlds, stories within stories, characters within characters, phantasms within phantasms – this is a majestic maze of mythmaking, a fiction that questions all assumptions of reality. Eddison thus proves more than a dreamer; like the very best writers of the *fantastique,* he saw this fiction of (im)possibilities as the truest mirror of our lives, one that shines back brightly the depths of the human spirit as well as the surfaces of the flesh.

Eddison's prose is archaic and often difficult, an intentionally affected throwback to Elizabethan and Jacobean drama. His characters are thus eloquent but long-winded; they speak not of killing a man, but of 'sending him from the shade into the house of darkness' [*The Worm Ouroboros*]. In his finest moments, Eddison ascends to a sustained poetic beauty; listen, for example, to the haunting premonition of the renegade Goblin Gro:

> 'For as I lay sleeping betwixt the strokes of night, a dream of the night stood by my bed and beheld me with a glance so fell that I was all adrad and quaking with fear. And it seemed to me that the dream smote the roof above my bed, and the roof opened and disclosed the outer dark, and in the dark travelled a bearded star, and the night was quick with fiery signs. And blood was on the roof, and great gouts of blood on the walls and on the cornice of my bed. And the dream screeched like the screech-owl, and cried, *Witchland from thy hand, O King!*' [*The Worm Ouroboros*]

At other times the reader is virtually overwhelmed with words. Palaces and armoury were Eddison's particular vices; he describes them with such ornate grandeur that page after page is lavished with their decoration. The reader should not be deterred by the density of such passages; like a vintage wine, a taste for Eddison's prose is expensively acquired, demanding the reader's patience and perseverance – and it is worthy of its price. These are books to be savoured, best read in the long dark hours of night, when the wind is against the windows and the shadows begin to walk – books not meant for the moment, but for forever.

The Zimiamvian trilogy inevitably has been compared with J. R. R. Tolkien's *Lord of the Rings,* but apart from their narrative ambition and epic sweep, the books share little in common. (Eddison, like Tolkien, disclaimed the notion that he was writing something beyond mere story: 'It is neither allegory nor fable but a Story to be read for its own sake' [*The Worm Ouroboros*' preface]. But as the reader will no doubt observe, he proves much less convincing.)

If comparisons are in order, then I suggest Eddison's obvious influences – Homer and the Icelandic sagas – and that most controversial of Jacobean dramatists, John Webster, whose blood-spattered tales of violence and chaos (from which Eddison's characters quote freely) saw him chastised for subverting orthodox society and religion. The shadow of Eddison may be seen, in turn, not only in the modern fiction of heroic fantasy, but also in the writings of his truest descendants, such dreamers of the dark *fantastique* as Stephen King (whose own epics, *The Stand* and *The Dark Tower,* read like paeans to Eddison) and Clive Barker (whose *The Great and Secret Show* called its chaotic forces the *Iad Ouroboros*).

Eddison would have found this line of succession, like the cyclical popularity of his books, the most natural order of events: the circle, ever turning – like the worm Ouroboros, that eateth its own tail – the symbol of eternity, where 'the end is ever at the beginning and the beginning at the end for ever more'.

Welcome to that fabled paradise, Zimiamvia: Once you have entered these words, this world, you may never leave.

DOUGLAS E. WINTER
1991
in memory of Phil Grossfield

WINIFRED GRACE EDDISON
To you, madonna mia,
and to my friend
EDWARD ABBE NILES
I dedicate this
Vision of Zimiamvia

Proper Names the reader will no doubt pronounce as he chooses. But perhaps, to please me, he will keep the *i*'s short in *Zimiamvia* and accent the third syllable: accent the second syllable in *Zayana*, give it a broad *a* (as in 'Guiana'), and pronouce the *ay* in the first syllable – and the *ai* in *Laimak* – as in 'aisle': keep the *g* soft in *Fingiswold*: let *Memison* echo 'denizen' except for the *m*: accent the first syllable in *Rerek* and make it rhyme with 'year': remember that *Fiorinda* is an Italian name, *Amaury, Amalie,* and *Beroald* French, and *Antiope, Zenianthe,* and a good many others, Greek: last, regard the *sz* in *Meszria* as ornamental, and not be deterred from pronouncing it as plain 'Mezria'.

Mère des souvenirs, maîtresse des maîtresses,
O toi, tous mes plaisrs! ô toi, tous mes devoirs!
Tu te rappelleras la beauté des caresses,
La douceur du foyer et le charme des soirs,
Mère des souvenirs, maîtresse des maîtresses!

Les soirs illuminés par l'ardeur du charbon,
Et les soirs au balcon, voilés de vapeurs roses.
Que ton sein m'était doux! que ton cœur m'était bon!
Nous avons dit souvent d'impérissables choses
Les soirs illuminés par l'ardeur du charbon.

Que les soleils sont beaux dans les chaudes soirées!
Que l'espace est profond! que le cœur est puissant!
En me penchant vers toi, reine des adorées,
Je croyais respirer le parfum de ton sang.
Que les soleils sont beaux dans les chaudes soirées!

La nuit s'épaississait ainsi qu'une cloison,
Et mes yeux dans le noir devinaient tes prunelles,
Et je buvais ton souffle, ô douceur, ô poison!
Et tes pieds s'endormaient dans mes mains fraternelles.
La nuit s'épaississait ainsi qu'une cloison.

Je sais l'art d'évoquer les minutes heureuses,
Et revis mon passé blotti dans tes genoux.
Car à quoi bon chercher tes beautés langoureuses
Ailleurs qu'en ton cher corps et qu'en ton cœur si doux?
Je sais l'art d'évoquer les minutes heureuses!

Ces serments, ces parfums, ces baisers infinis,
Renaîtront-ils d'un gouffre interdit à nos sondes,
Comme montent au ciel les soleils rajeunis
Après s'être lavés au fond des mers profondes?
– O serments! ô parfums! ô baisers infinis!

BAUDELAIRE

THE OVERTURE

LET me gather my thoughts a little, sitting here alone with you for the last time, in this high western window of your castle that you built so many years ago, to overhang like a sea eagle's eyrie the grey-walled waters of your Raftsund. We are fortunate, that this should have come about in the season of high summer, rather than on some troll-ridden night in the Arctic winter. At least, I am fortunate. For there is peace in these Arctic July nights, where the long sunset scarcely stoops beneath the horizon to kiss awake the long dawn. And on me, sitting in the deep embrasure upon your cushions of cloth of gold and your rugs of Samarkand that break the chill of the granite, something sheds peace, as those great sulphur-coloured lilies in your Ming vase shed their scent on the air. Peace; and power; indoors and out: the peace of the glassy surface of the sound with its strange midnight glory as of pale molten latoun or orichalc; and the peace of the waning moon unnaturally risen, large and pink-coloured, in the midst of the confused region betwixt sunset and sunrise, above the low slate-hued cloud-bank that fills the narrows far up the sound a little east of north, where the Trangstrómmen runs deep and still between mountain and shadowing mountain. That for power: and the Troldtinder, rearing their bare cliffs sheer from the further brink; and, away to the left of them, like pictures I have seen of your Ushba in the Caucasus, the tremendous two-eared Rulten, lifted up against the afterglow above a score of lesser spires and bastions: Rulten, that kept you and me hard at work for nineteen hours, climbing his paltry three thousand feet. Lord! And that was twenty-five years ago, when you were about the age I am today, an old man, by common reckoning; yet it taxed not me only in my prime but your own Swiss guides, to keep pace with you. The mountains; the unplumbed deeps of the Raftsund and its swinging tideways; the unearthly darkless Arctic summer night; and indoors, under the mingling of natural and artificial lights, of sunset and the windy candlelight of your seven-branched candlesticks of gold, the peace and the power of your face.

Your great Italian clock measures the silence with its ticking: 'Another, gone! Another, gone! Another, gone!' Commonly, I have grown to hate such tickings, hideous to an old man as the grinning *memento mori* at the feast. But now (perhaps the shock has deadened my feelings), I could almost cheat reason to believe there was in very truth eternity in these things: substance and everlasting life in what is more transient and unsubstantial than a mayfly, empirical, vainer than air, weak bubbles on the flux. You and your lordship here, I mean, and this castle of yours, more fantastic than Beckford's Fonthill, and all your life that has vanished into the irrevocable past: a kind of nothingness. 'Another, gone! Another, gone!' Seconds, or years, or aeons of unnumbered time, what does it matter? I can well think that this hour just past of my sitting here in this silent room is as long a time, or as short, as those twenty-five years that have gone by since you and I first, on a night like this, stared at Lofotveggen across thirty miles of sea, as we rounded the Landegode and steered north into the open Westfirth.

I can see you now, if I shut my eyes; in memory I see you,

staring at the Lynxfoot Wall: your kingdom to be, as I very well know you then resolved (and soon performed your resolve): that hundred miles of ridge and peak and precipice, of mountains of Alpine stature and seeming, but sunk to the neck in the Atlantic stream and so turned to islands of an unwonted fierceness, close set, so that seen from afar no breach appears nor sea-way betwixt them. So sharp cut was their outline that night, and so unimaginably nicked and jagged, against the rosy radiance to the north which was sunset and sunrise in one, that for the moment they seemed feigned mountains cut out of smoky crystal and set up against a painted sky. For a moment only; for there was the talking of the waves under our bows, and the wind in our faces, and, as time went by with still that unaltering scene before us, every now and again the flight and wild cry of a black-backed gull, to remind us that this was salt sea and open air and land ahead. And yet it was hard then to conceive that here was real land, with the common things of life and houses of men, under that bower of light where the mutations of night and day seemed to have been miraculously slowed down; as if nature had fallen entranced with her own beauty mirrored in that sheen of primrose light. Vividly, as it had been but a minute since instead of a quarter of a century, I see you standing beside me at the taffrail, with that light upon your lean and weather-beaten face, staring north with a proud, alert, and piercing look, the whole frame and posture of you alive with action and resolution and command. And I can hear the very accent of your voice in the only two things you said in all that four hours' crossing: first, 'The sea-board of Demonland.' Then, an hour later, I should think, very low and dream-like, 'This is the first sip of Eternity.'

Your voice, that all these years, forty-eight years and a month or two, since first I knew you, has had power over me as has no other thing on earth, I think. And today – But why talk of today? Either today is not, or you are not: I am not very certain which. Yesterday certainly was yours, and those five and twenty years in which you, by your genius and your riches, made of these islands a brighter Hellas. But today: it is as well, perhaps, that you have nothing to do with today. The fourteenth of July tomorrow: the date when the ultimatum expires, which this new government at Oslo sent you; the date they mean to take back their sovereign rights over Lofoten in order to reintroduce modern methods into the fisheries. I know you were prepared to use force. It may come to that yet, for your subjects who have grown up in the islands under the conditions you made for them may not give up all without a stroke. But it could only have been a catastrophe. You had not the means here to do as you did thirty-five years ago, when you conquered Paraguay: you could never have held, with your few thousand men, this bunch of islands against an industrialized country like Norway. Stir's, 'Shall the earth-lice be my bane, the sons of Grim Kogur?' They would have bombed your castle from the air.

And so, I think fate has been good to you. I am glad you died this morning.

I must have been deep in my thoughts and memories when the Señorita came into the room, for I had heard no rustle or footfall. Now, however, I turned from my window-gazing to look again on the face of Lessingham where he lay in state, and I saw that she was standing there at his feet, looking where I looked, very quiet and still. She had not noticed me, or, if she had, made no account of my presence. My nerves must have been shaken by the events of the day more than I could before have believed possible: in no other way can I explain the trembling that came upon me as I watched her, and the sudden tears that half blinded my eyes. For though, no doubt, the feelings can play strange tricks in moments of crisis, and easily confound that nice order which breeding and the common proprieties impose even on our inward thoughts, it is yet notable that the perturbation that now swept my whole mind and body was without any single note or touch of those chords which can thrill so loudly at the approach of a woman of exquisite beauty and presumed accessibility. Tears of my own I had not experienced since my nursery days. Indeed, it is only by going back to nursery days that I can recall anything remotely

comparable to the emotion with which I was at that moment rapt
and held. And both then as a child, and now half-way down the
sixties: then, as I listened on a summer's evening in the drawing-
room to my eldest sister singing at the piano what I learned to
know later as Schubert's *Wohin?*, and now, as I saw the Señorita
Aspasia del Rio Amargo stand over my friend's death-bed, there
was neither fear in the trembling that seized me and made my
body all gooseflesh, nor was it tears of grief that started in my
eyes. A moment before, it is true, my mind had been feeling its
way through many darknesses, while the heaviness of a great
unhappiness at long friendship gone like a blown-out candleflame
clogged my thoughts. But now I was as if caught by the throat
and held in a state of intense awareness: a state of mind that I
can find no name for, unless to call it a state of complete purity,
as of awaking suddenly in the morning of time and beholding the
world new born.

For a good many minutes, I think, I remained perfectly still,
except for my quickened breathing and the shifting of my eyes
from this part to that of the picture that was burning itself into
my senses so that, I am very certain, all memories and images will
fall off from me before this will suffer alteration or grow dim.
Then, unsurprised as one hears in a dream, I heard a voice (that
was my own voice) repeating softly that stanza in Swinburne's
great lamentable *Ballad of Death*:

> By night there stood over against my bed
> Queen Venus with a hood striped gold and black,
> Both sides drawn fully back
> From brows wherein the sad blood failed of red,
> And temples drained of purple and full of death.
> Her curled hair had the wave of sea-water
> And the sea's gold in it.
> Her eyes were as a dove's that sickeneth.
> Strewn dust of gold she had shed over her,
> And pearl and purple and amber on her feet.

With the last cadence I was startled awake to common things, as often, startling out of sleep, you hear words spoken in a dream echo loud beyond nature in your ears. I rose, inwardly angry with myself, with some conventional apology on the tip of my tongue, but I bit it back in time. The verses had been spoken not with my tongue but in my brain, I thought; for the look on her face assured me that she had heard nothing, or, if she had, passed it by as some remark which demanded neither comment on her part nor any explanation or apology on mine.

She moved a little so as to face me, her left hand hanging quiet and graceful at her side, her right resting gently on the brow of the great golden hippogriff that made the near bedpost at the foot of Lessingham's bed. With the motion I seemed to be held once again in that contemplation of peace and power from which I had these hours past taken some comfort, and at the same time to be rapt again into that state of wide-eyed awareness in which I had a few minutes since gazed upon her and Lessingham. But now, just as (they tell us) a star of earthly density but of the size of Betelgeuze would of necessity draw to it not matter and star-dust only but the very rays of imponderable light, and suck in and swallow at last the very boundaries of space into itself, so all things condensed in her as to a point. And when she spoke, I had an odd feeling as if peace itself had spoken.

She said: 'Is there anything new you can tell me about death, sir? Lessingham told me you are a philosopher.'

'All I could tell you is new, Doña Aspasia,' I answered; 'for death is like birth: it is new every time.'

'Does it matter, do you suppose?' Her voice, low, smooth, luxurious (as in Spanish women it should be, to fit their beauty, yet rarely is), seemed to balance on the air like a soaring bird that tilts an almost motionless wing now this way now that, and so soars on.

'It matters to me,' I said. 'And I suppose to you.'

She said a strange thing: 'Not to me. I have no self.' Then, 'You,' she said, 'are not one of those quibbling cheap-jacks, I think, who hold out to poor mankind hopes of some metaphysical perduration (great Caesar used to stop a bung-hole) in exchange for that immortality of persons which you have whittled away to the barest improbability?'

'No,' answered I. 'Because there is no wine, it is better go thirsty than lap sea-water.'

'And the wine is past praying for? You are sure?'

'We are sure of nothing. Every path in the maze brings you back at last to Herakleitos if you follow it fairly; yes, and beyond him: back to that philosopher who rebuked him for saying that no man may bathe twice in the same river, objecting that it was too gross an assumption to imply that he might avail to bathe once.'

'Then what is this new thing you are to tell me?'

'This,' said I: 'that I have lost a man who for forty years was my friend, and a man great and peerless in his generation. And that is death beyond common deaths.'

'Then I see that in one river you have bathed not twice but many times,' she said. 'But I very well know that that is no answer.'

She fell silent, looking me steadfastly in the eye. Her eyes with their great black lashes were unlike any eyes that I have ever seen, and went strangely with her dark southern colouring and her jet-black hair: they were green, with enormous pupils, and full of fiery specks, and as the pupils dilated or narrowed the whole orbs seemed aglow with a lambent flame. Frightening eyes at the first unearthly glance of them: so much so, that I thought for an instant of old wild tales of lamias and vampires, and so of that loveliest of all love-stories and sweet ironic gospel of pagan love – Théophile Gautier's: of her on whose unhallowed gravestone was written:

> Ici gît Clarimonde,
> Qui jut de son vivant
> La plus belle du monde.

And then in an instant my leaping thoughts were stilled, and in awed wonderment I recognized, deep down in those strange burning eyes, sixty years in the past, my mother's very look as she (beautiful then, but now many years dead) bent down to kiss her child good night.

The clock chiming the half hour before midnight brought back time again. She on the chime passed by me, as in a dream, and took my place in the embrasure; so that sitting at her feet I saw her side-face silhouetted against the twilight window, where the darkest hour still put on but such semblance of the true cloak of night as the dewdrops on a red rose might wear beside true tears of sorrow, or the faint memory of a long forgotten grief beside the bitterness of the passion itself. Peace distilled upon my mind like perfume from a flower. I looked across to Lessingham's face with its Grecian profile, pallid under the flickering candles, facing upwards: the hair, short, wavy, and thick, like a Greek God's: the ambrosial darknesses of his great black beard. He was ninety years old this year, and his hair was as black and (till a few hours ago, when he leaned back in his chair and was suddenly dead) his voice as resonant and his eyes as bright as a man's in his prime age.

The silence opened like a lily, and the Señorita's words came like the lily's fragrance: 'Tell me something that you remember. It is good to keep memories green.'

'I remember,' answered I, 'that he and I first met by candlelight. And that was forty-eight years ago. A good light to meet by; and a good light for parting.'

'Tell me,' she said.

'It was Easter time at Mardale Green in Cumberland. I had just left school. I was spending the holidays with an aunt of mine who had a big house in the Eamont valley. On Easter Sunday after a hard day by myself on the fells, I found myself looking down on Mardale and Haweswater from the top of Kidsty Pike. It was late afternoon, and the nights still closed in early. There was leavings of snow on the tops. Beneath my feet the valley was obscure purple, the shadows of night boiling up from below while weak daylight still walked the upper air and the mountain ridges. I ran down the long spur that Kidsty Pike sends down eastwards, dividing Randale from Riggindale. I was out of breath, and half deaf too after the quick descent, for I had come down about fifteen hundred feet, I suppose, in twelve minutes by the time I came to cross the beck by the farmhouse at Riggindale. Then I saw the light in the church windows through the trees. I remembered that Haweswater and all its belongings were condemned to be drowned twenty feet deep in water in order that some hive of civilization might be washed, and I thought I would go in to evening service in that little church now while I might, before there were fishes in its yew-trees instead of owls. So I stumbled my way from the gathering dusk of the quiet lane through the darkness of those tremendous yews, and so by the curtained doorway under the square tower into that tiny church. I loved it at first sight, coming in from the cold and darkness outside: a place of warmth and gentle candles, with its pews of oak blackened with age, its little Jacobaean gallery, its rough whitewashed walls, simple pointed windows, low dark roof-beams: a glamorous and dazzling loveliness such as a child's eyes feed upon in its first Christmas tree. As I found my way to a seat half-way up the aisle on the north side, I remember thinking of those little earthenware houses, white, green, and pink, that you can put a night-light inside; things I had forgotten for years, but I had one (as I remembered) long ago, in those lavender and musk-smelling days of childhood, which seemed far more distant to me then, when I was nineteen, than they do now; German things, I fancy: born of the old good German spirit of Struwwelpeter and Christmas trees. Yes, it was those little earthenware houses that I thought of as I sat there, sensuously loving the candlelight and the moving shadows it threw: safe shadows, like those there used to be in the nursery when your nurse was still there; not the ghostly shadows that threatened and hovered when she had gone down to supper and you were left alone. And these shadows and the yellow glamour of the candles fell on kind safe faces, like hers: an old farmer with furrowed, strong, big-boned, storm-weathered features, not in his Sunday-go-to-meeting suit, but with heavy boots nailed and plastered with mud, as if he had walked a good distance to church, and rough strong tweed coat and breeches. Three or four farmers, a few farm men, a few women and girls, an old woman, a boy or two, one or two folk in the little gallery above the door: that was all the congregation. But what pleased me most of all was the old parson, and his way of conducting the service. He was white-haired, with a bristly moustache. He did everything himself single-handed: said the prayers, read the lessons, collected the offertory, played the harmonium that did duty for an organ, preached the sermon. And all these things he did methodically and without hurry or self-consciousness, as you might imagine him looking after a roomful of friends at supper in the little rectory across the road. His sermon was short and full of personalities, but all kindly and gentle-humoured. His announcements of times of services, appointments for weddings, christenings and what not, were interspersed with detailed and homely explanations, given not in the least *ex cathedra* but as if across the breakfast-table. One particularly I remember, when he gave out: "Hymn number one hundred and forty: the one hundred and fortieth hymn: *Jesus lives! No longer now Can thy terrors, death, appal us.*" Then, before sitting down to the harmonium, he looked very benevolently at his little flock over the tops of his spectacles, and said, "I want everybody to try and get the words right. Some people make a mistake about the first line of this hymn, and give it quite a wrong meaning. Remember to pause after 'lives': 'Jesus lives!' Don't do like some people do, and say 'Jesus lives no longer now': that is quite wrong: gives quite a wrong meaning: it makes nonsense. Now then: 'Jesus lives! No longer now';" and he sat down to the harmonium and began.

'It was just at that moment, as we all stood up to sing that innocent hymn with its difficult first line, that I first saw Lessingham. He was away to my right, at the back on the south side, and as the congregation rose I looked half round and saw him. I remember, years later, his describing to me the effect of the sudden view you get of Nanga Parbat from one of those Kashmir valleys; you have been riding for hours among quiet richly wooded scenery, winding up along the side of some kind of gorge, with nothing very big to look at, just lush, leafy, pussy-cat country of steep hillsides and waterfalls; then suddenly you come round a corner where the view opens up the valley, and you are almost struck senseless by the blinding splendour of that vast face of ice-hung precipices and soaring ridges, sixteen thousand feet from top to toe, filling a whole quarter of the heavens at a distance of, I suppose, only a dozen miles. And now, whenever I call to mind my first sight of Lessingham in that little daleside church so many years ago, I think of Nanga Parbat. He stood half a head taller than the tallest man there, but it was the grandeur of his bearing that held me, as if he had been some great lord of the renaissance: a grandeur which seemed to sit upon every limb and feature of him with as much fitness, and to be carried with as little regard or notice from himself, as the scrubby old Norfolk jacket and breeches in which he was dressed. His jacket was threadbare, frayed at the cuffs, strapped with leather at the elbows, but it was as if lighted from within, as the flame shows in a horn lantern, with a sense of those sculptured heroes from the Parthenon. I saw the beauty of his hand where it rested on the window-sill, and the ruby burning like a coal in the strange ring he wore on the middle finger. But just as, in a snow mountain, all sublimities soar upwards to the great peak in the empyrean, so in him was all this majesty and beauty and strength gathered at last in the head and face; that serene forehead, those features where Apollo and Ares seemed to mingle, the strong luxurious lines of the mouth showing between the upcurled moustache and the cataract of black beard: that mouth whose corners seemed the lurking-places of all wild sudden gleams, of delightful humour, and melancholy, and swift resolution, and terrible anger. At length his unconscious eyes met mine, and, looking through me as lost in a deep sadness, made me turn away in some confusion.

'I thought he had been quite unaware of me and my staring; but as we came out into the lane when church was over (it was starlight now, and the moon risen behind the hills) he overtook me and fell into step beside me, saying he noticed that we wore the same tie. I hardly know which was to me the more astonishing, that this man should deign to talk to me at all, or that I should find myself within five minutes swinging along beside him down the lake road, which was my way home, and talking as easily as if it had been to an intimate friend of my own age instead of a

man old enough to be my father: a man too who, to all outward
seeming, would have been more in his element in the company
of Cesare Borgia or Gonsalvo di Cordova. It was not, of course,
till some time after this that I knew he traced his descent through
many generations of English forefathers to King Eric Bloodaxe
in York, the son of Harald Hairfair, that Charlemagne of the
north, and, by the female line, from the greatest ruler of men that
appeared in Europe in the thousand years between Charlemagne
and Napoleon: the Emperor Frederick II, of whom it has been
written that "the power, which in the rout of able and illustrious
men shines through crannies, in him pours out as through a rift
in nature". In after years I helped Lessingham a good deal in
collecting material for his ten-volume *History of Frederick II*,
which is of course today the standard authority on that period,
and ranks, as literature, far and away above any other history
book since Gibbon.

'We talked at first about Eton; then about rowing, and riding,
and then about mountains, for I was at that time newly bitten
with the climbing-madness and I found him an old hand at the
game, though it was not for a year or so that I discovered that
he was among the best (though incomparably the rashest) of
contemporary climbers. I do not think we touched on the then
recent War, in which he attained great distinction, mainly in East
Africa. At length the wings of our talk began to take those wider
sweeps which starlight and steady walking and that aptness of
mind to mind which is the basis of all true friendship lead to; so
that after a while I found myself telling him how much his presence had surprised me in that little church, and actually asking
him whether he was there to pray, like the other people, or only
to look on, like me. Those were the salad-days of my irreligious
fervour, when the strange *amor mortis* of adolescence binds a
panache of glory on the helmet of every unbelief, and when books
like *La Révolte des Anges* or Swinburne's *Dolores* send a thrill
down the spine that can never be caught again in its pristine vigour
when years and wisdom have taught us the true terrors of that
drab, comfortless, and inglorious sinking into not-being which

awaits us all at last. He answered he was there to pray. This I had
not expected, though I had been puzzled at the expression on his
face in church: an expression that I thought sat oddly on the face
of a pagan God or an atheistical tyrant of the renaissance. I
mumbled some awkwardness about his not looking to me much
like a churchman. His laughter at this seemed to set the whole
night a-sparkle: he stopped, caught me by the shoulder with one
hand and spun me round to face him. His mouth was smiling
down at me in the moonlight in a way which made me think of
Pater's essay about Mona Lisa. He said nothing, but I felt as if I
and my half-fledged impieties shrank under that smile to something
very naked and nerveless: a very immature Kapaneus posturing
before Thebes; a ridiculous little Aias waving a toy sword against
the lightning. We walked on beside the dark lake. He said nothing,
neither did I. So completely had he already bound me to his
chariot-wheels that I was ready, if he had informed me that he
was Anabaptist or Turk, to embrace that sect. At length he spoke,
words that for some reason I have never forgotten: "No doubt",
he said, "we were both in that little place for the same reason.
The good, the true, the beautiful: within that triangle (or rather,
upon that point; for 'truth' is but to say that beauty and goodness
are the ultimate reality; and goodness is servant to beauty), are
not the Gods protean?" Rank bad philosophy, as I soon learned
when I had made some progress in metaphysics. And yet it was
out of such marsh-fires that he built up in secret places of his
mind (as, from time to time in our long friendship, I have from
fleeting revelations and rare partial confidences discovered), a
palace of pleasure or house of heart's desire, a creed, a myth,
a fabric of pure poetry, more solid in its specifications and more
concrete in its strange glorious fictions and vanities beyond opium
or madness than this world is, and this life that we call real. And
more than that, for he moulded life to his dreams; and, besides
his poems and writings "more lasting than brass", his paintings
and sculptures that are scrambled for by the picture-galleries of
Europe, and those other (perhaps the most astounding) monuments
of his genius, the communities of men who have felt the iron and

yet beneficent might of his statecraft, as here in Lofoten – besides all these things, I know very well that he found in this Illusion of Illusions a something potent as the fabled unction of the Styx, so that no earthly loss, pain, or grief, could touch him.

'It was not until after many years of friendship that I got some inkling of the full power of this consolation; for he never wore his heart for daws to peck at. The bare facts I was soon informed of: his marriage, when he was not yet twenty-six, and she barely twenty, to the beautiful and brilliant Lady Mary Scarnside, and her death fifteen years later in a French railway accident along with their only child, a girl. This tragedy took place about two years before our meeting in Mardale church. Lessingham never talked of his wife. I learned that he had, soon after her death, deliberately burnt down their lovely old house in Wastdale. I never saw her portrait: several, from his own brush, were destroyed in the fire; he told me, years later, that he had subsequently bought up every picture or photograph of her that he could trace, and destroyed them. Like most men who are endowed with vigorous minds and high gifts of imagination, Lessingham was, for as long as I have known him, a man of extreme attractiveness to women, and a man to whom (as to his imperial ancestor) women and the beauty of women were as mountain air and sunshine. The spectacle of the unbroken succession and variety of ladies, who crowned, like jewels, the ever increasing splendour and pomp of his exist-ence, made me think that his marriage had been without significance, and that he never spoke of his wife because he had forgotten her. Later, when I heard about the burnt portraits, I changed my mind and supposed he had hated her. It was only when our friendship had ripened to a deep understanding in which words were scarcely needed as messengers between our minds, that I realized how things stood: that it was only his majestic if puerile belief in her personal immortality, and his own, beyond the grave, that upheld him in all the storm and peace and magnifi-cence and high achievement of the years (fifty, as it turned out) that he was to live on without her.

'These pragmatical sophisters, with their loose psychology and their question-begging logic-chopping that masquerades as meta-physic! I would almost give them leave to gag truth and lead the world by the nose like a jackass, if they could but be men as this man, and bend error and self-deception to high and lofty imaginings as he did. For it is certain mankind would build better if they built for themselves; few can love and tender an unknown posterity. But this man, as I have long observed him, looked on all things *sub specie æternitatis*; his actions all moved (like the slow procession of this northern summer night) to slow perfection, where the common run of men spoil all in their makeshift hurry. If he followed will-o'-the-wisps in metaphysics, they proved safe lights for him in practical affairs. He was neither deceived nor alarmed by the rabble's god, mere Quantity, considering that if you inflate it big enough the Matterhorn becomes as insignificant as a grain of sand, since the eye can no longer perceive it, and that a nebula in which our whole earth would be but as a particle in a cloud of tobacco-smoke is (unless as a whetter of imagination's appetite), more unimportant than that smoke, because further divorced from life. And so, with sound wisdom, he applied all his high gifts of nature, and that sceptre which his colossal wealth set ready in his hand, not to dissipate them in the welter of the world, but to fields definite enough to show the effect. And for all his restless vigour and love of action, he withheld himself as a rule from action in the world, except where he could find conditions, as in Paraguay and again in Lofoten, outside the ordinary texture of modern life. For he felt, I think, by a profound instinct, that in modern life action swallows up the individual. There is no scope for a good climber, he said, to show his powers in a quagmire. Well, it is night now; and no more climbing.'

It was not until I had ended that I felt I had been making something of a fool of myself, letting my thoughts run away with my tongue. For some minutes there was silence, broken only by the solemn ticking of the clock, and now and then a sea-bird's desolate cry without. Then the Señorita's voice stole on the silence as a meteor steals across darkness: 'All must pass away, all must break at last, everything we care for: lips wither, the bright brain grow dim, "the vine, the woman, and the rose": even the names, even the mention and remembrance of created things, must die and be forgotten; until at last not these only, but death and oblivion itself must – cease, dissipated in that infinite frost of illimitable nothingness of space and time, for ever and ever and ever.'

I listened with that sensation of alternating strain and collapse of certain muscles which belongs to some dreams where the dreamer climbs insecurely from frame to frame over rows of pictures hung on a wall of tremendous height below which opens the abyss. Hitherto the mere conception of annihilation (when once I had imaginatively compassed it, as now and then I have been able to do, lying awake in the middle of the night) had had so much power of horror upon me that I could barely refrain from shrieking in my bed. But now, for the first time in my life, I found I could look down from that sickening verge steadfastly and undismayed. It seemed a strange turn, that here in death's manifest presence I, for the first time, found myself unable seriously to believe in death.

My outward eyes were on Lessingham's face, the face of an Ozymandias. My inward eye searched the night, plunging to those deeps beyond the star-shine where, after uncounted millions of light-years' journeying, the two ends of a straight line meet, and the rays complete the full circle on themselves; so that what to my earthly gaze shows as this almost indiscernible speck of mist, seen through a gap in the sand-strewn thousands of the stars of the Lion, may be but the back view of the very same unknown cosmic island of suns and galaxies which (as a like unremarkable speck) faces my searching eye in the direct opposite region of the heavens, in the low dark sign of Capricorn.

Then, as another meteor across darkness: 'Many have blasphemed God for these things,' she said; 'but without reason, surely. Shall infinite Love that is able to wield infinite Power be subdued to our necessities? Must the Gods make haste, for Whom no night cometh? Is there a sooner or a later in Eternity? Have you thought of this: you had an evil dream: you were in hell that night; yet you woke and forgot it utterly. Are you tonight any jot the worse for it?'

She seemed to speak of forgotten things that I had known long ago and that, remembered now, brought back all that was lost and healed all sorrows. I had no words to answer her, but I thought of Lessingham's poems, and they seemed to be, to this mind she brought me to, as shadows before the sun. I reached down from the shelf at my left, beside the window, a book of vellum with clasps of gold. 'Lessingham shall answer you from this book,' I said, looking up at her where she sat against the sunset. The book opened at his rondel of *Aphrodite Ourania*. I read it aloud. My voice shook, and marred the reading:

> Between the sunset and the sea
>   The years shall still behold Your glory,
> Seen through this troubled fantasy
>   Of doubtful things and transitory.
>
> Desire's clear eyes still search for Thee
>   Beyond Time's transient territory,
>   Upon some flower-robed promontory
> Between the sunset and the sea.
>
>   Our Lady of Paphos: though a story
> They count You: though Your temples be
>   Time-wrecked, dishonoured, mute and hoary—
> You are more than their philosophy.
> Between the sunset and the sea
>   Waiteth Your eternal glory.

While I read, the Señorita sat motionless, her gaze bent on Lessingham. Then she rose softly from her seat in the window and stood once more in that place where I had first seen her that night, like the Queen of Love sorrowing for a great lover dead. The clock ticked on, and I measured it against my heart-beats. An unreasoning terror now took hold of me, that Death was in the room and had laid on my heart also his fleshless and icy hand. I dropped the book and made as if to rise from my seat, but my knees gave way like a drunken man's. Then with the music of her voice, speaking once more, as if love itself were speaking out of the interstellar spaces from beyond the mists of time and desolation and decay, my heart gave over its fluttering and became quiet like a dove held safe in its mistress's hand. 'It is midnight now,' she said. 'Time to say farewell, seal the chamber, and light the pyre. But first you have leave to look upon the picture, and to read that which was written.'

At the time, I wondered at nothing, but accepted, as in a dream, her knowledge of this secret charge bequeathed to me by Lessingham through sealed instructions locked in a fireproof box which I had only opened on his death, and of which he had once or twice assured me that no person other than himself had seen the contents. In that box was a key of gold, and with that I was at midnight of his death-day to unlock the folding doors of a cabinet that was built into the wall above his bed, and so leave him lying in state under the picture that was in the cabinet. And I must seal the room, and burn up Digermulen castle, and him and all that was in it, as he had burnt up his house in Wastdale fifty years before. And he had let me know that in that cabinet was his wife's picture, painted by himself, his masterpiece never seen by living eye except the painter's and the sitter's; the only one of all her pictures that he had spared.

The cabinet doors were of black lacquer and gold, flush with the wall. I turned the golden key, and opened them left and right. My eyes swam as I looked upon that loveliness that showed doubtfully in the glittering candlelight and the diffused rosy dusk from without. I saw well now that this great picture had been painted for himself alone. A sob choked me as I thought of this last pledge of our friendship, planned by him so many years ago to speak for him to me from beyond death, that my eyes should be allowed to see his treasure before it was committed, with his own mortal remains, to the consuming element of fire. And now I saw how upon the inside panels of the cabinet was inlaid (by his own hand, I doubt not) in letters of gold this poem, six stanzas upon either door:

A VISION OF ZIMIAMVIA

I will have gold and silver for my delight:
    Hangings of red silk, purfled and worked in gold
With mantichores and what worse shapes of fright
    Terror Antiquus spawn'd in the days of old.

I will have columns of Parian vein'd with gems,
    Their capitals by Pheidias' self design'd,
By his hand carv'd, for flowers with strong smooth stems,
    Nepenthe, Elysian Amaranth, and their kind.

I will have night: and the taste of a field well fought,
    And a golden bed made wide for luxury;
And there – since else were all things else prov'd naught –
    Bestower and hallower of all things: I will have Thee.

—Thee, and hawthorn time. For in that new birth though all
    Change, you I will have unchang'd: even that dress,
So fall'n to your hips as lapping waves should fall:
    You, cloth'd upon with your beauty's nakedness.

The line of your flank: so lily-pure and warm:
    The globéd wonder of splendid breasts made bare:
The gleam, like cymbals a-clash, when you lift your arm;
    And the faun leaps out with the sweetness of red-gold hair.

My dear – my tongue is broken: I cannot see:
    A sudden subtle fire beneath my skin
Runs, and an inward thunder deafens me,
    Drowning mine ears: I tremble. – O unpin

Those pins of anachite diamond, and unbraid
  Those strings of margery-pearls, and so let fall
Your python tresses in their deep cascade
  To be your misty robe imperial—

The beating of wings, the gallop, the wild spate,
  Die down. A hush resumes all Being, which you
Do with your starry presence consecrate,
  And peace of moon-trod gardens and falling dew.

Two are our bodies: two are our minds, but wed.
  On your dear shoulder, like a child asleep,
I let my shut lids press, while round my head
  Your gracious hands their benediction keep.

Mistress of my delights; and Mistress of Peace:
  O ever changing, never changing, You:
Dear pledge of our true love's unending lease,
  Since true to you means to mine own self true—

I will have gold and jewels for my delight:
  Hyacinth, ruby, and smaragd, and curtains work'd in gold
With mantichores and what worse shapes of fright
  Terror Antiquus spawn'd in the days of old.

Earth I will have, and the deep sky's ornament:
  Lordship, and hardship, and peril by land and sea—
And still, about cock-shut time, to pay for my banishment,
  Safe in the lowe of the firelight I will have Thee.

Half blinded with tears, I read the stanzas and copied them
down. All the while I was conscious of the Señorita's presence at
my side, a consciousness from which in some irrational way I
seemed to derive an inexplicable support, beyond comprehension
or comparisons. These were things which by all right judgement
it was unpardonable that any living creature other than myself

should have looked upon. Yet of the lightness of her presence (more, of its deep necessity), my sense was so lively as to pass without remark or question. When I had finished my writing, I saw that she had not moved, but remained there, very still, one hand laid lightly on the bedpost at the foot of the bed, between the ears of the great golden hippogriff. I heard her say, faint as the breath of night-flowers under the stars: 'The fabled land of ZIMIAMVIA. Is it true, will you think, which poets tell us of that fortunate land: that no mortal foot may tread it, but the blessed souls do inhabit it of the dead that be departed: of them that were great upon earth and did great deeds when they were living, that scorned not earth and the delights and the glories of earth, and yet did justly and were not dastards nor yet oppressors?'

'Who knows?' I said. 'Who dares say he knows?'

Then I heard her say, in her voice that was gentler than the glow-worm's light among rose-trees in a forgotten garden between dewfall and moonrise: *Be content. I have promised and I will perform.*

And as my eyes rested on that strange woman's face, it seemed to take upon itself, as she looked on Lessingham dead, that unsearchable look, of laughter-loving lips divine, half closed in a grave expectancy, of infinite pity, infinite patience, and infinite sweetness, which sits on the face of Praxiteles's Knidian Aphrodite.

ZIMIAMVIA

PRINCIPAL PERSONS

LESSINGHAM
BARGANAX
FIORINDA
ANTIOPE

I

A Spring Night in Mornagay

A COMMISSION OF PERIL • THE THREE KINGDOMS
MASTERLESS • POLICY OF THE VICAR • THE PROMISE
HEARD IN ZIMIAMVIA.

'By all accounts, 'twas to give him line only,' said Amaury; 'and if King Mezentius had lived, would have been war between them this summer. Then he should have been boiled in his own syrup; and 'tis like danger now, though smaller, to cope the son. You do forget your judgement, I think, in this single thing, save which I could swear you are perfect in all things.'

Lessingham made no answer. He was gazing with a strange intentness into the wine which brimmed the crystal goblet in his right hand. He held it up for the bunch of candles that stood in the middle of the table to shine through, turning the endless stream of bubbles into bubbles of golden fire. Amaury, half facing him on his right, watched him. Lessingham set down the goblet and looked round at him with the look of a man awaked from sleep.

'Now I've angered you,' said Amaury. 'And yet, I said but true.'

As a wren twinkles in and out in a hedgerow, the demurest soft shadow of laughter came and went in Lessingham's swift grey eyes. 'What, were you reading me good counsel? Forgive me, dear Amaury: I lost the thread on't. You were talking of my cousin, and the great King, and might-a-beens; but I was fallen a-dreaming and marked you not.'

Amaury gave him a look, then dropped his eyes. His thick eyebrows that were the colour of pale rye-straw frowned and bristled, and beneath the sunburn his face, clear-skinned as a girl's, flamed scarlet to the ears and hair-roots, and he sat sulky, his hands thrust into his belt at either side, his chin buried in his ruff. Lessingham, still leaning on his left elbow, stroked the black curls of his mustachios and ran a finger slowly and delicately over the jewelled filigree work of the goblet's feet. Now and again he cocked an eye at Amaury, who at last looked up and their glances met. Amaury burst out laughing. Lessingham busied himself still for a moment with the sparkling, rare, and sunset-coloured embellishments of the goldsmith's art, then, pushing the cup from him, sat back. 'Out with it,' he said; ''tis shame to plague you. Let me know what it is, and if it be in my nature I'll be schooled.'

'Here were comfort,' said Amaury; 'but that I much fear 'tis your own nature I would change.'

'Well, that you will never do,' answered he.

'My lord,' said Amaury, 'will you resolve me this: Why are we here? What waiting for? What intending?'

Lessingham stroked his beard and smiled.

Amaury said. 'You see, you will not answer. Will you answer this, then: It is against the nature of you not to be rash, and against the condition of rashness not to be 'gainst all reason; yet why (after these five years that I've followed you up and down the world, and seen you mount so swiftly the degrees and steps of greatness that, in what courts or princely armies soever you might be come, you stuck in the eyes of all as the most choice jewel there): why needs must you, with the wide world to choose from, come back to this land of Rerek, and, of all double-dealers and secretaries of hell, sell your sword to the Vicar?'

'Not sell, sweet Amaury,' answered Lessingham. 'Lend. Lend it in cousinly friendship.'

Amaury laughed. 'Cousinly friendship! Give us patience! With the Devil and him together on either hand of you!' He leapt up, oversetting the chair, and strode to the fireplace. He kicked the logs together with his heavy riding-boots, and the smother of flame and sparks roared up the chimney. Turning about, his back to the fire, feet planted wide, hands behind him, he said: 'I have you now in a good mood, though 'twere over much to hope you reasonable. And now you shall listen to me, for your good. You do know me: am I not myself by complexion subject to hasty and rash motions? Yet I it is must catch at your bridle-rein; for in good serious earnest, you do make toward most apparent danger, and no tittle of advantage to be purchased by it. Three black clouds moving to a point; and here are you, in the summer and hunting-season of your youth, lying here with your eight hundred horse these three days, waiting for I know not what cat to jump, but (as you have plainly told me) of a most set obstinacy to tie yourself hand and heart to the Vicar's interest. You have these three months been closeted in his counsels: that I forget not. Nor will I misprise your politic wisdom: you have played chess with the Devil ere now and given him stalemate. But 'cause of these very things, you must see the peril you stand in: lest, if by any means he should avail to bring all things under his beck, he should then throw you off and let you hop naked; or, in the other event, and his ambitious thoughts should break his neck, you would then have raised up against yourself most bloody and powerful enemies.

'Look but at the circumstance. This young King Styllis is but a boy. Yet remember, he is King Mezentius' son; and men look not for lapdog puppies in the wolf's lair, nor for milksops to be bred up for heirship to the crown and kingdom of Fingiswold. And he is come south not to have empty homage only from the regents here and in Meszria, but to take power. I would not have you build upon the Duke of Zayana's coldness to his young brother. True, in many families have the bastards been known the greater spirits; and you did justly blame the young King's handling of the reins in Meszria when (with a warmth from which his brother could not but take cold) he seemed to embrace to his bosom the lord Admiral, and in the same hour took away with a high hand from the Duke a great slice of his appanage the King their father left him. But though he smart under this neglect, 'tis not so likely he'll go against his own kindred, nor even stand idly by, if it come to a breach 'twixt the King and the Vicar. What hampers him today (besides his own easeful and luxurious idleness) is the Admiral and those others of the King's party, sitting in armed power at every hand of him in Meszria; but let the cry but be raised there of the King against the Vicar, and let Duke Barganax but shift shield and declare himself of's young brother's side, why then you shall see these and all Meszria stand in his firm obedience. Then were your cousin the Vicar ta'en betwixt two millstones; and then, where and in what case are you, my lord? And this is no fantastical scholar's chop-logic, neither: 'tis present danger. For hath not he for weeks now set every delay and cry-you-mercy and procrastinating stop and trick in the way of a plain answer to the young King's lawful demand he should hand over dominion unto him in Rerek?'

'Well,' said Lessingham, 'I have listened most obediently. You have it fully: there's not a word to which I take exceptions. Nay I admire it all, for indeed I told you every word of it myself last night.'

'Then would to heaven you'd be advised by't,' said Amaury. 'Too much light, I think, hath made you moon-eyed.'

'Reach me the map,' said Lessingham. For the instant there was a touch in the soft bantering music of his voice as if a blade had glinted out and in again to its velvet scabbard. Amaury spread out the parchment on the table, and they stood poring over it. 'You are a wiser man in action, Amaury, in natural and present, than in conceit; standing still, stirs your gall up: makes you see bugs and hobthrushes round every corner. Am I yet to teach you I may securely dare what no man thinks I would dare, which so by hardness becometh easy?'

Lessingham laid his forefinger on this place and that while he talked. 'Here lieth young Styllis with's main head of men, a league or more be-east of Hornmere. 'Tis thither he hath required the Vicar come to him to do homage of this realm of Rerek, and to lay in his hands the keys of Kessarey, Megra, Kaima, and Argyanna, in which the King will set his own captains now. Which once accomplished, he hath him harmless (so long, at least, as Barganax keep him at arm's length); for in the south there they of the March openly disaffect him and incline to Barganax, whose power also even in this northern ambit stands entrenched in's friendship with Prince Ercles and with Aramond, spite of all supposed alliances, respects, and means, which bind 'em tributary to the Vicar.

'But now to the point of action; for 'tis needful you should know, since we must move north by great marches, and that this very night. My noble cousin these three weeks past hath, whiles he amused the King with's chaffer-talk of how and wherefore, opened unseen a dozen sluices to let flow to him in Owldale men and instruments of war, armed with which strong arguments (I have it by sure intelligence but last night) he means tomorrow to obey the King's summons beside Hornmere. And, for a last point of logic, in case there be falling out between the great men and work no more for learned doctors but for bloody martialists, I am to seize the coast-way 'twixt the Swaleback fells and Arrowfirth and deny 'em the road home to Fingiswold.'

'Deny him the road home?' said Amaury. ''Tis war, then, and flat rebellion?'

'That's as the King shall choose. And so, Amaury, about it straight. We must saddle an hour before midnight.'

Amaury drew in his breath and straightened his back. 'An hour to pack the stuff and set all in marching trim: and an hour before midnight your horse is at the door.' With that, he was gone.

Lessingham scanned the map for yet a little while, then let it roll itself up. He went to the window and threw it open. There was the breath of spring in the air and daffodil scents: Sirius hung low in the south-west.

'Order is ta'en according to your command,' said Amaury suddenly at his side. 'And now, while yet is time to talk and consider, will you give me leave to speak?'

'I thought you had spoke already,' said Lessingham, still at the window, looking round at him. 'Was all that but the theme given out, and I must now hear point counterpoint?'

'Give me your sober ear, my lord, but for two minutes together. You know I am yours, were you bound for the slimy strand of Acheron. Do but consider; I think you are in some bad ecstasy. This is worse than all: cut the lines of the King's communications northward, in the post of main danger, with so little a force, and Ercles on your flank ready to stoop at us from his high castle of Eldir and fling us into the sea.'

'That's provided for,' said Lessingham: 'he's made friends with as for this time. Besides, he and Aramond are the Duke's dogs, not the King's; 'tis Meszria, Zayana, all their strings hold unto; north winds bring 'em the cough o' the lungs. Fear not them.'

Amaury came and leaned himself too on the window-sill, his left elbow touching Lessingham's. After a while he said, low and as if the words were stones loosed up one by one with difficulty from a stiff clay soil, ''Fore heaven, I must love you; and it is a thing not to be borne that your greatness should be made but this man's cat's-paw.'

Sirius, swinging lower, touched the highest tracery of a tall ash-tree, went out like a blown-out candle behind a branch, and next instant blazed again, a quintessential point of diamond and sapphire and emerald and amethyst and dazzling whiteness. Lessingham answered in a like low tone, meditatively, but his words came light on an easy breath: 'My cousin. He is meat and drink to me. I must have danger.'

They abode silent at that window, drinking those airs more potent than wine, and watching, with a deep compulsive sense of essence drawn to essence, that star's shimmer of many-coloured fires against the velvet bosom of the dark; which things drew and compelled their beings, as might the sweet breathing nearness of a woman lovely beyond perfection and deeply beyond all soundings desired. Lessingham began to say slowly, 'That was a strange trick of thought when I forgot you but now, and forgot my own self too, in those bubbles which in their flying upward signify not as the sparks, but that man is born for gladness. For I thought there was a voice spake in my ear in that moment and I thought it said, *I have promised and I will perform*. And I thought it was familiar to me beyond all familiar dear lost things. And yet 'tis a voice I swear I never heard before. And like a star-gleam, it was gone.'

The gentle night seemed to turn in her sleep. A faint drumming, as of horse-hooves far away, came from the south. Amaury stood up, walked over to the table, and fell to looking at the map again. The beating of hooves came louder, then on a sudden faint again. Lessingham said from the window, 'There's one rideth hastily. Now a cometh down to the ford in Killary Bottom, and that's why we lose the sound for awhile. Be his answers never so good, let him not pass nor return, but bring him to me.'

II

THE DUKE OF ZAYANA

PORTRAIT OF A LADY • DOCTOR VANDERMAST • FIORINDA:
'BITTER-SWEET' • THE LYRE THAT SHOOK MITYLENE

THE third morning after that coming of the galloping horseman
north to Mornagay, Duke Barganax was painting in his privy garden
in Zayana in the southland: that garden where it is everlasting
afternoon. There the low sun, swinging a level course at about that
pitch which Antares reaches at his highest southing in an English
May-night, filled the soft air with atomies of sublimated gold,
wherein all seen things became, where the beams touched them,
golden: a golden sheen on the lake's unruffled waters beyond the
parapet, gold burning in the young foliage of the oak-woods that
clothed the circling hills; and, in the garden, fruits of red and yellow
gold hanging in the gold-spun leafy darkness of the strawberry-
trees, a gilding shimmer of it in the stone of the carven bench, a
gilding of every tiny blade on the shaven lawn, a glow to deepen
all colours and to ripen every sweetness: gold faintly warming the
proud pallour of Fiorinda's brow and cheek, and thrown back in
sudden gleams from the jet-black smoothnesses of her hair.

'Would you be ageless and deathless for ever, madam, were
you given that choice?' said the Duke, scraping away for the third
time the colour with which he had striven to match, for the
third time unsuccessfully, the unearthly green of that lady's eyes.

'I am this already,' answered she with unconcern.

'Are you so? By what assurance?'

'By this most learn'd philosopher's, Doctor Vandermast.'

The Duke narrowed his eyes first at his model then at his picture: laid on a careful touch, stood back, compared them once more, and scraped it out again. Then he smiled at her: 'What? Will you believe him? Do but look upon him where he sitteth there beside Anthea, like winter wilting before Flora in her pride. Is he one to inspire faith in such promises beyond all likelihood and known experiment?'

Fiorinda said: 'He at least charmed you this garden.'

'Might he but charm your eyes,' said the Duke, 'to some such unaltering stability, I'd paint 'em; but now I cannot. And 'tis best I cannot. Even for this garden, if 'twere as you said, madam (or worse still, were you yourself so), my delight were poisoned. This eternal golden hour must lose its magic quite, were we certified beyond doubt or heresy that it should not, in the next twinkling of an eye, dissipate like mist and show us the work-a-day morning it conceals. Let him beware, and if he have art indeed to make safe these things and freeze them into perpetuity, let him forbear to exercise it. For as surely as I have till now well and justly rewarded him for what good he hath done me, in that day, by the living God, I will smite off his head.'

The Lady Fiorinda laughed luxuriously, a soft, mocking laugh with a scarce perceptible little contemptuous upward nodding of her head, displaying the better with that motion her throat's lithe strong loveliness. For a minute, the Duke painted swiftly and in silence. Hers was a beauty the more sovereign because, like smooth waters above a whirlpool, it seemed but the tranquillity of sleeping danger: there was a taint of harsh Tartarean stock in her high flat cheekbones, and in the slight upward slant of her eyes; a touch of cruelty in her laughing lips, the lower lip a little too full, the upper a little too thin; and in her nostrils, thus dilated, like a beautiful and dangerous beast's at the smell of blood. Her hair, parted and strained evenly back on either side from her serene sweet forehead, coiled down at last in a smooth convoluted knot which nestled in the nape of her neck like a black panther asleep. She wore no jewel nor ornament save two escarbuncles, great as a man's thumb, that hung at her ears like two burning coals of fire. 'A generous prince and patron indeed,' she said; 'and a most courtly servant for ladies, that we must rot tomorrow like the aloe-flower, and all to sauce his dish with a biting something of fragility and non-perpetuity.'

The Countess Rosalura, younger daughter of Prince Ercles, new-wed two months ago to Medor, the Duke's captain of the bodyguard, had risen softly from her seat beside her lord on the brink of a fountain of red porphyry and come to look upon the picture with her brown eyes. Medor followed her and stood looking beside her in the shade of the great lime-tree. Myrrha and Violante joined them, with secret eyes for the painter rather than for the picture: ladies of the bedchamber to Barganax's mother, the Duchess of Memison. Only Anthea moved not from her place beside that learned man, leaning a little forward. Her clear Grecian brow was bent, and from beneath it eyes yellow and unsearchable rested their level gaze upon Barganax. Her fierce lips barely parted in the dimmest shadow or remembrance of a smile. And it was as if the low golden beams of the sun, which in all things else in that garden wrought transformation, met at last with something not to be changed (because it possessed already a like essence with their own and a like glory), when they touched Anthea's hair.

'There, at last!' said the Duke. 'I have at last caught and pinned down safe on the canvas one particular minor diabolus of your ladyship's that hath dodged me a hundred times when I have had him on the tip of my brush; him I mean that peeks and snickers at the corner of your mouth when you laugh as if you would laugh all honesty out of fashion.'

'I laugh none out of fashion,' she said, 'but those that will not follow the fashions I set 'em. May I rest now?'

Without staying for an answer, she rose and stepped down from the stone plinth. She wore a coat-hardy, of dark crimson satin. From shoulder to wrist, from throat to girdle, the soft and shining garment sat close like a glove, veiling yet disclosing the breathing loveliness which, like a rose in crystal, gave it life from within. Her gown, of the like stuff, revealed when she walked (as in a deep wood in summer, a stir of wind in the tree-tops lets in the sun) rhythms and moving splendours bodily, every one of which was an intoxication beyond all voluptuous sweet scents, a swooning to secret music beyond deepest harmonies. For a while she stood looking on the picture. Her lips were grave now, as if something were fallen asleep there; her green eyes were narrowed and hard like a snake's. She nodded her head once or twice, very gently and slowly, as if to mark some judgement forming in her mind. At length, in tones from which all colour seemed to have been drained save the soft indeterminate greys as of muted strings, 'I wonder that you will still be painting,' she said: 'you, that are so much in love with the pathetic transitoriness of mortal things: you, that would smite his neck who should rob you of that melancholy sweet debauchery of your mind by fixing your marsh-fires in the sphere and making immortal for you your ephemeral treasures. And yet you will spend all your invention and all your skill, day after day, in wresting out of paint and canvas a counterfeit, frail, and scrappy immortality for something you love to look on, but, by your own confession, would love less did you not fear to lose it.'

'If you would be answered in philosophy, madam,' said the Duke, 'ask old Vandermast, not me.'

'I have asked him. He can answer nothing to the purpose.'

'What was his answer?' said the Duke.

The Lady Fiorinda looked at her picture, again with that lazy, meditative inclining of her head. That imp which the Duke had caught and bottled in paint awhile ago curled in the corner of her mouth. 'O,' said she, 'I do not traffic in outworn answers. Ask him, if you would know.'

'I will give your ladyship the answer I gave before,' said that old man, who had sat motionless, serene and unperturbed, darting his bright and eager glance from painter to sitter and to painter again, and smiling as if with the aftertaste of ancient wine. 'You

do marvel that his grace will still consume himself with striving
to fix in art, in a seeming changelessness, those self-same appear-
ances which in nature he prizeth by reason of their every mutability
and subjection to change and death. Herein your ladyship,
grounding yourself at first unassailably upon most predicamental
and categoric arguments in *celarent*, next propounded me a syllo-
gism in *barbara*, the major premiss whereof, being well and exactly
seen, surveyed, overlooked, reviewed, and recognized, was by my
demonstrations at large convicted in fallacy of simple conversion
and not *per accidens*; whereupon, countering in *bramantip*, I did
in conclusion confute you in *bokardo*; showing, in brief, that here
is no marvel; since 'tis women's minds alone are ruled by clear
reason: men's are fickle and elusive as the jack-o'-lanterns they
pursue.'

'A very complete and metaphysical answer,' said she. 'Seeing 'tis
given on my side, I'll let it stand without question; though (to be
honest) I cannot tell what the dickens it means.'

'To be honest, madam,' said the Duke, 'I paint because I cannot
help it.'

Fiorinda smiled: 'O my lord, I knew not you were wont to do
things upon compulsion.' Her lip curled, and she said again, privately
for his own ear, 'Save, indeed, when your little brother calleth the
tune.' Sidelong, under her eyelashes, she watched his face turn red
as blood.

With a sudden violence the Duke dashed his handful of brushes
to the ground and flung his palette skimming through the air
like a flat stone that boys play ducks and drakes with, till it
crashed into a clump of giant asphodel flowers a dozen yards
away. Two or three of those stately blooms, their stems smashed
a foot above the ground, drooped and slowly fell, laying pitifully
on the grass their great tapering spikes of pink-coloured waxen
filigree. His boy went softly after the palette to retrieve it. He
himself, swinging round a good half circle with the throw, was
gone in great strides the full length of the garden, turned heel at
the western parapet, and now came back, stalking with great
strides, his fists clenched. The company was stood back out of

the way in an uneasy silence. Only the Lady Fiorinda moved not at all from her place beside the easel of sweet sandalwood inlaid with gold. He came to a sudden halt within a yard of her. At his jewelled belt hung a dagger, its pommel and sheath set thick with cabochon rubies and smaragds in a criss-cross pattern of little diamonds. He watched her for a moment, the breath coming swift and hard through his nostrils: a tiger beside Aphrodite's statua. There hovered in the air about her a sense-maddening perfume of strange flowers: her eyes were averted, looking steadily southward to the hills: the devil sat sullen and hard in the corner of her mouth. He snatched out the dagger and, with a savage back-handed stroke, slashed the picture from corner to corner; then slashed it again, to ribbons. That done, he turned once more to look at her.

She had not stirred; yet, to his eye now, all was altered. As some tyrannous and triumphant phrase in a symphony returns, against all expectation, hushed to starved minor harmonies or borne on the magic welling moon-notes of the horn, a shuddering tenderness, a dying flame; such-like, and so moving, was the transfiguration that seemed to have come upon that lady: her beauty grown suddenly a thing to choke the breath, piteous like a dead child's toys: the bloom on her cheek more precious than kingdoms, and less perdurable than the bloom on a butterfly's wing. She was turned side-face towards him; and now, scarce to be perceived, her head moved with the faintest dim recalling of that imperial mockery of soft laughter that he knew so well; but he well saw that it was no motion of laughter now, but the gallant holding back of tears.

'You ride me unfairly,' he said in a whisper. 'You who have held my rendered soul, when you would, trembling in your hand: will you goad me till I sting myself to death with my own poison?'

She made no sign. To the Duke, still steadfastly regarding her, all sensible things seemed to have attuned themselves to her: a falling away of colours: grey silver in the sunshine instead of gold, the red quince-flowers blanched and bloodless, the lush grass grey where it should be green, a spectral emptiness where an instant before had been summer's promise on the air and the hues of life and the young year's burden. She turned her head and looked him full in the eye: it was as if, from between the wings of death, beauty beaconed like a star.

'Well,' said the Duke, 'which of the thousand harbours of damnation have you these three weeks been steering for? What murder must I enact?'

'Not on silly pictures,' said she; 'as wanton boys break up their playthings; and I doubt not I shall be entreated sit for you again tomorrow, to paint a new one.'

The Duke laughed lightly. 'Why there was good in that, too. Some drowsy beast within me roused himself and suddenly started up, making himself a horror to himself, and, now the blood's cooled, happily sleeps again.'

'Sleeps!' Fiorinda said. Her lip curled.

'Come,' said the Duke. 'What shall it be then? Inspire my invention. Entertain 'em all to a light collation and, by cue taken at the last kissing-cup, let split their weasands, stab 'em all in a moment? Your noble brother amongst them, 'tis to be feared, madam; since him, with a bunch of others, I am to thank for these beggar-my-neighbour sleights and cozenage beyond example. Or shall't be a grand night-piece of double fratricide? yours and mine, spitted on one spit like a brace of woodcock? We can proceed with the first today: for the other, well, I'll think on't.'

'Are you indeed that prince whom reputation told me of,' said she, 'that he which did offend you might tremble with only thinking of it? And now, as hares pull dead lions by the beard—'

The Duke swung away from her a step or two, then back, like a caged beast. His brow was thunderous again. 'Ever going on beyond your possession,' he said, 'beyond your bounds. 'Tis well I am of a cool judgement. There's more in't than hold up my hand, or whistle in my fist. Content you that I have some noble great design on foot, which in good time shall prove prodigious to 'em all: and once holding good my advantage over them, in their fall I'll tempt the destinies.'

With an infinite slow feline grace she lifted up her head: her nostrils widening, the flicker of a smile on her parted lips: from beneath the shadow of long black lashes, half-moons of green lambent fire beheld him steadily. 'You must not speak to me as if I were a child or an animal,' she said. 'Will you swear me all this?'

'No,' answered he. 'But you may look back and consider of time past: I have been so sparing to promise, that (as your ladyship will bear me out) I have ever paid more than either I promised or was due.'

'Well,' she said: 'I am satisfied.'

'I must to the throne-room,' said the Duke. ''Tis an hour past the hour of audience, and I would not hold 'em too long tarrying for me; 'tis an unhandsome part, and I use it but to curb the insolencies of some we spoke on.' The Lady Fiorinda gave him at arm's length her white hand: he bowed over it and raised it to his lips. Standing erect again, still unbonneted before her, he rested his eyes upon her a moment in silence, then with a step nearer bent to her ear: 'Do you remember the Poetess, madam?—

Ἔρος δαὖτέ μ' ὁ λυσιμελης δόνει,
γλυκυπικρον αμαχανον ορπετον.

As if spell-bound under the troublous sweet hesitation of the choriambics, she listened, very still. Very still, and dreamily, and with so soft an intonation that the words seemed but to take voiceless shape on her ambrosial breath, she answered, like an echo:

Once more Love, the limb-loosener, shaketh me:
Bitter-sweet, the dread Worm ineluctable.

'It is my birthday, I am reminded,' said the Duke in the same whispered quietness. 'Will your ladyship do me the honour to sup with me tonight, in my chamber in the western tower that looks upon the lake, at sunset?'

There was no smile on that lady's lips. Slowly, her eyes staring into his, she bent her head. Surely all of enchantment and of gold that charged the air of that garden, its breathless promise, its storing and its brooding, distilled like the perfume of a dark red rose, as 'Yes,' she said. 'Yes.'

III

The Tables Set in Meszria

MEANWHILE, for nearly two hours in the great throne-room in
Zayana had the presence begun to fill against the Duke's
appearing. Now the fashion of that hall was that it was long,
of a hundred cubits the length thereof and the breadth forty
cubits. The walls were of pale hammered mountain gold, rough
with an innumerable variety of living things graven some in
large some in little, both hairy kinds and feathered, and scaly
kinds both of land and sea, oftenest by twos and twos with their
children beside their nests or holes, and the flowers, fruits, leaves,
herbs and water-weeds native to each kind winding in the inter-
spaces with a conceited formal luxurance. Massy columns, four
times a man's height, of carved black onyx with milky veins,
made caryatides in form of monstrous snakes, nine lengthwise
of the hall on either side and four at either end. These supported
on their hooded heads a frieze of tesselated jet four cubits deep,

whereon were displayed poppies and blooms of the aloe and the forgetful lotus, all in a cool frail loveliness of opals and rose-coloured sapphires as for their several blooms and petals, and as for their stalks and leaves of green marmolite and chalcedony. Above this great flowered frieze the roof was pitched in a vault of tracery-work of ivory and gold, so wrought that in the lower ranges near the frieze the curls and arabesques were all of gold, then higher a little mingling of ivory, and so more and more ivory and the substance of the work more and more fine and airy; until in the highest all was but pure ivory only, and its woven filaments of the fineness of hairs to look upon, seen at that great height, and as if a sudden air or a word too roughly spoken should be enough to break a framework so unsubstantial and blow it clean away. In the corners of the hall stood four tripods of dull wrought gold ten cubits in height, bearing four shallow basins of pale moonstone. In those basins a child might have bathed, so broad they were, and brimming all with sweet scented essences, attar of roses and essences of the night-lily and the hyperborean eglantine, and honey-dew from the glades beyond Ravary; and birds of paradise, gold-capped, tawny-bodied, and with black velvet throats that scintillated with blue and emerald fire, flitted still from basin to basin, dipping and fluttering, spilling and spreading the sweet perfumes. The hall was paved all over with Parian marble in flags set lozenge-wise, and pink topaz insets in the joints; and at the northern end was the ducal throne upon a low dais of the same marble, and before the dais, stretching the whole width of the hall, a fair great carpet figured with cloud-shapes and rainbow-shapes and comets and birds of passage and fruits and blossoms and living things, all of a dim shifting variety of colours, pale and unseizable like moonlight, which character came of its cunning weaving of silks and fine wools and intermingling of gold and silver threads in warp and woof. The throne itself was without ornament, plainly hewn from a single block of stone, warm grey to look on with veins of a lighter hue here and there, and here and there a shimmer as of silver in the texture of the stone; and that stone was dream-stone, a thing beyond price, endowed with hidden virtues. But from behind, uplifted like the wings of a wild-duck as it settles on the water, great wings shadowed the dream-stone; they sprang twenty cubits high from base to the topmost feather, and made all of gold, each particular feather fashioned to the likeness of nature that it was a wonder to look upon, and yet with so much awfulness of beauty and shadowing grace in the grand uprising of the wings as made these small perfections seem but praise and worship of the principal design which gave them their life and which from them took again fulfilment. Thousands of thousands of tiny precious stones of every sort that grows in earth or sea were inlaid upon those mighty wings, incrusting each particular quill, each little barb of each feather, so that to a man moving in that hall and looking upon the wings the glory unceasingly changed, as new commixtures of myriad colours and facets caught and threw back the light. And, for all this splendour, the very light in the throne-room was, by art of Doctor Vandermast, made misty and glamorous: brighter than twilight, gentler than the cold beams of the moon, as if the light itself were resolved into motes of radiance which, instead of darting afar, floated like snow-flakes, invisible themselves but bathing all else with their soft effulgence. For there was in all that spacious throne-room not a shadow seen, nor any sparkle of over-brilliance, only everywhere that veiling glamour.

Twenty-five soldiers of the Duke's bodyguard were drawn up beside the throne on either hand. Their byrnies and greaves were of black iron, and they were weaponed with ponderous double-edged two-handed swords. Each man carried his helm in the crook of his left arm, for it was unlawful even for a man-at-arms to appear covered in that hall: none might so appear, save the Duke alone. They were all picked men for strength and stature and fierceness; the head of every man of them was shaven smooth like an egg, and every man had a beard, chestnut-red, that reached to his girdle. Save these soldiers only, the company came not beyond the fair carpet's edge that went the width of the hall

before the throne; for this was the law in Zayana, that whosoever, unbidden of the Duke, should set foot upon that carpet
should lose nothing but his life.

But in the great spaces of the hall below the carpet was such
a company of noble persons walking and discoursing as any
wise man should take pure joy to look upon: great states of
Meszria all in holiday attire; gentlemen of the Duke's household,
and of Memison; courtmen and captains out of Fingiswold
holden to the lord Admiral's service or the Chancellor's or Earl
Roder's, that triple pillar of the great King's power in the south
there, whereby he had in his life-days and by his politic governance not so much held down faction and discontents as not
suffered them be thought on or take life or being. But now, King
Mezentius dead, his lawful son sudden where he should be wary,
fumbling where he should be resolute; his bastard slighted and
set aside and likely (in common opinion) to snatch vengeance
for it in some unimagined violence; and last, his Vicar in the
midland parts puffed up like a deadly adder ready to strike, but
at whom first none can say: these inconveniences shook the royal
power in Meszria, patently, for even a careless eye to note, even
here in Duke Barganax's presence-chamber.

A bevy of young lords of Meszria, standing apart under the
perfume tripod in the south-eastern corner whence they might
at leisure view all that came in by the great main doors at the
southern end, held light converse. Said one of them, 'Here comes
my lord Admiral.'

'Ay,' said another, 'main means of our lingering consumption:
would the earth might gape for him.'

'Nay,' said a third, that was Melates of Vashtola, 'I do love
my Jeronimy as I love a young spring sallet: cold and safe. I
will not have you blame him. Do but look: as puzzled as a cod-
fish! For fancy's passion, spit upon him. Nay, Roder and Beroald
are the prime blood-suckers, not he.'

'Speak lower,' said the Lord Barrian, he that spoke first; 'there's
jealous ears pricked all-wheres.'

With a grave salutation they greeted the High Admiral, who

with a formal bow passed on. He was somewhat heavy of build, entered a little into the decline of years; his pale hair lay lankish on the dome of his head, his pale blue eyes were straight and honest; the growth of his beard was thin, straggling over the great collar and badge of the kingly order of the hippogriff that he wore about his neck; the whole aspect of the man melancholy, and as if strained with half-framed resolutions and wishes that give the wall to fears. Yet was the man of a presence that went beyond his stature, which was but ordinary; as if there hung upon him some majesty of the King's power he wielded, of sufficiency (at least in trained and loyal soldiery under arms) to have made a fair adventure to unseat the Duke upon Acrozayana, red-bearded bodyguard and all.

When he was passed by, Zapheles spake again, he that had spoken second: 'Perfidiousness is a common waiter in most princes' courts. And so, in your ear, were't not for loyal oblige-ment to a better man, I'd call it time to serve, though late, our own interest: call in him you wot of: do him obedience, 'stead of these plaguish stewards and palace-scullions that, contrary to good cupping-glasses, must affect and suck none but the best blood.'

Melates looked warily round, 'I taught you that, my lord: 'tis a fine toy, but in sober sadness I am not capable of it. Nor you neither, I think.'

Zapheles said, ''Twill yet bear thinking on. You have here your natural sovereign lord (o' the wrong side of the blanket may be; no matter, that's nor here nor there); you yield him service and upholding: well. You look for quiet, therefore, and to be lord of your own, being suffered to enjoy these borders whereof you have right and particular dominion. Good: then behold your payment. He is practised upon most devilishly; even ladies will shortly scoff and prattle of it, that he is grown as tractable to't as stock-fish. You'll say that's his concernment; in the midst of idleness and deliciousness, fanned with the soft gales of his own flatterers' lips, he sitteth content. Good. But must we take cold too, 'cause he hath given his cloak away?

Must I smile and sit mum (and here's a right instance hot upon me like new cakes) when that Beroald taketh up a man I ne'er saw nor heard on, took in his lordship's own private walks with a great poisoned dagger in his breeches; a pretty thing it was, and meant beyond question for my lord Chancellor; they hanged him where he stood, on a mulberry-tree; and, 'cause the vile murderer said with a lie that this was by County Zapheles his setting on, I am at short warning cited before the justiciars to answer this; and the Duke, when I appeal to him under ancient right of signiory to have the proceedings quashed under plea of *ne obstes* and carried before him in person (which should but have upheld his authority, too much abridged and bridled by these hireling office-nobility), counsels me kindly waive the point of jurisdiction. And why? but that he will not be teased with these matters; which yet ensueth neither the realm's good nor his.'

'To amend which,' said Barrian, 'you and Melates would in plain treason give over all to the Vicar?'

'Would if we were wise,' replied Melates; 'but for fond loyalty sake, will not. May be, too, he is loyal, and would not have us.'

Zapheles laughed.

Barrian said: 'Your own men would not follow you in such a bad enterprise.'

''Tis very true,' said Zapheles. 'And indeed, were't otherwise, they should deserve to be hanged.'

'And you and I too,' said Melates.

'And you and I too. Yet in the Parry you may behold a man that knoweth at least the right trick to govern: do't through lords of land, like as we be, bounded to's allegiance, not parchment lords of's own making.'

'Were the Duke but stiffened to't!' said Melates. 'You are his near friend, Barrian: speak to him privately.'

'Ay,' said Zapheles. 'Nay, I mock not: choose but the happy occasion. Say to him, "You are Meszria: our centre whereto all lines come, all things look. Who depriveth this merchandise of reverence, defaceth all lustre of it. To it, then: out with Beroald, out with Roder and Jeronimy: throw the fowl to the Devil that hatched it."'

'Great and thumping words,' said Barrian. 'But 'tis mere truth a hath not the main strength to do it and he would. But hist, here's the Chancellor.'

The company by the door made way right and left with many courtesies and loutings, which the Lord Beroald acknowledged with a cold and stately smile. His gait was direct and soldierly, he carried his head like a mettled horse, and on his lean countenance, flat in the cheekbones, wide between the eyes, clean cut about the jaw, close shaven save for the bristly brown mustachios, sat that look which, as lichens grow on rock-faces, comes but with years of constant lordship over men and their long customed obedience. 'See how the spongy sycophants do hang on his steps,' said Zapheles. 'You'd swear they feared he should have 'em called in question for simple being here in Acrozayana. And the Duke will not put down his foot, it shall soon come to this indeed; a main crime to do him this empty courtesy, attend the weekly presences, without leave asked of this great devil and his fellows. See how he and Jeronimy do draw to a point of secret mischief as the lode-stone draweth iron.'

For the Chancellor, ending now his progress up the hall, was stood with the Lord Jeronimy on the great carpet before the throne. To them, as presenting in their high commission, along with Earl Roder, the King's very person and authority in Meszria, was accorded these many years the freedom of the carpet; and that was accorded to none other in all the land who was not of the Duke's own household or of the ducal line of Memison.

'I am glad to see you here, my lord Admiral,' said Beroald; 'and indeed it is a joy I scarcely looked for: thrice in three weeks, and you were not formerly given to great observance of this ceremony.'

The Admiral looked at him with his dog-like eyes, smiled slowly, and said, 'I am here to keep the peace.'

'And I on the same errand,' said Beroald: 'and to please my lady sister. I would have you look a little more starved, as I

myself do study to do. It is nought useful to remind him how
we made new wood when the young King pruned away his
appanage.'

'There's that needs no reminding on,' said Jeronimy.

'Will your lordship walk a little?' said Beroald, taking him
by the arm, and, as they paced slowly to and fro, cheek by cheek
for convenience of private conference: 'I still do hear it opinioned
that it was not without some note or touch of malice these
things were brought about; and you are named in that particular,
to have set the King's mind against him.'

Jeronimy blew out his cheeks and shook his head. 'May be I
was to blame; but 'twas in the King's clear interest. I'd do it,
were't to do again tomorrow.'

'This country party love us the worse for it,' said Beroald.

'A good housewife,' answered Jeronimy, 'was ever held in bad
report with moths and spiders.'

'We can show our teeth, and use them, if it were come to
that,' said Beroald. 'But that were questionable policy. Too many
scales stand in too uncertain balance. Roder's long tarrying in
Rerek: I like it not, ha?'

'As if the King should think he needed men there.'

'You have no fresh despatches?'

'Not since that I showed you, a-Thursday sennight.'

'That was not so bad, methought. My lord Admiral, I have
a question I would move to you. Are we strong enough, think
you, to hold off the Vicar if need were?'

Jeronimy looked straight before him awhile; then, 'Yes,' he
said, 'with the Duke of our side.'

'You have taken me?' said Beroald. 'Supposition is, things fall
out worst imaginable: war with him in Rerek, and the King's
forces overthrown. You are confident then?'

'With the Duke of our side, and with right of our side, I
should hope to do it.'

'I too,' said the Chancellor, 'am of your opinion.'

'Well, what's the matter?' The Lord Jeronimy came to a stop
in his slow deliberate pacing. A gentleman of his household

waited below the carpet: he seemed short of breath, as one that hath run a course: with a low leg he made obeisance, drawing a packet from his doublet. Jeronimy came to him, took it, and looked carefully at the seal with the gold-mounted perspective-glass that hung by a fine chain about his neck. Men marked how his sallow face turned sallower. 'Just,' he said: 'it hath all the points in it.' He undid the seal and read the letter, then handed it to Beroald; then, scowling upon the messenger: 'How hapt, ninny-hammer, that you delivered this no sooner?'

'Lord,' answered he, 'his lordship, all muddied from hard riding, did write it in your own house; and upon his sudden injunction strung with threats and filthy speeches innumerable, I did fly a-horseback and upon admittance at the fortress gate did with such leaps flee up the stairs as I was in point to have been laid hands on for a madman, so had all my charge miscarried.'

'Away then: to him again and say I had it, and my lord Chancellor too.' Then, walking apart once more with Beroald: 'We were best act on this, albeit to see us openly on a sudden go from the chamber may give occasion that the people may buzz and talk of it. Yet these commends do directly say we are in peril here until he speak with us.'

'Roder,' said Beroald, 'is not a man to start at his own shadow. Go we while the way's yet open.'

Those two lords, presenting to curious eyes a studied show of untroubled and careless ease, were but even come forth to the grand staircase, when the lofty doors clanged to behind them, and in the throne-room trumpets sounded a sennet. And now in great pomp and splendour, an hour and a half past the just time of audience, the Duke opened the presence. There went before him, entering by a door behind the throne, six blacks with silver trumpets, sounding to the sennet as aforesaid, and thirty peacocks, walking two by two with their tails displayed, who, after their progress forth and back before the throne, ranged themselves fifteen on either hand beneath the black onyx pillars, making with their tails a screen of shimmering green and

blue and gold. Medor, Egan, and Vandermast, and a dozen other
of the Duke's household, took each his appointed station beside
the throne, Medor in his bronze byrny with gorget and shoulder-
pieces inlaid with silver and bearing as symbol of his office a
long double-handed two-edged sword; and now the trumpets,
after a long baying blast that seemed to shake the gossamer
tracery of the roof, suddenly fell silent as Barganax appeared.

His kirtle was of corded silk, rose-coloured, slashed with
velvet of a darker hue, and gathered about the waist with a belt
of sea-horse hide lapped at the edge with thread of gold and
bossed with balas rubies and cat's-eye chrysoberyls; he had
thick-woven silken hose of the like rose-colour, and a long cloak
of dark grey brocaded silk lined with cloth of silver; the collar
of the cloak was of black cormorants' feathers cunningly sewn
and fitted to make an even smoothness, cross-striped at every
span with lines of rubies and fastened with golden clasps. Yet
was all this but shadows in water beside the man himself. For,
alike in his lithe tall frame, and in his carriage noble and debo-
nair and of a cat-like elegance, this Duke was beautiful to look
upon beyond the example of men; his skin marvellous fair and
smooth, his hair the colour of burnished copper, short and curly,
his nose clean cut and straight, his brow wide, his eyebrows
sleek and thick and with a scarcely to be seen upward slant,
that cast a quality of somewhat pensive and of somewhat faun-
like across his face; his shaven chin delicate but strong, his
mouth a little large, firm-lipped under daintily upcurled mustachios, sensitive, apt for sudden modulations of mood and passion;
his eyes brown, contemplative, and with profound obscurities
of pulsing fire. And as, with that easy simplicity of magnificence
which seemed in him nature bred clean beyond the range of art,
he took his seat upon the dream-stone, it was as if the richness
of his jewelled apparel, the shadowing of those wings, and all
the sumptuous splendours of that hall were to him but as the
flower on the blackthorn or the rainbow across a mountain
peak: graces wedded to a substance worthy their own unsubstantial loveliness.

Now when the ceremonial business of presentations, petitions, sealings of placets and decrees was concluded, the Duke spake to them of his council that stood beside him: 'Is't not some wonder there should be no legate nor envoy here to represent the Vicar?'

'May be,' answered Medor, 'that he liked not your grace's sending away of Gabriel Flores a month ago.'

Barganax lifted an eyebrow: ''Twas pure charity, and indeed a compliment, to let him know I thought his honour too basely travestied by such a villain. Nor was it fit I should accept as envoy but his master of the horse, one that is besides but a patent hired intelligencer, and scarcely a gentleman by birth.'

'There's one more cloud against the sun,' said Egan; 'so have I seen storms a-brewing. Your grace was informed ere you did enter the presence-chamber how that the Admiral and the Chancellor, that were here but a little before, were gone forth in a flutter of seeming urgency upon word brought them from without. Be advised: leave your custom, and go not today among the general throng below the carpet.'

Barganax said, 'It is seven year today since I did come of age and take power here in Zayana, and never yet have I omitted the custom I did that day begin.'

He stood up to go, but now Medor spoke against it: 'There were no harm to change it; and remember, did aught go miss, 'twere more than your own life you laid in hazard. Go not, Lord.'

'Vandermast,' said Barganax, 'what say you?'

'They have given their reasons,' answered that ancient man. 'I would hear your grace's reasons on the contrary part.'

'Imprimis,' said the Duke, 'whose turn should it serve to yerk me one under the fifth rib? Not old Jeronimy's, nor theirs that stayed with him: it should raise a cloud of wasps about their ears should in three days sweep 'em out of Meszria. Nor yet our discontented lords: they cry for action, and that were a strange road, to murder me: by my soul, they can look for no other to lead 'em. The King's? True, there's some coldness betwixt us, but I'll not suspect him of things myself would not soil my hands withal. But indeed I do know all these men. Pew! I am not to begin Duke.'

'Horius Parry,' said Medor then, 'would not stick to murder you.'

'His hands are full, playing spoil-five with the King for Rerek,' the Duke replied. 'Come, Medor,' he said: 'I am minded to go my own gate; and when I must skulk and beware in my own presence-chamber, then were I best slain indeed, and high time to say adieu. Attend me, Medor. But is not this right reason?' said he over his shoulder, passing by, to Doctor Vandermast. Vandermast made no reply, but as he and the Duke crossed glances it was as if two diverse wisdoms of age and of hot youth rose from their wells, recognized each his make, and clipped hands together.

Now was Duke Barganax come about three-quarters of his way down from the throne to the lower end of the chamber, walking and discoursing with this man and that, with Medor at his elbow, when there came a stir about the main doorway, as if some would have entrance but, because of the lateness and because the Duke had voided the throne, was denied. The Duke sent one to inquire and see; that one came back on the instant to say that here was the Earl Roder craved audience and would not take their no for it. 'Let him come in,' said the Duke, and received him where he stood.

'My lord Duke,' said Roder, 'I am obliged to kiss your hand; and, ere I go further in a business which in this public place I dare not pronounce but between my teeth, I would entreat you of a matter, easy for you to grant, and condition absolute of our more large and secret conference.'

'Our fashion is not curious,' answered the Duke, marking his disordered countenance. 'Yet do I wonder a little, if the matter crieth so loud for urgency, why you came not sooner. Or why sent you with so much parade of secrecy (for I saw it, my lord, through eyes that serve me) to fetch away the Admiral and the Chancellor, already pricked off for the presence? Or why, for a last point of wonder, you now come here without them.'

'That is the condition I spoke on,' answered he. 'I am to beseek you confirm us, under your royal word, safe conduct and assurance all and severally of our lives and persons, which done we shall straight to the matter, but until then we may not.'

To this the Duke listened with apparent wonder, then fell a-laughing. 'What coil's here?' he said. 'Sure, the man's frantic. What, Medor, I shall be apt to think they mean me mischief indeed, if their own sick minds do make 'em start like rabbits at such fairy-babes o' their own imagining. Howbeit, content you, Earl; I do swear you peace and grith, safe conduct to come and to go with liberty of life and of body on all lawful occasions in my dukedom of Zayana, for you and for my lord High Admiral Jeronimy and for my lord Chancellor Beroald; and unto this you have my royal word, as I do trow on the high and blessed Gods and Goddesses Who keep the wide heavens.'

'I am beholden to your grace,' said the Earl. 'And yet, were it ask a further boon, I think they would treasure it much in writing.'

The Duke's eye gleamed. 'You have witnesses, my lord. And indeed, if my bond were better than my word, you might stand in some peril now.'

'Forgive me,' said Roder then. 'We are content with your royal word, and in this I am the mouthpiece of all three of us. And truly,' said he, chuckling in his beard, 'I may now disclose to your grace the inwardness of my calling of 'em out: 'twas because we should not all three be in your hand afore we had ta'en assurance of our safety. But now, had you been minded to entreat me evilly, he and Beroald do stand at your doors without the citadel with enough stout lads mustered under arms as—'

The blood rushed to Barganax's face and neck, and his hand leapt to the dagger at his belt. Roder said, 'I am sorry. But your grace will not forget your oath, nor you will not strike a weaponless man. Will't please you enter your closet and suffer me bring in the Admiral and the Chancellor, when we shall confer with you about matters of most weighty consequence.'

'You are a brave man, Roder,' said Barganax at length, folding

his arms and speaking close in the Earl's face. 'Bring in your
friends. This circumspection of peace-pledges, and this armed
alertness when we were never yet at variance, are clean past my
understanding. But tell 'em, for their better counsel, 'twas well
you had my oath before I knew you threatened force against
me. Had I known or seen it, my answer had been pat and to
the purpose.'

The Earl Roder, as a man that hath escaped a danger the full
menace of which he had not apprehended till the danger was
past, went forth somewhat shaken from before the face of the
Duke.

When they were set in Duke Barganax's closet, the lord Admiral
took up the word: they were but five there, those three great
officers of state, the Duke himself and Doctor Vandermast. 'It
was unadvisedly done,' said the Admiral; 'and we will first
tender to your grace our large regrets and most humbly crave
your pardon. Yet shall you consider, when you know all, that
these be great news and sudden, and something in a manner to
root up all past custom and example, so as we know not where
we stand, in a manner; and albeit we do well think, my lord
Duke, that it shall still lie to our interest, both yours and ours,
to hold each by other, sith it well may so come about as that
like dangers from the like quarter should menace us both, yet
in a manner—'

'My good lord Admiral,' said the Duke, 'I pray you put out
of mind this of the soldiers. I am satisfied: not another thought
will I give it. But, for the matter in hand, we shall the more
readily follow your argument if you will first tell us these news
you speak on.'

'Earl Roder,' said Jeronimy, 'hath rid from the north this
morning with tidings of sudden and great import.'

'Give me in a word, what is it?' said the Duke.

'Then,' said Roder, 'in a word: the King is dead.'

'Heavy news; but 'tis ten months old.'

'Nay, nay: King Styllis is dead,' said Roder. 'Four days since, in Rerek, in's camp a little beside Hornmere. I was by his bed, held his hand in mine when his soul took flight.'

Those three lords narrowly watched the Duke who, from his late posture of careless ease, was sat upright at these tidings, his strong and delicate hands grasping the edge of the table of carved sandalwood. His eyes were on Roder's, but seemed to gaze through and beyond him: for a minute he was silent. At length he spoke, saying, 'He died young. The Gods rest his soul. He was my brother, though he ne'er was good to me.' He lowered his gaze and was silent again, his fingers drumming on the table. None spoke. Then, as if waking to common things, he looked up and said sharply: 'Dead, by what means?'

'Eating of some venomous confection,' answered Roder. He paused an instant, then blurted out, 'The common tittle-tattle doth loudly say your grace did poison him.'

Barganax narrowed his eyes. He fell a-drumming once more on the table. Then, 'I doubt not, my lord Admiral,' said he, 'you have surveyed the field anew ere you came to me with this, and perceived that it is well that you and I should have Meszria solid behind us in our next business. Were it the Vicar had took him off with poison, 'twas first to be looked for he should lay the blame to me.'

None spake. Jeronimy leaned forward on the table, spreading out his hand palm upwards, and cleared his throat once and again as if in prelude to a speech. Beroald saved his embarrassments by saying, 'Your grace will wish to see all the circumstances before you would determine what were best to do. It were fit you now produce the King's testament, my lord.'

Roder at that word drew from his bosom a parchment sealed with the royal sign manual. The blood came and went under his swarthy skin, though there was small space to mark it, for the beard grew nigh up to his eyes, and the hair of his head, stiff like a brush, began scarce an inch above his eyebrows. Uneasily he looked at the Duke and said, 'I would desire your grace have patience; and lest you should be deceived to suppose these dispositions coloured any whit by my advisements, be sure

you lay your time aright: this testament was executed this fourth
of April, as the King's highness' own hand under his seal doth
testify, and your grace knoweth well that 'twas not till three
days later I did upon commandment go to him in Rerek.'

'Well, well,' said the Duke, 'what's this to the purpose? Let
me have it; as sour as it is, my lips are primed for it.'

Therewith the Lord Roder, bracing himself as a man in posture
to dive into an ice-cold tarn in winter time, read out the parchment, that was writ in manner following:

'By me STYLLYS, sonne of MEZENCIUS of glorous memorye
uppon whome be pece, greatt Kyng of Fingyswold and of
al stattes and domynyons apparteigning thereunto, bee it
by riht of guift or lawfull inheretaunce or costom of prynses
or riht of conquest by the destroyenge swherde of my greatt
Father or mine owne, in wycch large discrypcioun without
dowbt casten or throwen uppon the fullness of the same
is imbrased or concluded the domynyons places and pryn-
cipalites foloing naymely that is to sayne my holle maine
territorie and kyngdame of Fingyswold and the citty of
Rjalmar being the capital citty thereof and prencipall sette
or syedge of my statte and gouernement; and my territorie
or londe of Reerec and places cytuate and plaste ther
withynne being in especially but not exclusively the forte-
laces or strangg houlds of Laimac, Cessary, Maegra, Caima,
and Argjanna; and my marche of Ulba now gouerned undir
my direccion and for my soole behoolfe and sarvys by the
after naymed my Vicare of Rerec as aforn sayde; and my
cuntree or lond of Mezria and the citees castills fortrasses
towneshyps ballywekes herborowes ylands and in a generaltie all the places there withynne buylt or unbuylt dwellid
in or unhabyted, but not to exclud aught that is not naymed
or emplyed in this large generaltie save and exept only the
ducall apponage of Zajana whereof I doo of my brotherly
loove and affectione renounse al claymes of soverainty in
fauour and for enjoyment of BARRGANAX, reputed sonne of

*the sed Kyng Mezencius of glorous memorie vpon whome
be peace, wycch sed Barrgnax I doo heereby irreuocably
indue and envest and the heiers of his bodye for euer with
the sayde apponage, being nycely and puntyvally limitted
by the bundaries or limytts descrived or delineate on the
mappe wycch by this My roialle Seall of fingyswold is made
faste unto this My roialle testament—'*

'Let me see it,' said the Duke. He looked carefully at the map,
nodded, showed it to Vandermast, then passed it back to Roder.
Roder proceeded:

*'I the sayde Kyng Syllys do beqwithe and giue my roiall
estatt and name of Kyngdam and al my holle Realme and
Pocessyons afore sed or what somever save as exepted unto
my Systyr* ANTIOPE *Prynsace of Fingyswold being besydis
myself the soole suruiuing Chylde borne in wedloke of the
sayde greatt Kyng Mezencius vpon Whome bee pece. And
considering how that the mortality of kynges is subgette
unto the inconsederat and fyckle stoopes and strypes of
Fate noe les miserablely than comon mens mortallity, ther-
fore in cace the sayde Prynsace Antiopy should bee in time
of My deth nat yet come unto full aage of* XVIII *yeeres,
with addycyon of* III *yeeres in consideracion that shee is a
wommon and that I doo coumpt hir as nat fit to euse full
dyscreccion and awtoritee tyll shee be full* XXI *years of
aage, I do dyrect and wylle that the lorde* HOORIUS PARRYE
*my wel loued and trusted servaunt being in some degrie
of My kynnedred or affinitie and being heereby confirmed
by Me in his estatt and roialle offyce as Vicaire on my
behalve and my successours in my befoare naymed kyngdame of Reerec shalbe protectour and wardeyne of my
systyr during her minorite and shall in Her name rewll the
realme as Regent during that time afoare sed and shall
charisshe and care for Her diligently and louyngly in al
poincts as a Father should and in al things estudie hir*

propper good and saftie and the inhansement of hir realme and soverainty. But as touching my sayde kyngdam of Mezria—'

'Proceed, as touching Meszria,' said the Duke. ''Tis thus far i' the bounds of reasonable surmise; though I might a looked to see my royal sister entrusted to my care sooner than to so questionable a tutor. True it is, I ne'er set eyes upon her, but I am far nearer by blood and (or I should hate myself else) far more to trust to.'

'Ere I proceed,' said Roder, 'I would inform your grace of this; hard for me to say, but I pray bear with me. The King on's death-bed did directly say to me that though he was at odds with the Vicar, he did believe so great an honour as this is should bind him faithfully to the royal interest, but your grace he did misdoubt (as he did openly say, but I did speak against it) of a secret determination to usurp the kingdom, and so feared to entrust the Princess unto you.'

'Proceed, man,' said the Duke. Roder proceeded:

'As touching my sayde kyngdam of Mezria, save and exept the sayde apponage of Zayjana as heerin befoare prouided, I do point my wel beloued faythfull sarvante the Lorde Hy Amerall IERONIMY *to rewill all the londe as Regent therof during my sed Systyrs minorite and therafter as Shee shall of Hir roiall wylle and pleasire determine of. And who some ere shall neglect contempne or sette on syde any dysposicion of this My Testment, lat his life haue an erly a suddant and an euill endinge and lat the Angre of the Goddes reste vpon him. Giuen under my roiall seall and under myne hande in my pauylyoun bisyde Hornmeere in Rerec this fourt day of Aprelle in the yeere of my raighne I,*

STYLLYS R.'

A silence of little ease fell on their council when Roder ended his reading of that testament. Except old Vandermast's not an eye was raised: those others shrank, in that silence, from meeting Barganax's glance: Barganax himself sat staring downward with a cat-like intention on the void table-top before him. When he spoke at last it was in a strained voice, as if he rode wrath on the curb, tight held yet ready to overleap at the least slackening of control all bounds, all reason. 'You will libel me out a copy of that, my lord Chancellor, certified under your hand and under his and his,' pointing with his eye at Roder and Jeronimy.

Beroald answered and said, 'I will.'

'I must have half an hour to consider of this ere we pursue it further,' said the Duke, still with that frightening tenseness in his voice. 'Vandermast, fill out Rian wines for these lords and then attend me. And to you, sirs, I will say this: I have warranted you safety and freedom in Acrozayana. But this shall you know, and consider well of it: in case you shall not wait for me in this room until I come back to talk with you, and in case I find you not here all three when I do come again, that shall be in my eyes an act of war, my lord Admiral, and I shall answer it as such.' With that word, as if the reins he had held at such horrid tension had slipped on a sudden through his fingers, he leapt to his feet, smote with his dagger into the table-top so mighty a downward stabbing blow that the steel stood a hand-breadth deep in the wood and snapped off short, hurled the broken weapon in the fireplace, and in that gusty extremity of fury flung open the door, swapped it to behind him, and was gone. Doctor Vandermast, who alone of that company maintained a demeanour of detachment and imperturbability, silently set wine before them according to his master's bidding and silently departed.

'Sure, the Duke's much incensed,' said Jeronimy, wiping the sweat from his brow with a silken handkercher and blowing out with his mouth.

'It was, in my conceit, a prime error in judgement,' said Beroald, 'not to have given him the regency. Unless I do grossly mistake him, he was ready to let go the rest had he had but that. You must pardon me, my lord Admiral; the time calls for bare truth, not glosing compliment.'

'I would in pure joy give it him today,' said the Admiral, wiping his brow anew.

Roder drank a great draught of wine, then turned square upon them as if upon revelation suddenly to announce an important truth. 'Why, this is very much to the purpose, my lords. Give it him: 'tis a bargain, and he is ours.'

'You do forget your gravity,' said the Chancellor. 'Lieth it in us to alter and set aside the King's will?'

'Ay, indeed,' said Roder: 'I had forgot.'

''Tis not to be thought on,' said the Admiral. 'But, that provided, it is the more instant we waste not our powers in a manner with private bickerings. I am strangely puzzled. I think we be all of an accord, though, in this: that the main purport of the matter and our only thought is to uphold the young Queen as we are bound to do, and serve her wholly and throughly?'

'We be weaponless here,' said Beroald, 'else would I kiss my sword to that. Take up the regency, my lord Admiral, and I at least will sustain and comfort you in this 'gainst all continent impediments and unto death itself.'

'Thanks, noble Beroald,' said the Admiral, taking his hand and Earl Roder's, who on the motion sware him the like upholding. 'And now, 'tis to make firm accord with the Duke if we may, and then keep open eyes on Rerek. But there there's difficult going and need, in a manner, to go frost-nailed, since we were much to blame went we in aught against the King's testament, and by that testament the Vicar must have the Queen in ward and be Regent for her in Rerek.'

'Suffer me,' said the Chancellor, reaching out his hand for the document, 'to peruse it again. Ha! Come hither,' he said: 'note a strange accident. It saith "shall in her name rule the realm as Regent" (this of the Vicar), and then concerning you, my lord Admiral, "to rule all the land" (that is, of Meszria) "as Regent thereof." It might be nicely argued that, he being in terms named Regent of all the realm and you but of Meszria only, effect is you shall be subject unto him as Regent of all the realm.'

''Twas never so intended,' said Roder.

'Nay,' said the Chancellor; 'but 'twill be argued by the letter, not upon supposition of intention. How came it, Roder, that you had the original?'

'The Vicar hath it too,' said he: ''Twas execute in duplicate. O there's no doubt on't, my lords, the Vicar meaneth not sit content in Rerek. 'Twas most observable with what a cloak of seeming loyalty he wrapped himself withal soon as the King 'gan sicken, and with what eagerness he did haste to wipe out of men's sight and memories all evidences of strife betwixt them. As witness, a thing I knew by secret and most trusty intelligence: 'twas come so nigh a breach betwixt 'em, that he had privily posted his cousin german, the great Lord Lessingham, with near a thousand horse at Mornagay of Rerek to hold the ways north-ward 'gainst the King should they come to open differences; but straight upon the King's sickening (for well he knew the hellish virtue of the drug that would obey no antidote) a sent his Gabriel Flores, a close instrument of his, galloping a whole night and day, to call off Lessingham and fetch him home again. And put it about forthright (with circumstances to be witness in't) that 'twas Barganax in a jealous vengeful cruelty did procure 's young brother's taking off.'

'And will you say,' asked Jeronimy, 'that Barganax did not indeed procure it?'

'I rest but on hearsay and what my own judgement tells me,' answered he. 'I am persuaded the Vicar did it. And hath the mind too to use the sister as a stalk to catch birds with, and that's the whole kingdom for's own usurping and enjoyment.'

'You mind what we spoke on but now i' the throne-room?' said Jeronimy to the Chancellor. 'With right of our side, and with the Duke of our side?'

Beroald nodded a grave assent, saying, 'We need both.'

The Lord Jeronimy fingered his thin beard a moment in silence: 'And yet,' he said, with a twitch of his mouth, 'I would not trust him out of all-ho! His thoughts do soar too high, in a manner, for sober deed to follow. I would trust him discreetly.'

The door opened, and those lords stood up in a formal defer-
ence. It was easy to read in Jeronimy's most tell-tale eyes how
all his prudent and scrupulous withholdings discandied quite,
only to look on Barganax that now entered to them with so
lovely a taking grace as, after the foul storm he had gone out
with, seemed a new man, a new day. 'My lord Admiral,' he said,
standing in the door: 'I have now thought on't. I will stand in
alliance with you to uphold the King's testament unto last fulfilment. Let your scriveners draw it in form, my lord Chancellor:
we'll set our hands to it. And if you will dine with me tomorrow,
'tis a pleasure I shall set store by. I'd say tonight, but – tonight
I am bespoke already.'

IV

ZIMIAMVIAN DAWN

LIGHT ON A DARK LADY

THE beginnings of new light, fanned with little winds that had slept all night long on the gentle spring-time sea, entered through the wide-open windows of the Duke's private lodging in Acrozayana and so by open doors into the outer chamber and so, passing out by western windows, were lost upon distances of the hueless lake below. Upon their passage, ambrosial Night, who had first trailed her mantle of dusk and enchantery over the white damask and the wine-cups rough with jewels, and over the oysters and crayfish in hippocras, jellied ortolans, peaches, queen-apples, and strange passion-fruits filled with seeds afloat in a thin delicious juice, and had later watched, under the silver lamps, such preenings and soarings of the bird delight as even holy Night can find no name to name them, now furled plume by plume her downy wings, ready to repair for yet another diurnal span to her chambers of the west. And now morning stood awake in those rooms; loosing hand from departing Night's, even as Fiorinda, rising in a like silence, loosed her hand from her sleeping lover's late fallen asleep a little before the dawn.

Motionless at the great crystal mirror, her hands gathering behind her head the night-black heavy and scented softnesses of her unbound hair, she surveyed for a while her own naked loveliness:

marvels of white, proud, Greek, modelled to the faintest half-retracted touch, pure as snows that dream out the noonday on the untrod empyreal snow-dome of Koshtra Belorn; and, as in the sweet native habit of such hair, thrones whence darkness shines down darkness to the failing of vision. Compounded and made up of two things she seemed: day and sable night; only in her eyes shone that coolness of aquamarine, and as tempestuous dawns wear their rose-flowers, so she.

After a time, with a sudden melting movement, unseizable as a hummingbird's flight in its shimmer of moods and motives, voluptuous languor, half-surprised acceptance, self-surrender, disdain, she pronounced her name *Fiorinda*, delicately, as if caressing with tongue and lips the name's very beauty as she framed the syllables. She spoke it strangely, as if that name, and the looking-glass image itself, were not her own but somewhat other: somewhat of her making, it might be, as a painter should paint a picture of his heart's desire; yet not her, or at least not her complete. And, so speaking, she laughed, very light and low, all unlike to that mocking laugh that so pricked Barganax's sense, as if (by his saying yesterday) she would laugh all honesty out of fashion. For there was now in this laugh of hers a note of quality alien to all human kind, so honeysweet it was, fancy-free, yet laughter-loving of itself: so might a sudden rift in the veil between time and eternity let through a momentary light sound of the honey-sweet imperishable laughter. On the instant, it was gone. But the memory of it remained like the ringed ripple on water where a bird has dived.

The sun rose, and shot its first beam against that lady's brow, as she turned towards the morning. And now befell a great wonder. Even as she, standing so in the first beams of day, began to put up her hair and pin it with pins of chrysolite, she seemed on the sudden grown taller by a head, to out-top the tallest of men in stature; and whereas, since there is no increase beyond perfection, the beauty of her body might not increase, yet was the substance of it as if transmuted in a moment to pure light, of a like brightness and essence with the heavenly fires of sunrise. No man could in that time have named the colour of Her eyes or of Her hair: the shifting of the dark and light was become as a blinding glory too awful for mortal eye to look upon, too swift for the mind of man to seize or read. For upon Her cheek in that hour was the beauty that belongs to fair-crowned Aphrodite; and that beauty, thus made manifest in its fulness, no eye can bear or see, not even a God's, unless it be possible for the great Father of All Who sitteth in secret, that He might behold it and know it.

The rays touched Barganax's lids. He turned in his sleep: reached out a searching hand and spoke her name in his sleep. She took from the silver-studded stool where it lay her loose gown of diaphanous silken stuff spangled with silver stars and with diamonds and sapphires tiny as grains of sand, and put it about her. The marvel was overpast, as a meteor trails across heaven in the common sight of men and their lowly habitations a light never seen till now in earth or sky, and in a count of ten is gone. On the edge of the great bed upon the fair-worked lace border she sat down, placidly and gracefully as a she-leopard might sit. There was a new look in her eyes now as she watched him asleep: a simple human look, but yet as it were from above, detached and virginal, regarding as if in a tender pitiful wonder these toys of circumstance and greatness and magnificence, and him like a child asleep among them, and her own presence as part of them, sitting there. Suddenly she took his hand that lay there where it had abandoned its dreaming quest, and prisoned it, under both hers, in her bosom. The Duke opened his eyes upon her. He lay very still. Her side-face wore the cool loveliness of a windless lake at sunrise; her gaze was downward, the upper lid level and still, the eye still and wide, yet as if attending to no seen object but to some inside music. His imprisoned hand stirred: he said, under his breath, her name.

Her echo, scarce audible, upon a self-accepting Olympian faint upward nod, came with a kind of hushed assent: *Fiorinda*. And as still she sat with that downward gaze listening, the thing at the corner of her mouth, very beguiling and faun-like now, turned on its back and looked at him sideways.

V

THE VICAR OF REREK

A DOG-WASHING IN LAIMAK • GABRIEL FLORES •
AMENITIES BETWIXT COUSINS • THE CURST HORSE FEELS
THE BRIDLE • 'AN HONEST STATESMAN TO A PRINCE.'

THAT same eye of day, which three hours ago had opened upon
wonder in Acrozayana, was now climbed so high in the eastern
heavens as to top, fifty leagues to the northward, the far-shadowing
backbone of the Forn, and shine clear into Owldale where, upon
a little steep hill solitary among grazing-lands betwixt mountains
eastward and westward, the hold of Laimak lay like a sleeping
wolf. So steep was that hill that it rose naked in cliffs three or
four hundred feet high on every side, and the blind walls of the
fortress, built of huge blocks quarried from the crown of the hill,
followed the line of the cliffs' brow round about. Only to the
north an arched gateway broke the walls, opening on a path hewn
zig-zag up through the cliffs to give passage for men and horses;
but always upon sufferance, since at every step the walls or towers
commanded that passage way for shooting and casting down of
fire or boiling pitch; and a gatehouse bestrode the passage way at
its coming forth into the fields below, with towers and machicola-
tions and a portcullis of iron. Wolf-grey it was all to look upon,
as well the cliffs as the walls that frowned above them, being
of one substance of stubborn crystalline rock, of the earth's

primordial crust, wolf-grey and of an iron hardness. And this was from antique times the castle of the Parrys, that now for thirty generations had been lords in Rerek.

Upon the champaign north and east under Laimak there lay in tents that army, not yet disbanded, which the Lord Horius Parry had drawn to a head for dealing with the King if need were, and which, that necessity now being past, he in his prudent husbandry thought it not good too hastily to lay aside; meaning it should yet, haply for argument in the southlands, haply otherwise, nicely serve his turn.

Within the hold, thus early, he himself was up and doing, while most men yet slept. Under the mighty archway called Hagsby's Entry, that led from one of the inner courts beneath two towers into the inmost court of all, which was outer ward of the great square keep, he stood, all in dirt, stripped to the waist, aproned like a smith, with a long wooden vat or tub before him full of steaming soapy water, taking his pleasure with washing of his cursed dogs. Two or three that he had already dealt with rushed hither and thither about the narrow courtyard, yelping and barking and tumbling in a wild gladness of release; the rest skulked in shadowy corners of the archway, as hoping against hope to escape notice, yet daring not to slink away, coming each in turn when his name was called, grovelling and unwilling to his master's feet. Bushy-tailed prick-eared heavy-chested long-fanged slaver-mouthed beasts were they all, a dozen or more, some red, some black, some grey, some yellow, as big as wolves and most wolfish to look upon. Each as his turn came the Vicar seized by the scruff of the neck and by the loose skin above the haunches and, lifting it as it had been a kitten, set it in the bath. He was a huge, heavy, ugly man, nigh about fifty years of age, not tall as beside tall men, but great-thewed and broad of chest and shoulder, his neck as thick as a common man's thigh, his skin fair and full of freckons, his hair fiery red, stiff like wires and growing far down on his neck behind; he wore it trimmed short, and it had this quality that it stood upright on his head like a savage dog's if he was angry. His ears were strangely small and fine shaped, but set low; his jaw great

and wide; his mouth wide with pale thin lips; his nose jutting
forth with mighty side-pitched nostrils, and high and spreading in
the wings; his forehead high-domed, smooth, and broad, and with
a kind of noble serenity that sorted oddly with the ruffianly lines
of his nose and jaw; his beard and mustachios close-trimmed and
bristly; his eyebrows sparse; his eyelids heavy, not deep set. He
had delicate lively hazel eyes, like the eyes of an adder. He had
none of his servants by him at this dog-washing, save only his
secretary, Gabriel Flores, for his mind was sprightly and busy
a-mornings, and he would have the convenience to talk, if occasion were, secretly with this man, who were aptly styled (to overpass
his swarthy hue, and lack of all nobleness in his softer and more
bloated look) for his highness *in duodecimo*.

'Come hither, Pyewacket!' shouted the Vicar, letting go that
dog that was then in the bath and turning to peer into the shadows
of the gate. 'Pyewacket! Satan's lightnings blast the bitch! Woo't
come when th'art called?' He hurled the heavy scrubbing-brush
at a brindled shadowy form that stole away in hoped obscurity:
a yelp told him that his aim was true. The great beast, her tail
between her legs, trotted away; he shouted to her again; she
glanced back, a harried reproachful glance, and trotted faster;
the Vicar was upon her with a lion-like agility; he kicked her;
she laid back her ears, snarled, and snapped at his leg; he caught
her by the neck and beat her with his fist about the ribs and
buttocks till she yelped for pain; when he had done she growled
and bared her teeth; he beat her once more, harder, then waited
to see what she would do. She gave in, and walked, but with no
good grace, to the distasteful bath. There, standing shoulder-deep
in the steaming suds, grown thin to look on beyond nature, and
very pathetical, with the water's soaking of her hair and making
it cling close to the skin, she suffered sulkily the indignities of
soap and brush, and the searching erudite fingers that (greatly
indeed for her good) sought out and slew the ticks that here and
there beset her. All the while her staring eyes were sullen with
bottled-up anger, like a bull's. The Vicar's eyes had the like look
in them.

'Well,' said he in a while, 'is he coming? You did say I would have speech of him, and that instantly?'

'I did give him your highness' very words,' said Gabriel. He paused: then, "Tis a strange folly, this tennis: racket away a hundred crowns afore breakfast, and till that's done all sober business may go hang.'

'Did he not answer you?' asked the Vicar after a minute.

Gabriel smiled a crooked smile. 'Not to say, answer,' he said.

'What said he, then?' said the Vicar, looking up.

Gabriel said, 'Faith, 'twas not for your ear intended. I were to blame did I blab to your highness every scurvy word, spoke in unconsiderate haste, that your highness should magnify past all reason.'

At that word, came Lessingham hastily towards them out of the low dark passage that sloped upward into the long and narrow yard, at the far, or eastern, end whereof was Hagsby's Entry where the washing was. And at that word, whether seeing him or no, the Vicar gave his Pyewacket a damnable slap across the nose, grabbed her fore and aft, and flung her out in the way of Lessingham that walked hastily to greet him. She, with the gadflies of pain and outraged dignity behind her and a strange man before, sprang at his throat. Lessingham was in his shirt, tennis-racket in hand; he smote her with the racket, across the fore-leg as she sprang: this stopped her; she gave way, yowling and limping. 'God's death!' said the Vicar, 'will you kill my brach?' and threw a long-bladed dagger at him. Lessingham avoided it: but the singing of it was in his ear as it passed. He leapt at the Vicar and grappled him. The Vicar wrestled like a cat-a-mountain, but Lessingham held him. Gabriel, at his master's skirt, now kept off the dogs, now pleased himself with looking on the fight, ever side-stepping and dodging, like a man caught in a hill-forest in a whirlwind when the tall pines loosened at root reel and lock together and lurch, creaking and tottering, towards the last downward-tearing ruinous crash. The Vicar's breath began to come and go now in great puffs and hissings like the blowing of a sea-beast. Lessingham rushed him backwards. The edge of the wash-tub caught him behind the knees, and he fell in, body and breeches, with Lessingham a-top of him, and with that violence the tub was overturned.

They loosed hold and stood up now, and in that nick of time came Amaury into the yard. The Vicar barked out a great laugh, and held out his hand to Lessingham, who took it straight. There was in Lessingham's eye as it rested upon his cousin a singular look, as if he fingered in him a joy too fine for common capacities: such a look as a man might cast, unknowingly and because he could not help it, on his dear mistress. And indeed it was strange to consider how the Vicar, standing thus in nasty clothes, but even risen from a rude tussling-bout and a shameful fall, stood yet as clothed upon with greatness like a mantle, sunning in his majesty like adders in warm beams.

Lessingham said, 'You did send for me.'

'Yes,' answered he: 'the matter is of weight. Wash and array us, and we'll talk on't at breakfast. Gabriel, see to't.'

'I'll meet you straight in my lodging, Amaury,' said Lessingham.

When they were alone, 'Cousin,' said Lessingham, 'you did throw a knife at me.'

The Vicar was ill at ease under Lessingham's secure and disturbing smile. 'Tush,' he said, ''twas but in sport.'

'You shall find it a dangerous sport,' said Lessingham. 'Be advised, cousin. Leave that sport.'

'You are such a quarrelling, affronting—' the words ceased in his throat as his eye met Lessingham's. Like his own great hell-hound bitch awhile ago, he, as for this time, bared fang yet owned his master. And in that owning, as by some hidden law, he seemed to put on again that greatness which but even now, under Lessingham's basilisk look, had seemed to fall off from him.

That was an hour later when those kinsmen brake their fast together on the roof of the great main keep, over the Vicar's lodging: a place of air and wide prospect; and a place besides of secrecy; for when the door in the north-west turret was shut, by which alone was a way up to the roof and the battlements, there was none save the fowls of the air and the huge stones of the floor and parapet to be eavesdroppers at their conference. Here in the midst of the floor was a narrow table set under the sky, with musk-millions and peaches in silver dishes, and a great haunch of cold venison, and marmalades of quince and crab-apple, and flagons of white and red hippocras, with chased gold goblets; and there were diapered linen napkins and silver-handled knives and silver forks to eat withal; all very noble and sumptuously arrayed. Two heavy armchairs of old black oak were set at the table; the Vicar sat at the northern side, and over against him Lessingham. They were washen now, and in fair and fine clothes. The Vicar had put on now a kirtle of dark brown velvet edged with rich embroidery of thread of gold, but frayed and dirted and rubbed with wearing; it was cut wide and low about the neck, with a flat collar of white pleated lace tied with silken cord. Lessingham was in a buff-coloured kirtle of soft ribbed silk with a narrow ruff and narrow wristbands of point-lace spangled with beads of jet of the bigness of mustard seeds, and tight-fitting black silk breeches and velvet shoes.

For a time they ate in silence. Every other while, the Vicar's sudden eye glinted upon Lessingham; it was as if he had a mind to propound some matter, but would be besought for it first. But Lessingham sat sphinx-like and unconcerned in his pleasant ease, as wanting nothing, desiring nothing, at peace with himself and the hour and the fresh morning. At length the Vicar spoke: 'You are as unquiet and restless as an October stag: but three days here, and already I see you in a fever for some new action.'

Lessingham smiled.

After a time the Vicar spoke again: 'For my own part, I had as lief sit quiet now: enjoy that fortune hath given us.'

'I praise your resolution,' said Lessingham: 'a most pious and fine humility in you, whom fortune hath so much blest, without all seconding of your proper action.'

The Vicar took a peach and skinned it. 'Could we but count,' he said, 'on others for the like temperate withholding.'

Lessingham said nothing.

'The south breedeth hot bloods and hot livers like summer flies,' said the Vicar after a pause. He poured out some more wine. ''Tis that gives me stay,' he said. ''Tis that makes me think may be we should do somewhat,' he said, after another mouthful.

Lessingham waited.

The Vicar smote his fist on the table. 'I am master of the game, by this lucky turn,' he said: 'play off the fat Admiral 'gainst the Duke, and all the poppets of Meszria 'gainst each in turn: cheap as kissing, and twice as profitable. But it needs suasion, cousin, specious arguments; butter 'em, tickle 'em, conycatch 'em; you must go to 'em like coy wenches: amuse 'em, feed 'em with pathetical flim-flams, flout 'em, then seem to forget 'em, then be somewhat bold with 'em, laugh at 'em; last, i' the happy instant, ring up the grand main piece. Now I, cousin, am a loose, plain, rude talker: call a spade a spade. But you, and you would, should do this to admiration.'

'I have handled such a matter ere now,' said Lessingham, 'and have not spoilt things utterly.'

'Cousin,' said the Vicar: 'harkee, I would have your head in this. I would have you fare south and play this game for me. You shall be my ambassador. And, so you magnify it not beyond all reason, you shall name your own reward.'

'I did think you knew,' said Lessingham, 'that it is not my way to do aught upon reward. Reason why, that to such things only am I wont to set my hand as the reward thereof lieth in the doing of 'em.'

''Twould make a dog laugh to hear such fiddle-faddle,' said the Vicar. 'Go to, I shall give you wide choice of dominion and treasure when the time comes. Will you do it?'

'I will do it,' answered Lessingham: 'but upon conditions.' His eyes were a-sparkle.

'Well,' said the Vicar.

Lessingham said, 'First is, that you uphold the King's testament.'

'That,' replied he, 'proceedeth without question. It is my open proclaimed policy to uphold it throughly, and if you will I'll swear to it.'

'Second is,' said Lessingham, 'that you own and acknowledge

to me, for my private ear only, here in this place, that 'twas by your rede, more, your direct commandment, the King was lately thus miserably murdered.'

The Vicar laughed. "'Las cousin, will you, too, give credit to that slanderous rumour and obloquy now going abroad?'

'I see,' said Lessingham: 'you will not fulfil my second condition. Good. Get you another ambassador.'

The Vicar's face was scarlet to look upon. He said, 'I swear to you by God, the very founder, furtherer, and finisher of truth—'

Lessingham brake in upon him: 'Give over, cousin. Indeed, if you be not damned already 'twere pity damn yourself for so hopeless an attempt as make me credit what I well know to be a lie. Be not angry, cousin: here we be close as the grave: surely 'twixt you and I 'tis stretch courtesy past use and reason to pretend I know you not for a most approved liar and forswearer.' He ate a bit of marmalade, and leaned back in his chair. 'To be open with you,' he said, 'you have put me into such a gog of going. I would not stay now for the world. Yet see the pass we stand in: if it be as hard for you to tell the truth as for me to go back from my word, I'm sorry for it, for then all goeth miss.'

'Put case it were true,' said the Vicar. 'Were it not rash in you to desire a knowledge might hurry you to ruin? Like to that great man's mistress, wheedled him to confess a horrid murder, which done, he swore her to silence upon a poisoned book: knowing it lay not in her to conceal his counsel, bound her to't by death.'

Lessingham looked at him with the flicker of a smile in his eyes. 'When I am grown so useless to you, cousin, as you should afford to lose me, I'll think it danger to receive such secrets of you. Till then, no. I'll trust no man's affections, but I trust your wisdom most securely. Most securely, cousin.'

The Vicar toyed with his wine-cup. 'Be that as it may,' he said at last. 'This you talk on is a monstrous folly. Where's the reason of the thing? I were a fine fool to a murdered the young suck-egg, when 'twas in my hand to have overthrown him with force of arms.'

'There,' replied Lessingham, 'you do much belie your prudent mind. It had been folly indeed to stand in the eyes of the world a usurping rebel, when 'twas the readier way, with some devilish pothecary stuff, stibium, henbane, I know not what, to whiffle him off and then put on your mourning and say his jealous brother did it.'

'Ay, and did he,' said the Vicar. 'And did set too the lying tongues a-wag to say 'twas I.'

Lessingham yawned and studied the back of his hand, the little silky black hairs that grew fine and smooth on the shapely finger-joints, and the heavy ancient golden worm that he wore on his middle finger, scaly, eating of its own tail, its head a cabochon ruby big as a sparrow's egg, that glowed with inward fires like the blood-red fires of sunset.

'You will go then?' said the Vicar.

'But upon condition of confession,' answered he.

The Vicar lurched up from the table and began to pace about. Lessingham yawned again and played with his ring. Neither spoke. After a minute the Vicar, grinding his teeth, came and stood over against him. Lessingham looked up. 'Dear cousin,' he said, 'how long will you stay this matter's going into action, of so much worth and moment? And how long will you seek to cast suds in my eyes that am long since satisfied of the truth, but will have it of you in friendship? You did send me out of the way to Mornagay whiles it was done. But I know it.'

The Vicar laughed with anger. 'Know it? Upon what evidence?' He ground his teeth. 'Gabriel, that filth, was't he told you this? I'll have him hewn in pieces.'

'O spare your pains,' said Lessingham. 'Should Gabriel tell me at noonday 'twas twelve o'clock, I'd have evidence corroborative ere I'd believe it. No, cousin, I am satisfied you did act this murder; not by your own hand, indeed: that were too simple: but yours the deed was. And since you will be so strange with me as deny the thing: well, the Gods be with you, I'll have no further hand with you.'

The Vicar sat down again and leaned across the table, glowering at him awhile in silence. Lessingham returned his gaze steadily; the eyes of Lessingham were grey with brown and golden speckles. The Vicar at length turned away his gaze. 'Well,' he said betwixt his teeth: 'I did it.'

Slowly and luxuriously Lessingham stretched his arms, yawned, and then sat up. He reached out a leisurely hand to the golden flagon and filled his goblet with red hippocras. 'Truth hath been long time a-coming out,' he said. 'I'll pledge her, so.' He drank, looking over the cup at the Vicar with a slow smiling contentment, a strange, clouded look, in which came suddenly an alteration as if the red sun had glared out through a rift in the clouds. 'This murder,' said he, and there were now undertones and overtones in his voice that made it terrible, for all it was so quiet and came on so even and undisturbed a breath: 'This murder was one of the most filthiest acts that ever was done.'

The Vicar faced him like a bull of Nineveh.

'You did show me the testament,' said Lessingham. 'Was that some fine counterfeit device of yours, or was it real and true?' The Vicar made no answer. Lessingham said, 'Well, I know it was true, by tests beyond your protestations, cousin. And I remarked it very particularly, wherein it did name you vicar and vice-regent of the Queen and lord protector of her minority, and did enjoin you in all points study her proper good and safety and the enhancement of her sovereign power and dominion, and tender and cherish her lovingly as a father should. You are not much practised in a father's part, I think. Since you did drive your sons away into exile. This will be hard for you.'

He paused, looking the Vicar straight in the eye. It was as if across that silent table two thunder-clouds faced each other in an awful calm. Lessingham spoke: 'You have promised me to uphold that testament. Well, I'll help you, as I have done before. I'll go on this embassage for you. I'll follow and uphold you as Vicar of the Queen. But this testament shall be to you as a thing enskied and holy. Which if in any jot or tittle you shall offend against, or one finger's breadth depart from it: no more, but you shall bitterly aby it.'

The Vicar ran his tongue over his lips. For a minute he was

silent, then in a kind of cold tart pride he said, 'I were poorly paid then for my goodness and forbearance; seeing these five minutes past I have had a more than most intolerable lust to murder you, yet, I know not why, forbore.' He stood up with a laugh, and with a forced pretence of jolly-scoffing bravery. 'What squibs be these, for men of our kidney to tease ourselves withal of a spring morning! And, cousin, this is the maggot in the oak-apple: you are clean fallen in love with yonder little wagtail at mere hearsay.'

Lessingham answered and said, 'With you, cousin, I have long fallen in love.'

VI

LORD LESSINGHAM'S EMBASSAGE

THE ADMIRAL AND THE CHANCELLOR • DISCORDS OF
LESSINGHAM'S PLANTING • THE ADMIRAL MUCH PERPLEXED
• DIVIDED POLITICS • LESSINGHAM AND VANDERMAST •
CONFERENCE IN ACROZAYANA • THE DUKE BROUGHT
TO BAY • A BROKEN CONSORT • THE DUKE AND
LESSINGHAM: STRANGE CONCORDS.

THAT was of an evening of late May-time, the fourth week after
these things but now spoken of, that the Lord Beroald sat alone
at the upper edge of a clearing in the oak-woods that clothe the
low Darial hills south of the lake, looking northwards to Zayana.
From his feet the ground fell gently away for a hundred paces or
more to the bridle-path. Below that, the tree-clad face of the hill
dropped sharply to the lake seven or eight hundred feet beneath.
The sky was fair, and the weather smooth and calm. His horse
grazed at ease, moving to and fro amid the lush grasses. Save for
that munching sound, and the sound of falling water, and now
and then the note of a cuckoo calling, and now and then the
noise of the horse's hoof against a stone, there was silence. A
marmot came out of a heap of fallen rocks behind him on his left
and sat up with little fore-paws hanging down as if in a helpless
soft dismay, viewing the Chancellor. She whistled and retired back
to her hole when the silence was broken by a fresh noise of

Mistress of Mistresses

horse-hooves, and the lord Admiral rode up into the clearing, greeted the Chancellor, and dismounted beside him.

'It is very much,' said the Lord Jeronimy, when they were sat down together upon a great stone, 'that we should be fain to take counsel under the sky like owls or moor-dogs.'

Beroald smiled his cold smile. 'I am much beholden to your lordship for suffering this inconvenience. In the city, a flea shall not frisk forth unless his intelligencers comment upon her. And this new business both calleth for speedy action, and needs that both you and I examine and consider of it o'erheard by none.'

'Will he not take my no for an answer?' said Jeronimy. 'Why, what a loose hot corrupter of virtue have we here. First getteth no from me; then no from the Duke; and now sueth to your lordship to be in a manner his go-between, as if I were a silly maid to comply at last, with oftener scenting of the flower. What new conditions now then?'

''Tis not altogether thus,' said the Chancellor. The offer is now to me in my own particular.'

Jeronimy opened his lips as if to speak, but there was a moment ere the words came: 'To you, my lord? Good: and upon like condition?'

'Upon like condition.'

'Of suzerainty?' said Jeronimy. 'Well, and do you mean to take it? No, no,' he said, meeting the Chancellor's cold eye: 'I meant not that. I meant, in what estate left you this business with him? did you in a manner temporize?'

Beroald answered, 'I did handle the thing in such a vein as that I must give him yea or nay tomorrow.'

The Admiral pulled off his black velvet cap plumed with a white estridge-feather set in a diamond brooch, mopped his head, and put on his cap again.

The Lord Beroald gazed steadily before him on Acrozayana, two or three miles away, mirrored in the glassy lake. His speech came cool and glassy, like the thing he looked on, remote and passionless as if it were his own thought speaking to itself. 'It is needful,' he said, 'in this business, that we hold heedy guard, and reckon well our strength. Now is ten days today that this Lessingham, treating with full powers on behalf of the Vicar, hath dealt with us touching the Meszrian regency; and if there be any alteration made in these ten days, 'tis to their advantage, not ours. First his offer unto you, my lord Admiral, that the Vicar would receive and acknowledge you as regent in Meszria conformably in all points to the King's testament, and upon condition (which he stiffly maintained to be in that same testament supposed and implicit) that you should do him homage as, pending the Queen's minority, your overlord. That condition you did, in agreement with the Duke, with Roder, and with myself, after mature deliberation of counsel, flatly refuse. The next day after your so refusing, he did offer the regency upon like condition to the Duke, who did refuse it. That was but yesterday. And now, this very morning, did send for me and propound to me the self-same offer; which I, forbearing all private closer conference, fobbed off until tomorrow. Thus standeth it, then. What follows? If I refuse,' (upon that 'if' the Admiral pulled out his handkerchief and mopped his head), 'next move belike is overture of regency to Roder, and then, if he'll not take it, war. I like it not. The Duke I do trust but as you do, my lord: very discreetly. These Meszrian lords, not at all. The Vicar hath a fair solicitor, hath got the right ear of Zapheles, and Melates, too, or I am much mistook: young fools, that have not the wit to see in all the Vicar's promises but fair sunshining, sweetly spoken and but sourly to be performed. Prince Ercles in the north, too, is not so good to rest on, even if Barganax be safe: if the Vicar make war upon the Duke and us upon pretext of enforcing of the King's testament, you shall not see Ercles nor Aramond put their finger too far in the fire o' the Duke's behalf; Lessingham, I am told, hath made friends with 'em both of late.'

'That Lessingham is a subtle devil,' said Jeronimy.

'This latest offer thus made to me,' said the Chancellor, 'hath given us the chance if need be to afterthink us. That were pity were it appear in the end that our eyes were greater than our bellies. I would remember you of this, my lord Admiral, that in point of construction the Vicar's claim of suzerainty is good in law. We are precisely bound to uphold the testament. It can be said that, going against him in this, we do merely violate it. The Parry himself none but a ninny would trust further than a might see him; but here 'tis not to deal with him direct, but through Lessingham.'

'As 't should be handed us,' said Jeronimy, 'in a fair gilded cup, to make his poison go down the smoother.'

'I see it not altogether so,' said Beroald. ''Tis a young man of most supposed abilities both in the council and a soldier of renown. I have these ten days studied him like a book, and I find no point to question, but all to confirm and justify what reputation saith of him: an honourable man, and a man with the power to hold his principal to whatsoever he shall stand warrant for of his behalf. And he hath, in no qualified way but at large, took it upon his honour that upon agreement made betwixt us the Vicar will perform the King's testament unto the littlest letter.'

Jeronimy said, 'He is a subtle devil.'

'It is for you, not me, to determine,' said the Chancellor. 'Only I would have you consider of all this, not as somewhat to be swept up with a sudden and tumultuous judgement, but as a thing of heaviest import. For you see, you may, upon this offer thus made to me, open your dealings anew with him, and take up the regency upon condition of suzerainty and upon his proper warranty of the Vicar's performance.'

'And so, in a manner—' said the Admiral slowly, and fell silent. The Chancellor said no more, judging it good to give time for these matters to digest.

They sat in shadow. The sun had for some time now gone behind the hill on their left. The shadows lengthened over the lake. The horses munched on. After a while the Chancellor spoke: 'Will you not change your mind?'

The Lord Jeronimy rose heavily from his seat and stood looking at him a minute in silence; then said, 'No. And no more must you, my lord Chancellor.'

'We stand together,' said Beroald, and rose up too. 'Yet

remember, things worsen as time goeth by. These country lords
are quite debauched by him. 'Tis time to end talking and fall to
action.'

The Admiral's black mare, at her lord's stirring, came to him
and nuzzled her nose in his neck. He fondled and petted her. ''Tis
time indeed,' he said. 'Time indeed.'

'Better we were not seen too much in conference tonight,' said
Beroald. 'Better not enter the gates together.'

'Will you ride first,' said the Admiral, 'or shall I? Truth is, I had
been minded for Sestola tonight, 'bout some business of the fleet.
But as things shape, I will let that go by and sleep in Zayana.'

'I pray you ride first,' said the Chancellor.

The Admiral came down through the wood at a walking pace,
his mind heavy with thought. His men, that had waited this while
in the wood with the Chancellor's, rode a score of paces or so
behind him. 'Lessingham,' he said in himself. 'A very subtle devil:
a devil full of all seduction and charm. Hath a not charmed me
too? Ay, but not too far: not to danger. Like to that son of mine,
drowned in the Sound of Tabarey: should a been of about his
years too, had he lived. Pish! 'Tis foolery. And yet, 'tis in the Duke
too. Lessingham: Barganax. Strange: so unlike, and yet, in a manner,
so like; both of the grape, as 'twere. Red wine: white wine. Away,
'tis foolery. Still, like a shying horse: ride her up to it, let her see
and examine it well as to its nature: it frighteth her not another
time.' His mind stood still awhile. Then he said again in himself,
'Hath charmed Beroald. Nay, but that's not true neither. Nay, I
trust Beroald.'

He drew rein for a moment as the path rounded the verge of
a jutting cliff giving a fair wide prospect over the water. An owl
hooted. Jeronimy said in himself, 'If he can handle Horius Parry,
as folk say he can: tickle him, make him serve his turn; what
wonder in the world can he not do then?' He rode on. 'Beroald
is a man of law. There's his element. But with me 'tis substance
and intention, not form and accident. And yet indeed, a great wise
man; prudent and foreseeing. Ay, "time to afterthink us", that's
wisdom. Worse weather than that we put to sea in: ay, 'tis pure

truth. There's many would take his rede and think no more on't. Safer. Safer take his rede.

'Ay, but I do know 'tis wrong. In my bones I know it.' He struck spurs into the mare's flanks: she started forward violently: he leaned forward calming her, patting her neck. 'No, I'll not change my mind. Nor you must not neither, my lord Chancellor. But then, what next? Action, next. An end of these talkings: 'tis time indeed.' He stroked her neck again, softly, meditatively. 'And I the main actor. Regent of Meszria. Lieth upon me. Well, we have long since considered on't. With right of our side; and with the Duke of our side. "I am of your opinion," said he. Well: now cometh this silver to the trying. Barganax: is he to trust to? 'Tis a doubt whereon hangeth all, on this one thin thread. Trust him discreetly. The word is wiser than the deed, now I consider on't. O, the down-bearing weight of this immense charge. Tis a fine toy, make up alliance with a royal prince on terms he must but figure bass for such a man as me to run the divisions on't; comfort and uphold me at all points whiles I sit i' the seat he looked for as his by right. If he have a spice of pride in him still (and he is made up and compounded of pride, opinion, and disdain), shall he not hate me every while, and seek but first fair occasion to ding me down and take his own back? And yet the man's mind is so noble, I'd trust him, where his word's engaged, even to breaking-point. And yet, no, 'tis midsummer madness: 'tis but the spell of his masterful youth and grace, like t'other's. I had done with this ten minutes since: 'tis 'foolery. And yet, and yet: have I not proof of's loyal mind within reason: his refusing on't when Lessingham did offer it? Nay, but 'twas but stinking fish then: 'twas under suzerainty. And he of the royal ancient family of Fingiswold.'

He halted, as with a sudden thought then with a shake of the rein went on. 'Of Fingiswold. Ay, and of Memison. I'll do it. Better hazard sinking there, than sink for sure where we stand. And there's some hope. Say they be corrupted indeed, these young quats, with Lessingham's words and promises: 'tis certain their corruption, even as their fealty, is but skin-deep. They'll follow their own liege sovereign prince of Meszrian blood and line a

thousand times, where, were it but me, they'd take but the happy
instant to throw me off and so rid them at last of the prime
scourge and hate of all their liberties for years. I'll do it. Ay, I'll
do it tonight.'

That same night after supper the Chancellor was sat in his chamber
writing out fair this letter, which being writ he signed by his name
and sealed with his seal. And the letter was conceived in terms
following:

'*Unto thonorable my very goode Lo. Lessynghame as wyth
fulle powre and awtoritee dymysed and prorogate to speke
trette and determyn on byhalve of his hyghnes Horyus Parye
Lo. Protector and Vicker of the Qwene in Reyrek:*
*I have bin carefull my Lo. to waighe and conseder of hys
Highnes proposes wherewithall hys hyghnes hath honored
me thorow your lops, mowth to thende that for the bettere
setlying and doynge awaie of these presente diffrences I
schold in myn owne persoun accept of the Regensy of Meszrya
upon condicyons exposed att lardge bi your lop., and bi
asspeciall thus condicyon that the Regent schalbe in al
poyntes His Hyghnes subgytte and uery leage man. Al whilke
I hauing with carefull mind perpended and revuiewed am
lefte att length wyth noe other choys that semeth to me
agreable unto my propre honor and my dwte ylike to the
Qwene (hoom the Goddes tender and preserue) and to
thadmerall bi royalle testement named regent but bi hys
hyghnes set asyde upon refusell of condicyoun a forseyd,
saue to conclud that yt is nat fytt I schold accept of the
sed Regensy. Whilke resolue thus consederately taken I will
vnmoueably stand upon, and wold dessire your lop. to
acqweynt Hys Highnes accordynge.*
The Goddes leade your lop. bi the hande.
*I haue thonor to bee with greatt trewth and respecte your
lops, most obedient humble Servaunt,*

BEROALD'

The ink was scarce dry and the wax yet warm when there came in a gentleman of his to say the High Admiral was here and would have speech of him. The Chancellor smiled. 'That saveth me a journey,' he said: 'I was this instant upon going to see him;' and he bade admit him straight. When they were private, 'My lord Chancellor,' said Jeronimy, and his face was flushed, 'I bring you good tidings. I have seen the Duke upon this matter we talked on.'

The Chancellor lifted a cold eye upon him. 'You have seen the Duke?'

Jeronimy's eyes took on that look that a dog's eyes have when, under a detecting gaze, he suddenly bethinks him that this eating of that bit of meat or chewing up of that bird, albeit good and reasonable in his estimation, was yet questionable in the sight of others, and fraught, may be, with consequences he till then ne'er thought upon. 'I'm sorry,' he said. 'I am come straight from him to you. Perhaps I should a seen you first. I'm sorry, my lord.'

'You are dark to me yet,' said the Chancellor. 'Did your lordship inform the Duke of this last turn: I mean this offer I told you of?'

'In a manner, yes,' answered Jeronimy.

'Had I stood in your shoes, my lord Admiral,' said the Chancellor, 'I should have given you the opportunity to come with me upon such an errand.'

'You and I,' said the Admiral, 'did conclude upon speedy action. A-riding home I did view the matter from all points, and did at last conceive in a manner but one safe way betwixt these quicksands. Brief, I did resign but now into the Duke's hand, as well for present as prospectively, the office of Regent: bade him take it up and defend it, and we would go through and second him.'

He paused. The Chancellor's jaw set, and his lean face turned ashy. He stood up from his chair, pushed the letter across the table to Jeronimy, and stalked to the window. The Admiral took out his perspective-glass and read the letter, blowing softly with his cheeks the while. 'Your lordship hath an art in drafting of such matters,' he said: ''tis beyond admiration excellent.' He looked cautiously up, met the Chancellor's eye, and looked away.

For a minute the Lord Beroald abode silent. When he mastered himself to speak, the words came like chips of ice clinking down an ice-slope. 'Lessingham,' he said, 'is an able politician. You and me, my lord, he but turneth to his purpose. You have made a fine hand of it.'

Jeronimy slowly shook his head. 'I did play for a firm line and no stragglers,' said he. 'We should not have held the Duke with us had we ta'en, in a manner, the course you formerly thought on: had I complied and ta'en up the regency 'pon Lessingham's conditions.'

'You have now by your act,' said Beroald, 'disburdened him of all conditions, and left us open to all injuries. You have, in face of dangerous enemies, set aside the law, which was our strength and our justification; you have struck wide division in our counsels, when a single mind was most needful; you have unleashed the Duke on a course may be shall prove his ruin and ours. Had you gone cap in hand to my Lord Lessingham and professed yourself ready to do his bidding so as to make fair success of his mission hither, he could a thought on no better means to bid you take than these you have taken.'

Jeronimy's face became drawn and his kindly eyes darkened with anger. He rose from his chair. 'This talk,' he said, thickly, 'doth more disgrace than it helpeth or graceth us. Let us say no more but good night, my lord Chancellor. May be morning shall bring us riper wisdom.'

On the morrow towards midday the Lord Lessingham took horse and rode with Amaury from his lodgings in the old Leantine palace in the northern quarter down through the market-place, and so, turning right along Stonegate and Paddockgate, up into the driving-road that ran by the water-side along the top of the town wall of old red sandstone for a quarter of a mile or more; thence, turning inland at the Heugh, through some winding cobbled streets, they came out into the sunlight of the piazza of the Winds, and, crossing that from north to south, took the Way of the Seven Hundred Pillars. At a walking-pace they climbed its wide zig-zags, pleasant with the shade of ancient holm-oaks and the heavy scent of the mimosa-trees, and came at length a little before noon up to the main gate of the citadel. A guard of honour, of seven of the Duke's red-bearded swordsmen, conducted them up the shining stairs that were built of panteron stone, black green and purple, and so by many courts and colonnades to silver doors and through them to a narrow and high-roofed corridor which opened at its far end, with silver doors, upon that garden of everlasting afternoon. Here, in the low slanting rays under the tufted shade of strawberry-trees, that ancient man stood to do them welcome, Doctor Vandermast.

He said, 'You are late, my lord.'

Lessingham, that had not before beheld the wonder of this garden, bit in his admiration and said, 'I am, on the contrary, upon the very point of noon. His grace is late, for his own time appointed.'

'His grace,' answered Vandermast, 'is always late. That is to say, he o'errunneth the just time by an hour or so; and that is not blameworthy in a royal Duke. But here indeed is a strange impertinent jest of your lordship's, to come hither some four or five hours behind your set time, and look to find him waiting upon your pleasure.'

Amaury said, 'Will you make game with my lord, sir? Be more civil; for in truth you are but an old fantastical scholar, with a beard like a crow with two or three dirty straws in her mouth, going to build her nest.'

'Hold your tongue, Amaury,' said Lessingham. 'Scandal not the reverend signior. Doctor, I heard tell ere now of this garden, that 'tis one of the wonders of the world, and that you did make it. And now I see it indeed, I am astonished.'

'It is a natural garden, my lord,' answered that old man. 'This is very sky, and very sun, very clouds and lake, and you and I here in our bodies. You may touch, smell, walk and discourse, inhale the airs. It is natural present.'

'Come,' said Lessingham: 'that is over high meat for my weak stomach. Why, the sun in a golden bush of glory standeth but a handbreadth above yonder woody hills beyond the water; and yet, ten minutes since, it was white noon, blazing on our heads from the meridian.'

Vandermast said: 'Save for birds or reremice, winged emmets, wasps, flies, and such manner of filths, there is but one only way into this garden, and it is through the lobby of the silver doors. Your lordship and this froward young man did pass the further door at noon, but the hither door some five hours after noon. It is a nice point of disputation whether you did with tortoise-like slowness transambulate that lobby, so as in five hours to proceed but twenty paces, or whether *per contra* those five hours did, with a speed whipped to ten thousand times its natural, blow by you as you walked. *Experimentum docet*: you are here, and 'tis late afternoon.'

'And if I shall instantly go back again?' said Lessingham. 'What then?'

'You shall find it then but a little past midday without. The Duke expects you, my lord. He will be here ere long.'

Lessingham walked and stood by the parapet, looking south. Amaury followed him. For a minute or two Lessingham abode there, then turned, leaning with an elbow on the parapet behind him, so as to face that garden. Amaury watched the look in his eyes as they wandered from yellow lily to rose and alkanet and honeysuckle, from bee-haunted lime to strawberry-tree with night-dark foliage, wine-red twisted branches, and jewel-like flower and fruit; shaven sward, porphyry seat, doves at the fountains; all in a sleepy plenitude of golden air and cool long shadows. But once in his life before had Amaury seen that look, and that was a month ago, when Lessingham had stared into the wine in Mornagay. He turned, and saw that that learned man was gazing on Lessingham with a strange intention, and that the look in the eyes of him and the look in the eyes of Lessingham were the same.

The silver doors opened in the blind northern wall, and one came to say that the council was set now in the Duke's closet and he would there receive them. As they turned to go, Lessingham halted and looked down at Doctor Vandermast. 'One thing I would know,' he said, 'that hath strangely puzzled me since first I came hither to Zayana. What are you, old sir?'

Vandermast was silent for a moment, looking straight before him to those sunshiny hills beyond the lake, through half-closed lids, as if remarking and appraising some strange matter. He smiled. 'I, my lord,' he said slowly, 'am one that am wont to pry beneath the unstable course and fickle flower of man's affairs. Somewhat, may be, I have digged up in my searchings. And I am an old faithful servant of the Duke of Zayana.' Then, looking Lessingham in the eye, he said, 'Forget not, my lord, that all things work together. If, spite all, his grace should bid you guest here this night, in Acrozayana, be very sure you do it.'

So now came they to the Duke's closet. He himself sat on the north side of the table, his back to the fireplace, with the Admiral on his right, the Chancellor on his left, and beyond the Chancellor Earl Roder. On the Earl's left was Count Zapheles, and the Lords Melates and Barrian to the right of the Admiral. Lessingham sat midmost of the table over against the Duke, Amaury and Doctor Vandermast took notes. Amaury said privately as they sat down, 'Now that we are gotten safe away, sir, out of yon sorcery-witched garden, I'll say I'm sorry I was rude with you. I would not say it there. I would not you should think I was afeared of you.'

Vandermast answered and said, 'I have an eye to find out good, even as the margaret is found growing in the meat of certain shell-fishes, in howsoever curious a sort it shall disguise itself. Therefore, be at ease, young gentleman.'

But even while he so spoke with Amaury, the eagle glance of him was busy with the faces of the great men met about that table, and most of all with the Duke's face and the Lord Lessingham's. The Duke, under his cloak of disdainful ease, seemed as if gathered for his spring. Lessingham, stroking his black beard, looking through half-dropped lashes now at the Duke, now at the Admiral or the Chancellor, and still at the Duke again, seemed waiting for that spring should land the springer in a pit he himself had digged for him.

'Will you speak first, my Lord Lessingham?' said the Duke.

'Willingly,' answered he, with a grave inclination of the head. 'But it can but be to invite your grace to set forth the business you have called us to consider of upon so much urgency.' There was in his voice as he spoke a lazy bantering music, full of charm, redolent too of sleeping dangers. Amaury, that had been bred up with him to manhood, knew it like his native air. Vandermast knew it too, but not till now in a man's voice. For it bore, even as the troubled image in a lake at midnight to the star it mirrors, some kinship to that languorous mocking lazy music that awoke so often in the Lady Fiorinda's voice; and Vandermast thought he knew, looking at the Duke, that the Duke too felt the spell of it, albeit without recognition, as a man listening to an air which he knows yet cannot place.

'It is now going upon the eleventh day,' said the Duke, 'that your lordship hath gladdened us with your company. In respect of persons, we could wish no end to't. But in respect of matters of state 'tis not convenient.'

'For your princely entertainment I am greatly beholden,' answered Lessingham. 'For the delays, they are none of mine. So far forth as it lay in me to do it, all might a been done and goodbye the first morning.'

'Yet it draggeth on,' said the Duke. 'And thence ensueth idleness. And from idleness, mischief. My lord, I mean this offer of yours unto my lord Chancellor: I but heard on't this morning.'

'Your grace will not hold me answerable,' said Lessingham, 'for this failure to tell good news round the family. Howsoever, I've not been answered yet;' and he turned to Beroald.

'There, my lord, is my answer,' said Beroald; and gave it him across the table.

Lessingham took the letter: 'Is it yes?'

Beroald replied, 'Your lordship hath the wit to know very well 'tis no.'

'That is by so much the worser answer for us all,' said Lessingham, 'by how much it is the shorter: by a letter. What next, then? May be your grace hath thought on some way to please us all?'

Barganax sat suddenly forward in his chair. 'We shall now,' said he, 'play no more at fair-and-softly, or king-by-your-leave. The Vicar's offers please nobody. You are grown too bold, my lord. Or did you think I should sit content ever in my curious pretty gardens, my delicate groves, while you fob me up with fair speeches? Lie sunning myself for ever, while you hawk the regency about the town to find a higher bidder? Will you not offer it to my Lord Roder next? There he is. Come, ask him.'

Lessingham said nothing, but folded his arms.

Barganax said, 'You shall find my patience but a gathering deadly cloud. And thus it lightens into action: these great officers of state to right and left of me, bound by old allegiance to uphold the house of Fingiswold, stand in firm league with me to say nay to the Vicar when he requireth abatement of our powers for his behoof, whom we do utterly refuse and mistrust. Under the threats and wrongfulness of whose tyranny, the lord Admiral hath solemnly resigned and given over into my hand the regency of Meszria by testament royal conferred upon him. My Lord Lessingham, I take up that regency, but under suzerainty of no man. If the Vicar will receive me as his equal, lord of Meszria as he of Rerek: good, we are at one. If not, shortest is to say to him that I will maintain my dominion in his despite: in the midst of all his bloody ruff, I'll cope with him.'

Lessingham, albeit strangely surprised and put out of his reckonings by this sudden turn, yet kept his countenance, thinking swiftly with himself. He swept his gaze from one to other, facing him across that table: the Duke like a warhorse that sniffs the morning: the Chancellor, lean-visaged and inscrutable, sitting upright and staring straight before him: Jeronimy with downcast look, elbows on table, his left hand propping his chin, his right twisting and untwisting a strand of the lank spare hair above his forehead: Roder, black and scowling: Barrian with flushed countenance, playing with his pen: Zepheles with jaw thrust forward, looking steadily at the Duke: Melates, half sprawled on his folded arms upon the table, looking steadily at Lessingham. 'My lord Admiral,' said Lessingham at length, 'what will you say to this?'

'You were best address yourself to me, my lord,' said Barganax. 'From henceforth it is me you have to do with.'

But Lessingham said, 'Under your favour, my lord Duke, I must press this. You, my lord Admiral, not his grace, are named regent in the testament.'

'I have resigned it up into his grace's hand. That, in a manner, endeth it,' said Jeronimy. He did not raise his eyes to meet Lessingham's levelled steely gaze.

Then said Lessingham to the Chancellor, 'Your lordship did write me a letter. By his grace's leave I will read it.' He spread it upon the table and read it out. 'I note this,' he said, 'in the Chancellor's letter: that it dealeth not at all with the point of law.'

Beroald said: 'It did not need.'

'No,' said Lessingham. 'Yet to have argued the thing unlawful should much have strengthened it. My lord Chancellor, did you leave out that argument, because you were satisfied that the Vicar's claim of suzerainty is right in law?'

Beroald, looking steadily before him, made no reply.

'Much lieth on this. I pray you, answer,' said Lessingham.

Beroald said, 'I am nowise bounden to advise your lordship on points of law.'

'That is true,' said Lessingham. 'And it must have tried your temper very much, my lord, when they whom you do, as in duty bound, advise, do the one (I mean my Lord Jeronimy) take your advice but durst not act upon't, whiles t'other doth but put it by like idle chatter, and acteth clean contrary.'

The Chancellor said in an acid voice, 'By these ifs and supposings you may gather against us what proofs you list. But since your lordship hath not had my advice upon these matters, nor any authority whereby to conclude what my advice would be, your lordship's observation wanteth substance, whether in fact or probability.'

'My lord, I would but have your answer on point of fact: were you, or were you not, satisfied?' The Chancellor held his peace.

'No need to bandy words on this,' said Barganax, to end it. 'We will not take our law from the Vicar.'

'Nor from my lord Chancellor neither, as now appeareth,' said Lessingham.

Out of an angry silence, Jeronimy spoke and said, 'It is, in a manner, clean 'gainst all likelihood, nay, and not to be imagined, the King should have given over clean everything unto his Vicar, seeing the unkindness there was between them. Even grant the law were in a manner doubtful—'

But Lessingham brake in upon these pleasantnesses. 'My lord Duke,' said he: 'I stand upon the law. Be not angry if I leave velvet words and oily compliment, and talk open. You have set at naught the King's testament. You have brow-beat the High Admiral until he is become your tool. The Chancellor will not answer me, but his silence hath damned by default your rotten pretences before all the world. Be not deceived,' he said, and in the pauses between his words men were ware of each other's breathing: 'the beginnings of things are weak and tender; but I do very well discern your grace's end and purpose, and it is to usurp the whole kingdom 'gainst your harmless sister. It resteth with my noble kinsman, as Lord Protector, to foil you in this. Your answer to me is war. In his highness' name, the Vicar, I do defy you. And I do call upon these great officers (upon you, my lord, and you, and you) to come back to their true allegiance unto the Queen's serenity, to the overthrow of you and your unlawful usurpation.'

Now ever as he spoke, for all the heat of his words and violence, his perceptive mind was cool and busy, marking how much and in what diverse ways these sayings wrought alteration in them that heard them: what jealous mutual doubtings and inward questionings arose to insinuate, like ivy-shoots betwixt the stones of some tottering wall, divisions betwixt the Duke and his sworn confederates: how, perceiving such rifts to open or but the danger of their opening, the Meszrian lords seemed to draw back and view again their own security: how in the Admiral's eyes, as in an open book, was writ in great characters the digging up again of all the old doubts he had but so lately buried, of the Chancellor's truth and of the Duke's: and how, as unkind and nipping winds will find way through every cloak, the Duke himself seemed to be touched, behind all his jaunting bravery, by such unspoken uncertainties in these that he needs must trust to. These effects Lessingham, while he spoke, conjured and swayed but with the spell now here, now there, of a justly chosen word or look; not otherwise than as a master playing on the treble viol will lead the whole consort and build up so a living presence of music: from the deep theorbo such a figure, from the recorders such, and so the treble lutes to take up the canon, and the hautboy, the dulcimer, and the rebeck, every one in his turn, and so with a ritornello, each thus and thus, and always even exact as he, leading the broken consort, would have it. Even so, perceiving these motions, these ruinous doubts and questionings, leap to life at his touch, did Lessingham taste in them a delicate pleasure.

With those last words spoken he ended, and the voice of his speech was like the rattle of iron swords. The Duke, whose chin had risen little by little higher and yet higher as, with smouldering eyes fixed on Lessingham, he had hearkened to these injuries, stood up now with the smooth and measured stateliness of a leopard rising from sleep. With a high and noble look upon his friends to left and right of him, 'Is my hand the weaker,' he said, 'because it is divided into many fingers? No, 'tis the more strongly nimble.' So saying, and turning again to Lessingham, he now with a formal courtesy unsheathed his sword, raised it point upwards till the hilt was level with his lips, kissed the hilt, and laid it naked on the table with the point towards Lessingham. Lessingham stood up in silence and, going through the like ceremony, laid his bare sword beside the Duke's, pointing towards the Duke. So for a minute they stood, facing each other across that table, eye to eye; as if the levin-shot dark splendour of a storm-cloud, towering from the east, faced across listening earth the many-coloured splendour of the westering golden sun. And when at last the Duke spoke, it was as out of that unfathomed harmony which is at once condition of such discords and by them conditioned; ensphered and incarnate by them to a more diviner music. There were but two only at that table who, hearing him so speak, were not taken with wonderment, or with fear, or dismay: and that was Lessingham and Doctor Vandermast.

The Duke said, 'My Lord Lessingham, sith our friendship must be but a summer friendship and its leaves drop off in autumn, let's end it as fitteth persons of our quality. Let us trust each to other's honour until noon tomorrow: you to me, that I will do no dastard's work against your life or freedom: I to you, that, whether by word nor deed, you will meddle no more with these high matters until this day's truce be past.'

'My lord Duke,' said Lessingham, 'I am content.'

Then said the Duke, 'I do intend a masque tonight, and a water banquet upon the lake. Will your lordship honour me to be my guest, and lie tonight in Acrozayana? Until tomorrow at noon we will expel all affairs of state, chase all difficulties from our society: one more day to sun it in pleasures in this hot summer-blink, last merriment 'fore winter. Then you must go. And thereafter we shall bloodily try out by war these differences we have these ten days to so little purpose debated.'

Amaury said in Lessingham's ear, 'Beware, my lord. Let us be gone.'

But Lessingham's eye still met the Duke's, and he remembered the counsel of Doctor Vandermast. 'This offer,' answered he, 'is what was to be looked for in so high-minded a prince, and I embrace and accept it. I well think there is not any other prince extant should have made me the like offer, nor at whose hand I would have accepted of it.'

VII

A NIGHT-PIECE ON AMBREMERINE

ZAYANA LAKE AT EVENING • CAMPASPE: COMMERCE WITH
A WATER NYMPH • MOONRISE • QUEEN OF NIGHT •
THE PHILOSOPHER SPEAKS • SONG OF THE FAUN •
OUR LADY OF BLINDNESS • ANTHEA: COMMERCE WITH
AN OREAD • THE NATURE OF DRYADS, NAIADS,
AND OREADS • THE DEAD SHADOW • DIVINE
PHILOSOPHY • COUNSEL OF VANDERMAST.

PEACE seemed to have laid her lily over all the earth when, that
evening, eight gondolas that carried the Duke and his company
put out from the water-gate under the western tower and steered
into the sunset. In the open water they spread into line abreast,
making a shallow crescent, horns in advance, and so passed on
their way, spacing themselves by intervals of some fifty paces to
be within hail but not to the overhearing of talk within the
gondolas. Three or four hundred paces ahead of them went a little
caravel, bearing aboard of her the Duke's bodyguard and the last
and most delicate wines and meats. Her sweeps were out, for in
that windless air her russet-coloured silken sails flapped the masts.
From her poop floated over the water the music of old love-ditties,
waked in the throb of silver lute-strings, the wail of hautboys, and
the flattering soft singing of viols.

North and north-eastward, fainter and fainter in the distance, the foot-hills took on purple hues, like the bloom on grapes. High beyond the furthest hills, lit with a rosy light, the great mountains reared themselves that shut in the habited lands on the northward: outlying sentinels of the Hyperborean snows. So high they stood, that it might have been clouds in the upper air; save that they swam not as clouds, but persisted, and that their architecture was not cloud-like, but steadfast, as of buildings of the ancient earth, wide founded, bastion upon huger bastion, buttress soaring to battlement, wall standing back upon wall, roof-ridge and gable and turret and airy spire; and yet all as if of no gross substance, but rather the thin spirit of these, and their grandeur not the grandeur of clouds that pass, but of frozen and unalterable repose, as of Gods reclining on heaven's brink. Astern, Acrozayana faced the warm light. On the starboard quarter, half a mile to the north, on a beach at the end of the low wooded promontory that stretches far out into the lake there towards Zayana town, two women were bathing. The sunset out of that serene and cloudless sky suffused their limbs and bodies, their reflections in the water, the woods behind them, with a glory that made them seem no women of mortal kind, but dryads or oreads of the hills come down to show their beauties to the opening eyes of night and, with the calm lake for their mirror, braid their hair.

In the outermost gondola on the northern horn was Lessingham, his soul and senses lapped in a lotus-like contentment. For beside him reclined Madam Campaspe, a young lady in whose sprightly discourse he savoured, and in the sleepy little noises of the water under the prow, a delectable present that wandered towards a yet more delectable to come.

'The seven seas,' he said, answering her: 'ever since I was fifteen years old.'

'And you are now – fifty?'

'Six times that,' answered Lessingham gravely; 'reckoned in months.'

'With me,' she said, 'reckonings go always askew.'

'Let's give over reckonings, then,' said he, 'and do it by example. I am credibly informed that I am pat of an age with your Duke.'

'O, so old indeed? Twenty-five? No marvel you are so staid and serious.'

'And you, madam?' said Lessingham. 'How far in the decline?'

'Nay, 'tis me to ask questions,' said she; 'you to answer.'

Idly Lessingham was looking at her hand which rested on the cushion beside him, gloved with a black scented gauntlet with falling cuff of open-work and flower-work of yellow zircons. 'I am all expectation,' he said.

Campaspe stole a glance at him. Her eyes were beady, like some shy creature's of the fields or woods. Her features, considered coldly one by one, had recalled strange deformities as of frogs or spiders; yet were they by those eyes welded to a kind of beauty. So might a queen of Elfland look, of an unfair, unhuman, yet most taking comeliness. 'Well,' said she: 'how many straws go to goose-nest?'

'None, for lack of feet.'

'O, unkind! You knew it afore. That cometh of this so much faring 'twixt land and land: maketh men too knowing.' After a little, she said, 'Tell me, is it not better here than in your northlands?'

''Tis at least much hotter,' said Lessingham.

'And which liketh you better, my lord, hot or cold?'

'Must I answer of airs, or of ladies' hearts?'

'You must keep order: answer of that you spoke on.'

'Nay,' said Lessingham, ''tis holiday. Let me be impertinent, and answer of that I set most store by.'

'Then, to be courtly, you must say cold is best,' said she. 'For our fashion here is cold hearts, as the easier changed.'

'Ah,' he said: 'I see there is something, madam, you are yet to learn.'

'How, my lord? I' the fashion?'

'O no. Because I am a soldier, yet have I not such numbed and so clumsy hands for't as tell a lady she's out of fashion. I meant 'tis warm hearts, not cold, are most apt to change: fire at each fresh kindling.'

'Here's fine doctrine,' said she. 'Do you rest it, pray, upon experience?'

He smiled. "'Tis a first point of wisdom,' he replied, 'to affirm nought upon hearsay.'

Campaspe sat suddenly forward, with a little murmur of pleasure: 'O, my friend!' addressed, as Lessingham perceived, not to him but to a lady-duck with her seven young swimming close by in column ahead. For a fleeting instant, as she leaned eagerly across to watch them, her hand, put out to steady her, touched Lessingham's knee: a touch that, sylph-like and immaterial as a dream, sent a thousand serpents through his veins. The duck and her children took fright at the gondola, and, with a scutter of feet and wings, left a little wake of troubled water which showed the better, as a foil sets off a diamond, the placid smoothness of that lake.

'And how many foolish ladies ere now,' said Campaspe, very demurely, 'have you found to give open ear to these schoolings?'

'There, madam,' said he, 'you put me to a stand. They come and go, I suppose, with the changing of the moon.'

'I was a fine fool,' said she, 'to come into this boat with you, my lord.'

Lessingham smiled. 'I think,' he said, 'I know an argument, when we come to it, shall satisfy you to the contrary.' His eyes, half veiled under their long lashes, surveyed her now with a slow and disturbing gaze. It was as if the spirit that sat in them tasted, in a profound luxurious apprehension beyond the magic of mortal vintages, the wine of its own power: tasted it doubly, in her veins as in his own, attuning blood to blood. Then, turning his gaze from her to the back of his own hand, he looked at that awhile in silence as if there were there some comic engaging matter. 'Howe'er that be,' he said lightly at last, 'you must remember, 'tis the same moon. That were a quaint folly, for love of last month's moon at the full, to have done with moonlight for ever.'

'O, you can a game beside tennis, my lord, there's n'er a doubt,' she said.

'I have beat the Duke ere now at tennis,' said Lessingham.

'That is hard,' said she. 'But 'tis harder to beat him at this.'

''Tis but another prime article of wisdom,' said Lessingham, 'ne'er to let past memories blunt the fine point of present pleasures. I am skilled,' he said, 'to read a lady's heart from her hand. Let me try.' Campaspe, laughing, struggled against him as he would have drawn off her glove. 'Moist palms argue warm hearts,' he said in her ear. 'Is that why you wear gloves, madam?'

'Nay, but I will not. Fie, shall the gondolier see us?'

'I am discretion itself,' said Lessingham.

'You must learn, my lord,' she said, putting away his hands, 'if you would have me to spread your table, to fall to it nicely, not swallow it like flapdragons.'

Lessingham said, close at her ear, 'I'll be your scholar. Only but promise.'

But Campaspe said, 'No promises in Zayana: the Duke hath banned them. As for performance, why, respectful service, my lord, hath its payment here as in other lands.'

Her voice had taken on a new delicacy: the voice of willow-trees beside still water when the falling wind stirs them. The great flattened ball of the sun touched the western hills. Lessingham took her under the chin with his hand and turned her face towards his. 'I like little water-rats,' he said. Her eyes grew big and frightened, like some little fieldish thing's that sees a hawk. For a minute she abode motionless. Then, as if with a sudden resolution, she pulled off her glove: offered her bare hand, palm upwards, to his lips. The gondola lurched sideways. The lady laughed, half smothered: 'Nay, no more, my lord. Nay, and you will not have patience, you shall have nought, then.'

'Jenny wrens: water-rats: willow-leaves sharp against the moon like little feet. Why is your laugh like a night breeze among willows? Do I not descry you? behind your mask of lady of presence: you and your "friend". Are you not these? Tell me: are you not?'

Each soft stroke of the gondolier's paddle at the stern came like one more drop in the cup of enchantment, which still brimmed and still did not run over. 'It is not time, my lord. O yes, these, and other besides. But see, we shall land upon the instant. I pray you, have patience. In this isle of Ambremerine is bosky glades removed, flowery headlands; in two hours the moon will ride high; and she, you know—'

'And she,' said Lessingham, 'is an ancient sweet suggester of ingenious pleasures.' He kissed the hand again. 'Let us turn the cat in the pan: say, If I have patience I shall have all, then?'

In Campaspe's beady eyes he read his passport.

Their landing was near about the south-east point of that isle, in a little natural harbour, half-moon shaped and with a beach of fine white sand. The sun had gone down, and dusk gathered on the lake; eastward, pale blue smoke hung here and there over Zayana and the citadel; the walls and the roofs and towers were grown shadowy and dim; their lamps came out like stars. In the north, the great peaks still held some light. A wide glade went up into the isle from that harbour in gently sloping lawns, shut in on all but the water side by groves of cypress-trees: pillar-like boles and dense spires so tangled, drenched, and impregnate with thick darkness that not midday itself might pierce nor black night deepen their elemental gloom. In the midst of that glade, on a level lawn where in their thousands daisies and little yellow cinquefoils were but now newly folded up and gone to sleep, tables were set for the feast. The main table faced south to the harbour, where the gondolas and the caravel, with their lofty stems and stern-posts and their lights, some red some green, floated graceful over their graceful images in the water. Two shorter tables ran down from that table's either end: the one faced Zayana and the night, and the other westward to the leavings of the sunset, above which the evening star, high in a pellucid heaven of pale chrysolite, burned like a diamond from Aphrodite's neck.

The tables were spread with damask, and set forth with a fish dinner: oysters and lobsters, crayfish both great and small, trout, tunny, salmon, sturgeon, lampreys and caviare, all in fair golden dishes, with mushrooms besides and sparrow-grass, cockscombs and truffles, and store of all manner of delicious fruits, and wines of all kind in great bowls and beakers of crystal and silver and gold: dry and ancient wines golden and tawny, good to sharpen the stomach and to whet the edge of wit; and red wines the heavy sweetness whereof, full of the colour of old sunsets and clinging to the goblet like blood, is able to mellow thought and steady the senses to a quiet where the inner voices may be heard; and wines the foam whereof whispers of that eternal sea and of that eternal spring-time towards which all memories return and all hearts' desires for ever. Fifty little boys, yellow-haired, clothed all in green, planted and tended torches behind the tables to give light to the feasters. Steady was the burning of those torches in the still summer air, with ever a little movement of their light, like the fall and swell of a girl's bosom; and the scent of their burning mingled in wafts with the flower scents and wood scents and the dew-laden breath of evening.

So now they made merry and supped under the sky. Scarcely was the sunset's last ember burned out westward, and night scarce well awake in the eastern heavens behind Zayana town, when from that quarter a bower of light began to spread upward, into which stepped at length, like a queen to lead night's pageant, the lady moon, and trailed her golden train across those sleeping waters. At that, their talk was stilled for a minute. Barganax, sitting in the midst of the cross table with Lessingham on his right, looked at Fiorinda, beside him on his left, as she looked at the moon. 'Your looking-glass,' he said, under his breath. Her face altered and she smiled, saying, with a lazy shrug of the shoulders, 'One of!'

'My Lord Lessingham,' said Campaspe: 'imagine me potent in art magic, able to give you the thing you would. Whether would you then choose pleasure or power?'

'That question,' answered he, 'in such company and on such a night, and most of all by moonrise, I can but answer in the words of the poet:

'My pleasure is my power to please my mistress:
My power is my pleasure in that power.'

'A roundabout answer,' said the Duke: 'full of wiles and guiles. Mistrust it, madam.'

'Can your grace better it then?' said Campaspe.

'Most easily. And in one word: pleasure.'

Fiorinda smiled.

'Your ladyship will second me,' said the Duke. 'What's power but for the procuring of wise, powerful and glorious pleasures? What else availeth my dukedom? 'Las, I should make very light account thereof, as being a thing of very small and base value, save that it is a mean unto that rich and sunny diamond that outlustreth all else.'

'Philosophic disputations,' said Fiorinda, 'do still use to awake strange longings in me.'

'Longings?' said the Duke. 'You are mistress of our revels tonight. Breathe but the whisper of a half-shapen wish; lightning shall be slow to our suddenness to perform it.'

'For the present need,' said that lady, 'a little fruit would serve.'

'Framboises?' said the Duke, offering them in a golden dish.

'No,' she said, looking upon them daintily: 'they have too many twiddles in them: like my Lord Lessingham's distich.'

'Will your ladyship eat a peach?' said Melates.

'I could,' she said. 'And yet, no. Clingstone, 'tis too great trouble: freestone, I like them not. Your grace shall give me a summer poppering.'

The Duke sent his boy to fetch them from the end of the table. 'You shall peel it for me,' she said, choosing one.

Barganax, as drunk with some sudden exhalation of her beauty, the lazy voice, the lovely pausing betwixt torchlight and moonlight of fastidious jewelled fingers above the dish of pears, was taken with a trembling that shook the dish in his hand. Mastering which, 'I had forgot,' he said with a grave courtesy, 'that you do favour this beyond all fruits else.'

'Forgot? Is it then so long ago your grace and I reviewed these matters? And indeed I had little fault to find with your partialities, nor you I think with mine.'

Lessingham, looking on at this little by-play, tasted in it a fine and curious delight; such delight as, more imponderable than the dew-sparkles on grass about sunrise or the wayward airs that lift the gossamer-spiders' threads, dances with fairy feet, beauty fitted to beauty, *allegretto scherzando*, in some great master's music. Only for the whim to set such divisions a-trip again, he spoke and said: 'If your ladyship will judge between us, I shall justify myself against the Duke that, would pleasure's self have had me, I should a refused to wed her. For there be pleasures base, illiberal, nasty, and merely hoggish. How then shall you choose pleasure *per se*?'

'By the same argument, how power *per se*?' replied the Duke. 'What of the gardener's dog, that could not eat the cabbages in the garden and would suffer none else to do so? Call you that power good? I think I have there strook you into the hazard, my lord. Or at least, 'tis change sides and play for the chase.'

'The chase is mine, then,' said Lessingham. 'For if power be but sometimes good, even so is pleasure. It must be noble pleasure, and the noblest pleasure is power.'

Fiorinda daintily bit a piece out of her pear. 'Pray you honour us, madam, to be our umpire,' said Lessingham.

She smiled, saying, 'It is not my way to sit in judgement. Only to listen.'

Barganax said, 'But will you listen to folly?'

'O yes,' answered she. 'There was often more good matter in one grain of folly than in a peck of wisdom.'

'Ha! that hath touched you, Vandermast,' said the Duke.

That aged man, sitting at the outer end of the eastern table betwixt Anthea and the young Countess Rosalura, laughed in his beard. The Lady Fiorinda lifted her eyebrows with a questioning look first upon him, then upon the Duke, then upon Lessingham. 'Is he wise?' she said. 'I had thought he was a philosopher. Truly, I could listen to him a whole summer's night and ne'er tire of his preposterous nonsense.'

'An old fool,' said Vandermast, 'that is yet wise enough to serve your ladyship.'

'Does that need wisdom?' she said, and looked at the moon. Lessingham, watching her face, thought of that deadly Scythian queen who gave Cyrus his last deep drink of blood. Yet, even so thinking, he was the more deeply aware, in the caressing charm of her voice, of a mind that savoured the world delicately and simply, with a quaint, amused humour; so might some demure and graceful bird gracefully explore this way and that, accepting or rejecting with an equable enjoyment. 'Does that need wisdom?' she said again. And now it was as if from that lady's lips some unheard song, some unseen beauty, had stolen abroad and, taking to itself wings, mounted far from earth, far above the columnar shapes of those cypresses that, huge and erect, stood round that dim garden; until the vast canopy of night was all filled as with an impending flowering of unimagined wonder.

'There is no other wisdom than that: not in heaven or earth or under the earth, in the world phenomenal or the world noumenal, *sub specie temporali* or *sub specie aeternitatis*. There is no other,' said Vandermast, in a voice so low that none well heard him, save only the Countess close by on his right. And she, hearing, yet not understanding, yet apprehending in her very bowels the tenour of his words, as a reed bending before the wind might apprehend dimly somewhat of what betided in the wind-ridden spaces without to bend and to compel it, sought Medor's hand and held it fast.

There was silence. Then Medor said, 'What of love?'

Vandermast said, as to himself, but the Countess Rosalura heard it: 'There is no other power.'

'Love,' said Lessingham, cool and at ease again after the passing of that sudden light, 'shall aptly point my argument. Here, as otherwhere, power ruleth. For what is a lover without power to win his mistress? Or she without power to hold her lover?' His hand, as he spoke, tightened unseen about Campaspe's yielding waist. His eyes, carelessly roving, as he spoke, from face to face of that company, came to a stop, meeting Anthea's where she sat beside the learned doctor. The tawny wealth of her deep hair was to the cold beauty of her face as a double curtain of fulvid glory. Her eyes caught and held his gaze with a fascination, hard, bold, and inscrutable.

'I have been told that Love,' said Fiorinda, 'is a more intricate game than tennis; or than soldiership; or than politicians' games, my Lord Lessingham.'

Anthea, with a little laugh, bared her lynx-like teeth. 'I was remembered of a saying of your ladyship's,' she said.

Fiorinda lifted an eyebrow, gently pushing her wine-cup towards the Duke for him to fill it.

'That a lover who should think to win his mistress by power,' said Anthea, 'is like an old dried-up dotard who would be young again by false hair, false teeth, and skilful painting of his face: thus, and with a good stoup of wine, but one thing he lacketh, and that the one thing needful.'

'Did I say so indeed?' said Fiorinda. 'I had forgot it. In truth, this is strange talk, of power and pleasure in love,' she said. 'There is a garden, there is a tree in the garden, there is a rose upon the tree. Can a woman not keep her lover without she study always to please him with pleasure? Pew! Then let her give up the game. Or shall my lover think with pleasing of me to win me indeed? Faugh! He payeth me then; doth he think I am for hire?'

Barganax sitting beside her, not looking at her, his shoulder towards her, his elbow on the table, his fingers in an arrested stillness touching his mustachios, gazed still before him as though all his senses listened to the last scarce-heard cadence of the music of that lady's voice.

Fiorinda, in that pause, looked across to Doctor Vandermast. Obedient to her look, he stood up now and raised a hand twice and thrice above his head as in sign to somewhat to come out of the shadows that stirred beyond the torchlight. The moon rode high now over Zayana, and out of torchbeam and moonbeam and starbeam was a veil woven that confounded earth and sky and water into an immateriality of uncertain shade and misty light. At Vandermast's so standing up, the very night seemed to slip down into some deeper pool of stillness, like the silent slipping of an otter down from the bank into the black waters. Only the purr of a nightjar came from the edge of the woods. And now on the sudden they at the tables were ware of somewhat quick, that stood in the confines of the torchlight and the shadowy region without; of man-like form, but little of stature, scarce reaching with its head to the elbow of a grown man; with shaggy hairy legs and goat's feet, and with a sprouting of horns like a young goat's upon its head; and there was in its eyes the appearance as of red coals burning. Piercing were the glances of those eyes, as they darted in swift succession from face to face (save that before Fiorinda's it dropped its gaze as if in worship), and piercing was the music of the song it sang: the song that lovers and great poets have ravished their hearts to hear since the world began: a night-song, bittersweet, that shakes the heart of darkness with longings and questionings too tumultuous for speech to fit or follow; and in that song the listener hears echoing up the abysses of eternity voices of men and women unborn answering the voices of the dead.

Surely, hearkening to that singing, all they sat like as amazed or startled out of sleep. Lover clung to lover: Amaury to velvet-eyed Violante, Myrrha to Zapheles, Bellafront to Barrian. Lessingham's encircling arm drew closer about his Campaspe: her breast beneath the silk under his hand was a tremulous dove: her black eyes rested as though in soft accustomed contemplation upon the singer. Pantasilea, with heavy lids and heavy curled lips half closed, as in half eclipse of the outward sense, lay back sideways on Melates's shoulder. Medor held gathered to him like a child his sweet young Countess. Beyond them, in the outermost place of the eastern table, Anthea sat upright and listening, her hair touching with some stray tendrils of its glory the sleeve of old Vandermast's gaberdine where he stood motionless beside her.

Only the Lady Fiorinda seemed to listen fancy-free to that singing, even as the cold moon, mistress of the tides, has yet no part in their restless ebb and flow, but, taking her course serene far above the cloudy region of the air, surveys these and all earthly things with equal eye, divine and passionless. The Duke, sitting back, had this while watched her from the side from under his faun-like eyebrows, his hand moving as if with chalk or brush. He leaned nearer now, giving over that painting motion: his right elbow on the table, his left arm resting, but not to touch her, on the back of her chair. The voice of the singer, that was become as the echoes of a distant music borne on the breeze from behind a hill, now made a thin obbligato to the extreme passionate love that spoke in the Duke's accents like the roll of muffled thunder as, low in her ear, he began to say:

'O forest of dark beasts about the base
　Of some white peak that dreams in the Empyrean:
O hare's child sleeping by a queen's palace,
　'Mid lily-meadows of some isle Lethean:
Barbaric, beastly, virginal, divine:
　Fierce feral loveliness: sweet secret fire:
Last rest and bourne of every lovely line:
　—All these Thou art, that art the World's Desire.'

The deep tones of the Duke's voice, so speaking, were hushed to the quivering superficies of silence, beneath which the darkness stirred as with a rushing of arpeggios upon muted strings. In the corner of that lady's mouth, as she listened, the minor diabolus, dainty and seductive, seemed to turn and stretch in its sleep. Lessingham, not minded to listen, yet heard. Darkly he tasted in his own flesh Barganax's secret mind: in what fashion this Duke lived in that seeming woman's life far sweetlier than in his own. He leaned back to look upon her, over the Duke's shoulder. He saw now that she had glow-worms in her hair. But when he would have beheld her face, it was as if spears of many-coloured light, such light as, like the halo about the moon, is near akin to darkness, swept in an endless shower outward from his vision's centre; and now when he would have looked upon her he saw but these outrushings, and in the fair line of vision not darkness indeed but the void: a solution of continuity: nothing.

As a man that turns from the halcyon vision to safe verities, he turned to his Campaspe. Her lips invited sweetly: he bent to them. With a little ripple of laughter, they eluded him, and under his hand, with soft arched back warm and trembling, was the water-rat in very deed.

About the north-western point of that island there was a garden shadowed with oaks ten generations old and starproof cedars and delicate-limbed close-tufted strawberry-trees. Out of its leafy darknesses nightingale answered nightingale, and nightflowers, sweet-mouthed like brides in their first sleep, mixed their sweetness with the breath of the dews of night. It was now upon the last hour before midnight. From the harbour to the southward rose the long slumbrous notes of a horn, swelling, drawing their heavy sweetness across the face of the night sky. Anthea stood up, slender as a moonbeam in those silent woods. 'The Duke's horn,' she said. 'We must go back; unless you are minded to lodge in this isle tonight, my Lord Lessingham.'

Lessingham stood up and kissed her hand. For a minute she regarded him in silence from under her brow, her eyes burning steadily, her chin drawn down a little: an unsmiling lip-licking look. Then giving him her arm she said, as they turned to be gone, 'There is discontent in your eyes. You are dreaming on somewhat without me and beyond.'

'Incomparable lady,' answered he, 'call it a surfeit. If I am discontented, it is with the time, that draweth me from these high pleasures to where, as cinders raked up in ashes—'

'O no nice excuses,' she said. 'I and Campaspe are not woman-kind. Truly, 'tis but at Her bidding we durst not disobey we thus have dallied with such as you, my lord.'

His mustachios stirred.

'You think that a lie?' she said. 'The unfathomed pride of mortals!'

Lessingham said, 'My memories are too fiery clear.'

They walked now under the obscurity of crowding cypresses. 'It is true,' said Anthea, 'that you and Barganax are not altogether as the common rout of men. This world is yours, yours and his, did you but know it. And did you know it, such is the folly of mortals, you would straight be out of conceit with it and desire another. But you are well made, not to know these things. See, I tell it you, yet you believe it not. And though I should tell you from now till dawn, yet you would not believe.' She laughed.

'You are pleasantly plain with me,' said Lessingham after a pause. 'You can be fierce. So can I. I do love your fierceness, your bites and scratches, madam. Shall I be plain too?' He looked down; her face, level with his shoulder, wore a singular look of benign tranquillity. 'You,' he said, '(and I must not omit Mistress Campaspe) have let me taste this night such pleasures as the heroes in Elysium, I well think, taste nought sweeter. Yet would I have more; yet, what more, I know not.'

Without looking at him, she made a little mow. 'In your erudite conversation, my lord, I have tasted this night such pleasures as I am by nature accustomed to. I desire no more. I am, even as always I am, contented.'

'As always?' said he.

'Is "always" a squeeze of crab-orange in your cup, my lord? 'Tis wholesome truth, howsoe'er. And now, in our sober voyaging back to Zayana, with the learn'd doctor conducting of us, I do look for no less bliss than – But this you will think ungracious?'

She looked up, with a little pressure of her arm on his. His eyes, when he turned his face to hers, were blurred and unseeing.

The path came into the open now, as they crossed the low backbone of the island. They walked into a flood of moonlight; on their left, immeasurably far away, the great snow ranges stood like spirits in the moon-drenched air. Anthea said, 'Behold that mountain, my lord, falling away to the west in saw-toothed ridges a hand-breadth leftward of the sycamore-tree. That is Ramosh Arkab; and I say to you, I have dwelt there 'twixt wood and snowfield ten million years.'

They were now come down to the harbour. The cypress-shadowed glade lay empty: the tables taken up where their banquet had been: the torches and the feasters gone. Far away on the water the lights of the gondolas showed where they took their course homeward to Zayana. Under an utter silence and loneliness of moonlight the lawns sloped gently to the lake. One gondola only lay by the landing-stage. Beside it waited that aged man. With a grave obeisance he greeted Lessingham; they went aboard all three, loosed, and put out. There was no gondolier. Doctor Vandermast would have taken the paddle, but Lessingham made him sit beside Anthea in the seat of honour, and himself, sitting on the fore-deck with his feet in the boat's bottom, paddled her stern-foremost. So they had passage over those waters that were full of drowned stars and secret unsounded deeps of darkness. Something broke the smoothness on the starboard bow; Lessingham saw, as they neared it, that it was the round head of an otter, swimming towards Ambremerine. It looked at them with its little face and hissed. In a minute it was out of eyeshot astern.

'My beard was black once,' said Vandermast. 'Black as yours, my lord.' Lessingham saw that the face of that old man was blanched in the moonlight, and his eyes hidden as in ocean caves or deep archways of some prison-house, so that only with looking upon him a man might not have known for sure whether there were eyes in truth within those shadows or but void eye-sockets and eclipsing darkness. Anthea sat beside him in a languorous grace. She trailed a finger in the water, making a little rippling noise, pleasant to the ear. Her face, too, was white under the moon, her hair a charmed labyrinth of moonbeams, her eyes pits of fire.

'Dryads,' said Vandermast, after a little, 'are in two kinds, whereof the one is more nearly consanguineous with the more madefied and waterish natures, naiads namely and nereids; but the other kind, having their habitation nearer to the meteoric houses and the cold upper borders of woods appropinquate to the snows and the gelid ice-streams of the heights, do derive therefrom some qualities of the oreads or mountain nymphs. I have indulged my self-complacency so far as to entertain hopes, my lord, that, by supplying for your entertainment one of either sort, and discoursing so by turns two musics to your ear, *andante piacevole e lussurioso* and then *allegro appassionato*, I may have opened a more easier way to your lordship's perfect satisfaction and profitable enjoyment of this night's revelries.'

That old man's talk, droning slow, made curious harmonies with the drowsy body of night; the dip and swirl and dip again of Lessingham's paddle; the drip of water from the blade between the strokes.

'Where did your lordship forsake my little water-rat?' he asked in a while.

'She was turned willow-wren at the last,' answered Lessingham.

'Such natures,' said Vandermast, 'do commonly suck much gratification out of change and the variety of perceptible form and corporeity. But I doubt not your lordship, with your more settled preferences and trained appetites, found her most acceptable in form and guise of a woman?'

'She did me the courtesy,' answered Lessingham, 'to maintain that shape for the more part of our time together.'

They proceeded in silence. Vandermast spoke again. 'You find satisfaction, then, in women, my lord?'

'I find in their society,' Lessingham answered, 'a pleasurable interlude.'

'That,' said that learned man, 'agreeth with the conclusion whereunto, by process of ratiocination, I was led upon consideration of that stave or versicule recited by your lordship about one hour since, and composed, if I mistake not, by your lordship. Went it not thus?

> Anthea, wooed with flatteries,
> To please her lover's fantasies,
> Unlocks her bosom's treasuries—
> Ah! silver apples like to these
> Ne'er grew, save on those holy trees
> Tended by nymphs Hesperides.'

'What's this?' said Lessingham, and there was danger in his voice.

'You must not take it ill,' said Vandermast, 'that this trifle, spoke for her ear only and the jealous ear of night, was known to me without o'erhearing. Yourself are witness that neither you nor she did tell it me, and indeed I was half a mile away, so scarce could a heard it. A little cold: a little detached, methought, for a love-poem. But indeed I do think your lordship is a man of deeds. Do you find satisfaction, then, in deeds?'

'Yes,' answered he.

'Power,' said that learned doctor: 'power; which maketh change.

Yea, but have you considered the power that is in Time, young man? to change the black hairs of your beard to blanched hairs, like as mine: and the last change of Death? that, but with waiting and expecting and standing still, overcometh all by drawing of all to its own likeness. Dare your power face that power, to go like a bridegroom to annihilation's bed? Let me look at your eyes.'

Lessingham, whose eyes had all this while been fixed upon Vandermast's, said, 'Look then.'

The face of the night was altered now. A cool drizzle of rain dimmed the moon: the gondola seemed to drift a-beam, cut off from all the world else upon desolate waters. Vandermast's voice came like the soughing of a distant wind: 'The hairless, bloodless, juiceless, power of silence,' he said, 'that consumeth and abateth and swalloweth up lordship and subjection, favour and foulness, lust and satiety, youth and eld, into the dark and slubbery mess of nothingness.' Lessingham saw that the face of that old man was become now as a shrivelled death's-head, and his eyes but windows opening inwards upon the horror of an empty skull. And that lynx-eyed mountain nymph, fiercely glaring, crouching sleek and spotted beside him, was become now a lynx indeed, with her tufted slender ears erect and the whiskers moving nervously right and left of her snarling mouth. And Vandermast spake loud and hoarse, crying out and saying, 'You shall die young, my Lord Lessingham. Two years, a year, may be, and you shall die. And then what help shall it be that you with your high gifts of nature did o'ersway great ones upon earth (as here but today you did in Acrozayana), and did ride the great Vicar of Rerek, your curst and untamed horse, till he did fling you to break your neck, and die at the last? What is fame to the deaf dust that shall then be your delicate ear, my lord? What shall it avail you then that you had fair women? What shall it matter though they contented you never? Seeing there is no discontent whither you go down, my lord, neither yet content, but the empty belly of darkness enclosing eternity upon eternity. Or what shall even that vision beyond the veil profit you (if you saw it indeed tonight, then ere folk rose from table), since that is but impossibility, fiction and vanity, and shall then be less than vanity itself: less than the dust of you in the worm's blind mouth? For all departeth, all breaketh and perisheth away, all is hollowness and nothing worth ere it sink to very nothing at last.'

'I saw nought,' said Lessingham. 'What is that Lady Fiorinda then?' His voice was level; only the strokes of his paddle came with a more steadier resolution, may be, of settled strength as that old man spoke.

The gondola lurched sideways. Lessingham turned swiftly from his outstaring of that aged man to bring her safe through a sudden turmoil of the waters that rose now and opened downward again to bottomless engulfings. Pale cliffs superimpended in the mist and the darkness, and fires burned there, with the semblance as of corpse-fires. And above those cliffs was the semblance of icy mountains, and streams that rolled burning down them of lava, making a sizzling in the water that was heard high above the voice of the waves; and Lessingham beheld walking shrouded upon the cliffs faceless figures, beyond the stature of human kind, that seemed to despair and lament, lifting up skinny hands to the earless heaven. And while he beheld these things, there was torn a ragged rift in the clouds, and there fled there a bearded star, baleful in the abyss of night. And now there was thunder, and the noise as of a desolate sea roaring upon the coasts of death. Then, as a thought steps over the threshold of oblivion, all was gone; the cloudless summer night held its breath in the presence of its own inward blessedness: the waters purred in their sleep under the touch of Anthea's idly trailing finger.

Lessingham laid down his paddle and clapped his right hand to his hip; but they had gone unweaponed to that feast. Without more ado he with an easy swiftness, scarcely to rock the boat, had gotten in his left hand the two wrists of Vandermast: his right hand slid up beneath the long white beard, and fumbled the doctor's skinny throat. 'Scritch-owl,' he said, 'you would unman me, ha, with your sickly bodings? You have done it, I think: but you shall die for't.' The iron strength of his fingers toyed delicately about that old man's weasand.

Very still sat Doctor Vandermast. He said, 'Suffer me yet to speak.'

'Speak and be sudden,' said Lessingham.

Surely that old man's eyes looked now into his with a brightness that was as the lifting up of day. 'My Lord Lessingham,' he said, *'per realitatem et perfectionem idem intelligo*: in my conceit, reality and perfection are one. If therefore your lordship have suffered an inconvenience, you are not to revenge it upon me: your disorder proceedeth but from partial apprehension.'

'Ha! But did not you frame and present me, with fantasticoes? Did not you spit your poison?' said Lessingham. 'Do not mistake me: I am not afeared of my death. But I do feel within me somewhat, such as I ne'er did meet with its like aforrow, and I know not what it is, if it be not some despair. Wherefore, teach me to apprehend fully, you were best, and that presently. Or like a filthy fly I'll finger you off to hell.' Upon which very word, he strangely took his fingers from the lean weasand of that old man and let go the lean wrists.

Vandermast said, as if to himself, *'Cum mens suam impotentiam imaginatur, eo ipso contristatur*: when the mind imagineth its own impotence, it by that only circumstance falleth into a deep sadness. My lord,' he said, raising his head to look Lessingham in the face, 'I did think you had seen. Had you so seen, these later sights I did present you, and these prognostications of decay, could not have cankered so your mind: they had been then but as fumadoes, hot and burning spices, to awake your appetite the more and prepare you for that cup whereof he that drinketh shall for ever thirst and for ever be satisfied; yea, and without it there is no power but destroyeth and murdereth itself at last, nor no pleasure but disgusteth in the end, like the stench of the dead.'

'Words,' said Lessingham. 'The mouth jangleth, as lewd as a lamp that no light is in. I tell you, I saw nought: nought but outrushing lights and dazzles. And now, I feel my hand upon a latch, and you, in some manner I understand not, by some damned sleight, withholding me. Teach me, as you said but now, to apprehend fully. But if not, whether you be devil or demigod or old drivelling disard as I am apt to think you: by the blessed Gods, I will tear you into pieces.'

Anthea widened her lips and laughed. 'Now you are in a good vein, my lord. Shall I bite his throat out?' She seemed to slaver at the mouth. 'You are a lynx, go,' said Lessingham. It was as if the passion of his anger was burnt out, like a fire of dead leaves kindled upon a bed of snow.

Vandermast's lean hands twisted and unclasped their fingers together in his lap. 'I had thought,' he said, to himself aloud, in the manner of old men, 'her ladyship would have told me. O inexorable folly to think so! Innumerable laughter of the sea: ever changing: shall I never learn?'

'What is that lady?' said Lessingham.

Vandermast said, 'You did command me, my lord, to learn you to apprehend fully. But here, *in limine demonstrationis*, upon the very threshold, appeareth a difficulty beyond solution, in that your lordship is instructed already in things contingent and apparent, *affectiones, actiones*, phenomenal actualities *rei politicae et militaris*, the council chamber and the camp, *puella-puellae* and matters conducive thereunto. But in things substantial I find you less well grounded, and here it is beyond my art to carry you further seeing my art is the doctor's practice of reason; because things substantial are not known by reason but by perception: *perceptio per solam suam essentiam*; and *omnis substantia est necessario infinita*: all substance, in its essence, infinite.'

'Leave this discourse,' said Lessingham, 'which, did I understand its drift, should make me, I doubt not, as wise as a capon. Answer me: of what *substantia* or *essentia* is that lady?'

Doctor Vandermast lowered his eyes. 'She is my Mistress,' he said.

'That, to use your gibberish, old sir, is *per accidens*,' said Lessingham. 'I had supposed her the Duke's mistress: the Devil's mistress too, belike. But *per essence*, what is she? Why did my eyes dazzle when I would have looked upon her but at that moment tonight? since many a time ere then I easily enough beheld her. And why should aught lie on it, that they did so dazzle? Come, we have dealt with seeming women tonight that be nymphs of the lakes and mountains, taking at their will bird-like shapes and beastly. What is she? Is she such an one? Tell me, for I will know.'

'No,' said Vandermast, shaking his head. 'She is not such as these.'

Eastward, ahead, Lessingham saw how, with the dancings of summer lightnings, the sky was opened on a sudden behind the towers and rampires of Acrozayana. For that instant it was as if a veil had been torn to show where, built of starbeams and empyreal light, waited, over all, the house of heart's desire.

That learned man was searching now beneath the folds of his gaberdine, and now he drew forth a little somewhat and, holding it carefully in his fingers, scanned it this way and that and raised it to view its shape against the moon. Then, giving it carefully to Lessingham, 'My lord,' he said, 'take this, and tender it as you would a precious stone; for indeed albeit but a little withered leaf, there be few jewels so hard to come by or of such curious virtue. Because I have unwittingly done your lordship an ill service tonight, and because not wisdom itself could conduct you to that apprehension you do stand in need of, I would every deal I may to serve and further you. And because I know (both of my own judgement and by certain weightier confirmations of my art) the proud integrity of your lordship's mind and certain conditions of your inward being, whereby I may, without harm to my own fealty, trust you thus, albeit tomorrow again our enemy: therefore, my Lord Lessingham, behold a thing for your peace. For the name of this leaf is called *sferra cavallo*, and this virtue it hath, to break and open all locks of steel and iron. Take it then to your bed, my lord, now in the fair guest-chamber prepared for you in Acrozayana. And if, for the things you saw and for the things you saw not tonight, your heart shall be troubled, and sleep stand iron-eyed willing not to lie down with you and fold her plumes about your eyelids, then if you will, my lord, taking this leaf, you may rise and seek. What I may, that do I, my lord, giving you this. There shall, at least, no door be shut against you. But when night is done and day cometh you must by all means (and this lieth upon your honour) burn the leaf. It is to do you good I give it unto you, and for your peace. Not for a weapon against my own sovereign lord.'

Lessingham took it and examined it well in the light of the moon. Then, with a noble look to Vandermast, he put it away like a jewel in his bosom.

VIII

SFERRA CAVALLO

PURSUIT OF A NIGHT VISION • FIORINDA ON THE
DREAM-STONE • WHIRLPOOL • MISTRESS OF
MISTRESSES • 'NORTH, IN RIALMAR.'

IN the deep and dead time of the night there went forth a dream through the gate of horn, by permission of Her that is, and is to come. And the dream, treading the viewless ways, came down to the land of Meszria and to the citadel that overlooks Zayana town, and entered and stood in the fair guest-chamber at the foot of the golden bed, the posts whereof were fashioned in the likeness of hippogriffs, gold and with eyes of sapphire. And upon that bed was the Lord Lessingham but even now fallen into an uncertain slumber. And the dream put on beauty, and, to temper that beauty, the appearance of moonlight as a gown and of a girdle as of silvery moonlight upon snow mountains, and the appearance as of a bodice woven of those stars which men call Berenice's Hair: stars of so delicate a shimmering brightness that the gross direct look may ill perceive it, but is best gazed on askance or indirect. But by ordainment of the Gods, there was drawn about the head of that dream and across its face a veil of light, as darkness inscrutable, or as wonder overwritten upon wonder so as none might read. And the dream spake with the voice that a sleeper may hear, too fine for waking ears (unless, indeed, for a moment they wake and dream at once), saying: *I promised and I will perform.*

Lessingham, hearing these words, and knowing that voice, moved and opened his eyes and awoke to the night and the lonely chamber.

It was not as if a dream had fled: rather truth, that had stood but a moment since ready to cast off her cloak. Like a man over-taken by swift-darkening night in a bog through which a path leads, hard to find even by day and now lost though but a moment since he trod it, he seemed to plunge and stagger without a guide. Betwixt sleeping and waking, he clad himself, girt on his sword, took from beneath the pillow that little leaf, and, filled with that vision, blundered towards the door. The great iron key stood in the lock where, upon going to bed, he had turned it. With the touch of that leaf the locked door swung open before him like a door that opens in a dream. As a dreamer with hastening undi-rected noiseless footsteps follows an unknown quest, Lessingham, not knowing well whether he dreamed or no, followed he knew not what, save that, may be, there was nought else in earth or heaven worth the following. And as he strode or stumbled along dim corridors, up winding shadowy stairs, across moonlit courts, still there sprang open before him both lock and bolt in a sudden-ness of dream-like stillness. And ever as each door opened, it opened upon emptiness: quiet empty rooms of darkness or silent moonlight.

In the meantime, not Lessingham alone waked in Acrozayana. In the spacious throne-room the wings that lifted their glory above the dream-stone seemed to quiver a little. The blackness of the great twisted pillars, the poppied frieze, the walls, the very floor of marble, seemed to waver like the texture of a dream. It was as if, in that midnight hour, some deeper drowsiness of moonset, that held its breath to listen to its own stillness, hung in the perfumed air, circling, tending in slow eddies ever to one centre. And there, as it had been glamour's self-made flesh for a season, to be queen of all scents and furry wings, dews, and

silences, and star-shimmering depths, and of all wild hearts'
desires that cry to the heart of summer night, Fiorinda sat throned
upon the dream-stone.

She had let fall her cloak, which lay tumbled in waves of sea-
green velvet and silver about her feet and about the cushions
where she sat. Her arms, bare to the shoulder, had an ivory
pallour and an ivory smoothness: pillars at the temple door. Her
fingernails were as shells new-taken from some enchanted sea:
the fingers as branched white coral from that sea's treasure-groves,
marvellously transmuted from its native insensate elegance to be
the ornament and living instrument of that lady's life and her
inward thought, and wearing the livery of her own aching loveliness. Her gown was of gauzy silk coloured like moonlight, pleated
with a hundred pleats and a-glitter with silver sequins and a
maze of spiral tendrils made of little beads of jet. A girdle of
corded silver lace curved low on her hips. Her bodice, of the like
stuff save that here were diamonds instead of sequins amid the
spirals, barely contained as with a double cup its warm and
breathing treasures. Betwixt bodice and girdle the sweet bare
interspace was a thing to shame all jewels, to make driven snow
seem sullied, and magnolia petals coarse and common, beside
the lily of its heavenly purity.

Upon her left, below her, a pace or so removed, Barganax sat
sideways on the steps of the throne, whence he might behold all
at a look her beauty: strange, complex, discordant in its elements,
yet in the living whole satisfying and perfect.

'More,' he said.

'I am tired of talking,' answered she.

'Look at me, then,' said the Duke.

She did so, with a little finical inclination of the head, as a rose
might take notice of a butterfly, and looked away again.

'Were it not that I do suspect 'twas your own devilish device
to trip me up, the better to flaunt your power upon me, I should
be sorry,' said the Duke, after a minute's silence.

'Repentance,' said Fiorinda, 'is a thing not easy to forgive, in a
great man.'

'Will you forgive the deed?' he said. 'For your forgiveness, may be, shall be a sunshine to drink up these mists.'

'I'll have it named first,' she said.

'I'll not name it,' said the Duke. 'It was an abomination, a woe, a miscreative dream.'

'A nameless abomination! I must pursue this.' There was in her voice a voluptuous lazy languor. 'And it befell – when?'

'Upon Friday of last week.'

'And this is Monday!' she said. A whole masque of little gadflies of unseizable conscient comedy danced forth in her eyes and were gone. 'And yet,' she said: 'Anthea: one of my most happiest devisements. And yet: was it fit indeed to sup a falcon with straw?'

Barganax looked at her, and as he looked his brow lightened and his eyes grew dark. 'O, you are beyond soundings,' he said. 'Do you laugh? Or do you nurse it against me? Well, there it is: and I swear to you, there was not an instant in it but my thought and my sense were nailed to you: but only to prove for the thousandth time your power, that outparagons all.'

'Well,' he said: 'do you know that?'

Her eyebrows, like brooding wings beyond nature long and slender of some far-flown bird, informed the serene purity of her brow with an air of permanent soft surprise touched sometimes with contemplation, and now with a faint mockery. 'Yes,' she said.

'Will you forgive me?'

'Yes,' she said.

'I would give much,' said Barganax, 'but to see your mind. Do you understand, that every road I tread leads to you?'

'I have heard you say so,' she said. 'No doubt your grace will accept the same comforting assurance from me.'

'It is true I am a proud man,' said Barganax then; 'yet I doubt my pride for this. For this, I must know in myself perfection.'

Fiorinda smiled. It was as if the termlessness of some divinity, clear, secure, pitiless, taking its easeful pleasure in the contemplation of its own self, lay veiled in that faint Olympian smile.

'But with you,' said the Duke, 'no such matter. You are perfect. You know it. Most devilishly you know it.'

He stood up and paced back and forth upon the carpet, then came to a stop beside her. 'But no. Jealousy,' he said, 'is a distemper of little men. Puff! 'Tis gone. I play even, madonna. And – well, I hold my own.'

Slowly, after a minute, she turned her head: gave him her green eyes. As she looked they widened, and it was as if fire leapt in their deeps and then flickered down to quiet embers. She turned away, giving him now, from black hair to silver shoulder, the virginal sweet line of her bended neck; the side view of her chin, firm and proud, and of lips, where her thought seemed to rest like a lily on still water.

One foot upon the highest step of the throne, he stood looking down at her. 'I have a mind,' said he, 'to turn sculptor: chryselephantine work: no, jet and ivory: ivory and black diamonds, rather: or the old man shall conjure up from the treasure-beds of Tartarus some new such thing, since earth hath nought precious enough. And I will fashion therein the likeness of each particular hair. Listen,' (bending a little nearer): 'I made this for you last week.' And he began to speak the lines, it was as though her dark troublous beauty was turned to music in his voice. As in secret antiphone to that music, her bosom mounted and fell with a quickened breathing.

> 'Some love the lily, some the rose
> Which in the summer garden blows;
> Some daisies shy, some mignonette,
> Some the sweet-breathed violet.
> But I a statelier Flower do owe,
> Doth in a heav'nlier garden grow:
> The Lily of sphinxian mystery,
> Too fair, too perilous-sweet to see,
> With curious work of filigree
> Trac'd in a thousand crimps and rings
> On her softly spreading wings.
> Upon the mountain of delight
> Bloometh my wild Flower, black like night.

> Her petals, curl'd luxuriously,
> Ravish the live soul forth of me.
> Her perfum'd darkness sets, like wine,
> My veins a-throb with fire divine—
> Fate, take all: yet leave me this:
> The Flower of Flowers, my Flower-Delice.

She made no sign, but remained with her downward, listening look. 'I wonder?' Barganax said: 'Did I ask you, no matter what, would you give it me? Were I bid you do, no matter what, would you do it?'

She nodded twice or thrice, without turning her head. 'All of me,' she answered softly. 'What you will.'

'Ah, then you shall swear this. For there is a favour you have till now refused me.'

'O,' said she, and the thing that dwelt in the corner of her mouth was awake and ready; 'if you must chaffer with me for oaths and blind bargains, I'll take back my words. We'll start fair.'

'No, no,' said the Duke. 'No oaths, then. I'll not cheapen the sweet bounty of your word already spoken.'

'But I've taken it back,' said she.

'Then,' he said, 'we begin again. First: will you not smile me a thank for today's proceedings?'

'I'll think on't,' she said. 'I might. But I'll be besought more prettily for it ere I do it.'

''Twas but to pleasure you, so I will at least be thanked,' said the Duke. 'For myself, why, I'd see the Admiral and my silly sister and the whole bunch of cards drowned together in the Styx ere I'd a stirred a foot in it. And so, for my payment—'

'You will unthank yourself with such talk,' she said. 'And besides, it is all lies.'

Barganax laughed. Then, looking in hers, his eyes became dark and masterful. 'It is lies,' he said. 'But only because of this, that I cannot do without you. You have taken it back?' He was suddenly kneeled at her feet: his hands shut like shackles upon her ankles, prisoning them. 'I have never bended knee to man or woman,' he said; 'and now I will have my way. At this hundredth time of asking, will you be my Duchess in Zayana?'

She made as if to rise, but his grip tightened. He said in a low fierce voice, 'Answer.' In his hands he felt her answer before she spoke: 'Never that.'

'That is an old stale answer,' he said. 'Try again.'

Fiorinda threw up her head with a little silent laugh. 'If you have your hour,' she said, 'to begin or to refuse, so have I mine.'

'But why?' said the Duke fiercely. She looked stonily down upon him. 'Why?' he said again.

'Because I had rather be my own mistress,' she said. 'And yours.'

'Ha! And I must starve still, save at the horning of the moon? And then oft but live on supposings; and every handwhile the chance you may forsake me? By heavens, but I will have more of you, madam.'

She shook her head. The Duke, letting go her feet now, clasped his arms about her below the knees. 'I know you care not a rush for the ducal crown. You are not dissevered by places, nor altered by times, nor subject unto to and fro. Do it for my sake. For indeed I am most venomously in love with you' (here he buried his forehead in her lap): 'were I lose you, as well tear out my heart roots.'

She sat very still. Then her fingers softly stroked, the wrong way, the thick, short-cropped, coppery, curling hair at the back of his head. 'O folly of men!' she whispered. 'How often, my lord, have you not exclaimed against safety and enduring goods? And now will you, like a peevish boy, provoke me to dwindle into your Duchess, and poison all our bliss? I'll sit in a shed with madge howlet and catch mice first.'

It was as if he had not heard her. The grip of his arms was tenser about her knees. His face, when he now looked up at her, had the look of a man dazzled from sleep. He said, 'I am sick with love of you.'

Fiorinda met his eyes for a minute in silence. Then she trembled: her laughter-loving imperial lips parted a little: the long black eyelashes half veiled her eyes: her eyelids quivered. With a little sudden catch of her breath, she bent forward; her chin lifted a little; her throat and bosom became in that instant the pure benediction of beauty, the opening of heaven, the coming down. 'Love me, then,' she answered. 'I am here to be loved.'

The Duke, now upon that throne beside her, had her now in his arms. As a sweet in the goblet, as pearls when the silken thread is broken, all her fierce lithe pride and queenship was unstrung: fallen loose: melted away. In the nape of her neck, where her hair was done in a knot that nestled there black and sleek like a sleeping leopard, he kissed, a dozen times, the last lowest little hairs, too young to be commanded, which, finer than gossamer-spiders' silk, shadowed the white skin with their delicately ordered growth: little hairs prophetic of all perfections. And now his bee-winged kiss, hovering below her ear, under the earring's smouldering of garnet, passed thence to where neck and shoulder join, and so to the warm throat, and so by the chin to that mocking spirit's place of slumber and provocation; until, like the bee into the honeyed oblivion of some deep flower incarnadine, it was entertained at last into the consuming heaven of that lady's lips.

Now opened the last door of all before that leaf of virtue, the high double door that led from the main staircase to the throne-room, and Lessingham, striding out of darkness into the very presence, checked in the threshold. In the first bright glimpsing, indeed, he beheld the Lady Fiorinda thus in Duke Barganax's arms; but, ere foot or hand might act on his will, shut doors and be gone, she had stood up and turned her eyes upon him: and with that he was like a man ensorcelled.

For now in her, so facing him from beside the dream-stone, he beheld no longer that lady, but another. In her hair, too pale for gold, too golden for silver, braided with strings of pearls, light itself seemed fallen a-dreaming, caught and stung asleep by the thousand little twisting tendrils that floated, hovered, vanished, and glinted again, with every stir of the quiet air. Feature by feature so might have been Barganax had he been born woman: a golden girl, in the sweet holiday spring-time of her awakening beauty.

Her grey eyes drew to far spaces, like the sea. On her cool lips, full, clean cut, pure of curve, everything desirable on earth or heaven seemed delicately to slumber: As a man out of the death-like sleep of some drug comes to his senses at first with a disordered perception, wherein familiar things stand new, with no root in time, no perfume, no promise, no echo: so Lessingham beheld her but as a vision uncurdled from the phantasmagoria of some dream: a thing which the awakening sense, making as yet no question of perduration or possession, or of a world beyond the charmed present, accepts without surprise. Then on the sudden he noted the fashion of her dress, strange, fitter for a lover's eye than for the common gaze of the court, and knew it, with a knowledge that seemed to shut fingers about his naked soul, for that very dress and garb which that dream had worn, standing but a half hour since at his bed's foot.

Up the empty hall he came to her, slowly, not to frighten away this wonder, but resolute. The Duke sprang up, his eyes shining like a lion's surprised. But Lessingham, as marking him not, was come now within ten paces of them, still with that unwavering noiseless stride, and now his foot was even upon the carpet. He halted with the prick of Barganax's sword against his chest. He stepped back a pace, and drew. For the second time in a day and a night they stood as opposites; and this time in a witched kind of stillness, wherein each leaned towards other across the kindling instant that should let them together, point and edge, like two great strokes of lightning and thunder. And for the second time, and now strangelier still, for the hotter occasion that was now than in the council chamber for bloody rages, the moment passed.

Lessingham lowered his sword. 'Who you are,' he said, 'I know not. But I'll not fight with you.'

'Nor I with you,' said the Duke, yet with thunder on his brow. 'Nor I with you.'

With the look on the face of each of them that a man's face wears when he strives to remember some forgotten tune, each fell back yet another pace or two from the other, each staring at the other still. And so staring, both slowly put up their swords, and, with the double click of them going home in the scabbards, both turned as upon a common impulse towards Fiorinda.

Like a man's beside himself, Barganax's eyes leapt from that other to Lessingham, from him to her, and his sword was jumped half-bare from the scabbard again. 'What mummery's this?' he said. 'Where is my lady? God's death! Speak, you were best, man, and you, woman, whoever you be.'

But Lessingham, looking too at that lady, and standing as if drunk, said, in a starved voice unlike his own, 'Give me her back': then bit it in and set his jaw. Barganax, with a dazed look, passed his hand across his eyes.

'My cloak, my lord,' she said, turning for the Duke to put it about her shoulders. He paused a moment. Her presence, thus strangely snatched away and as strangely restored, and in so serene an unconcernment; the curve of neck and hair; her skin; the sweet smell of her: these things shook the fierce blood in him so that he scarce dared trust his hand upon her, even through the cloak. But Lessingham near her too, and more, face to face with her dark and alluring loveliness, bore himself with a cold formal courtesy.

She thanked the Duke with a look: that slow, unblinking, unsmiling, suddenly opening and then fading, stare, with which upon his birthday she had promised herself in the garden. It mastered and then steadied his senses like wine. In that moment, so near the high climacteric, his eyes looking over her shoulder met the eyes of Lessingham in a profound recognition. In Lessingham's face, the masculine of hers by many particulars, he read a promise; not indeed, as in hers, the world-dissolving epithalamion of sense and spirit, but a promise of something scarcely less deep in the blood, albeit without arrows and without fire: of brotherhood beyond time and circumstance, not to be estranged, but riveted rather together, by mutual strife upon the great stage of the world and noble great contentions.

'My Lady Fiorinda,' said Lessingham, 'and you my lord Duke: inconsiderate excuses are no better than accusations. I could not rest. I will say no more.'

'In this world-without-end hour,' said the Duke, 'let us say but good night.'

Fiorinda spoke: 'You go north, my Lord Lessingham?'

'Tomorrow, madam.'

'Today, then: it is past midnight. Ere you go, I would know a thing. Were you ever a painter of pictures?'

'No. But a doer of deeds.'

'My lord the Duke painteth past admiration. Of me he hath painted forty pictures, but not yet one to's liking, and so burnt all.'

'There was a man I knew did so,' said Lessingham: 'burnt all save one. Yet no,' he said, with a strange half-waked look at her. 'What was't I said?'

'It is hard, I suppose,' said that lady, as if, in the enjoyment of her own thoughts' stoops and hoverings, she had no eye to note the lightless gaze with which he seemed to search inward in himself: 'It is hard, I suppose, for a lover, if he be a very lover, to paint his mistress. For then that which he would paint, if he be a very lover, is not appearance, but the thing which is. How can he paint her? Seeing that his picture, when it is painted, changeth then no more; but that which is, changeth unceasingly: and yet changeth not.'

'And yet changeth not,' said Lessingham.

'This ring of mine,' she said: 'see, it is wine-red tonight, but a-daytime sleepy green. And such, as Doctor Vandermast affirmeth, is beauty: ever changing, never changing. But truly it is an old prating man, and I think hardly knoweth what he prateth of.'

'Ever changing, never changing,' said Lessingham, as if he felt his way in the dark. Once more his gaze met the Duke's.

Her slanting green eyes, snakish, veiled with their silky dark-nesses, turned upon Barganax and then again upon Lessingham.

Lessingham, after a little silence, said, 'Good night.'

'And yet,' said she, as he bent to kiss her hand; and surely everything of that lady, the least turn of her finger, the least falling tone of her lazy voice, was as a stirring of mists ready to blow away and open upon wonder: 'what riddle was that you did ask me but now, my lord? A man's Self, said you? Or his Love?'

Lessingham, who had asked no riddle, made no answer.

'I think it is both,' Fiorinda said, looking steadily at him. He was ware of a settled quality of power in her face now, diamantine, older and surer than the primal crust, older than the stars: a quality that belonged most of all to her lips, and to her eyes: lips that seemed to close upon antique secrets, memories of flesh and spirit fused and transfigured in the dance of the daughters of the morning; and eyes yet blurred from looking upon the very bed of beauty, and delights unconceived by the mind of man. Those eyes and those lips Lessingham knew as a child knows its mother, or as the sunset knows the sea. In a dizziness of conflicting yeas and nays, he recognized in her the power that had drawn him but now up the hall, on to Barganax's sword-point. Yet she who had had that power so to draw him was strangely not this woman, but another. He bethought him then of their supper under the moon, and of her *allegretto scherzando* that had then so charmed his mind. The movement was changed now to *adagio molto maestoso ed appassionato*, but the charm remained; as if here were the lady and mistress of all, revealed, as his very sister, the feminine of his own self: a rare and sweet familiarity of friendship, but not of love; since no man can love and worship his own self.

Again she spoke: 'Good night. And you are well advised to go north, my Lord Lessingham; for I think you will find there that which you seek. North, in Rialmar.'

In a maze, Lessingham went from the hall.

And now Barganax and Fiorinda, standing under the shadowing glory of those wings, for a minute regarded one another in silence. The Duke, too, knew that mouth. He, too, knew those upper lids with their upward slant that beaconed to ineffable sweets. He, too, knew those lower lids, of a straightness that seemed to rest upon the level infinitude of beauty, which is the laying and the consolation and the promise on which, like sleeping winds on a sleeping ocean, repose all unfulfilled desires. And now at the inner corners of those eyes, as she looked at him, something stirred, ruffling the even purity of that lower line as the first peep of the sun's bright limb at morning breaks the level horizon of the sea.

'Yes,' she said: 'you have leave to resume our conversation where it was broke off, my friend. Yet this throne-room perhaps is not the most convenientest place for us, considering the lateness; considering too the subject, which, once thus raised between us, was never, as I remember, well laid again ere morning.'

IX

THE INGS OF LORKAN

THE RUYAR PASS • OWLDALE AND THE STRINGWAY •
THE VICAR PREPARES WAR; SO ALSO THE DUKE •
LESSINGHAM INVADES MESZRIA • BURNING OF LIMISBA •
RODER MOVES • BATTLE OF LORKAN FIELD • BEROALD
AND JERONIMY IN THE SALIMAT.

LESSINGHAM in the same hour, not to fail of his word, burnt up that leaf. On the morrow he rode north by way of Reisma Mere and Memison, going, as he had come south three weeks ago, but twenty in company, but so fast that now he was his own harbinger. So it was that the Duke's safe conduct procured him welcome of all men and speeding on his journey, while at less than a day's lag behind him was shearing up of the war-arrow and the countryside ablaze with rumours of war. So by great journeys he came at evening of the third day up through the defiles of the Ruyar to the windy stony flats that tail away north-westward between the glacier capped cliffs of the Hurun range on the right and Sherma on the left, and so to where, in the cleft of the Ruyar pass where it crosses the watershed to Outer Meszria and the north, the great work of Rumala leaves not so much as a goat's way between cliff and towering cliff.

'This were a pretty mouse-trap,' said Amaury, as they drew rein in the cold shadow of the wall: 'if he had bethought him

out of prudence, may hap, say a Monday last, soon as you broke
with him, to send a galloper whiles we dallied and gave him
time for it: enjoin his seneschal of Rumala shut door upon us,
hold us for's disposal upon further order. Had you thought on
that?'

'I thought on't,' said Lessingham, 'when I took his offer.'

'So I too,' said Amaury, and loosened his sword in its scabbard.
'And I think on't now.'

'And yet I took his offer,' said Lessingham. 'And I had reason.
You are prudent, Amaury, and I would have you so. Without my
reason, my prudence were in you rashness. And indeed, my reason
was a summer reason and would pass very ill in winter.'

In Rumala they were well lodged and with good entertainment.
They were up betimes. The seneschal, a gaunt man with yellow
mustachios and a pale blue eye, brought them out, when they were
ready after breakfast, by the northern gate to the little level saddle
whence the road drops northwards into Rubalnardale.

'The Gods take your lordship in Their hand. You are for Rerek?'

'Ay, for Laimak,' answered Lessingham.

'By the Salimat had been your easiest from Zayana.'

'I came that way south,' answered he; 'and now I was minded
to look upon Rumala. 'Tis as they told me; I shall not come this
way again.'

Amaury smiled in himself.

'You are bound by Kutarmish?' said the seneschal.

'Yes.'

'I have despatches for the keeper there. If your lordship would
do me the honour to carry them?'

'Willingly,' said Lessingham. 'Yet, if they be not of urgency, I
would counsel you keep 'em till tomorrow. You may have news
then shall make these stale.'

The seneschal looked curiously at him. 'Why, what news should
there be?' he said.

'How can I tell?' said Lessingham.

'You speak as knowing somewhat.'

'Tomorrow,' said Lessingham, 'was always dark today. Today

is clear: so enjoy it, seneschal. Give Amaury your letters: I'll see 'em delivered in Kutarmish.'

They were come now to the edge of the cliff upon the face whereof the road winds in and out for two thousand feet or more before it comes out in the bottom of Rubalnardale, plumb below the brink they stood on as a man might spit. The seneschal said, 'You must walk and lead your horses, my lord, down the Curtain.'

'Can a man not ride it?'

'Nor ever did, nor ever will.'

Lessingham looked over and considered. 'Maddalena hath carried me, and at a good racking pace, through the Hanging Corridors of the Greenbone ranges in nether Akkama: 'twas very like this.' He began to mount: 'Nay, touch her not: she will bite and strike with her forelegs at an unknown.'

The seneschal backed away with a wry smile as Lessingham leapt astride of his dangerous-eyed red mare. With him barely in the saddle, she threw a capriole on the very verge of the precipice; tossed her mane; with a graceful turn of her head took her master's left foot daintily between her teeth; then in a sudden frozen stillness waited on his will.

'I had heard tell,' said the seneschal, as the mare, treading delicately as an antelope, carried her rider down and out of sight, 'that this lord of yours was a mad fighting young fellow; but never saw I the like of this. Nay,' he said, as Amaury mounted and his men besides, 'then give me back my letters. As well send 'em later with the party must take up your corpses.'

'We shall now show you a thing: safe as flies on a wall,' said Amaury.

Lessingham shouted from the bend below, ''Tis a good road north by Rumala: a bad road south.' Amaury, smiling with himself, rode over the edge, and the rest followed him man by man. The seneschal stood for a while looking down the cliff when they were gone. There was nothing to be seen: only on the ear came a jangling of bits and the uneven clatter of horse-hooves fainter and fainter from the hollows of the crags. Far below, an eagle sailed past the face of that mountain wall, a level effortless sweep on still wings brazen in the sunshine.

Dusk was confounding all distances, smoothing away all shadows, smudging with sleepy fingers the clear daylight verities of whinbush and briar and thorn, mole-hill and wayside stone, outcropping rock and grassy hummock, fern and bent, willow and oak and beech and silver birch-tree, all into a pallid oneness and immateriality of twilight, as Lessingham and Amaury came at a walking-pace over the last stretch of the long open moorland sparsely grown with trees that runs up north from Ristby, and took the road north-eastward for Owldale. The westermost outlying spur of the Forn impended in a precipitous gable on their right; beyond it, north and round to the west, gathered by the dusk into a single blue wall of crenelled and ruined towers, the Armarick peaks and the fells about Anderside and Latterdale were a vastness of peace against the windy sky. There had been showers of rain, and thunder among the hills. Great Armarick, topping the neighbouring peaks, had drawn about his frost-shattered head a coverlet of sluggish and slate-hued cloud.

They had long outridden their company. Amaury's horse was blown. Even Maddalena had quieted her fiery paces to the unrelenting plod that draws on to corn and a sweet bed and sleep at night. Lessingham in a graceful idleness rode sideways, the slacked reins in his left hand, his right flat-palmed on the crupper. Turning his head, he met Amaury's eyes regarding him through the dusk. Something in their look made him smile. 'Well,' he said: 'grey silver aloft again, Amaury?'

'There's more in't than that,' said Amaury. 'You are stark mad these five days I think, since we set out north from Zayana. I cannot fathom you.'

Lessingham's eyes took on their veiled inward-dreaming look and his lips their smile that had first snared Barganax's fancy, holding a mirror as it were to Fiorinda's smile. 'I was never more sober in my life,' he said, his hand softly stroking Maddalena's back. There was a secret beat of music in his voice, like as had been in the Duke's when, upon Ambremerine to the singing of the faun, he had spoken that stave into his mistress's ear.

They rode the next league in silence, up the deep ravine of Scandergill above which the valley spreads out into wide flats, and the road strikes across to the north side through oak-woods that turned with their overarching shade the cloudy May night to inky darkness. A drizzling rain was falling when they came out of the forest and followed the left bank of Owlswater up to the bridge above the waters-meet at Storby, where Stordale opens a gateway into the hills to the north and the Stordale Beck tumbles into Owldale white over a staircase of waterfalls. The keeper of the bridge-house took the password and came down to offer his duty to Lessingham: he flew an owl to carry tidings of their approach to the Vicar in Laimak, and another, because of the darkness, to Anguring that they should have lights to light them over the Stringway. Two hours above Storby they halted half an hour for their company, left behind in their wild riding beyond Ristby. Now the road narrowed and steepened, climbing in zig-zags under the cliffs at the base of Little Armarick and tapering at last to a four-foot ledge with the jutting rock of Anguring Combust above it and the under-cut wall of the gorge below. At the bottom of that gorge, two hundred feet beneath the road, Owlswater whitened in foam and thunder over the ruins of old Anguring castle, that twenty years ago the Lord Horius Parry had flung down there from its rock, when after a long siege he had by stratagem won it and burnt it up along with his brother and his brother's wife and their sons and daughters and all their folk, glad to have rooted out at last this tree that had stood as a shadow against the sun to mar the fair growth of his own lordship in Laimak. Then had he let build, over against it on the left bank of the gorge, his own new fortalice of Anguring, upon a backward and upward running crest, to command at close range both the road below the former castle, and the Stringway. Upon this Stringway Maddalena now delicately stepped, her soul calm, amid the flurry of winds and unseen furious waters and flare-lit darknesses, with the comfort of a familiar master-mind speaking to her through pressure of

knee and through sensitive touch of bit upon lips and tongue. The
gorge was here barely twenty paces broad, and a huge slab, fallen
in ancient times from the mountain face above, was jammed like
a platter or meat-dish caught and gripped there up on edge: one
edge of the platter jammed where the road ended under old
Anguring, and the other jammed against the gorge's brink where
new Anguring sat perched like a preying bird. Along that slab's
upturned edge ran the road: an arched footway of rock, too narrow
for two horses meeting to pass one another: the inexpugnable
gateway from the south into upper Owldale and the pasture lands
of Laimak. Lessingham rode it unconcerned, giving Maddalena
her head and letting her take her time, in the smoky glare of a
dozen torches brought down to the cliff's edge out of Anguring.
Amaury and the rest were fain to lead their horses across.

A little before midnight Lessingham blew horn under Laimak.

The Vicar received Lessingham by torchlight in the great main gate
above the gatehouse. He advanced three steps to meet Lessingham,
and embraced and kissed him on both cheeks. Lessingham said,
'Your highness is to thank me indeed. I have set 'em all by the ears,
and in that suspectuous squabbling insecurity declared war upon
them. It resteth now but to raise force and crush them ere they run
together again. I'll tell you all at large, but first I would bathe and
shift me; and indeed I have not eat these eight hours, since dinner-
time at Ketterby.'

''Tis provided,' said the Vicar. 'Let's hold more chat over the
supper table.'

Half an hour past midnight supper was set in the great banquet-
hall which was shapen like an L, the main member forty cubits
in length and the shorter twenty-five. Amaury and they of
Lessingham's company had place at the far end of the long table
by the door at the end of the main body of the hall that opened
on the great court. The Vicar sat with Lessingham at a little round
table at the northern corner whence they might see everywhere in
the hall both ways, left and right, and be out of earshot of the
rest and talk at ease. The hall was of black obsidian-stone, with

deep mullioned windows along its north-western wall. Devilish heads, five cubits in bigness from brow to chin, were carven in high relief along the five other walls: thirteen heads in all, very deformed and uglisome, laying out their tongues; and on the end of each tongue was stood a lamp brightly burning, and the eyes of the great faces were looking-glasses nicely cut up with facets to throw back the rays of the lamps, so that the whole banquet-room was lit with a brilliance of lamplight. It was mizzly weather, very cold for the time of year; the Vicar bade light a fire of logs in the great hearth that stood on the inner angle opposite their table.

Lessingham, in a pleasant ease now after nigh five days' riding, sat eating of his supper, a neat's tongue, some jellied quails, a sallet of endives lettuces and salsify, with hippocras and a quince pie to end it, while the Vicar, leaning over the table at his cousin's elbow and drinking chill wine, talked long and low in his ear. Gabriel Flores, upon pretext of hospitable attentions, tarried by the table. 'Care not for Gabriel, he is inward in my counsels,' said the Vicar.

'Not in mine,' said Lessingham.

'Well, pug, begone,' said the Vicar then; 'we have no love for you.'

'O I do love my little Gabriel,' said Lessingham; 'yet sometimes he is dearest to me in absence. And that humour's on me now; and so, Gabriel, good night.' Gabriel gat him gone with an ill grace.

'Filth and damnation of these free towns in the north there!' said the Vicar, reaching out a broad and hairy hand for the leavings of the tongue, which he threw to a great dog that, prick-eared and alert, watched their meal as a peri should watch the things of Paradise. 'I trust ere long to wash my hands in the umbles of the knaves; but all taketh time, and here's trouble upon trouble ever since the old King died. And, like a fool, I laughed to think my hands were untied then.'

'I would you had not needed act so suddenly,' said Lessingham. 'These soldiers you have packed off north I could a used to your great vantage in the south now. Tella, Lailma, Veiring, and Abaraima, you told me, swapt up a roguish bargain with Ercles; opened their gates to him; called him their captain?'

'Ay: 'stead of Mandricard, that held it in my interest these five years.'

'Mandricard,' said Lessingham, 'was never the man to serve your turn; I told you that five years ago, cousin. Too irresolute, fawning on the tag-rag people for favour today, putting 'em down with a bloody petulance tomorrow; such an uncertain seat: such jaggings on the bit: spoil your best of horses.'

'Pah! 'Twas not one man's insufficiency raised this smother,' said the Vicar. 'Hath been brewing for years. I have had my finger on their pulses. I saw it afore yesterday. And Veiring, worst of all. God's body! I tell you Prince Ercles' self did say to my face (when there was less coolness 'twixt us than nowadays befalleth): said if they of Veiring did trouble him as they did me, he would send his men with shovels and pickaxes and throw it into the sea.'

'You have despatched Arcastus, you say, and a thousand men?'

'Twelve, no, fifteen hundred: not as upon serious action: only to cow 'em with a show of strength: stop other sheep from following of those through the same gate. But harkee, I have yet one good cogging die ready upon the cast,' and his voice fell to a growling whisper: 'a likely lad with a good point to his knife and a well shut mouth and a good habit of miching round by unseen ways: tickled his belly with two hundred gold pieces, and five hundred more upon performance: if he but wriggle his way into Eldir—' the Vicar drank. 'Gabriel procured him, and that at some third remove. My hand's not seen in't. If aught miscarry, should slander blow hitherward I can securely 'gainst all contradictions disown him.'

Lessingham leaned back in his chair and stretched. He regarded his cousin with a look of profound enjoyment which, when the adder eyes met his, livened to the shadow of a smile. 'I do sadly fear, cousin, this most taking simple-heartedness of yours,' he said. 'Consider: 'tis barely two months since the Chancellor took up one of your instruments in his garden in Zayana and hanged him there. I know 'twas given out 'twas Zapheles worked that poppet's strings, not to make too much pother of it; but in all their private counsels there was no question made but you did do it. And now Ercles: that old dog-fox is not to be caught with your springes, cousin. I would you had been in Zayana; you should a seen the labour I had untying of those bands of alliance your known ways had knit them together withal; and but for that, little enough of trust or friendship amongst 'em. My work had been easy else.'

The Vicar turned upon him eyes of stone. 'You have your ways,' he said. 'I mine.'

'What strength have you in Owldale?' asked Lessingham, as a falcon leaves playing with her mate in the upper air to stoop at her proper prey. 'Four thousand men?'

'Just, if you'll drink drunk and see each man double,' answered he.

'Two thousand? and my own riders, eight hundred more.'

'Nay, I reckoned them in,' said the Vicar.

'I must have more,' said Lessingham, and sprang up. 'We must come down upon them like a thunderbolt ere they have time to consider too much and stick together again, else is all this work wasted.'

'Softly, softly,' said the Vicar. ''Tis but boys and women count to go through presently their designments a royal point; my policy runneth deeper. I'll clear my rear in the north first. Besides, I've thought on a business for you north-away; but that must wait again. For this present matter, I will first make sure of Ercles and Aramond.'

Lessingham paced a dozen times to and again from the table to the fire. 'Cousin,' he said then, coming to a stop before the table, 'you have taken my rede ere now, and have you ever fallen down by it?' The Vicar shrugged his shoulders. Lessingham's eyes were a-sparkle. 'Seeing I have begun,' said he, 'I will stoutly go through. You can hold Laimak and Anguring with as many men as chestnuts you could carry in two fists. Give me the rest, and your warrant to raise what more I may. Ere a month be past I'll grab you Outer Meszria in the hollow of my hand.'

'You've a sweet vein in speech,' the Vicar said; 'but you know as well as I we cannot now lay hand on above two thousand five hundred men, and there's four or five thousand needed for such an enterprise.'

'Yet shall you see me undertake it,' said Lessingham. Things least feared are least defended and observed. And remember, one great stroke i' the southlands, and these factions that vex you i' the north there shall fizzle like a lamp when the oil is out. Time enough then to sort them, put 'em to rights.'

The Vicar's great spreading nostrils widened and the red blood flushed his face, as if set a-boiling with the heat of the imperious eager and resolute imaginings that burned in Lessingham's speech and bearing. He stood up now heavily, and for a minute faced Lessingham in silence. Then, clapping a heavy hand upon either shoulder of Lessingham, 'We'll sleep on't,' he said. 'The more spacious that the tennis-court is, the more large is the hazard. And if you think, cousin, to thrust all this down my pudding-house at a gob, well, the Devil eat your soul for me then, for you are sadly mistook.'

That was the twenty-seventh of May. Upon the twenty-ninth Duke Barganax, his scheme well laid now, moved north with his bodyguard of five hundred picked men-at-arms to Rumala, there to wait Barrian and Melates with the levies of Krestenaya and Memison ere he should descend into Outer Meszria and the marches. Here was good hopes, soon as the ducal banner should be shown north of the Zenner and the Vicar's garrison shut up by siege in Argyanna, that the whole March of Ulba should rise to resume their old affinities and fling off the yoke of Rerek. So upon the fifth day from Zayana, being now the second of June, came the Duke to Rumala. Upon that same day at evening the lord Admiral weighed anchor and put out from Sestola with sixteen fighting ships all manned and six ships of burden, a great and redoubtable power of men: two thousand five hundred of his own sailors, men inured to war by land as well as by sea, besides two thousand footmen of the royal garrison in Meszria and the Earl Roder himself on board with the Admiral. Roder's chosen riders, three hundred strong, veterans all of ten years' service, fared by land for lack of room a-shipboard. The like was Egan to do, with four hundred Meszrian horse. The Salimat was set for their meeting-place, of the power that went by sea, and the horse, and the Chancellor with nigh two thousand more old levies of Fingiswold. These tarried in Zayana yet a day or two for Zapheles, who was raising of forces south in Armash and Daish. All these were appointed to meet on Wednesday the seventh of June upon the Salimat, where the highway from Zayana to Ulba crosses Nephory Edge at its lowest; and that is the best vantage ground for an army to stand against an enemy faring from the north, for it gives a clear wide prospect west and north and east over the low-lying marchlands of Outer Meszria and Ulba, and the lie of the land is good for falling upon him if he will attack up the pass, and it is a strong place too to hold upon defence if need be, and a place well apt by nature for hidden ambushes and espial of any army that should fare by that road whether south or north.

The High Admiral put out upon the flood-tide from Sestola and dropped down the firth with a favouring wind. But at nightfall the wind had freshened so that it was dangerous sailing among the islands. The fleet lay up till dawn in sheltered water behind Lashoda; by then was a high sea running, and when they were come out into the open they must beat up northwards all day against a headwind and at night were glad to run for shelter in to Spruna mouth. With these delays and adverse winds it was not until the evening of the third day that they made Peraz Firth and anchored about supper-time at the head of the firth over against the town. Here were sumpter horses and mules and bullock carts to meet them, and the next day they landed the army and the stuff, and, leaving a thousand of Jeronimy's men to mind the ships, came on the morrow in a day's march up through the flowering valley of Biulmar and camped the same evening in the Salimat. Roder's three hundred horse, punctual to the day appointed, came in before night. The Meszrian horse with Egan were late: nought

known of them since these had set forth without them from
Zayana, after six hours' vain waiting. Roder cursed them. Of
Beroald, with his two thousand, there was no sign, nor no word.

Morning rose abated with cloud and mist. A blanket of vapour
rolling down the smooth rock hummocks east of the pass lay
damp about the tents. The Admiral sent a man of trust east through
the hills to Rumala to advertise the Duke that the Salimat was
held and all well, and another to find out the Chancellor.
Intelligencers had gone well a week before into Outer Meszria
and the borderlands. An hour before noon came in tidings by one
of these, that upon Sunday Lessingham had crossed the Zenner
with no great strength of men and appeared before Fiveways: that
the accursed people of that town had, against expectation, opened
their gates to him: that there he lay as late as Tuesday, and there
men drew to him, by twos and threes, here a score and there a
score; mainly, 'twas thought, from the March, but some few, 'twas
spoken, from the Meszrian border upon pretext he did owe their
allegiance, bearing the Queen's warrant and upholding her right.
An hour later came in others with more fresh advertisement, how
but yesterday, upon their own observation, Lessingham was
marched out of Five-ways, in strength some fifteen hundred foot
and a thousand horse: that 'twas said seven hundred of the footmen
were veterans of the Parry's, the rest raw levies: the horse mainly
Lessingham's own: that with these he was turned north-east along
the road by the river, as if his intents were aimed for Kutarmish.
Upon which tidings, Roder took Jeronimy by the sleeve and walked
out of earshot of their officers.

'What rede will you take now, my lord Admiral? One mischief
never comes alone. Here you have the Chancellor a day behind
time and still no news of him, and we with our powers thus
clipped sit but and look on. If Kutarmish fall, then is Outer
Meszria lost without a stroke, and that the richest land of all in
the south here.'

'Ibian will hold Kutarmish, never doubt it,' said the Admiral.

'Say he do,' replied Roder. 'Shall then these ram-cats of Meszria
reap all the honour, whiles we of the Queen's true party sit

quittering here? 'Twill breed discontent i' the army, too, forget not. I have felt it ere now: ears pricked up for every air that bloweth a doubt if it be we truly or these of the other party do truly uphold her interest.'

'That,' said Jeronimy, 'is a main uncertainty of currents and shifting sands we needs must in a manner sleep and eat withal since first he was deputed overseer of her nonage, whose innocent right doth so justify his wrong.'

'It lieth upon us, saving your reverence, my lord Admiral,' said Roder, 'not but eat and sleep only, but stand up and act. Consider: if this intelligence (and 'tis well seconded) be not all out, we be now two to one against him.'

'He is strong in horse, and of great reputation in that arm,' said Jeronimy.

'I redoubt him not,' said Roder, 'in that particular.'

'All in all,' said Jeronimy, 'his force, be it little, is well strengthed. A little gold overvalueth much lead or iron.'

Roder spat on the ground and scowled. 'Were't mine alone to command,' said he, after a minute, 'I'd down into the flats today: with my new broom sweep him one swap, and sweep him out of Meszria.'

The Admiral softly blew out his cheeks and shook his head. 'Let us wait, my lord, till tomorrow. The Chancellor will sure be come then.'

The morrow dawned fair. All the morning fog hung over the countryside to the northwards, so that it showed dull like the bloom on a black grape; above it the sky was blue and tender, and all the near stretches of the wide vale of the Zenner lay bright under the' sun, but in a soft brightness, with the dwellings of men and the paleness here and there of a winding stream, and the winding empty high-road coming south across the low land till at length it breasted the slopes of these southern hills and came up to cross the Salimat. At noon came hot news of the vicarian army marching west again. By the third hour past noon they were in sight, coming south-east over the brow two leagues away, above Aptyssa. The camp in the Salimat was pitched a little to the south

below the hause, not to let it be known from the northward how
strongly the road was held. In the hause and upon the northern
slope it was jopplety ground of rock and heather: little knolls and
dingles, in which Jeronimy and Roder now disposed their army
on either side of the road, hidden and well posted for overwhelming
of Lessingham should he assay the pass. He came on but slowly.
It was three hours more ere he began to drive in Jeronimy's outposts
on the Hazanat beck. Roder's patience was long since drained
away, and he was for setting upon them then and there while
daylight lasted. 'Nay, we must bide fast,' said Jeronimy. 'Would
you throw away the advantage we do hold upon him and fight
on ground of his own choosing; aptest too for cavalry, wherein
we are weakest?'

Roder drew up his lip. 'Wisdom,' he said, 'hath her excesses,
and no less need of moderation, than folly. Take your course, my
lord; but for my own part I will not be held answerable for these
delays.'

It was seen now that Lessingham halted and pitched camp in
the meadows west of Limisba, the hither side of the Hazanat,
about a mile short of where the ground began to rise. And now
he arrayed his army before the camp as if for battle. Jeronimy
said, 'He doth now in a manner draw the straw before the cat.
But we shall not play withal.' Roder ground his teeth and went
to his quarters. Little content it brought him to see his own summer
palace of Limisba, given him lately by King Mezentius in payment
of his services in peace and war, lie thus under the claws of
Lessingham. When supper was cooked, Jeronimy bade damp out
all fires, so as it should not be known from below whether he lay
there still in the Salimat or whether he was marched away. There
was yet no tidings of the Chancellor, now full two days behind
the time appointed. This lay like an ill-digested meal on their
bellies. Jeronimy chose him out a prudent close and faithful
messenger: sent him back by the Zayana road to seek tidings. All
night long Lessingham's camp-fires smoked to the stars from glimmering
points of flame. Roder said, 'Are they girl-children, then,
these riffraff of Rerek, that they must coddle by the fire these

summer nights, though we upon the hill can sleep in the cold?' He was snoring in his tent and so saw not, an hour before dawn, his own house of Limisba in a lowe, like Antares amid the lesser fires of night.

At daybreak Limisba sparkled merrily, so as even here in the Salimat a man might doubt he heard not the crackle, throwing up vast eddying clouds of smoke that were yet but as a wreath from a snuffed-out candle facing the clouds of the dawn. The camp-fires burned yet, but the camp was struck. Along the winding waters towards the Zenner new fires beaconed to the sky, as if Lessingham, having done with his feint against the Salimat, would say, 'Come down then and deal with me, or I will burn up all Meszria under your noses.' Word was brought hastily to the generals: Roder rushed out in his shirt, sputtering a stream of blasphemies: called up the guard to summon the captains to council: gave order to strike camp and make all ready to march in posture for battle upon short warning. In the midst of which haste and fury he was met with the Lord Jeronimy with letters in his hand. 'From the Chancellor: put in my hands this instant by's messenger ridden day and night,' said the Admiral: 'these commends express he hath had delays for cause we spoke on: doubtful allegiance 'mongst his men: but all ended now and their minds well satisfied. Doubted not to set forth from Zayana on Thursday (that's four days late)' – 'Damnation of hell! What good's in that?' said Roder. – 'And by forced marches should be here ere tomorrow night.'

'Then is our way clear,' said Roder: 'we wait no longer;' and he flung off to his tent to clothe himself. The lord Admiral looked after him with pursed lips and an anxious brow.

Ten minutes later was their council called in the Admiral's tent. Earl Roder came in in full battle-gear. He said, 'There is first the point of policy, my lord, and that's for you and I. Pray you let's be private.'

'As shall please you,' said Jeronimy.

When they were private the Lord Jeronimy took him by the arm and said, 'I would have you in a manner overview the thing serenely. I am no jot less eager than yourself to strike; but remember, 'tis his plain game to make us put our finger in a hole. There is hazard in't today. Tomorrow, with the Chancellor and near another two thousand men, no hazard at all. Hasty fruits, my lord, be a pleasure for the time; but their time is but a cherry-fair.'

Roder said, in a strained quietness, 'Your lordship must forgive me if I speak my mind, and 'tis, of this that you have spoke now, that a lewder and feebler skill or argument can no man make: if in sober sadness you would wait till tomorrow and suffer this Lessingham slip through our fingers.'

'Nay, pray you, my lord,' said Jeronimy, 'you must not wrest my words. Wait till tomorrow, and I will securely promise you there shall not one tail of them return again into Rerek.'

'Were it speak my thought,' said Roder, and grew crimson, 'I should a said you did seek an argument to cloak your – nay, but I know 'tis not chicken-hearted-ness: I mean your pig-headedness – like a filthy fly that seeketh all over the body for a sore.'

'Rude incivilities, my Lord Roder,' said the Admiral, taking his hand away, 'shall stand us in little stead in our search for wise counsel. In a manner, 'tis a main need for us to be of one mind in this pass we are come to: to fail of that were a ruin worth all men's pity.'

'My good lord Admiral,' said Roder, 'give me your hand. I'm sorry my cursed words should so outrun my meaning. Only, a shame have we with so much strength at our back, when that a pawn saith to the king checkmate. Well, let him go his ways then. I reck not. And when his grace shall see, from his high vantage point of Rumala, this Lessingham fare like a king through Outer Meszria, and none to nay-say him, and we by just presumption lost or gone to sleep, he will soon down on him from Rumala, and himself do the thing we boggled at.'

The Admiral listened with hands clasping and unclasping behind his back, his head bent, as if studying his own feet. At mention of the Duke he gave a little start: a deep flush overspread his countenance. 'Nay, but I had forgot that,' he said, after a pause. 'And yet 'tis present danger, Lessingham heading east. In the mad-brain violence of his valour, to come down: cope Lessingham in the plains.' Still avoiding Roder's eye, he walked slowly to the tent door and stood looking out. 'Whereupon should most assuredly his too little force be incontinently overthrown and eaten up.'

Roder pricked his ears. Jeronimy abode there, silent and thoughtful, twirling his gold perspective-glass on the end of its slender chain. Roder spoke: 'Which if't befall, you and I should have but one shift left, my lord Admiral: that's straight go hang ourselves.'

The Admiral said nothing: only ceased from twirling of his glass. Roder waited a little. Then he said. 'There is yet good time to head him off, bring him to battle. After a few hours, not so easy; yet even that were better, follow at his heels through Meszria: better than sit here.'

There was a long silence. Roder breathed thickly through his nose; his jowl, under the bristles of his cropped black beard, swoll above the collar of his gorget. At last, without looking round, Jeronimy spoke. 'The considerations are too much different. Time: 'tis that spoils all. No time to bring word to the Duke in Rumala. And so, impulsive necessity: not your other reasons, my lord,' he said, turning and coming in; ''tis this persuadeth me to that which were else great folly. You shall have your way, my lord. Call in the rest.'

'Ha! Then 'tis day!' said Roder, and took him by both hands. 'Now have I the bloody man upon the anvil: shall be pulp ere sundown.'

Lessingham, from a rise of ground beside the Zenner where he had now halted his army, beheld at four miles' distance how Roder came down in force from the Salimat. 'The Gods be praised,' he said: 'here's an end of bonfires. Yet with such sluggish foxen, no way but smoke 'em out. And now we must not seem too eager, while they have yet the choice to run to earth again.'

'You have roused a bed of bears, not foxen,' said Amaury.

'When the bear was met with the tiger cat, then was there fur a-flying,' said Lessingham. 'Time is of our side. They outnumber us, but not past coping with. Give 'em time to gather all their power, we durst not stand them; but now 'tis not beyond adventure.'

He issued command now, and they fell back slowly south-eastwards. The Earl turned east on this, as if to intercept them in the lava at the skirts of the hills above Nephory. After an hour's march the armies were drawn within two miles of one another. Lessingham altered his course and headed due north, hugging at last the eastern edge of the wood of Orasbieh as if he would make for the bridge at Lorkan, where the Kutarmish road running in from the north crosses the shallow and muddy river Ailyman a little above its falling into the Zenner. Here betwixt wood and river was a stretch of meadow land, firm and level: and here, resting his left upon the river a few hundred paces above the bridge and his right upon the border of Orasbieh wood, Lessingham halted and made ready for battle. Of his main battle, of footmen, he made a crescent, centre advanced, horns curving back toward the road. A great part of these were raw levies, raised, some hundreds, within the week from the country-side inland about Argyanna and seaward about Kessarey, others raised by the Vicar two months since, when he drew power to him in Owldale because of King Styllis. But nine hundred, of all the sixteen hundred foot, were veterans of the Vicar's old army, hard as bears and inured to war: these had seen service under Lessingham too ere now, seven or eight years ago when, not without discreet countenance from the princes and (as was commonly said) from Barganax, the great rebellion had shaken all Rerek nearly to the unseating of the Vicar and the conquering might of Fingiswold. With some of these veteran troops Lessingham stiffened his centre, but posted them in the main upon the wings, held well back as aforesaid: ten score he kept in reserve under his own hand for more security in the dangerous purpose he did intend. Four hundred of his own horse, under command of Amaury, made his left battle, resting on the river. Three hundred more, under Brandremart, along with the squadrons lent from Argyanna, went on the right beside the wood.

When the Earl's outriders came round the south-east neb of the wood and saw these dispositions, they sent word back to let him know that Lessingham stood there in the ings of Lorkan, and in what posture, offering battle. Upon which the Earl straightway called a halt, arrayed his host as he had determined with himself before, and advanced in order of battle. He had with him the whole army that was that morning gathered in the Salimat, save only five hundred sailors from the fleet who abode still in the pass there with the High Admiral, to hold it if need were and to await the Chancellor. His main strength, of two thousand heavy-armed spearmen of Fingiswold and a thousand of Jeronimy's sailors, so far outwent in his judgement Lessingham's foot, as well in weapons and goodness as in numbers, that he made little account of the odds against him in respect of horse. With that mind, he arrayed them in deep ranks, and commanded Peropeutes, who with Hortensius and Belinus captained the foot, to throw their whole weight, upon blowing of the horn for battle, against Lessingham's centre, and break it. He himself with his three hundred picked horsemen of the Wold fared against Amaury beside the river. Egan and the Meszrian horse, but new come in that morning, went upon the left.

Earl Roder without parley let blow up the war-blast, and the banners were borne forth, and with a great and horrid shout his main battle set on at a lumbering run. Lessingham bade his folk hold their ground till it was come to handystrokes and then to hold firm on the wings at all costs. When they were come within cast, each side let at the other with twirl-spears. Upon the next instant Peropeutes and the pick of the royal guard, bearing great oblong shields and armed alternately with long thrusting-spears and two-handed swords, crashed like a battering-ram against Lessingham's centre. In the roar of that onset and the clatter of steel and grinding of edge upon edge, the levies of Rerek, under the weight of deep columns so thrown upon them, shook and bent. Many were hurt and many slain of either side in that first clash of the battle; for fair in the centre had Lessingham set with each raw young man an old fighter of the Vicar's, and these, with their short two-edged swords good for thrusting and hewing alike, and their smaller shields light but tough, made play where Roder's spearmen might scarce find weapon-room in the close mellay. With main ponderous weight of numbers thrusting in serried ranks from behind, the battle front bent northwards, until Lessingham's half-moon was clean reversed: horns reaching forward on either side, belly buckled inward. And little by little into that deepening pocket Roder's battering-ram, with ever narrowing front, crowded and battered its way.

Lessingham had under his hand a hundred picked riders and a hundred of his veteran foot, men trained to go into battle with the horsemen, holding to the stirrup when they charge. With these he hung about the backward-buckling centre as a gannet follows a shoal of mackerel. His lips were set: his eyes dancing fires. By runners and riders, where he might not see for himself, he knew minute by minute how things fared: of the Meszrian horse now broken and put to flight beside the wood: of Amaury heavily engaged with Roder on the left. For the main action, his tried troops, two hundred and fifty on either part, were now, with the passage between them of that battering-ram, posted where he would have them: upon the enemy's flanks. Even as the gannet, half closing her wings, drops like a white broad-barbed arrow to the sea, cleaving the waters with a blow that flings up spray with a swish as of a spouting whale, so, suddenly, seizing the moment, Lessingham struck. Himself, with his two hundred, rushing forth now from between the ranks of the unbroken but battered and far-driven centre, turned back the advance of Roder's main front as with a blast of murdering wild-fire. In that same nick of time, the Vicar's veterans closed upon Roder's flanks like the claws of a crab. They took his right flank at open shields, so that great was the man-fall, and men cast down in heaps: some smothered under their fellows' carcasses, some cut to death with their own weapons or their fellows' or ever their foes might come at them. The horse upon Lessingham's right, leaving the pursuit when they heard his horn blow up the battle-call, took a sweep south and about and fell upon the foot from flank and rear. Amaury in a last charge flung the half of Roder's famous horsemen into the river and utterly overthrew them.

The sun was a flattened ball of crimson fire touching the sea between the Quesmodian isles, when the High Admiral walked up from his tent with the Lord Beroald to a place of prospect whence they might overlook far and wide the vale of the Zenner, misty in the warm and sleepy sunset light. 'Well, I have told you, I think, every tittle,' he said. 'And now it is the eighth hour past noon. And no news these three hours.'

'And then to say he had come up with him in the ings of Lorkan?'

Jeronimy nodded his head. 'Should a been more news ere now.'

The Chancellor with a swift glance sideways, not to be seen, noted the Admiral's face clouded with anxious thought. 'I would not think so,' he said lightly.

'A cat not to be caught without mittens,' said Jeronimy. He stood for a minute scanning the countryside below, then, as they turned again to their walking, 'When should your main body be here?' he said.

'Tomorrow night,' answered Beroald.

'And Zapheles?'

Beroald's lip curled. 'I will adventure upon no guesses as to that.'

'Tomorrow night,' said Jeronimy. 'And that's but lean relief, when 'tis being played out now, and for want of your army, three days dallied behind the day – nay, I blame it not on you, my lord: I know what ado you had. Nor I blame it not on myself.' He met the Chancellor's cold eye, squared his shoulders and laughed. 'Your lordship must forgive me. Pah! 'Tis barely sunset, and are the scritch-owls abroad already? But these land-fights, 'tis pure truth, have ever seemed a thing 'gainst nature to me, in a manner.'

A studied imperturbability informed the Chancellor's lean

countenance as, erect and soldier-like, he surveyed the landscape with folded arms. 'The odds of strength, my lord Admiral,' he said coldly, 'can alone resolve you of all doubts. And Roder is no untried boy, to walk into nets or aim ere he can strike. Come, let's go to supper.'

X

THE CONCORDAT OF ILKIS

AMAURY BEFORE THE DUKE • OUR LADY OF CYPRUS •
FIORINDA IN A JEWELLED SHADE • PHILOMMEIDES
APHRODITE • HER HIGH PIERIAN FLOWER
• THE DUKE PERCEIVES.

DUKE Barganax, the second night after that battle, sat in an upper
chamber above the guard-room in Rumala. Bolt upright he sat, in
a great stone chair, back to the wall, greaved and helmed, and
in his long-sleeved byrny, every link of which was damascened
with silver and gold. Black plumes of the bird of paradise shadowed his helm with their shifting iridescence of green and steel-blue
fires. His hands hung relaxed over the arms of the chair. Torn and
crumpled papers lay at his feet. A lamp on the table at his left
elbow lighted the room but dimly. His face was in shadow, turned
from the lamp towards the deep-set open window and its darkness
astir with starlight. He did not move at the clatter of Medor's
mailed footsteps on the stair nor at his coming in. For a full minute
Medor stood before him silent, as if afeared.

'Is he gone?'

Medor answered, 'I cannot move him. He is most stubborn set
to speak with your grace.'

Barganax neither spoke nor stirred.

'He will say nought to me,' said Medor: 'nought to any save to your grace alone.'

'Is he weary of his life?'

'I did instruct him at large. Yet nought will do but he shall have speech with you face to face. I have done my best.'

After a pause the Duke said, 'Admit him.'

Thereupon was guarded into the chamber, betwixt two of the Duke's red-bearded shaven-headed men-at-arms, Amaury. He was dirted to the knee from hard riding through the marshlands. They had made him leave his weapons. 'Was this well done, Amaury,' said the Duke, 'to come and make me your gazing-stock, and the glory of Zayana laid in the suds?'

'My lord Duke,' said Amaury, 'I see no such thing. If your grace will in your old used nobility meet my master, he doth most eagerly desire to treat with you, and upon such terms as shall be of more honour and advantage to you than those which he beforetime did offer, before war was betwixt you.'

'Do you see that goblet?' said the Duke then. 'Were you to set in it an invenomed toad and mash him to a jelly, then pour wine on't and drink it off, that were a thing likelier for your safety than come hither to insult over me with his words of peace.'

Amaury flushed like a girl under his fair skin. He said, 'If there is blame, blame me. Of myself, not sent, came I hither into your power; for I knew his strange and needless resolve to come himself tomorrow on the like errand, but I smelt danger in that. Therefore I came first, without leave asked, to be his taster; as great men will have the dish tasted first by another, if there be poison in it.'

'Then shall he thank me,' said the Duke, 'for chastising of his disobedient dog. And yet,' he said, 'you might a known there was little danger. You might a known I should have the wit to let you go: as men use with rat-traps: there is a way in with a snap-door, but another way out: let 'em go at will, in and out, for a few nights till they have lost all fear on't; then, one night, shut the way out, catch 'em all in a bunch. Dear Gods, could I have but that Roder and that Beroald amongst 'em: mince them all!'

'But I am not a rat,' said Amaury. 'I can judge; and if I judge so, warn him.'

The Duke's face was dark as blood. 'Take him out,' he said. 'Tie him hand and foot and throw him down the cliff. This may somewhat ease my rage.'

The guardsmen laid each a hand upon Amaury's shoulders. He turned pale. He said, 'If I come not back, there is this good in it, that 'twill yet give him pause. And his life is better to me than mine.'

'Make haste, as I bade you,' said the Duke, starting suddenly up, deadly white, terrible, like a wounded lion. 'If more come, I'll use the like liberty on them. It shall appear whether I be well tamed with the infortunity of this battle. Trokers and dastards: let them know me, too late.' He strode with great clanking strides to the window and stood there, stiff, his back to the room, his arms tight folded before his face and pressed against the wall, his temples pressed against the backs of his clenched fists. Medor, by a look, bade the guard stand still. Amaury waited.

'Medor,' said the Duke: he was now at the window, looking out. Medor went to him.

'Keep the man till morning: out of my sight. I will think more on this.'

Amaury spoke: 'May I, with your grace's leave, say but a word?'

The Duke made no answer, looking still out of the window, but his frame stiffened as he stood.

'If I be not returned ere morning, there be those will tell my lord whither I am gone. He will conclude your grace hath made away with me. That ruins all.'

The Duke swung round. 'Have him away, ere I afterthink me.' He plucked out his dagger.

'He was resolved to ride up the Curtain alone,' said Amaury loudly as they led him out: 'alone: in so high a trusting honour hath he held you.'

'Away!' said Barganax. His left hand shut upon Medor's wrist. The soldiers hurried Amaury through the door. 'O horrible ruin! Was ever prince betrayed as I am? O Medor I could bathe in blood: butcher their heads off with my own hands: cut their hearts out, eat 'em raw with garlic; then sink with stink *ad Tartara Termagorum*.

'Nay, that's foulness,' he said, again striding up and down. 'Damned Beroald: damned two-faced Zapheles: damned womanish Jeronimy: dregs of the Devil's cup. That's worst of all: I, that dared imaginarily place myself above the circle of the moon, to be the wide world's paragon, and only beauty's self to be my paramour: now baffled to extremest derision, changed to a bloody beast.

'Nay,' he said, 'but I'll prince it out;' and sat again in the stone chair. Medor was leaned on his elbows at the window surveying the night. 'What dost think on?' said the Duke.

'On your star-like nobleness,' answered he.

'What was that he said?' said the Duke suddenly: 'that Lessingham would trust himself all alone to treat with me here in Rumala? That was very like a lie.'

'I think it likely true,' answered Medor. 'He knoweth well enough your grace's firm-kept faith toward him lately in Zayana.'

The Duke was silent. Then, 'Why have they taken him away?' he said. 'Fetch him back! Must I be betrayed by you too, to do my bidding when I'm beside myself?'

'No,' replied he, and gave him a look. 'I will keep my old bargain with your grace as for that.'

Barganax put off his helm and set it beside him on the table with his iron gloves. The leavings of storm yet darkened and flickered about his eyes and about the lines of his mouth under the curled mustachios; but no longer so as to deform that face and brow which, clear seen now in the upward beaming of the lamp, seemed to contain the united sweet of heaven's graces. He said under his breath: 'Ζά δ' ελεξάμαν 'όναρ Κυπρογενήᾳ. In a dream I spake with Our Lady of Cyprus.'

When Amaury was come in again with Medor, 'You are a brave man, Amaury,' said the Duke; 'and that was to be looked for, since you serve a brave man; and he is a man to pick out men of strength and manliness to follow him, and men of his own bent of mind. And now lay open your former speeches, that I may understand your meaning.'

Amaury laid it all before him point by point.

'And now,' said the Duke then, 'I have bethought me of this matter betwixt me and your lord, what way it shall become. Here is a ring,' he said, and took it from his finger: 'the stone of it is called quandias: it is found in the vulture's head, and is man's friend, for it driveth from him all things that be hurtful. Give it him from me. Say to him, I will not be outdone by him in nobility: I'll meet with him, but not here. I'll meet him half way, at Ilkis in Rubalnardale. Today 'tis Monday; let it be Wednesday at noon. 'Tis best we go weaponed, seeing the countryside may well be up in a tumult after these doings. But let there be twenty of either side, and no more. And let truce hold, howsoe'er things fadge, till Thursday midnight.'

Amaury kissed Barganax's hand and took the ring. 'I am so far in my lord's counsels,' he said, 'that I can here confidently accept it all on his behalf, and say that your grace's noble dealing in this business hath opened an easy way unto honour and peace betwixt you.'

'Then fare you well, sir,' said the Duke. 'On Wednesday at noonday we shall confer in Ilkis. Soldiers, conduct him: a dozen torches down the Curtain.

'And now,' said he to Medor, when Amaury was gone: 'nor you nor no man speak to me. Lights and to bed.'

It was now about midday of Wednesday, that fourteenth day of June. In Acrozayana, in a jewelled shade of strawberry-trees, where the sun speckled the gravel path with moidores strewn upon a carpet of cool purple, the Lady Fiorinda rested as music rests when the lute is laid by. Her couch was cushions of wine-dark satin on a bench of porphyry. Her gown, very soft and fine, long-sleeved, close fitting, yellow of the pale cowslip petal and with narrow ruffs at throat and wrist, settled at every gently taken breath to some fresh perfection of her as she rested there, sweetly gathered up, upon her right side, her feet along the bench. A hood of black netted silk, rebated at the border with chrysoprases sewn upon cloth of gold, framed her face as with an aureole within which, betwixt white brow and jewelled tissue, her hair was like the mystery of night set betwixt bright sun and moon.

Below her to her left, on the step of the carved porphyry seat, sat Rosalura, her needlework fallen on the ground at her side, her hands clasped in her lap. Anthea, clothed in white, stood on the confines of the shade and the sunlight of the lawn without: the pupils of her eyes were slits against that brightness: there was in her bearing an alertness of expectancy: her hair, loosely gathered and knotted up in a disordered grace, was as fire burning. Bellafront, at the outer end of a low bench on the left, close to Anthea, caught the rays too on her coiled plaits of chestnut red. Pantasilea and Myrrha, Campaspe and Violante, reclined these upon this bench those upon that, of the two low benches to Fiorinda's left and right. All were as if listening to something afar off, or, may be, to the humming of the bees only that droned on the summer air, now louder now more dim, but never silent; listening not as hearing but rather hoping to hear some expected thing.

Doctor Vandermast, in russet-coloured gaberdine, walked in his meditation. The little arrows of sunlight, piercing the leaves, rained upon him ceaselessly in his measured walking.

Fiorinda spoke: 'That was a strange freedom in so grave a scholar as you, sir, to say that I was, of myself – but indeed now I have forgot what 'twas you said.'

He came to a stop at her side, looking past Anthea to the smooth sunny spaces of lawn and flower-bed beyond and, over the parapet, to mountains dim in the summer haze. 'It is a principle infringible of divine philosophy,' he said, 'to seek an understanding of all things *sub specie quadam aeternitatis*: holding them up, as to a lamp, to eternity, wherefrom they take illumination. Myself too did spend whole thirty-seven years together in studying of the Physicals and Ultramundanes, proceeding therein by concatenation of axiom with proposition and so through *demonstratio, scholium, corollarium*, to the union of all in a perpetual and uniform law: that vertical point above the pyramids of knowledge where the intellects may in momentary contemplation seize the truth of things. Yet was it, when all came to all, but an empty truth: *praeter verbum nihil est*, a vain breath. For it supposed further, if it must stand, a reason, understanding, and platform. But whensoever, leaving these toys, I have considered of your ladyship, then is all clear daylight; and whensoever I have been put to a stound, unable to understand of this or that in nature or in time, wherefore it should be thus and not thus, I need but view it under the light of your ladyship, and in an instant I see its very worth and its necessity.'

'As this late ruinous field of Lorkan?' said she, 'that hath cut the ground, from under his feet and sent him cap in hand to make peace with his great enemy?'

He replied: 'I behold it in your ladyship as in a glass. I embrace and accept it.'

'Mew!' said she, 'I would plague him. That is all.'

'I do discern you through a thicker cloud than that,' said Vandermast, meeting her eye.

'Do you so?' said she. ''Las! Were I not somewhat high-hearted I should be scared out of my senses, as if with such a cockatrice stare the old man would unclothe me where I sit. Horror of Apollonius upon Lamia! Are we safe indeed?'

'Apollonius,' said Vandermast, 'was but a very false philosopher, and had but a very superficial and poor understanding. In sum (and this was in my mind when by a trope or figure, madam, I permitted myself to liken you to *eternity*), I conclude that your ladyship is, of yourself, *omnium rerum causa immanens*: the sufficient explanation of the world.'

Fiorinda did not smile. 'But what needed it of explanations?' she said. 'Here it is. I like it.'

'Without you,' said that old man, 'it should fly in pieces and be gone. Like a drop of glass that I have seen, will crash instantly into dust if a man but nip its tail off.'

'And, sure, you will not say there ever lived a man so wicked,' said she, 'as dream it could be otherwise? A world without me? Or that hated me?'

'My Lady Fiorinda,' said he in a low voice: '*nemo potest Deum odio habere*: no man is able to hate God. I speak not of time and place and outward habit. In Rialmar, no less constantly than in Acrozayana, you do have your siege and presence. There may be more of you, three, nine, nine thousand thousand: I know not: *ex necessitate divinae naturae infinita infinitis modis sequi debent*: infinite shapes and ostentations. I know, in this world, but two. And you, albeit you change, yet change not.'

He fell silent. 'Nay, I would have you go on,' she said, in accents that seemed to draw a veil of mockery shot with starry sparkles across her thought, even as the long black lashes veiled her eyes. ''Tis very music to me, to smooth my ear: to listen to subtleties, fantastic queries, and speculations, discoursed so by so learn'd a doctor: like as the deceiving of the senses is one of the pleasures of the senses.'

Vandermast, immerst yet in his vision, and as if he had not heard her, said, 'It is an open-founded doctrine, which can scarce escape the notice even of the rudest; save that they note it and pass by, not knowing fully that which they noted. As they that go to and fro in the street behold a tower, and yet there be many steps and degrees to be ascended painfully, *per scientiam*, ere a man shall stand upon the top thereof and know the thing. And yet,' he said, 'this is to small purpose talking so, with laborious stumbling words, to your ladyship, as a child conning his lesson: to you that do know these things better than I and without all grammatication.'

'You may have a nose for metaphysicals,' said that lady; 'but here you cry out upon no trail. I know nothing. Only, I am.'

'Your ladyship doth play with me,' said Vandermast.

'I play with all things,' she said. It was as if that which dwelt in the corner of her mouth shot its arrow and then buried its face again for very sweetness of the place it dwelt in. Her right hand made a rest for her cheek; her left arm was thrown back and fallen behind her behind the proud arch of her hip, as in a carelessness and divine largesse of the treasure of her body, ethereal as the scented thought of a white rose, beautiful as golden flowers, the fairness of it and the Grecian pride. 'With all things,' she said.

'And rightly so,' said that ancient doctor, slowly, as if communing with his inward thought: 'seeing that it is for you that all things, *omnia quae existunt*, are kept and preserved by the sole power of God alone, *a sola vi Dei conservantur*.'

The bees' drowsy note conducted on the silence. Fiorinda's voice came like honey dropping from the hive on some Elysian Hymettus, saying, as in a dream, 'It may be you said true. It may be I do know. The Poetess:

σύ τε κἄμος θεράπων Ἔρος.

She was charier of words than you, most reverend doctor, and yet said it all, I think:

thou, and My servant Love.'

The Countess Rosalura, remembering Ambremerine, leaned suddenly forward to lay her head against the sandals of gold which, with broidered straps of fair Lydian work, covered Fiorinda's feet.

Fiorinda, with a little movement of her head, beckoned the learned doctor to bend nearer. 'Will you credit that old tale,' she said in his ear, 'of their speaking with King Hakon Athelstane's-fosterling, to summon him home, when he sat there a-dying, on the bloody battlefield of Fitiar in Stord? When

Gondul and Skogul the Goths'-God sent
To choose of the kings,
Which of Yngvi's line must with Odin fare,
In Valhall to won.

'And was not the king glad then, when he heard the words of the noble Valkyries, where they sat there a-horseback, and bare themselves so fairly, and sat helmed and with shield and spear?'

'It is not past credit,' answered Vandermast. '*Deus ex solis suae naturae legibus, et a nemine coactus agit*: God fareth according to the laws of His own nature, and under constraint of no man.'

She laughed and stood up. Surely the light of her beauty was upon that old man's face, to transfigure it, as sunlight the cold frosty season of December. Every line and thought-driven furrow, the wrinkled hollows of his eye-sockets, their bristling eaves, the lean beaked nose of him, and white beard, were as lighted with her beauty from withinward; and the peace of her beauty lay upon the fragile and vein-streaked smoothness of his brow, and all his countenance was made gracious with the holy spirit and power of that lady's beauty, which stirred now and glittered in the depths of his swift and piercing eyes.

'I will look on this meeting,' said she. 'A man shall not need be hurt to the death, as then at Fitiar, ere he may pluck the rose acceptable to the Gods and wear it: my roses of Pieria, reached tiptoe from the mere pinnacle of his hopes' defeat. Draw back the veil.'

There went with that word a shadow across the sunpath, and a coolness without wind was on the air. And now it was suddenly as if trees and flowers and daisied lawns, nay the very walls and solid ground here in Acrozayana, and the stablished mountains seen beyond the parapet, far off across the lake, were thinned to a tenuous immateriality, not wavering but steady in edge and texture, as if made all of clear livid-coloured glass of the thinness of thin parchment. Through this, as through a painted window, appeared now the naked anatomy of earth, blue and cold: cliffs which swept down to fearful silences, with the tide washing against the bases of the cliffs, and a welter of drowned treasure and sea-wrack and vast worms tearing at one another in the shallows of the sea. The air between the cliffs, ruffled in mists and rawky vapours, was troubled with iron wings of chimaeras that mounted ever upwards, as bubbles mount in wine, and vanished ever in the strip of sky high up between the lips of the precipices: night sky, for all that it was day here in the natural world; and in the night a blazing star with long hairs appeared. Vandermast and those ladies were becoming even as the things about them livid and translucent, like shadows in water or fetches of the dead. She alone, in that falling away of appearance from reality, retained yet the lovely hues of life and carnal substance.

So that to the Duke, facing Lessingham across the council table in Ilkis, it was in that moment as if he looked through layer upon layer of dream, as through veil behind veil: the thinnest veil, natural present: the next, as in a dumb-show strangely presented by art magic, the dappled path beneath the strawberry-trees in his own garden in Zayana and the company there gathered: and so, the firm frame of things and a jut of rock between the abysses, and, standing upon it, that woman, clothed upon with the fires of thunder and of night. From whose eyes as from starred heavens he took knowledge of the action he now went on; and, as through them, saw it; and was content.

XI

GABRIEL FLORES

TERMS OF THE CONCORDAT • THE HALF-FORGOTTEN
HARMONIES • TIDINGS BROUGHT TO THE VICAR • A GREAT
PRINCE AND HIS POOR SECRETARY • A FURY OF DOGS •
ENTRY OF LESSINGHAM INTO LAIMAK
• THE RIDER THROWN.

LESSINGHAM said, 'I have now laid the whole matter before your
grace. I hide it not, it goes better with my purpose to gather the
apples this battle's lucky cast hath brought down for me and enjoy
them with your grace's friendship, sooner than climb higher for
more and may be break my neck. Nor can any say, who hath any
forehead left, that you did draw sword and get nought by it; when
you are, upon sheathing of it, seized again of your whole appanage
as sovereign indefeasible, and regent besides of all Meszria, save
Outer Meszria only.'

'Regent,' said Barganax: 'and in that quality his man, vassal,
and subject. Leaveth a tang upon the tongue.'

'What man is not spoken of in this sense?' said Lessingham.
'All are subject to the Queen of Fingiswold.'

'And she,' said Barganax, 'to this tutor. But losers must not be
choosers; and I never reared a pig but that I was ready to eat his
bacon.'

'My lord Duke,' said Lessingham, 'we have looked each other

in the eye ere this. That I treat o' the Vicar's behalf, regard it not: 'tis me, not him, you deal withal. That I o'erthrew Roder in the ings of Lorkan, I have forgot it and do you, my lord, forget it. From the sweep of eagles' wings it becometh us overview the matter, and what's just and allowable of our greatness, choose that, suffering nought else in the world 'twixt that and our clear judgement.'

The Duke was sat forward in his chair, his chin thrust forward a little, right elbow on the table, forearm upright, hand propping his chin; his left arm akimbo, hand upon hip with fingers spread: all with a cattish reposeful elegance. His eyes, that seemed now hawk's eyes, now a deer's, all pupil, liquid and unfathomable, now again proud, serene and relentless, like a lion's, gazed not upon Lessingham but over Lessingham's shoulder. Lessingham, sitting back, watched them in their mutations, until, with their turning at last to engage his own, it was as if from those eyes his own secret spirit faced and regarded him from without.

The Duke spoke. 'Item, I subscribe my brother's testament (upon whom be peace); and sith the Admiral resigned it in my favour, take up the regency of South Meszria, doing homage therefor to my royal sister through person, during her minority, of the Lord Protector. Item, he, both for himself and for behalf of the Queen, receives me as lord of Zayana and of that whole duchy and dominion as in that testament set forth, without all suzerainty. To these I add two things further, my Lord Lessingham: first, that the Admiral is confirmed regent of Outer Meszria, 'cause 'tis in the testament so, and I'll be secured 'gainst strange fingers meddling in that pie upon my border; and secondly, the Vicar must give full amnesty to all took up weapons against him for sake of me, and especially I mean to Earl Roder and to the Chancellor.'

'Let them go,' said Lessingham. 'They have stood your grace in little stead. 'Tis well if your dealing should measure their deserving.'

'It shall rather hold measure with my own mind,' replied he. 'I'll not forsake them.'

'Then goeth the matter out of all measure, if our agreement fall to the ground for sake of men that, with bunglings and delays—'

'My Lord Lessingham,' said the Duke, 'you may spare your argument. Be it the wasting and last downthrow of all my fortune, I'll not agree without this.'

Then said Gabriel Flores in Lessingham's ear, from a stool at his left elbow, a little behind him, 'My lord, 'twere not fit to concede this. His highness will never stand for't.'

'Nature, my lord Duke, stood ever on this point,' said Lessingham without heeding him: '"Kae me, I'll kae thee." The cushion of my cousin's throne is stuffed with thorns, and the stiffest are of your grace's stuffing in: Ercles and Aramond. He will give peace to Beroald, Roder, and Jeronimy, and all them of their following,' here Gabriel put a hand upon his sleeve, but withdrew it under swift terror of Lessingham's eye-flash, 'and confirm besides Jeronimy, upon homage done therefor unto his highness, in Outer Meszria, upon condition you do call off those princes from practice 'gainst him in the north there; for the world knoweth 'tis your hand works 'em, and at your bidding they can be made to do or to forbear.'

'Put it in,' said the Duke then: ''tis a bargain. But you must not set me down for more than I can perform. That I will be neither aiding nor comforting and so forth: good; and that I will use all suasions: good. But if they lay deaf ear to my counselling—'

Lessingham threw out his hands. 'Shall I expect your grace then with armed hand to enter their dominions? I thought of no such thing. Countenance is enough: 'tis matter of course with them, as eat and drink, meditating how they may with favour benefit you, or be wary how to offend you. Let's set down largely that you will not lend your shadow for these contrivings. Where the stream is clear, not too much scriveners' preciseness: vomit up ink to trouble the waters.'

'Then 'tis fitted,' said the Duke, and stood up.

'Will you appoint someone: County Medor if you please: to draw it out for us with Gabriel Flores?'

'Yes, Medor: he hath noted down all for my behalf,' said Barganax. 'And remember yet constantly of this,' he said, walking apart with Lessingham to the pavilion door while the others gathered up their papers: "Tis you and I make this peace, but 'tis you must keep it. Were't the Vicar alone, I'd not waste ink and parchment 'pon a concordat I'd know he should tear, soon as advantage should wink at him to the transgressing of it. But in this I see something, that you, my Lord Lessingham, have took it upon your honour, and stand warranty unto me, that this peace shall hold.'

'Here,' answered Lessingham, 'I must use a like licence as did your grace but now. He is not at my apron-strings as a child by his nurse. But so far as in me lies, I faithfully affirm by my solemned oath he shall in all points abide by this agreement.'

Upon this, said with great grandeur by the Lord Lessingham, they two struck hand together. As they so stood, handfasted for a moment upon that peacemaking, it was as if a third stood with them: not perceivably in distinction of bodily presence, yet with a strange certitude made known to each in the other and apparent so: so that to the sense of each the other was lost, drunk up, confounded, in this new presence. So they stood, not three but two. But to the Duke the black beard and masculine presence of Lessingham were become as a cloak only, cloaking but not hiding; or as some fortress of old night, strong to preserve that which, to the Duke familiar yet ever new, unseizable as some flower dreamt of by God but not yet unfolded in Elysium, looked from its windows. So too to Lessingham was the Duke become, but as a might of sunrise rather or of white noon; and that wonder seen at the window was for Lessingham as a forgotten music remembered again and lost again, as in that May night three weeks ago in Acrozayana.

Gabriel said at his elbow, 'Pray your worship, I had rather meddle no further in this. Amaury hath a more apter hand than I for't.'

Lessingham looked down coldly at him. 'Belike he hath. But his highness did design your presence mainly for such work as this. You were best go through with it.'

Gabriel stood uncertain. 'So please you, I had rather not. So please you, I see little of his highness' design in this,' he said, gathering boldness with speaking but to a shoulder. 'I am a simple poor servant of his: not a great lord. May be's some trick in it; but to sell his highness' interest, I'd rather not set my pen to it, no not to the drawing of it, so please you.'

'Well, begone then,' said Lessingham, tartly; 'for indeed I have suffered too long your impertinences in these proceedings, like a sparrow chirping and chittering to other sparrows. Begone, go.'

Gabriel stood yet in doubt. 'Yet, consider, my lord—'

Lessingham gave him a sudden look. 'Unless you mean to be kicked,' he said. 'Begone.'

And with great swiftness Gabriel went.

Gabriel went by chosen by-ways and with much circumspection, so that it was mid-evening when he rode down through the skirts of the forest where alders and birches increase upon the oaks, and came upon the Zenner a mile below Kutarmish bridge and scarce ten miles as the crow flies from Ilkis whence he had set forth. His little brown horse swam the river, and now in another mile he turned with secure mind up into the highroad and so, 'twixt gallops and breathing times, had by nightfall left behind him the long straight causeway through the fens that runs south and north past the solitary walled bluff of Argyanna. At Ketterby he halted to bait his horse and sup at the moated house: mutton pies, tripe, cheese, and garlic, and thick black beer; would not stay, but rode on and slept in his cloak under the moon on the open heath a little this side of Ristby; saddled up again before daylight; came to Storby when folk were first astir at the bridge-house; ate breakfast at Anguring, and, galloping hard, an hour later met the Lord Horius Parry riding with a half dozen of his gentlemen in the water-meadows a league below Laimak.

'Now we shall know somewhat,' said the Vicar, as Gabriel clambered down from the saddle, took his master by the foot, and with a clumsy reverence kissed it. 'Chatter and surmise these two days past have fleshed us: set teeth on edge to ask for truth. Give it me in a word: good or bad?'

'Highness, 'tis very good,' answered he. In the midst of the great dogs sniffing his boots and breeches he stood unbonneted, shifting from leg to leg, his eyes shifting but ever coming back to meet the Vicar's.

'That and no more?'

'I have been schooled by your highness to answer no more than your highness shall please to ask.'

The Vicar looked at him piercingly for a moment, then gave a great barking laugh. 'Good is enough,' he said. Then, 'Mandricard,' he said, swinging round in his saddle so that those others, edging and craning nearer for news, drew laughably back as if upon some danger: 'you and the rest go home: announce these tidings. I'll take air awhile yet, talk on some small matters concern not you. Fare you well.'

'May we not know, but largely—?' Count Mandricard began to say. He was a big bacon-faced side-lipped man with the carriage of a king and a voice like the undertones of bronze, but his words withered on his lips as he met the eye of the Vicar. 'Fare you well,' the Vicar said, after an instant's pause. And, being that they, like Gabriel, were not without schooling, they obediently departed.

'Well?' said the Vicar. 'The sum?'

He answered, 'Sum is, their whole power beat in pieces in a main battle beside the Zenner, at Lorkan, a three leagues down from Kutarmish 'pon the Meszrian bank; and yonder Duke laid at your highness' disposal, ready for treading like a frog beneath your boot.'

The Vicar, motionless in the saddle, head erect, gazing through half-closed eyelids down the valley, took in a breath through his nostrils, and the leather doublet creaked that encased his mighty chest. Under the freckons his face flamed like sunrise before stormy weather. 'That was well done,' he said. He shook the rein and turned at a walking pace east along a bridle-path that led to the mountain. Gabriel mounted and followed at his elbow.

'The Duke: ta'en, then? Or how?'

Gabriel answered, 'I would not have your highness fall to too sudden a conclusion. No, not ta'en; nor not like to be now. Yet was in hand to be.'

'In hand to be?' said the Vicar, looking round at him. Gabriel held his peace. 'When was this battle?' said the Vicar.

He answered, 'Upon Saturday: five days gone.' And now as they rode he told of it point by point, to the coming down of the Duke to Ilkis out of Rumala. 'By the blood of Satan!' said the Vicar, 'had I been there, I doubt I should a made so delicate fine-fingered a matter on't. This bastard line in Meszria springeth too rank a crop of weeds for my liking. Go, I'd a been sore tempted to take his head while God gave me opportunity; so by one gallon of blood save an ocean of cares to come.'

They rode on for a few minutes in silence. 'What's the end on't?' he said. 'Surrender without all conditions?'

'Scarcely thus,' said Gabriel.

'What then?' said the Vicar.

'Indeed,' said Gabriel, and showed his teeth like a ferret, 'it were fittest your highness should wait till my Lord Lessingham come home. He will resolve you of all this, ne'er a doubt on't.'

Their horse-hooves, clattering among the stones as they forded a beck, measured the laden silence. Gabriel, with a sidelong glance, noted how the Vicar, bull-like and erect in an inscrutability as of hewn granite, gazed steadily between his horse's ears; only there was a duller red showed now under his fair skin between the freckons. Gabriel hazarded no more glances. A bittern boomed in the marshes far away.

'Fittest I should wait?' said the Vicar in a slow purring quietness. Gabriel, biting his lip near until the blood came, rose stiff in his stirrups with head drawn back till his beard pointed skywards. The Vicar, regarding him snakishly, drew back his thin lips in a smile. 'I have not taken hold of you yet, my friend,' he said. His fingers like brazen clamps tightened their grip on Gabriel's elbow, while the thumbnail with an erudite cruelty searched the tissues between bone and bone, then at the one intolerable place bored in like a beak. Gabriel's leather sleeve spared him effusion of blood but not the torment. He writhed forward till his forehead hit the saddle-bow, then up again with a sudden motion as of a puppet worked by springs. 'I cannot bear it,' he said, 'I cannot bear it.'

The Vicar's hand relaxed but, like an iron gin, held him still. 'I can wait?' he said, still with that low purring; 'more patience than you, it seems, my little pigsnye? But I'll none of your michery; you shall lay yourself open to me, my pug, lest I open you indeed, see what colour your guts are of, as you've seen me do to others ere now. Well then, is't restore his appanage?'

'Yes,' said Gabriel, 'and without conditions: without suzerainty.'

'If you gape upon me,' said the Vicar, 'I'll make dogs'-meat of you. What's done, 'tis my doing, not for such vermin as you to question or pronounce upon.'

'Your highness yet needs not to eat and devour up me, that had neither hand nor part in't. For indeed there's worse to come too.'

'Make haste with it,' said the Vicar. ''Tis my doing, d'ye hear? Remember that, if you would keep your belly unripped.'

Gabriel said, 'First there's the regency.'

The Vicar reined in his horse: near threw him on his haunches. Gabriel paused, meeting his lord's eye that had the wicked look of a bull's about to charge. 'God's blood! and might I not give him the regency and ne'er ask leave of thee?' For the moment Gabriel's thoughts were so intent for his proper safety that he forgot his cue to speak. 'Regent of what, fool?' said the Vicar. They were bearing now down towards the road again. Gabriel answered, 'Great part of Meszria: but upon your highness' suzerainty.'

'Great part? What's that? The main south of Zayana, south of the neck? Memison? Doth it bar Sestola and ports besides that should give him the key to the sea? 'Twas a prime act of policy lodged the Admiral aforetime in Sestola to keep Zayana's wings clipped. Speak, fool? What part, fool?'

'All these,' said he, his flesh shrinking to feel the threat of that iron grip: 'all south of the mountains from Ruyar to Salimat.'

'What of the north?'

'Jeronimy confirmed regent, 'pon homage done unto your highness.'

'Ha, and was that well done, think you?'

''Twas your highness' doing: not for me to question.'

'Damned measled hog, answer to the matter, or we'll cut your tongue out: was it well done to entrust my borders to this nannicock, for Zayana to make use of as the monkey do the cat's foot?'

Gabriel faced him with the boldness of a weasel driven into a corner. 'Must I answer?'

'You must.'

'Then,' said Gabriel, 'I answer your highness. Yes: it was well done.'

'Why so?' said the Vicar. 'Answer me, filth, you were best.'

Gabriel said, 'Let go my arm then, and I'll answer.' The Vicar flung him off with so rude a violence, Gabriel near lost his saddle. 'Because,' said Gabriel then, 'sith your highness had given free peace and amnesty to Beroald and Roder both, and commissioned my Lord Lessingham too to pledge you body and soul to Barganax to yield up all, as if you, not he, had been the vanquished party: a thing I would not swallow, and therefore left him—'

''Tis a lie,' said the Vicar. 'When! Pyewacket! Illmauger! Pecki'-the-crown! Loo! Loo! Hie on! Tear him! Tear him!'

Gabriel was barely in time drawing of his hanger as the dogs charged. One he slew with a down-cut, but the next in the next instant had caught his wrist of the hand that gripped the hilt. His horse reared, fell backwards: Gabriel was fallen clear, but before he was gotten upon his feet they had pulled him down and, with a hideous din, set about worrying him like a fox. The Vicar leaped from his saddle, calling them off, smiting left and right among them with his riding-switch: in a moment they were in hand again, obedient, shamefaced, waiting for his eye. All save Illmauger, that with that bite had tasted blood: he, huge, yellow-heckled, wolfish, snarling and slavering at the lips, crouched for another spring. The Vicar grabbed him by the scruff of the neck and flung him aside. He stood his ground, bristling, savage-eyed, ears laid back, growling on a deep inward-taken breath. As the Vicar made a step towards him with uplifted switch, he gathered himself and leapt at the Vicar's throat. They went down together, rolling over and

over in an evil hugger-mugger as it had been of wolf and bear.
The Vicar for all his bigness scarce outwent the dog in weight of
bone and sinew, but it was swiftly seen that he was more deft and
agile than a wolf, in strength not overmatched, and in his present
mood as wolfish and as implacable. And now was an ill music of
the Vicar's snarls and pants and grunts and the clashing of the
great beast's teeth as he snapped at air; for the Vicar, now uppermost now under in their fight for the mastery, was never shaken
nor loosened from his grasp, of his right hand iron-fast upon the
throat. Little by little he tightened his grip to a better purchase,
then suddenly the music changed, as his left hand found its quarry,
a crueller and more ingenious hold. At length the stifled shrieks
died down into a gurgling and sodden quiet. The Vicar, uppermost
now, was grovelled face downwards on his adversary, and now,
as a whirlwind hushes upon the centre, the leaping medley of
limbs, part dog part man, began to be still. Gabriel marked how
the great muscles of the Vicar's neck worked under their low-
growing cropped stubble of red hair like the neck-muscles of a
preying lion, and how his breath came and went, in laboured
snuffs and snorts through his nostrils. At length he raised himself
on his hands and knees. The dog was dead, bitten clean through
the weasand.

The Vicar stood up. He spat, wiped his mouth upon his sleeve,
gave a hitch to his kirtle, walked to where his horse was, and
climbed leisurely into the saddle. Then, gathering the reins, he with
a look bade Gabriel mount too and come with him. They turned
now at a walking pace toward Laimak. For a full mile they rode
on without word spoken. Then, 'You, my pretty pigsnye,' the Vicar
said: 'study to be quiet and to meddle with your own business,
not with matters too high for you. And remember, or I'll kill you,
all these things were by my prescription and commandment to the
least tittle. D'ye hear?'

'I both hear, highness, and obey,' said he.

'And carry that hand of yours to the leech when we come home,'
said the Vicar: 'loadstone is available against dog-bites and
invenoming.'

So, without further word spoken, they came at length, and the Vicar's great dogs beside him, through the meadows home to Laimak.

It was now afternoon, the third day after these things aforesaid. Lessingham and Amaury came to a halt below the Stringway. Amaury said, 'I would give all I have would you but turn back now.'

Lessingham laughed.

'Had we but half the horse, your own tried men to follow you, that were security: but go alone with a bare dozen men, 'tis tempting of the Gods, stark folly: put your neck in the bear's mouth.'

'What's new in that, sweet nurse-mother? Have I not lodged in my cousin's house fifty times ere now as cousins should, not as an armed enemy?'

'He had not the cause he now hath.'

''Las, is it not a fair peace I bring him home then?'

'Too fair for him that's foul.'

''Tis a peace I'll justify,' said Lessingham, ''gainst all skilled advocates in the world.'

'He'll say you have been open-handed at his expense. And remember, the fox his secretary ran to him first with the tale: will a put the worst face upon it.'

Lessingham said, 'I'd a been as open-handed with my own. And for foxes, I deal not with 'em, neither regard 'em.' He touched the rein, and Maddalena stepped daintily upon the Stringway.

For a half-hour beyond Anguring the road was through beech-woods mixed with chestnut and oak and sycamore, a pleasant green shade: Owlswater ran between rocky banks on their left below them as they rode. Then the woods thinned away, and the river wound gleaming through water-meadows, where in scattered droves black cows grazed or lay, smaller and smaller in the distance, and fields bounded with dry walls stretched on either hand, with here and there a white farmstead, to the rough hill-pastures and the open fell. Here and there men made hay. Smoke went up blue

and still in the air where no breeze moved. All the skirts of the
mountains were spotted with browsing sheep. On the right,
the upper ridges of the Forn, shadowless in the afternoon sunlight,
were of a delicate peach-like colour against the blue. Lessingham
rode with Amaury a hundred paces or more ahead of his company.
Lessingham was in his byrny of black iron, ringed with gold links
about the neck and wrists. He wore a low honey-coloured ruff.
He went bare-headed for pleasure of the air, and carried his helm
at the saddle-bow. The folk in the fields stood up to salute him
as he rode by.

They came riding now round the curve of a hill to the last
house. It was built beside the road on their right. Upon the left,
three sycamore-trees, old and bare of branches below, made an
overarching shade before the house, so that, as they rode up, the
road went as through a gateway between those trees and the house,
and over the brow fell away out of sight. And through that arched
way, as in a picture framed, they might see now Laimak couchant
upon its rock, bare and unkind of aspect, pallid in the sunshine
and with cold blue shadows; beholding which, Amaury shivered
in the warm sun and, angry with himself for that, cursed aloud.
And now, beyond this last farmstead, the road became but a
bridleway, and there were fields no more, but moorish grounds
and marsh and rank pasture with sometimes stretches of lush grass
and sometimes sedges and peaty pools: the sharp squawk of a
water hen, the sudden flight of wild-duck, or a heron heavily taking
the air, borne swiftly on her slow flapping wings. Three black
crows rose from a grassy patch on the right a hundred paces ahead
and departed on furtive wing. Amaury kept his eye on the place.
'Carrion,' he said, as they came nearer. 'One of his cursed dogs;
and that's an omen,' as they came alongside.

Lessingham looked and rode on. 'I would have you learn a new
tune, dear Amaury,' he said; 'not melancholy yourself to melancholy's self and die of your apprehensions.'

So came they at length to the castle of the Parrys and rode
north-about to the gatehouse and up by the deep hewn passage
way to the main gateway, high upon the northern verge, and there

was the Vicar and his men to welcome Lessingham. The Vicar was in his brown velvet kirtle, with a belt about his middle of old silver. About his shoulders was his great robe or mantle of state, of red tartarine, and upon his brow a coronal of gold. With so much unexampled show of honourable respect he received Lessingham, as offer to hold the bridle while he dismounted; then took his arms about him and kissed him. Then he made him go up with him to his private chamber in the tower above Hagsby's Entry. 'Nay,' he said, when they were private there, 'I would hear no word from Gabriel. I would have it from your lips, cousin. And first, is it well?'

''Tis not altogether bad,' answered Lessingham, pouring out some wine.

''Tis victory?'

'My coming home should warrant you that. Did you ever know me put up my sword with the work half done?'

'You did promise me Outer Meszria in the hollow of my hand: that in a month. 'Tis bare three weeks since then. I'm not Grizell Greedigut to ask aught past reason, but somewhat I hope you have brought me.'

'Outer Meszria? Did I promise so little?' said Lessingham. 'If that should content you, cousin, you shall be more than content with this when you shall have understood it and considered of it;' and with that he pulled forth from his bosom a parchment and writing sealed with seals.

'I can read,' said the Vicar, 'though none of the best, yet meanly,' reaching out his hand for it.

'First I'll rehearse it to you at large,' said Lessingham.

'Nay,' said the Vicar, and took it: 'if any words seem dark, you shall make it more open, cousin. I like 'em best naked: you shall put the frills and furbelows on it anon.' He read it, sitting back easily in his great chair. His face as he read was open as a book, with the light full on it from the high window beside them, and Lessingham watched it, sipping his wine. There was not, as he read, so much as a passing shadow ruffled the noble serenity of the Vicar's brow or stirred the repose of those lineaments about the eyes and nose and jowl that could, upon an ill wind's blowing, wake to so much bestial ferocity. Nor was there any new note in his voice when, having read and read it again, at last he spoke. 'These articles express a concordat made 'twixt me of the one part, acting within my sovereignty vicarial and as Lord Protector for the Queen, and of t'other part Duke Barganax and ('pon their by instrument accepting of it) those other scum of the world, Jeronimy, I mean, Roder, and Beroald?'

'And in case any one of them shall not within fifteen days accept it,' said Lessingham, 'then falleth it to the ground, and our hands free of either part. That's why I hold the army still on the Zenner. But they'll accept, ne'er fear it.'

'And 'tis execute in duplicate, cousin, by you in virtue of your full powers on my behalf? And Zayana hath my seal, as I have his?'

'Yes,' said Lessingham.

The Vicar let fall the parchment and clapped his hands. Six men-at-arms upon the instant leaped out upon Lessingham from behind and ere he could raise finger clamped chains upon him that shackled him, wrist and elbow, knee and foot. Lessingham saw that Gabriel Flores was come in with them and was beside his master. The Vicar started from his chair like a ravening tiger. He smote Lessingham across the face with the parchment. The countenance of Lessingham was for a moment transported with terrible anger: he neither spoke nor moved, but he became white as death. The Vicar, mastering himself, sat down again. Under the clutch of his hands the arms of his chair shook and trembled. He glared with his eyes upon Lessingham who, of his right colour again, had now in his grey eyes the steadiness of levelled steel.

The Vicar opened his mouth and said, and his words came thick and stumbling as a man's that is drunk with wine: 'Overmuch have I trusted you. Yet this showed little wit, to come tell me to my face of this betrayal, that stinks more ugly in the sight of God than do all the carrion of this world. But you shall see I have a short way with such checking buzzards. A guard upon him! In an hour's time, cut his neck. Chop his carcase for the dogs, but spike up the head upon the main gate. I'll look on it before supper.'

Gabriel was shivering and twitching in all his body, like a little terrier dog at the edge of a duckpond. The Vicar looked around at him, then back at Lessingham who was stood up now, taller by a head than the soldiers that held him shackled. Even upon that brink of fate and death he stood with so good a grace and presence as if a soul of iron informed him; looking upon the Vicar as from above, and in his grey eyes, keen and speckled, something very like a smile, as if he knew something that was not true. 'Well,' said the Vicar, 'have you nothing to say?'

'Nothing but this,' answered he: 'that you were wont to act upon no great resolution without you first had slept upon it. It seems the Gods have infatuated your high subtle wisdom, if now you will do a wrong irrevocable both to yourself and me, and not e'en sleep upon it. Your matter hath not turned out so ill aforetime, following of my counsels.'

The Vicar glowered motionless as a bull in granite; his eyes were fixed no longer on Lessingham's eyes, but below them, on his mouth or beard. The guard, obedient to a covert sign from Gabriel, made a motion to take Lessingham away. The Vicar turned suddenly and Gabriel's elbow shrank in his brazen grip. 'Stay,' he said. 'I'll not let truth go by, albeit she were pointed out to me by a dissembling tyke. Tomorrow's as good as today. And to make sure, unto you, Gabriel, I commit him in charge; doubt not but that I shall call to you for a strict account of your dealing with him. For his life and safe keeping your life shall answer. Here are the keys,' and he threw them on the table.

Gabriel took them with a beaten scowling look.

XII

NOBLE KINSMEN IN LAIMAK

THE VICAR'S DREAM • ARGUMENT OF MIDNIGHT •
ADAMANT GRINDS ADAMANT • THE RIDER IN SADDLE AGAIN
• 'POLICY AND HER TRUE ASPECT' • NUPTIAL FLIGHT OF
THE PEREGRINES • LESSINGHAM CAPTAIN-GENERAL •
CONCEITS OF A LORD PROTECTOR • REVELRY; AND
A MEETING AT DAWN • NORTH.

THE Lord Horius Parry awoke between midnight and cock-crow, being troubled and vexed with a certain unpleasing dream. And this was the beginning of his dream: that Gabriel sat at his knee reading in a book of the *Iliad* wherein was told the fate of the lady Simë that she was (and here Gabriel, not knowing the meaning of the Greek word, asked him the meaning). And though upon waking he knew not the word, and knew besides that in the *Iliad* is no such tale and no such lady, it seemed to him in his dream that the word meant 'gutted like a dog'. Thereupon in his dream the Vicar was remembered of that old tale of Swanhild, Gudrun's daughter, wed in the old time to King Jormunrek, and by him, upon lying slanders of Bikki, adjudged to die and be trod with horses in the gate; but, for the loveliness of her eyes that looked upon them, the horses would not tread upon her, but still swerved and reared and spared her, until Bikki let do a sack about her head, hiding her eyes, and she was trodden so and so slain. And now was the dream troubled and made unclear, as a breeze ruffles water and does away the reflected shapes and colours; and when it cleared, there was a wide plain lay amid mountains, all in a summer's evening and pleasant sunshine air, and in the midst upon a little rise of ground a table, and before the table three thrones. And the Vicar thought he saw himself sitting upon the left-hand throne, and he thought he knew in his dream that he was a king; and the plain was filled with people assembled as for some occasion, and they waited there in silence in their multitude, innumerable as the sands of the sea. And the Vicar looked upon himself, upon the king, and saw that he was both in feature and in apparel like to the Assyrian kings in the great stone likenesses carved of them of old, and his beard long and tightly frizzed and curled, and his belted robe incrusted with every kind of precious stone, so that it glittered green and purple and with sparkles of fiery red; and he was cruel and fell to look upon, and with white glinting teeth. And behold there walked a woman before the thrones, fair as the moon, clothed in a like glittering garment as the king's; and he knew in his dream that this was that lady Simë, and when he beheld her steadfastly he saw (yet without mazement, as in dreams the singularest and superlative wonder, impossibilities and fictions beyond laughter, will seem but trivial and ordinary) that she was Lessingham. It seemed to him that this she-Lessingham did obeisance to the king, and took her seat on the right-hand throne; and immediately upon the third throne he beheld the queen that sat there betwixt them, as it had been a queen of hell. She was attired in a like garment of precious stones; her hair was the colour of wet mud, her eyes like two hard pebbles, set near together, her nose straight and narrow, her lips thin and pale, her face a lean sneak-bill chitty-face; she had a waiting, triumphing look upon her face; and he loathed her. And now went men before the thrones, bearing on a great stand or easel a picture framed, and showed it to that bright lady; and it seemed to the Vicar that she gave a terrible cry and covered her eyes; and the men turned the picture that all might see, and he could not discern the picture to understand it; but only the writing upon it, in great letters: UT

COMPRESSA PEREAT. And he thought the whole multitude in
their thousands took up those words and howled them aloud with
a howling like the howling of wolves. And he shouted and leapt
awake, sitting up in the dark in his great canopied bed in Laimak,
all shaking and sweating.

For a minute he sat so, listening to the darkness, which was as
if some vast body had been flung into the pool of night and made
waves upon it that were his own blood-beats. Then with an obscene
and blasphemous oath he felt for tinder, struck a light, and lighted
the candles on the table by his bed in the silver candlesticks that
stood there, and his sword beside them, and a goblet, and wine
in a great-bellied bottle of green glass with a stopper of gold. As
the new-kindled candleflames shrank dim in the moment before
the melting of the tallow, questionable shadows crouched in the
recesses of the walls and vaulted ceiling. A puff of wind stirred
the curtain by the window. Then the candles burned up. Pyewacket,
waked by his shout, was come from the foot of the bed and laid
her chin on his thigh, looking up at him with great speaking eyes
in the bright beams of the candles. The Vicar poured out wine, a
brimming goblet, and guzzled it down at one gulp. Then he stood
up and abode for a while staring at the candleflames and as if
listening. At length he clad himself in breeches and gown, buckled
on his sword, took and lighted a lantern, and unbolted the door.
Gabriel was in his place without, asleep on his bed made up upon
the floor across the threshold. The Vicar woke him with his foot
and bade him give him the keys. He gave them in silence and
would have come with him, but the Vicar with a kind of snarl
bade him remain. Gabriel, considering this, and his disordered
looks, and the sword at his thigh, watched him go with his bitch
at his heel, through the ante-room and through the further door,
that led to his private chamber, and when he was gone sat down
on his pallet bed again, licking his lips.

The Vicar went down by a privy passage of his own to the
prison where Lessingham was mewed up; went in by means of
his private key, and locked the door behind him. He held up the
lantern. Lessingham lay in the far corner, with his ankles shackled

to a ball of lead great as a man's two fists. His left arm was free, but the other wrist locked in a manacle with a long chain from that to his foot. His cloak of costly silken stuff was rolled for a pillow for his cheek. The Vicar came nearer. With his dream still upon him, he stood looking upon Lessingham and listening, as upon some horrid sudden doubt, for the sound of his breathing. In a deep stillness he lay there on the cobblestones, and with so much lithe strength and splendour of limb and chest and shoulder that the mould and dank of that place and the sweating walls, with trickles of wet that glistered in the lantern-light, seemed to take on an infection from his presence and put on a kind of beauty. Yet so still and without sound as he slept, had he been dead he could scarce have lain more still. Pyewacket gave a low growl. The Vicar caught her by the collar and flashed the lantern near Lessingham's face. Upon that, he sat up wide awake, and with great coolness looked upon the Vicar.

They kept silence, each waiting on the other. Lessingham's patience outstayed the Vicar's in that game, and the Vicar spoke. 'I have bethought me, cousin, and if there's aught you can say may extenuate the thing, I'll hear it.'

'Extenuate?' Lessingham said, and his voice was chilling as the first streak of a winter's dawn on a frozen sea. As the Vicar held the lantern, so his own face was shadowed, but the eye of Lessingham in full light: the eye of such a man that a prince would rather be afraid of than ashamed of, so much awfulness and ascendancy it lent to his aspect over other mortals. 'Is it morning then, outside of this hole you have thrust me in?'

'Two hours past midnight'

'It shall at least be set down to you for a courtesy,' said Lessingham, 'that at this time of night you are gotten up out of your bed to make me amends. Pray you unlock.' He held out his right wrist, chained: "Tis a kind of gewgaw I ne'er put on till now and not greatly to my liking.'

'There's time to talk on that,' said the Vicar. 'I'll first hear if there be any good face you can put on this ill trick you have played me.'

Lessingham's eye flashed. He held out his wrist, as might a queen to her tiring-woman. 'An ill trick you,' he said, 'have played me! By heavens, you shall unlock me first, cousin. We'll talk outside.'

The Vicar paused and there was a cloud in his face. 'You were a more persuasive pleader for your safety but now, cousin, when you lay sleeping. Be advised, for I have cause against you enough and beyond enough; and be sure you satisfy me. For except you do, be certain you shall never go from this place alive.'

'Indeed then you might a spared your sleep and mine,' said Lessingham then, shaking his cloak up as if to lie down again. The Vicar began pacing to and fro like a wolf. ''Tis simplicity or mere impudent malice to say I did betray you; and this an insolency past forgiveness, to use me so. So touching this concordat not a word will I say till I am loosed, and 'pon no conditions neither.'

The Vicar stopped and stood for a minute. Then he gave a short laugh. 'Let me remember you,' he said in a clear soft voice, glaring in Lessingham's face by the light of the lantern, 'of Prince Valero, him that betrayed Argyanna a few years since to them of Ulba and led that revolt against me. The Gods delivered him into my hand. Know you the manner of his end, cousin? No: for none knew it but only I and my four deaf mutes you wot of, that were here at the doing on't, and I have told no man of it until now. Do you see that hook in the ceiling?' and he swung the light to show it. 'I'll not weary you with particulars, cousin. I fear 'twas not without some note and touch of cruelty. Such a pretty toying wit had I. But we've washed the flagstones since.

'Well?' he said, after a silence.

'Well,' said Lessingham, and from now he held the Vicar constantly with his steel-cold eye: 'I have listened to your story. Your manner of telling of it does you credit: not so greatly the substance of it.'

'Be you ware,' said the Vicar with a loud sudden violence, and give him an ill look. 'The case you are in, this place you lie in, which is my hidden slaying-place in Laimak: think on't. And I can make that laughing face of yours turn serious.'

'I laugh not,' replied he. ''Tis not a laughing matter.' They looked one another in the eye without speaking. In that game too Lessingham outstayed the Vicar.

Then Lessingham said: 'Do not mistake me. If I fear you not, I am not so foolish as hold you for a man not worthy to be feared. But to threaten me with death, 'tis as the little boy that sat on a bough and would cut away from the tree the bough he sat on. I think you have more wit than do that.'

In a deadly stillness, with feet planted wide apart, the Vicar stood like a colossus looking down upon him. The Vicars' own face was now in shadow, so that when, after a long time, Lessingham spoke to him again, it was as a man might speak to an impending great darkness. 'I know it is a hard choice for you, cousin. Upon this side, you have no true friend in the world but me; lose me, and you stand alone amidst a world of enemies, your back bare. And yet, against this, you have done me a gross injury, and you know me for a man who, albeit I have looked upon this world for but half your span of years, have yet slain near as many men upon matter of honour alone, in single combats, as yourself have slain whether by murder or what not. I have slain a dozen, I think, in these eight years, since I was of years seventeen, not to reckon scores I have slain in battle. So, and to judge me by yourself, you must see great danger in it to release me. A hard choice. As if you must run hazard either way to lose me. And yet, my way you stand some chance of keeping me: your way, none.'

There was a pause when he ended. Then said the Vicar with his face yet in darkness, 'You are a strange man. Doth not death then terrify you?'

Lessingham answered, 'The horror and ugsomeness of death is worse than death itself.'

The Vicar said, 'Is it one to you: live or die? Do you not care?'

'O yes,' said Lessingham. 'I care. But this choice, cousin, is in the hand of fate now: for you even as for me. And for my part, if the fall of the dice mean death: well, it was ever my way to make the best of things.'

With the cadence of his voice falling away to silence, it was as if, in that quiet charnel under Laimak that knew not night nor day, scales were held and swung doubtful, now this way now that. Then the Vicar slowly, as if upon some resolution that came near to crumbling as he embraced it, turned to the door. Behind him his shadow as he went rushed up and stopped like a winged darkness shedding obscurity from wall and ceiling over half the chamber. Then he was gone, and the door locked, and all darkness; and in that darkness Lessingham saw Pyewacket's eyes, like two coals burning. He reached out a hand to her, open, palm downwards. He could not see her, save those eyes, but he felt her sniff cautiously and then touch the back of his hand lightly with her cold nose.

The Vicar was mid-part up the stairs when he missed her. He called her by name: then stood listening. Cursing in his beard, he was about turning back; but after a few steps down, halted again, swinging his keys. Then, very slowly, he resumed his mounting of the stairs.

Betimes in the morning the Vicar let fetch out Amaury from the place where he had been clapped up: gave him in charge to Gabriel and those six close men: made these wait in the ante-chamber: gave Amaury, in private audience, keys for Lessingham's prison by the secret door: walked the room a dozen turns, eyes still bent upon the floor, then said: 'You are free, lieutenant. Go to your master: conduct's provided, Gabriel and them: strike off his chains: here's keys, enlarge him. Tell him I'm sorry: a jest: went too far: he and I am friends, understand each other: therefore let us meet as if this ne'er had befallen. He and I be two proud men, tell him. I've took a long step to meet him: 'tis for him make it easy for me now.'

Amaury said with flaming face, 'I humbly thank your highness. I am a blunt soldier, and there is this to be said: my lord is your highness' true and noble friend. And strangely so. And a thousand times better than you deserve.'

'Have you got it by rote? Say it over,' said the Vicar, not hearing, or choosing not to be thought to have heard, that bearding boldness. Amaury said over his message, word by word, while the Vicar paced the room. 'Away then.'

Lessingham woke and came forth into the air and day with as much of careless equanimity as a man might carry who rises from the accustomed bed he has slept upon, night by night, for ten years in peace. Only there sat in his eyes a private sunbeamed look, as if he smiled in himself to see, like a sculptor, the thing shape itself as he had meant and imagined it. Amaury sat with him in his chamber while he bathed and donned clean linen. 'Praise be to the blessed Gods,' he said, leaping from the bath where he had rinsed away the suds, 'for curling of my hair by nature: not as yonder paraquitos, must spend an hour a day with barbers to do't by art.' His skin, save where the weather had tanned or the black hair shadowed it, was white like ivory. Then, when he was well scrubbed dry with towels: 'Boy! When, with orange-flower water for my beard! Foh! I smell her yet.' He gave his boy kirtle, hose, ruff: all the upper clothing he had worn in prison: bade him burn it.

Amaury spoke. 'What o'clock do you mean to set forward?'

'Set forward?'

'Leave this place,' said Amaury: 'out of his fingers: out of Rerek?'

'Not for some weeks yet. There's a mort of work I must first set in hand the conduct of.'

Amaury sprang up, and began to walk the room. 'You are preserved this time beyond natural reason. If a man take a snake or serpent into his handling – O he spoke true when he said you do understand each other. And there's the despair on't: and your eyes were not open to your danger, there were hope yet, by opening of 'em, to save you from it. But you do know your danger, most clearly, most perfectly and circumspectly: yet rejoice in it, and laugh at it.'

'Well, that is true,' said Lessingham, giving a touch to his ruff. 'What shall's do then?'

The heat of the summer noonday stood over Laimak when Lessingham at length came, with Amaury and two or three of his gentlemen attending him, to meet the Vicar on that long straight paven walk that runs, shaded at that hour by the tennis-court wall, along the battlements above the north face. Their folk, of either side, hung back a little, marking, these in the one, those in the other, their looks as each faced each: the Vicar a little put out of his countenance, Lessingham, under a generous noble courtesy, a little amused. After a while Lessingham held out his hand, and they shook hands without speaking. 'Give us leave,' said the Vicar and took him apart.

When they had measured a few paces in silence, 'I hope you slept well,' said Lessingham. 'It was prettily done to leave me your bitch for company.'

'What's this?' said the Vicar. 'The Devil damn me! I had clean forgot her.'

'I had thought,' said Lessingham, 'you were hard put to it to make up your mind, and conceited you might cast her for the part of Fate. A chained man: 'twas a nice poising of the chances. I admired it. And you feed 'em on man's flesh now and then I think? Of ill-doers and such like.'

'I swear to you, cousin, you do me wrong. By all the eternal Gods in heaven, I swear I had forgot her. But let's not talk on this—'

'Waste not a thought upon't. I ne'er slept better. Being of that sort, may be 'twas that made her take to me:

O we curl'd-haird men
Are still most kind to women.

'Or how think you?'

'Cousin,' said the Vicar: 'this concordat.' Here he took him by the arm. 'I would know the whole carriage on't. I question not there's good in't, for, by my soul, you have ever done me good: but let me die bursten if I understand the good of this.'

'An answer so fairly besought,' said Lessingham, 'should be fairly given. But first I would have you, as a politic prince who will not lay your foundations in the dirt but upon the archaean crust, refer the whole estate you are in to your highness' deliberate overviewing again. This kingdom, whiles the old King lived, was set in its seat unshakable: terrible to kings and peoples upon lengths of seas and shores. A main cause was, 'twas well knit: at one unto itself. True, at the last you had been already straining at the leash in new-conquered Rerek: unwisely, to my thinking, as I plainly told you. Then the King died, and that changed all: a hard-handed young fool in the saddle 'stead of a great wise man: and that shook all from withinwards. You had experiment then, cousin, of my mind towards you: did not I stand for you at Mornagay with my eight hundred horse, as a boy with a stick 'gainst a pack of wolves? Had you miscarried I mean; and that was not past likelihood. Then you took a means that both rid you of present danger and, 'cause men shrewdly guessed it, weakened you, 'cause it blasted your reputation (and a sickly browned flower was that already) – and then immediately, by direct bounty of Heaven, was all given into your lap by handfuls: named in the testament Lord Protector and Regent for the young Queen's minority. Why, 'tis all in your hand, cousin, and you will but use it. The realm is in your hand, like a sword; but all in pieces. And first is to weld the slivers: make it a sword again, like as King Mezentius had: then strip it out against Akkama, or what other heads were best plucked off that durst threaten you.'

They walked slowly, step with step, the Vicar with a brooding look, silent. Lessingham hummed under his breath a lilting southern song. When they came to the corner against the wall of the round north-western tower the Vicar stopped and, resting his elbows on the battlement, stood looking over the landscape where all colour was burnt to ashes under the sunlight. Near at hand, to the north-ward, a little crag rose solitary, a mimic Laimak, may be fifty feet above the marsh; and on its highest rock sat a falcon-gentle all alone, turning her head sharply every now and then to look this way and that. Once and again she took a short flight, and small birds mobbed her. And now she sat again on her rock, hunched, with a discontented look, glancing about this way and that. The Vicar watched her in his meditation, spitting at whiles thoughtfully over the parapet. 'Remember, I have taught 'em,' said Lessingham, 'first in Zayana, and now with sharp swords upon the Zenner, there's a higher here to o'ersway them if need be. Next is to reclaim 'em, call 'em to heel, be kind to 'em. By this, eased of your present fears lest they of your own house shall pluck the chair from under you, you may frown upon the world secure.'

After a while the Vicar stood up and began to walk again. Lessingham walked beside him.

Lessingham said: 'Once you have the main picture, the points of my concordat are as easily seen as we can discern flies in a milkpot. I know this Duke, cousin, as you do not. He is proud and violent: will stick at no extremity if you drive him and hold him at bay. But he is given to laziness: loveth best his curious great splendours, his women, voluptuousness, and other maddish toys, delicate gardens where he doth paint and meditate. And he is an honourable man, will hold firmly by a just peace; and this peace is just.'

'Will not she hound him on to some foul turn against me, that woman of his?'

'What woman?' said Lessingham.

'Why, is't not the Chancellor's sister? Zayana loveth her as his life, they say: 'can wind him to her turn, I'm told.'

'Again,' said Lessingham, not to follow this vein, ''tis weapons in your hand to a won Jeronimy, Beroald and Roder to your allegiance. The point of law hath stuck, I know, in the Chancellor's gullet since the testament was first made known: by this largesse of amnesty you purchase much secureness there.'

'Ay, but 'twas put in 'pon urgency of Zayana: he'll get the thanks for it when he shows it them, not I. And why needs he your warranty, cousin, as if you should compel me to abide by it? By Satan's ear-feathers! There's neither you nor any man on earth shall so compel me.'

'Compel's not in it,' answered he. 'He knows I am in your counsels and that you would listen to me: no more. Another great good: these vexations in north Rerek should go off the boil now, when he hath called off Ercles and Aramond from that business. Brief, we are not presently strong enough to hold down by force no more than Outer Meszria, and that but with his good will. By so much the more had it been folly to a carried the war south after this victory to Southern Meszria and Zayana.'

They walked the whole length of the parapet in silence, then the Vicar stopped and took Lessingham by both arms above the elbow. 'Cousin,' he said, and there sparkled in his eyes a most strange and unwonted kindness:

'That Friend a Great mans ruine strongely checks,
Who railes into his beliefe, all his defects.

'You have saved me, very matter indeed. By God, your behaviour hath not deserved such doggish dealing. Ask your reward: will you be Warden of the March of Ulba? I'd told Mandricard he should have it: 'tis yours. Or will you have Megra? What you will: you shall have it.'

Lessingham smiled at him with that measure of admiration, contented and undeluded, that is in a skilled skipper's eye when he marks, on a blue and sunny sea, the white laughter of breakers above a hidden skerry. 'A noble offer,' he said, 'and fitting in so great a prince. But I will not be a lord of land, cousin. Like those birds Mamuques, that fly upon wingless wings and the air only feeds them, such am I, I think: a storm-bird, and to no place will I be tied, but live by my sword. But, for such as I am I will take this good offer you have made me; and two things I will choose: one a great matter, and one little.'

'Good. The great one?'

'This it is,' said Lessingham: 'that wheresoever I may be within the realm I bear style and dignity of Captain-General of the Queen, having at my obedience, under your sovereignty as Lord Protector, all armed levies in her behalf whether by land or sea.'

The Vicar blew out with his lips.

Lessingham said, 'You see I can open my mouth wide.'

'Ay,' said the Vicar, after a minute. 'But I will fill it. Today there's no such office, save I suppose it vesteth in me by assumption, flowing from my powers vicarial. I cannot tell where I should better employ it than on you. Conceive it done. The next?'

'Thanks, noble cousin,' said Lessingham. 'After so high a thing, 'tis almost churlish ask you for more. Yet this goes with it. I wish your highness will, by decree general throughout your realm of Rerek, proclaim, as for my body, like dispensation and immunity as for your own particular. By this must all attempts 'gainst me, were they by your very commandment, carry from this time forth like guilt as attempts 'gainst you and your throne and state do carry: and like punishment.'

The Vicar gave a scoffing laugh. 'Come, you would be witty now.'

'I was never in plainer earnest,' said Lessingham.

'Then 'tis a saucy claim, deserveth no answer.'

Lessingham shrugged his shoulders. 'Be not sudden, cousin, the matter is of weight. Indeed, it is no more than need.'

'I wonder you will not ask me deliver up to you Gabriel and those six men: 'twere scarcely more monstrous.'

'That were one way,' said Lessingham, 'But I am reasonable. That were to shake your authority: a thing you could never grant. But this, easily. And this is as good for me.'

'Dear Gods!' The Vicar laughed in his anger. 'If you but heard yourself speaking with my ears! I'll tell you, cousin, you are like a kept woman: and the cost, I 'gin to think, beyond the enjoyment. Sink away to hell then, for this is a thing you could not in your senses hope for.'

The falcon was perched still on the crag, alone and unmerry. At an instant suddenly out of the sky there swept down at her a little unknown, as if she were his prey: barely avoided her as he stooped, swept up again, and stooped again. She, with wings half lifted and head lowered snakelike betwixt her shoulders, faced with sudden beak each teasing stoop of his; and now she took wing, and in ever widening spirals they rose skywards above Laimak, racing for height. Lessingham, imperturbable with folded arms, watched that play. The Vicar, following his eye, noted it too. And now as they swung wide apart, the tassel-gentle from a momentary vantage in height stooped at her in mid-air, avoiding her by inches as he dived past, while she in the same instant turned on her back to face his onset, scrabbling in air at him with her pounces and threatening with open beak. Twice and thrice they played over this battle in the sky: then he fled high in air eastward, she pursuing, till they were lost to sight.

'I have strained a note above Ela for a device,' said Lessingham upon an unruffled easy speech, 'but you can scarce expect me, for safety of my person, be content with less than this. I would not, by speaking on't, move an evil that is well laid; yet partnership betwixt us can scarce hold if I must get a good guard to secure me with swords and so forth, whensoever I am to lodge in your house of Laimak.'

The Vicar ground his teeth, then suddenly facing round at him, 'I know not,' he said, 'why I do not go through and murder you.'

'Why, there it is,' said Lessingham. 'Have you not this moment laid great trust and charge upon me, and will you sup up your words again? Have you not a thousand tokens of my love and simple meaning to your highness? Yet, like some girl ta'en with the green sickness, you will turn upon me: and as you are, so will you still persist. 'Tis pity. Our fortunes have bettered soonest, I think, when we have gone arm in arm.'

She was back again, perched. And now came her mate again and stooped at her; and again they mounted and went to their sport again, high in the blue. Lessingham said, 'I'll go take a walk: leave you to yourself, cousin, to employ your mind upon't.'

The Vicar replied neither with word nor look. Left to himself, he leaned upon folded arms looking north from the battlements: his brow smooth and clear, his mouth set hard and grim, and his jowl, under the red bristly clipped growth of beard, as if carved out of the unyielding granite. As a film is drawn at whiles over the eyes of a hawk or a serpent, thought clouded his eyes. The tassel-gentle was fled away again into the eastward airt, and the falcon at length, returning from the pursuit, perched once more on her little rock. She looked about, but this time he came not back again. And now she sat hunched, alone, discontented.

So it was in the end, that Lessingham had his way: confirmed by letters patent, under hand of the Lord Protector and sealed with the great seal, Captain-General of the Queen, with like inviolability of person and like guilt laid upon any that should raise hand or weapon or draw plot against him, as were it the Vicar's own person in question or one of the royal blood and line of Fingiswold. With so much honour was Lessingham now entertained and princelike estate in the open eye of the world, and proclaimed so, not in Laimak only but up and down the land. And now, for certain days and weeks, he was whiles with the Vicar in Laimak, and at whiles in the March, or south beyond the Zenner, putting in order matters that were necessary for carrying out of that concordat made at Ilkis. Nor was there found any man to speak against that measure, but it was accepted of by all of them: by the High Admiral Jeronimy, and by Earl Roder, and by the Chancellor. And all they with an industrious loyalty upheld the Duke and Lessingham in the conduct of this work, in so much that, as summer wore and July was turning toward August, things were well set in order for a good peace; and that seemed like to hold, since all were contented with it. With things in such case, Lessingham came north again to Owldale, and men thought that he, that had been great before, was by all these things grown greater.

Now the Lord Horius Parry made a feast for his cousin Lessingham in the great banquet-room in Laimak, and there were there mighty men of account from all the dales and habited lands in Rerek, and they of the Vicar's household and his great officers, and Amaury and others that followed Lessingham. And now when the feast was part done, the Vicar upon a pretext rose from his seat and made Lessingham go with him privately out of the banquet-hall, and so up upon the roof of the keep. Here they had many a time taken counsel together: as upon the morrow of Lessingham's coming from Mornagay, when he wrung from the Vicar the truth touching the taking off of King Styllis and undertook that embassage to Zayana. On this secret roof they walked now under stars which shone down with a mildness like sleep and with an untwinkling steadfastness through the region air that was woven in web and woof of moonlight and where no wind stirred.

Only Antares, sinking to the west above the ridges of Armarick, blinked red with sometimes a sparkle of green fire. The noise of feasting floated up faint from the banquet-hall. The hooting of owls, as they went about their occasions, sounded at whiles from the wooded hillsides and spaces of the sleeping valley afar. Breathing such airs, showered down upon with such influences, flattered with such music, that the season of sleep discourses and the ensphered peace of the summer's night, Lessingham talked with the Lord Horius Parry of men and their factions within the land and without, and of their actions and valour, and the ordering and grounding of their several estates and powers; deliberating which of these it were fit to encourage and rely upon, which were best coaxed and dallied withal, and last, which ought upon first occasion to be suddenly extinguished. After which mature deliberation they propounded to themselves this, that Lessingham should shortly go north and across the Wold to Rialmar, there to perform for a while his office of a commander, entertaining the people and assuring himself of the great men: a thing not to be done by the Vicar himself, in so much as they of those northern parts held him suspected and were not easily to be wooed to serve him faithfully or cancel that sinister opinion they had held of him. But Lessingham was not odious to them, but rather held in admiration, upon experience in late wars both by soldiers and people, for one of fair dealing, and for a man-at-arms fierce and courageous in his venturing upon and coming off from dangers.

And now while they walked, Lessingham, debating with himself of all these things, was ware that the Vicar talked now of women, and how unfit it was they should succeed to the government of states, where need was rather of princes that should be both venerable and terrible: and so forth of women in generality: 'In my conceit he understood it aright that said, "It is all but hogsflesh, varied by sauce." And I think you too are of that opinion, cousin?'

'Yes,' said Lessingham out of the starlight, as a man might answer a child: 'I am of that opinion.'

'And, by that, the sured man for this further purpose. Cousin, it would comfort my hand mightily could I bring this pretty

ladybird and emblem of sovereignty to dwell here in Rerek. I do
mistrust the folk about her in the north there. And remember, she's
of manable age: wooers, I hear tell on: that Derxis for one, newly
crowned in Akkama, a sweet young swanking: in Rialmar, I have't
upon sure intelligence, this very instant. Phrut! the cat will after
kind. Therefore, cousin, of this plain power I give you and make
you commissionary: use what means you will, but bring her south
to me in Laimak.'

Lessingham studied a season and at last said: 'In plain terms,
cousin: this is not an overture of marriage?'

'Footra! I ne'er dreamed on't.'

'That is well; for 'pon first bruit of that, you should incur the
hatred of them all, and all our work fly again in pieces. Well, I
will undertake it, if your highness will wisely give me a large
discretion: for it is a thing may seem mischievous or profitable,
and whether of the two we know not till I be there to try.'

'Enough: you know my mind,' said the Vicar. 'Try how she stands
affected to me, and do what you may. And now,' he said, 'let us
go down and drink with them. Cousin, I do love you, but by my
soul you have this fault: you do drink commonly but to satisfy
nature. Let's you and I this night drink 'em all speechless.'

Lessingham said, 'Wine measurably drunken delighteth best.
But to humour you tonight, cousin, I will drink immeasurably.'

So came they again to the feast, in the hall of the great carven
faces of black obsidian-stone whose eyes flung back the lamplight;
and straightway there began to be poured forth by command of
the Vicar cup upon cup, and as a man quaffed it down so in an
instant was his cup brimmed a-fresh, and the Vicar shouted at
every while that men should swiftly drink. And now he bade the
cup-bearers mix the wines, and still the cups were brimmed, and
swiftlier drank they, and great noise there was of the sucking down
of wines and clatter of cups and singing and laughing and loud
boastings each against each. And now were the wits of the more
part of them bemused and altered with so much bibbing and
quaffing as night wore, so that some wept, and some sang, and
some embraced here his neighbour, there a cup-bearer, and some

quarrelled, and some danced; some sat speechless in their chairs; some rolled beneath the table; and some upon it. The heat and sweat and the breath of furious drinking hung betwixt tables and rafters like the night mist above a mere in autumn. It was ever that the Vicar and Lessingham set the pace, carousing down goblet after goblet. But now the high windows, all wide open for air, began to pale, and the lamps to burn out one by one; and not a man remained now able to drink or speak or stand but all lay senseless among the rushes, or in their seats, or sprawled forward on the table: all save the Vicar and Lessingham alone.

The Vicar now dismissed the cup-bearers, and now they two fell again to their drinking, each against each, cup for cup. The Vicar's countenance showed scarlet in the uncertain light, and his eyes puffy like an owl's disturbed at noon; he spoke no more; his breath laboured; the sweat ran down his brow and down nose and cheeks in little runlets; his neck was bloated much beyond its common size, and of the hue of a beetroot. He drank slowlier now; Lessingham drank fair with him as before, cup against cup. All that night's quaffings had lighted but a moderate glow beneath the bronze on Lessingham's cheek, and his eyes were yet clear and sparkling, when the Vicar, lurching sideways and letting fall from nerveless fingers his half-drained cup, slid beneath the table and there lay like a hog, snoring and snouking with the rest.

Two or three lamps yet burned on the walls, but with a light that weakened moment by moment before the opening dawn. Lessingham set cushions under his cousin's head and made his way to the door, picking his steps amongst bodies thus fallen ingloriously beneath the cup-din. In the darkness of the lobby a lady stood to face him, goblet in hand, quite still, clothed all in white. 'Morrow, my Lord Lessingham,' she said, and drank to him. 'So you go north, at last, to Rialmar?'

There was a quality in her voice that swept memory like harp-strings within him: a quality like the unsheathing of claws. His eyes could not pierce the shadow more than to know her hair, which seemed to have of itself some luminosity that showed through darkness: her eyes, like a beast's eyes lit from within: a glint of teeth.

'What, dear mistress of the snows?' he said, and caught her. 'Under your servant's lips? Ha, under your servant's lips! And what wind blew you to Laimak?'

'Fie!' said she. 'Will the man smother me, with a great beard? I'll bite it off, then. Nay and indeed, my lord,' she said, as he kissed her in the mouth, 'there's no such haste: I have my lodging here in the castle. And truly I'm tired, awaiting of you all night long. I was on my way to bed now.'

He suffered her to go, upon her telling him her lodging, in the half-moon tower on the west wall, and giving him besides, from a sprig she had in her bosom, a little leaf like to that which Vandermast had given him in the boat upon Zayana mere, that month of May. 'And it is by leaves like this,' said she, 'that we have freedom of all strongholds and secret places to come and go as we list and accompany with this person or that; but wherefore, and by Whose bidding, and how passing to and fro from distant places of the earth in no more time than needeth a thought to pass: these are things, dear my lord, not to be understood by such as you.'

Lessingham came out now into the great court, with broadened breast, sniffing the air. In all the hold of Laimak none else was abroad, save here and there soldiers of the night-watch. Below the walls of the banquet-chamber he walked, and so past the guard-house and Hagsby's Entry and the keep, and so across to the tennis-court and beyond that to the northern rampire where they had had their meeting in June. Lessingham paced the rampart with head high. Not Maddalena treading the turfy uplands in the spring of the year went with a firmer nor a lighter step. The breeze, that had sprung up with the opening of day, played about him, stirring the short thick and wavy black hair about his brow and temples.

He stood looking north. It was a little past four o'clock, and the lovely face of heaven was lit with the first beams thrown upward from behind the Forn. The floor of the dale lay yet under the coverlet of night, but the mountains at the head of it caught the day. Lessingham said in himself: 'His Fiorinda. What was it she said to me? "I think you will find there that which you seek. North, in Rialmar."'

'Rialmar.' A long time he stood there, staring north. Then, drawing from the bosom of his doublet the leaf of sferra cavallo: 'And meanwhile not to neglect present gladness—' he said in himself; and so turned, smiling with himself, towards the half-moon tower where, as she had kindly let him know, Anthea had her lodging.

XIII

QUEEN ANTIOPE

ANOTHER KIND OF COUSIN • A ROYAL WOOER • MISERY OF
PRINCES • HAPPY DIVERSION • THE QUEEN AND HER
CAPTAIN-GENERAL • '—BUT LOOKT TO NEARE . . .' • A KING
IN WAITING • PRINCESS ZENIANTHE • USES OF FRIENDSHIP
• THE HALL OF THE SEA-HORSES • QUALITIES AND
CONDITIONS OF DERXIS • CAMPASPE LIFTS A CURTAIN •
THE QUEEN IN PRESENCE • ANTHEA: DERXIS: THE PAVANE •
VERTIGO • THE SEAHORSE STAIRCASE.

THROUGH the wide-flung casements of the Queen's bedchamber
in the Teremnene palace in Rialmar came the fifteenth day of
August, new born. Over a bowl of white roses it stepped, that
stood on the windowsill with dew-drops on their petals, and so
into the room, touching with pale fingers the roof-beams; the
milk-white figured hangings; the bottles on the white onyx table:
angelica water, attar of roses, Brentheian unguent made from the
honey of Hyperborean flowers; the jewels laid out beside them;
the mirrors framed in filigree work of silver and white coral; gowns
and farthingales of rich taffety and chamblet and cloth of silver that
lay tumbled on chairs and on the deep soft white velvet carpet; all
these it touched, so that they took form, but as yet not colour. And
now it touched Zenianthe's bed, which was made crossways
at the foot of the Queen's, betwixt it and the windows; and her

hair it touched, but not her eyes, for she was turned on her side away from the light, and slept on. But now the day, momently gathering strength, fluttered its mayfly wings about the Queen's face. And now colour came: the damask warmth of sleep on her face; her hair the colour of the young moon half an hour after sunset when the pale radiance has as yet but the faintest tinge of gold. With a little comfortable assenting sleepy noise she stirred, turning on her back. The day kissed her beneath the eyelids, a morning kiss, as a child might kiss awake its sleeping sister.

She threw back the clothes and leapt from the bed and, in her night-gown of fine lawn, stood in the window, looking out. Seventy feet beneath her the wall had its foundations in native rock, and the cliff, greatly undercut, fell away unseen. The drop from that window-sill was clear eight hundred feet to the sea of cloud, dusky, fluffed like carded wool, that overspread the river-valley of Revarm. North-westward, to her left where she stood, the walls and roofs swept down to Mesokerasin, where, in the dip between this horn Teremne and the lower horn Mehisbon, is the main of Rialmar town; horns which overhang the precipitous face north-westward, so that both the royal Teremnene palace and the houses and temples upon Mehisbon are held out over the valley dizzily in air. To her right, south-eastward, the blanket of mist hid the harbour and the river and the Midland Sea. Overhead, in a stainless sky, night still trailed a deeper intensity of blue westwards towards the zenith. The whole half circle of the horizon was filled with the forms, diamond-clear against the saffron of the dawn, of those mountains Hyperborean that are higher than all mountains else in the stablished earth. Upon all these things the Queen looked: beholding in them (but knew it not) her own image in a mirror. A lark singing mounted from height to height of air till it was level now with her window.

After a little, 'Cousin,' she said, without turning: 'are you awake?'

'No,' answered she. 'Are you asleep?'

'No.'

'Get up,' said the Queen.

'No,' she said, and snuggled down a little more, so that the sheet was nicely arranged to cover her mouth but not her nose.

The Queen came and stood over her. 'We will wake her up ourselves, then,' said she, picking up from the foot of her own bed a little white cat, very hairy, with blue eyes, and dangling it so that its paws were on the sheets above Zenianthe's chin. 'Now she is at our mercy. Wake up, cousin. Talk to me.'

Zenianthe took the little cat into her arms. 'Well, I am talking. What about?'

'You must think of something,' said the Queen. 'Something useful. "How best to rid away an unwelcome guest": a lesson on that would be good now.'

'You have nothing to learn from me there, cousin,' said Zenianthe.

Antiope's face was serious. 'I have flaunted flags enough,' she said, 'to show what way the wind blows. A year ago it should not have been so.'

'Perhaps,' said Zenianthe, 'a man might think it fit to stay till he had the Lord Protector's word to bid him be gone. But you might try with your own word. And yet some would like well to hold a king, and so goodly a young gentleman besides, at their apron-strings.'

'You can have him for me,' said the Queen.

'I am humbly beholden to your highness; but I think he is not a man to take the sorb-apple and leave the peach on the dish.'

Antiope said, 'You are both naughty and dull this morning. I think I'll send you away like the rest.' She surveyed her cousin's supine form, brown hair spread in sweet tangled confusion on the pillow, and morning face. 'No, you're not good,' she said, sitting down on the bed's edge. 'And you will not help me.'

'Do your hair in some nasty fashion. That may disgust him.'

'Well, give me a scissors,' said the Queen: 'I'll cut it off, if that might serve. But no. Not that: not even for that.'

'Might fetch you a back-handed stroke too, reverse the thing you played for. High squeaking voice: if he be but half a man (as you said t'other day), half a woman should be nicer to his liking than the whole.'

Antiope said, 'You shall not talk to me of his likings. Bad enough
to go through with it; no need to think on't and talk on't: to be
gazed on like a sweetmeat or a dish of caviare. Not all men,
Zenianthe, fall sick of this distemper.'

'But all sorts,' said Zenianthe.

'As a good horse may be took with the staggers. Yes, there
was—' She thought a minute. 'But not all our friends go bad.
Venton, Tyarchus, Orvald, Peropeutes, why, a dozen others, can
ride, be merry at table, go a-hunting, lead a coranto, and ne'er
spoil friendship with this moping eat-me-up folly: talk as good
sense as you, cousin: better. Zenianthe,' she said after a pause,
'why might we not stay children? Or if not, why could I not be
my own mistress, next month when I shall be of age eighteen, as
my brother was? What's a Protector, that sits in Rerek two weeks'
journey from us? And these great ones here, old Bodenay and the
rest: nought but for their own ends: they but play chess: if they
have a Queen, exchange her for a pair of castles and a pawn soon
as they see their vantage.' She fell silent, stroking the cat's cheeks
and putting its little ears together. Then, 'I believe they are playing
this king against the Vicar,' she said. 'Do you not think so, cousin?'

Zenianthe laughed. 'I should be sorry you should wed the Vicar.'

'Hark to the silly talk!' said the Queen, rolling the cat on its
back, this way that way with her hand, till it kicked and fought
with little velvet hind-paws and made pretence to bite her. 'You
at least, cousin, might keep your senses, and not think but and
talk but of wed, wed, wed, like a popinjay. Get up!' and she
suddenly pulled the bed-clothes and the princess with them onto
the floor.

The sun was high and the hour but an hour short of noon
when the king of Akkama, having broken his fast on a dish of
lobsters washed down with yellow wine, walked with two or three
of his gentlemen out by the back stair from his lodgings in the
southern wing of the palace of Teremne and so by paths he knew
of round to the Queen's garden, into which he entered by a way
well chosen as not observable from the windows. The garden was
designed so as none should overlook it; facing eastwards and

westwards, and with a great blind wall to shelter it from the north. Walls of hewn granite six cubits high shut it in, with deep wide embrasures at every few paces on the east side and on the west, to look, those upon the valley over the precipice brink and upon the great mountains afar, these upon the main garden pleasance with its silver birch-trees and fish-ponds and walks and bowers, and beyond it hills again and circling mountains, far beyond which lies Akkama. An oval pond gleamed in the midst of that little garden, with a paved walk about it of granite, and steps of granite going down to the walk from a double flight of terraces. Late-flowering lilies, creamy white and with red anthers and speckled with brown and dust of gold, filled the beds upon the terraces; there were sunflowers a-row along the northern side, lifting their faces to the noon, and little northern mountain plants, stone-crops and houseleeks and matted pinks, were in the joints of the walls and between the paving-stones; and under the east wall were chairs set out with cushions of silk, and an ivory chair for the Queen; and upon a carven pedestal rising from the middle of the water, a chryselephantine statue of Aphrodite Anadyomene.

'The presence 'gins to fill,' said the Lord Alquemen, throwing open the gate they entered by at the north-west corner and standing clumsily aside for the king to go in; 'yet the goddess tarries.'

Derxis walked moodily into the empty garden, flicking off a lily-head with his walking-stick as he passed. He was something above the middle height, well shapen and slender. His hair was straight, brushed back from the forehead, of the colour of mud: his eyes small and hard, like pebbles, set near together: his face a lean sneak-bill chitty-face, shaved smooth as a woman's, thin-lipped and with little colour about the lips, the nose straight and narrow. For all his youth (but three-and-twenty years of age), there was a deep furrow driven upright betwixt his brows. He wore a light cloak, and doublet with puffed sleeves after the Akkama fashion: loose breeches buckled below the knee: all of a sober brownish colour. There were bracelets of gold cut-work on his wrists and a linked collar of gold, broad and set with rubies between the links, hung on his chest.

Twice round that garden the king paced idly, with his gentlemen at his elbow mum as he, as if they durst not speak unbidden. 'You,' he said at length. 'Was it not you told me this was the place?'

'I pray your highness have but a little patience,' said Alquemen. 'I had it by surest ways (why, 'twas from you, my Lord Esperveris?) she cometh to this place four times out of five a-mornings 'bout this hour.'

'You were best get your intelligence more precise ere you serve it up to me,' said Derxis. His voice was soft, too high of pitch for a man's voice, effeminate. Yet Alquemen and those other lords, hard heavy and brutal to look upon, seemed to cringe together under the reproof of that voice as boys might cringe, lighting suddenly upon some deadly poisoned serpent.

The king walked on, whistling an air under his breath. 'Well,' he said, after a while, 'you're tedious company. Tell me some merry tale to pass away the time.'

Alquemen recounted the tale of the cook that turned fisherman: a tale of a nastiness to infect the sweet garden scents and taint the lilies' petals. The king laughed. They, as if suddenly the air were freer, laughed loudlier with him.

'You have remembered me,' Derxis said, 'of that conceit of the three women and the lamprey. Or how went it? It was yours, Orynxis, ha?'

Orynxis recounted that story. The king laid out his tongue and laughed till the tears started. 'Come, I am merry now,' said he, as they walked now westward beside the sunflowers. 'What's here? a toad? Give me a stone.'

Alquemen picked one from the flower-bed. The king threw and missed. Kasmon proffered him another. The king's hand was up for the second throw, when Antiope entered and, seeing him, halted in the gate, fair in the line of aim.

He dropped the stone and with a low leg wished her good morrow. 'I was not without hope, madam,' he said with great smoothness, as she came in with her ladies and some of her officers of state, 'to have had the happy fortune to have met you here. I see now 'tis a most heavenly garden; and yet but now I thought it but ordinary. Nay, 'tis plain fact: give me leave but to tear up these flowers, throw down the carven bauble standeth in the water there, you should see, gentlemen, it should seem fairer yet: you, madam, the queen-rose to grace it, and these ladies brier-roses about you to pay you honour with their meaner sweets.'

'Sir, I am infinitely full of business,' said the Queen. 'This is my summer council-chamber. I did send to let you know there was a hunt prepared for you this morning, but my gentleman of the horse told me you were not abroad yet.'

'My chamberlain was at fault, then,' said Derxis. 'How came it, Orynxis, you gave me not the message?'

Orynxis, that had given it punctually, excused himself that he ne'er heard of it till now: he would examine into it, and see him punished with whom the fault lay.

'See to it,' Derxis said. 'Cropping of the ears were too little a punishment for such oversight. Yet, for I mind me of your compassionate nature, madam, ask me to pardon it, 'tis done, forgot, at your sweet asking.'

'I pray report it to my justiciar, if aught's committed needeth correction. You are my guest, sir, in Rialmar, and I hold on the King my father's way (upon whom be peace); no private justice here.'

'You speak high, madam. And that becomes you.'

The Queen now espied at her feet the toad, where it cowered under the broad leaf of a saxifrage. She looked direct at Derxis, then at it, then again at Derxis.

He laughed. 'You did offer me a boar-hunt, madam. Praise my simple tastes, I am content with throwing at a toad.'

'At a toad?' said she, without smiling. 'Why?'

'For diversion, awaiting of you. It is a toad. I would kill it.'

He met in her eye an Artemisian coldness and displeasure. Then, with a sudden little lovely grace picking up the toad, she made sure it was unhurt, made as if to kiss it, then put it back in a safe place on the flower-bed.

Derxis followed her as she turned away. 'What a strange

pitifulness is this of yours,' he said, walking at her side, 'that taketh compassion of malefactors and nasty paddocks, but not of him that most needeth your dear pity.' He spoke low, for her ear alone. Their people, his and hers, walked behind them.

She came to a halt. 'I'm sorry, sir, but I must to business.'

'Then my suit standeth first in the list, so hear it.'

Antiope stood silent, with face averted. Alquemen was saying to the Princess Zenianthe, 'I pray you then scent this flower: can speak to your ladyship plainer words than I durst.' Zenianthe moved away. Derxis noted the Queen's lips. He gritted his teeth and said, with a persuasive sweetness, 'Will you not show me your garden?'

'I had thought you had seen it,' she said.

'How could I see it,' said Derxis, 'but with your beauteous self to show it me?'

Antiope turned to him. 'I have bethought me of a game,' she said. 'I will show you my garden, sir, for half an hour; in which time you shall not pay me no compliments. That will be a new thing indeed.'

'And the wager?'

'You may leave that to me.'

'Ha!' said he, softly, and his eyes surveyed her with a slow appraising stare: 'that raiseth hopes.'

'Let them not rise too high,' she said.

The lubricity that jumped pat upon Derxis's tongue he swallowed in again. He dropped a pace or so behind her for a moment, enough to say in the ear of Lord Alquemen, 'See to it you manage me some privacy.'

But now came into the garden a gentleman-usher and brought a packet to the Queen's chamberlain, who, reading the direction, handed it unopened to the Queen. 'I pray you hold me excused, sir,' she said to Derxis, 'while I read it.'

The king bowed assent. With a jealous sidelong look he watched her face light up as she read. 'But who's the carrier?' she said, looking up: 'of these letters, I mean?'

'Serene highness,' answered he that brought them: 'his lordship's self that writ it bare it, and waiteth on your disposals.'

'O entertain him hither straight,' said Antiope. Derxis's face grew dark. 'It is my great kinsman's kinsman, the great Lord Lessingham, come from the south upon some matters extraordinary,' she said, turning with a lovely courtly favour to Derxis. 'I have your leave, sir, to bid him join our company?'

The king stood silent. Then said the knight marshal Bodenay, 'Your serenity may be sure he had rather you gave him breathing-time to prepare himself: not come all clagged with mire and clay into your grace's presence.'

Antiope laughed. 'O court ceremonies! Have we seen ne'er a man yet in riding-gear? No, he shall come now.'

'Cry you mercy, madam,' said the king; 'I value not a courtesy hangeth long betwixt the fingers. You did engage to show me your garden. Surely this what's-his-name can wait our pleasure while you perform your engagement to me.'

'I must not,' she said, 'be gracious with one hand and ungracious with the other. This is a stranger, not in reputation, yet in person ne'er yet known to us. That your royal estate doth outgo his rank and place, 'tis more reason I use him honourably. No, you shall see the garden, sir, and he shall see it with us. Carry him hither straight,' she said, and the messenger went forth immediately.

Derxis said nothing, neither did the Queen look at him.

And truly to have looked in that moment upon that young king, even so little crossed, had been no sight of comfort.

'What's that Lessingham?' asked the Count Orynxis, privately in Alquemen's ear.

'Cousin to the Vicar of Rerek,' answered he.

'Why, 'tis that same spruce youth, is't not,' said Kasmon, 'captained Mezentius's horse six years ago? Catched you napping when all hung in hazard at the battle of Elsmo: broke up your squadrons and beat you round your own camp? Was't not Lessingham?'

'O hold your clack,' said Alquemen. 'You came not too well out of those doings.'

'Came as fast as his horse could carry him,' said Orynxis. 'Kasmon's ride they call it now: home through the outer Corridor, and near broke his neck i' the end. You two were best hold together, lest this fellow trounce you again. Nay, but sadly, know you aught else of him, Alquemen? The Parry is a hard man, I've heard tell.'

Alquemen answered, 'They are two notable knaves together: both of a hair, and both cousin germans to the Devil.'

The Queen sat now in her ivory chair: Zenianthe to right of her, and upon her left, standing, Bodenay. Raviamne, Paphirrhoe, and Anamnestra, ladies of honour, with half a dozen more, court-men and lords of Fingiswold, made a half circle behind her. Derxis and his troop of gentry stood a little apart upon her right. The Queen, looking round, noted how he, with an uncivil insolence, stood now with his back towards her. As moved by some sudden toy taking her in the head, she whispered Zenianthe to sit in the siege royal while she herself, spite of all protests of the old Lord Bodenay and other grave persons about her, took place among her girls behind it.

Lessingham, ushered in by the north-western gate, walked between the sunflowers and the sun, that even at cloudless midday made but a temperate heat in that mountain country of the north. He was bare-headed, in his mail-coat of black iron and gold, black silk hosen and black leather riding-boots, dusty from the journey. So came he towards them, with clanking silver spurs. And as he came, he gathered with the sweep of his eyes, resting with no inconvenient intensity upon this person or that, all the posture of their company: the staid elders that curiously regarded him; Derxis and his, haughty and uneasy like cattle when the dog comes towards them; Zenianthe in the chair and her companions, who lent to that stone-walled garden a delicacy, as of tender feet trampling the fine soft bloom of grass.

Now were greetings given and taken. Lessingham said, 'You must pardon me, noble ladies and you my lords of Fingiswold, to a come without all ceremony and even in my riding-clothes. But the message was, the Queen was here, and did desire me come instantly to present my service.'

'Well, sir,' said Zenianthe, 'and will you not present it? This is the siege royal.'

Lessingham bowed. 'You become it most excellent well, madam.'

'That is strangely spoken,' said she. 'Or did you look then to find some rustic girl, should know not how to draw the skirt about her ankles?'

Antiope, with a hand on Raviamne's arm, watched him very demurely.

'Your ladyship shall not find me so flat nor so stupid,' answered he. 'No, but I can tell 'twixt the dusky lily and the white. I am not colour-blind.'

Zenianthe laughed. 'You have seen my picture? May be the paint had faded.'

The eye-tricks and signs they bandied amongst them did not escape Lessingham. 'No, madam,' he answered, 'I have not seen her highness's picture. But I have heard.'

'Was "dusky lily" to say, uncomely?'

'Had your ladyship hearkened more carefully, you would have noted I stressed the "lily".'

Antiope spoke: 'It is a wonder you will not know the Queen, sir, when you see her.'

He looked at them in turn: Antiope, Paphirrhoë, Zenianthe, Anamnestra, Raviamne, Antiope again. 'Ah,' he said, 'not till she tell me I may. That were too unmannerly, find her out sooner than she meant.'

They fell a-laughing, and Zenianthe, catching Antiope's eye, stood up. 'The fox was near driven, your highness, when he took this muse,' she said.

'A most good and courtly answer, sir,' said the Queen. 'And cometh from the south: none here could have turned it so. And you'll not be angry with us for this game of play?'

'Serenissime princess and my sovereign lady,' said Lessingham, 'humbled on my knee I kiss your grace's hand.'

King Derxis, being turned about now, looked upon these actions. With an insolent stare he went over Lessingham from brow to boots and so back and so down to boots again. And now he came to them. 'Pray you present to me this gentleman, madam. I were loth to lose aught of his discourse, so pleasant as it seemeth.'

'Sir,' said the Queen, 'this is my cousin Lord Lessingham, he that must be my captain of war against my enemies. Your highness knows him by repute?'

'In my conscience, not I,' said Derxis. 'Yet, being your cousin, madam, should recommend a very cuckoo: by how much more a person of so much fame and nobility as my Lord— I've forgot your name, sir?'

'It is not yet so renowned,' said Lessingham, 'as that ignorance need disgrace your highness.'

They turned to walk now, looking on the garden and the flowers that were there. Derxis held close at the Queen's elbow, and spoke to her in undertones. Lessingham by and by fell behind, and walked now with the knight marshal and the old Countess of Tasmar and four or five others, talking of his journey north from Rerek and of matters indifferent. And first they looked askance and coldly, and cold was their talk; and then that coldness began to melt to him as morning frosts in autumn to the mounting sun, that makes warm the air, and the clouds disperse and mists are drunk up and the rime on a myriad twigs and grass-blades runs together to jewels. With so expert a touch he handled them, as one that himself at ease breathes ease into all the air about him.

And yet carried he little ease within him. To have fed in his thought these three months so many lusts and longings: to have come up to this much thought-on city of Rialmar, thus strangely held out that night to his desire: to have approved it but so, a plain walled hold, cold among northern mountains under ordinary daylight, and the dwellers in it, even to the Queen's self and her maidens, but ordinary: these things were an outshedding in his mind of wormwood and darkness. In the Queen indeed, he saw a girl gay and high-hearted, and one in whom, as they talked together, he thought he touched a mind his own rode in step with, laughing at things his laughed at, leaping where his leapt. But in this was neither recompense nor echo of that which with so much wonder had been permitted to stand for a little moment and with so much aching loss had been taken and gone, upon that midnight under the winged glory in Barganax's jewelled mansion of delights. Moreover, until now he had remembered and might feed on the memory of that moment; but now, from his first looking on very Rialmar, the memory was become as the thin lost perfume dreamed in a dream, that a man knows would restore him all, might he but breathe it again, but natural present walls him from it, as day is a wall to shut out the star-shine.

The Queen now, walking with Derxis, stopped at a bed of the yellow mountain-lily with spotted flower. 'Poor little lilies,' said she. 'I cannot please them.'

Derxis shrugged and, catching the sound of Lessingham's voice, would have walked on. But the Queen waited, so that, if with no good will, he must needs retrace his step.

'My Lord Lessingham,' said she: 'are you a gardener? What is it hurts my lilies?'

Lessingham viewed them. His eyes and ears were opened to the estate of more than lilies in that garden. 'Not the aspect,' answered he. 'Your grace hath given them sun for their faces, and these little mezereon bushes to shade their feet, and sheltered them from the winds.'

Derxis said apart to Alquemen, in such a whisper as all might hear, 'Hast not wit to keep the fellow away, but must be thrust still into my company? Go draw him apart.'

'But how of the soil?' said Lessingham. 'They have very particular likes. Mould of old oak-leaves, and—'

'A word with you,' said Alquemen, close to his ear.

Lessingham's eyes crossed with the Queen's. 'Or if your grace should be troubled with land-mice, little rude beasts that gnaw your lilies underground? I know a way with such.'

His back was turned upon Alquemen, and he gave no sign that he had heard him or was ware of his presence.

Derxis, looking at Lessingham's riding-boots, said to the Queen, 'Belike I understand not the right ceremony of your grace's court. It is custom, is't, to come into the presence in disarray?'

Again her eyes crossed with Lessingham's: a look sudden and gone like a kingfisher's flight between gliding water and overshadowing trees. He turned to Derxis with a grave courtesy. 'My lord the king of Akkama, I am a soldier. And it is custom, with a soldier, to obey his sovereign's command.'

The Queen had moved onwards a step or two. 'A soldier?' said Derxis. 'Go, and 'tis said women will love a soldier better than all other men?'

Lessingham lifted an eyebrow. 'I know not that. But this have I known,' said he, as if talking to the flowers: 'in many countries of the world I have known ladies plagued with uncivil persons have found a soldier excellent good as doorkeeper.'

With so little conscience and so leisurable a gravity had he spoken these words, the king was unready how to take it; and ere he was resolved, Lessingham was some paces from him walking with the Queen and them of her household. The Princess Zenianthe alone was left: she had turned aside suddenly, handkercher to mouth, to contemplate a bunch of water gladiole in the near corner of the pond. Derxis turned colour, the more at the sight of Zenianthe's shaking shoulders. With a hasty glance he satisfied himself that, save his own folk's, no eye was on him. Then with two steps he was at her side, took her about the neck from behind, bent back her head and kissed her upon the lips, well and strong. Alquemen flung up his chin with a great laugh. Lessingham looked round. She, freeing herself, took Derxis a box on the ear that he heard bells.

The Queen and her folk waited now by the sunflowers for the king to come up. He came, twirling his walking-stick idly as he walked, his gentlemen in his wake, his features well composed. A poisonsome look was in his eyes. 'And now, sir,' said the Queen, 'is my half-hour ended; and now must I be private in this garden to confer with my council 'pon matters of state.'

'Madam,' Derxis said: 'of all cruel ladies are not you the cruellest? Is not sunlight a darkness, and every minute a year of prison, out of sight of your life-giving eyes? Well, I am your slave to obey, then; asking but that your sweet lips that speak the sentence shall give me yet some promise of more private conference; haply this afternoon?'

'I pray you give us leave. And perhaps my huntsmen may find you the means to make life bearable.'

Zenianthe said with a levelled malice, 'And you, my Lord Lessingham, care not: we can offer you some sport here in the garden: a toad-hunt!' Derxis, kissing the Queen's hand, turned colour again at those words. Laughter sat in the Queen's eyes, but discretion locked it there.

As they of the king's company moved off now towards the gate, Lessingham overtook them, came beside Alquemen, who walked last, and touched him on the arm. 'My Lord Alquemen: this time, a word with you. Is it as it seemed to me but now, that you laughed, when a lady was put to an inconvenience?'

'Well, and if I did?' replied he, swinging round upon his heel and thrusting his face, with its full popping eyes, into Lessingham's. 'Shall need a better than thee to check me.'

King Derxis, ware of this jangling, paused in the gate and looked back. At a word from him, Kasmon, Orynxis, and Esperveris advanced menacingly towards Lessingham and stood scowling about him. Lessingham gathered their eyes with his and folded his arms. 'Let us make no jarring in this presence, my lords,' he said; and, to Alquemen, 'can you use a sword?' Amid their great burst of laughter Alquemen answered, with a bloody look, 'It hath been thought so.'

'Good,' said Lessingham. 'This then, and no more: You are a mannerless swine, and shall account to me for your unmannerly dealing.'

Alquemen said, 'A word is as good as a blow. I take you very well. My Lord Orynxis will take order for my part.'

'And for mine, my lieutenant, Amaury. I'll send him, my lord, to speak with you.'

The twenty-fourth day after these things just told of, a little past sunset, the Princess Zenianthe stood at that same window of the Queen's bedchamber. The room was all astir with lights and shadows of a log fire that blazed and sputtered on the hearth. To the left of the fire the deep-bayed window stood wide to the evening, which entered now with a tang of autumn and a tang of mountains and the sea. The roofs and towers of Mehisbon were a sharp screen of dark greenish violet against the west, where motes of a rosy radiance swam and shimmered suffusing the smoky blues and purples, and, for a last lighting to bed of day, the broad and tapering blade of the zodiacal light slanted up from the place of settle-gang. The beetle, winding his faint horn to Zenianthe as he travelled the paths of opening night beside that window, saw her as some titanic figure darkly fair against a background of fire. The firelight saw her as its own, spirit of its spirit, dream of its dream, that which itself would become, might it but be clothed upon with the divinity of flesh: a presence secure, protective, glad, warm, fancy-free; and so it made sure of her, touching with trembling sudden fingers now her breathing bosom, now a ringlet of brown hair that rested curled on her shoulder, now a ruby warm against her throat.

She turned as the doors swung open in the middle of the side-wall to the left of the great bay of the window, and, with four ladies of the bedchamber to bear the candles before her and behind, the Queen entered, like a lily, from her bath. Surely her eyes outdanced the shining candles as Raviamne and Paphirrhoë lighted them, a dozen candles by the mirror that stood on the table to the right of the fire and another dozen by the tall mirror, framed in silver and white coral, to the right again, in the corner; surely the warmth of her presence hushed the encircling firelight and outglowed its glow. Zenochlide brought from a chair beside the fire, one by one, garments fine as the spider's web, fragrant, delicate as the butterfly's wing, and the Queen put them on. Anamnestra brought her coat-hardy of rich sarsenet, with a silver taint like a lily, yielding and clinging, wide-skirted downward from the hips: the Queen, pointing her white arms above her head, bowed and entered it like a diver, and like a diver came up laughing and shaking the hair from her eyes. The silken sleeves ended an inch or two below the shoulder, continuing thence with pale blue transparent gauze cut wide, shimmering with dust of gold, and gathered at the wrists to bracelets of fretted silver and margery-pearls. The skirt was purfled upon its lower edge, two spans deep, with flower-work in seed-pearls and the soft blue of turkey-stones and thread of gold, upon pale rose-coloured silk. Raviamne brought her shoes, sewn all over with pearls and amber.

The Queen now, standing before the mirror, took out the pins and, with a shake of her head, let down her hair like a garment of netted sunlight falling nearly to the purfled flounce of her dress. Zenianthe came with the little white cat and held it out to be kissed: 'To salute your highness respectfully on your natal day, and ask you kindly admire my birthday collar Zenianthe gave me.' Antiope bent and kissed it between the blue eyes. 'And now,' she said, sitting down with it in her lap upon a long backless tapestry-cushioned seat of sandalwood before the table and mirror, 'you were best go and make ready yourselves. Zenianthe is dressed already: will help me do my hair.'

'The peace of it!' she said, when they were alone, parting and combing the masses of her hair with a golden comb: hair that was like to the pallid soul of gold breathed into a mist at the foot of some waterfall. 'It is most strange calm weather, cousin: i' the court, I mean.'

'Peace?' said Zenianthe, fingering the jewels on the table. 'Well, for a fortnight: since Lessingham's killing of those five, and the hubble-bubble that that made, and your making the whole pack of 'em lodge henceforth without Teremne; certainly it is more peacefuller now.'

'Ah, but I meant from our own folk,' said Antiope. 'Bodenay; old Madam Tasmar; our vulpine friend Romyrus; they let me have my way now. Do they give me line, but the readier to pluck me in? I know them too well, my puss,' she said, stroking it: 'twisty plots, but little sense. No, I am sure 'tis this: they are altogether carried by this man; and being by him taught sense, let me alone to go my ways. And for that,' she said, meeting Zenianthe's eyes in the glass with a most limpid, unconscious, and merry look, 'I am much beholden to him, and but wish he'd a come here sooner.'

'Must this Derxis be at your festivities tonight?' Zenianthe asked. 'Planted near two months, he begins to take root I think in Rialmar. Will you wear your sapphire comb, cousin, or the turkey-stone to go with your gown? Or will you have your hair low on the neck and no comb at all?'

'I'll have the little half-moon crown of flower-delices, and do it the Greek way, and with those long strings of margarets you did give me, dear cousin.' She was silent a minute, a dimple coining and going near to her mouth's corner. Then, 'Must have been wormwood in his mouth, that business of Alquemen.'

'These little margarets tangle in your hair, cousin, as if they were fain to wind cocoons in it and sleep themselves into fire-flies, or whatever 'tis margaret-chains turn to after their sleep.'

'White moths,' said the Queen: 'owly faces and furry wings.'

Zenianthe said, 'Methought I never saw so delicate playing as my Lord Lessingham's, when you did send for him after that affair, 'pon Derxis's complaint, and did confront them. So penitent and good as he bore himself toward the king, so's who could take exceptions at it? And yet never to leave you in doubt, cousin, that he knew your mind and purpose; as if he should look through his fingers and wink at it. Faith, I near gave away all by laughing, 'twas so pretty. So remorseful, cousin: "Yes, now 'twas put so, he did see indeed 'twas hardly to be pardoned: kill five of the king's men, and all in five minutes. And yet might he be indulged a little for ignorance sake; for truly he had not understood till now that Derxis, as a royal person, had free licence to set men in the dark under archways to kill and murder whom he pleased while guesting here in Rialmar."'

Antiope smiled. 'And there the other walked so neatly into it.'

'Yes,' said Zenianthe. '"By my soul, madam, I had nought i' the world to do with it!" And then you, so sweet and harmless, "O I see, sir, then 'twas not upon your business they went then?" And while he felt about for firm ground then Lessingham again, most courtly and submissive, remembering Derxis of that former passage with Alquemen (I was the distressed lady there, cousin: the beast had laughed when Derxis did me that insolency).

Precious heaven! I near burst myself keeping of my face, thinking (while Lessingham discoursed so formal and serious) of the true tale we had had of that encounter: of his snicking of the beastly fellow's wrist at the third pass and flicking the sword from his hand, contemptuous as dust away a fly: and this their notable great duellist with twenty men's deaths to's credit: and then,' she lowered her voice, that shook with suppressed merriment: 'and then making him put offs breeches, and slashing 'em to ribbons, and then bid him go in that pickle, and learn when and when not to laugh from henceforth—'

'O Zenianthe!' said the Queen.

'And then you,' said Zenianthe: '"O, I'm sorry, sir. I understand. You are as blameless as I am in these mischances. This Alquemen of yours I see hath broke leash, run past your controlling, and 'twas he, not you, did fee these ruffians to sit for my officer to perform his death. Shall I punish him for you?" Cousin, I never saw man so angry, nor so checkmated. Worst of all, when, 'pon pretext to avoid such pothers from henceforth, you did decree them all lodging henceforth without Teremne.'

Her hair being done, Antiope stood up now. 'What's good in Lessingham is right sense,' she said, 'and a wit so turnable for all things alike. What needs doing, this man doth it, and that often even before I knew I needed it. And best of all, a man that stands on's own feet in's own place. Not with your own self, cousin, was I ever more at ease; that I can talk to as 'twere my brother, and never shadow nor taint of that folly that ruineth all.'

The princess was silent. She fetched from the bed a girdle which Antiope now put on, of clouded pink tourmalines; and after that her outer dress of white crinkled silken gauze, transparent as an April shower. Little blue flowers of the squill and the blue-bell were worked on it here and there, and little specks of gold. Soft it was, fitting itself to every movement, even as loveliness itself. And about her delicate neck was a ruff, heart-shaped, open-cut, edged with pearls, going down to a point between her breasts where it was fastened with a flower-delice of little diamonds, so fine that it seemed to be made of mere light. 'As for this tedious king,' she said, 'I have in mind a way to rid us of him tonight, if aught may rid him.'

'What is that?'

'O, a nice and courteous point of precedence I am minded to show him. You shall see.'

'And but only this morning,' said Zenianthe behind her, settling the ruff, 'you did directly refuse, the third time, his offer of marriage. Poor king, he must be most pitifully fallen into your highness' toils.'

'Poor king. Well, shall I take him after all, Zenianthe? For indeed I am sorry for him. And indeed I find him most displeasing. And indeed it is pitiful to consider of a person so lost in the world: pleasing of himself, but displeasing of all other. Well, then, shall I take him then? – 'Las, cousin, you must not prick me with that pin so!'

The great Hall of the Sea-horses in the royal palace in Rialmar was shaped like a cross: a square central hall and four others, lower of roof, opening upon it: and each of these five was well thirty paces either way. The walls were panelled with green jasper between pillars of lapis lazuli. At the northern end, facing the main doors, was a staircase all of jasper; a broad flight leading down to the floor of the northern hall, and side-flights branching up right and left from it to the gallery. Windows, five times the height of a man, filled all the space upon the end walls east and west; in the west, the moon at this time looked in, three days old, a reaping-hook of silver fire. The main doors were in the southern side of the southern hall: doorways with pointed arches, and the doors all covered with leather of peacock blue, nailed all over with golden stars, and edged with rims of rose-pink crystal. The roofs of the side-halls were flat, of a dark stone full of fiery sparkles. Slender jasper columns, two rows down the middle of each hall, dividing it so into three aisles, bare up the ceilings. But of the main middle hall the roof was domed and exceeding high, and the whole floor of the middle hall empty and without pillars. Curtains or hangings of tapestry came down from the dome and, looped up at each corner at the level of the frieze, tumbled thence in billowy masses upon the floor: all of dusky stuff that showed blues or greens as the light moved or the eye that beheld them, and with streamed stripes of ultramarine, and roses worked in pink silk here and there, and at the converging of the stripes or streamers, bosses, broader than a man's arms might span, of cushioned black silk, sewn with vast sunflowers in gold thread. One enormous lamp swung high in the dome, of silver and topaz and yellow sapphires, shedding a radiance very warm and golden: and everywhere, suspended by iron chains, were censers of bronze hammered and damascened, some in green and white enamel, some dusky bronze, some lacquered red, and in the chains were flowers twined and the verdure of creeping plants and leaves and fruits. Alternating with the censers, scores of small hanging lamps burned with a rose-red light. The floor was of inlaid work of rare and sweet-smelling woods, divers-coloured, but with a general show of redness, bare in the main middle hall for dancing, but with crimson carpets in the four outer halls. And at the ends of the balustrades of that great staircase where it came upon the floor (and from these had the hall its name) were two sea-horses rampant, with webbed feet and finny wings and scaly fish-like bodies with fishes' tails. Bigger they were than the biggest horse that ever went upon the earth, and were carved each from a single stone of sea-blue rock-crystal.

Amid this magnificence hundreds of guests were now assembled to rejoice upon Queen Antiope's eighteenth birthday. And as they walked and mingled, it was as the shining forth of the sun after long and heavy rain, when the beams suck up from a wet hedge of box or yew a mist that shimmers with rainbow colours, and the drops upon the leaves change, as the wind shakes them, from emerald to amethyst, from that to ruby, from ruby to liquid gold. King Derxis, surveying the scene with the look of one that has yet in his mouth the taste of a sour mixture, stood with his folk in the main hall. Some saluted him with a formal respect as they passed by; more went about some other way; none joined his company. Every while, the furrow betwixt his brows knit at the sight of some young lord of Fingiswold or some proper man among the company; but his eyes turned oftenest towards the stairs. 'Rialmar fashions,' he said under his breath at last. 'I am nigh sickened of these meant discourtesies. The bitch! Am I her monkey to be led in a string? Esperveris!' he said, aloud.

'Humbly to your highness' wish.'

'Send in another messenger. Say the King of Akkama tarrieth, and 'tis not our custom to wait on women's leisures.'

'Hold thee. Send not.' Esperveris turned back. 'I've changed my mind.' Esperveris, bowing his obedience, had in his eyes that brightened cringing look (seen before in the little garden) of a man that has seen a sight behind the veil.

And now, turning to look towards the eastern doors, Derxis set eye for the first time that evening upon Lessingham, where he talked with old Bodenay and the Lord Romyrus, Constable in Rialmar, and some young lords about him, Orvald, Venton, and Tyarchus, and ladies besides, the Countess Heterasmene, Myrilla, daughter to the lord Admiral Jeronimy, and others. Gay and easy seemed Lessingham, and it was plain how their conversation danced to his tune and opened under his presence as flowers to a warm sun. His attire was of great richness and darkness: blacks and deep indigo blues, with figurings of silver trefoils. He wore a narrow three-double ruff, and ruffs at the wrists besides, below cuffs of silver lace. But a single jewel he wore, of the kingly order of the hippogriff, about his neck; and upon his thumb a ring in the figure of that worm Ouroboros, that eateth his own tail.

Not with the flicker of muscle nor eyelash did the countenance of Derxis uncover his mind as he, for a full minute, steadfastly regarded Lessingham across the hall. Then in that chill unruffled lady-like voice he said to Orynxis, taking his arm, 'Behold yonder woman-server, come to ruffian it out in the company of his betters. A soldier of fortune: hireth out his sword, and body too, for trash. How call you such an one, Orynxis?'

'So please your grace, how but shortly thus?' answered Orynxis: 'a male harlot.'

'O sweet and excellent!' said Derxis. 'Go, tell him so, from me.' His eyes, like pebbles, rested upon Orynxis, noting how the blood shrank, leaving the brutal face white and pappy, then rushed to it once more as under the lash of shame: noting the fumbling of irresolute fingers for the sword-hilt that was not there, for no man was admitted armed to that presence. Squaring his shoulders, Orynxis began to go, as a condemned man towards the beheading-block. The king stayed him with his hand. 'Thou fool,' he said, and there was a muted evil music of laughter in his voice that cut like the east wind: 'shall I unfeather me of all my friends, aids, and helps, because you are like pilled rabbits when't cometh to facing this bloody bully? Alquemen could eat up two such as thou: yet did not this fellow whip him? As I'll whip this puling girl, might I but come at her i' the happy occasion and where I would. Whip her flesh till the blood spurt.'

Almost in manner of a royal progress was Lessingham's passage among the guests: not by his doing, for he seemed ever as a man whose thoughts and looks went outwards, not busied with his own self. But, as the lily of the compass is turned always towards the pole, so of that throng of great court-men and ladies in their summer beauty and others of worship from up and down the land, were eyes turned towards him. 'So you live not always upon gondolas or islands?' said a light bantering voice at his elbow. He looked down into beady eyes whose strange shy gaze captured the gaze that looked on them, allowing it no liberty to look well at the face that owned them.

'My pleasure is my power to please my mistress
My power is my pleasure in that power.

'Are you still so roundabout in your philosophy, my Lord Lessingham?'

'I had thought, madam,' said he, bowing over her small hand, gloved to above the elbow in velvet-soft brown leather that had the sharp sweet smell of summer evenings amid rush-grown sleepy waters, 'that I had demonstrated to you that 'twas a philosophy agreeable to extreme directness of practice. May I have the honour to tread a measure with you when the music shall begin?'

'Please you, I'll be asked rather when that time shall come,' she replied. 'I know not yet what orders have gone forth for tonight. Care not, my lord: once had, you cannot lose me.' As she spoke, the brown paw had slipped from his fingers, and she in her brown fur-trimmed gown was lost among the press, as if she had slid noiselessly into water, and no ripple left behind.

Lessingham, under a singular unseizable exhilaration of spirit, looked round for her awhile in vain, then went on his way. It was as if the bright lights of that hall burned brighter, and as if secret eyes watched from the lamps themselves, and from the hangings and from the golden chapiters of the pillars, and from the walls themselves: a thousand eyes, unseen, that watched and waited on some event. Lessingham, stroking his black beard, bethought him that he had drunk no wine: bethought him then that wine has no effects like these. For now a tranquillity possessed him, and a clarity of thought and vision; wherein, as he looked round upon all that company, he was aware of a new grandeur come upon them. Zenianthe, passing through the hall, acknowledged his salutation: it seemed to him that he beheld for the first time her beauty, of her that he had thought but a princess among princesses, but clothed now with the perfection of the ancient earth, as on the hills shepherds trample the hyacinth under foot, and the flower darkens on the ground. A change, not of the like quality yet of like measure, was come upon a hundred fair women that he now gazed on, so that they seemed like Galateas in marble quickened to a cold stately movement of life and breathing: statuesque presences of nymphs, or of persons half divine, brought back to the visitations of the common earth, and that September evening, and the young moon setting. Yet had this alteration no character of dream nor vision: it was a hardening rather of sensual solid fact, as if some breath had passed, blowing away all dissembling mists and exhalations and leaving naked the verity of things. Lessingham now, without surprise, met, levelled at him from the re-entrant corner of the southern hall to the right of the seahorse staircase, the unblinking, cat-like stare of his oread lady, Anthea. In her, as flame held in flame remains flame still, he beheld no change.

Making his way towards her, he walked across that very place where Derxis and his gentlemen were standing: walked indeed through the midst of them, knowing not that he did so, nor that they in angry astonishment gave back right and left to let him pass. For they, under that alteration, were become so unremarkable that he did not, for the while, perceive their presence.

But ere, with mind a-surge now from memories of past love-sports in Ambremerine and lately in Laimak, he might come within speaking-distance of that lady, seven silver trumpets blew to a sennet, and upon the first blast was every person in that great hall stood still, and all eyes turned to the staircase. And now in a silence, under the shadowy splendours of the looped hangings and betwixt those mighty sea-horses, Queen Antiope came down the mid-stairway and, upon the last step, stood still.

The silence broke with a stir of soft music. Guests of honour were marshalled and presented before the Queen, to kiss hands upon her birthday: King Derxis first. Lessingham, from his place a little removed upon the left or eastern side, noted her face as Derxis, with a flowery ceremony, lifted her hand: her eyes caught Lessingham's in a private interchange, too slight for any else to detect it, of comic intelligence and resignation.

Upon the ending of these formalities, came a dozen waiting-men and spread a little carpet of black velvet with selvage of silver a few paces forward from the foot of the stairs, and set upon it a chair of mother-of-pearl and ivory. Thither came the Queen now, still in her cloak of dull cloth of silver, gleaming to all greys, and four little boys to bear up the train behind her, and sat in that chair, and her ladies of presence took place behind her and upon either side. Derxis came and stood at her right hand. She gave him short answers, and spoke most to Zenianthe upon her left. The company now danced the sarabande; and in this had Lessingham Madam Campaspe to his partner. Derxis craved the honour to dance it with the Queen. She answered, it was custom for her to dance but in the pavane only, since that was their royal dance. Derxis asked when would the pavane begin. She answered, 'When I shall give order for it.' He prayed her then give order now, soon as this dance was done, and so ease his impatient long-ings. 'If this can any way oblige you,' she said, ''tis a simple matter to do it;' and bade her sergeant of arms see it given forth accordingly.

As the last majestic chords of the sarabande grated, on the strings, and the dancers paused and sundered, Lessingham said to his Campaspe, 'Dear mistress of still waters and sallows and moonshine, may we dance again? The third from this, or what, will you grant me? Or, for your warm darknesses have charms beyond these bright lights, shall's walk then in a little garden I can find for you, where a statue of the blessed Goddess Herself stands amid water and lily-flowers?'

'So's there you may explore again the mysteries of divine philos-ophy?' she said, laughing in his eyes. 'As upon Ambremerine? But I'll be asked later. Nay, I'll not play kiss-and-begone, my lord. Nor I'll not nurse it against you if you find other 'ployment when the time comes. For indeed,' she said, very prim-mouthed and proper, her soft arm touching his above the elbow as she with tiny gloved fingers settled the pins in a loosening plait of her dark hair, 'the part, as we know, is but part of the whole.'

Mistress Anthea he now claimed for his partner in the stately pavane, kissing her hand (the nails whereof he noted were polished and sharpened to claw-like points) and looking across it as he did so, from under his brows, into her yellow lynx-like eyes: beacons that he had ere now learned well to steer by, into enchanted and perilous seas wherein he had approved her to be a navigator both practised and of adventurous resource. But, 'Madam,' he heard a man's voice say at his side; 'I pray you pardon me.' Then, 'My Lord Lessingham, her serene highness desireth your presence.'

'Madam,' said Lessingham, 'there's a sovereignty ruleth here higher than even yours, that you must let your servant go when that biddeth. Strengthen me to my duty by saying I may find you anon?'

'Why, here speaks a mortal truer than he knows,' said she, and the cold classic features of her fair face were chilled yet the more for a certain disdain. 'It must ever be an honour to me to be to your excellence – what was't you told the learned doctor? – a "pleasurable interlude"? But indeed, tonight there are changes in the air; and, were I you, my Lord Lessingham, I would not reckon too far ahead. Not tonight, I think.' The upright slits narrowed in her eyes that seemed to plunge into his own and read his thought there, and find there matter of entertainment. Then she laughed: then turned from him.

Lessingham, smoothing his tumbled thoughts and stifling in his mind, as he walked, his discontent and his disappointed designs, threaded his way in the wake of the Queen's chamberlain through couples that stood forth now for the pavane, and so came before the Queen. She, at that instant rising from her pearly chair, let fall her cloak that the little pages received as it left her shoulders, and so stood in her rich and lovely dress, mistinesses of silver and rose and faintest blue, like the new morning sky in gentle summer weather; and nobly she carried about her shoulders that which, of all raiment worn by woman, is test of a noble carriage: a shawl, of blue pale gauze, sprinkled with little diamonds and edged with a fringe of rose-pink silk. The stringed instruments began now, preluding in parts. Lessingham read in her eye swift advertisement, sudden and gone as he made his obeisance, that here was somewhat he must swiftly do for her, and be ready upon the instant to note and act it. Derxis, upon her right, turned to her with proffered arm. She, as if not seeing it, looked round upon Lessingham. 'Sir,' said she, 'you do here in person represent the Lord Protector, who is to me *in loco parentis*. In that quality pray you take place of honour in this company, and lead on for the pavane.'

Derxis, watching them go, stood rigid while a man might count ten. Amaury, chancing to pass at that moment with the Lady Myrilla on his arm, saw the look in the king's eye, and, seeing it, felt a sudden deadly weakness catch him behind the knees. Lessingham, too, had sight of that look: the Queen was ware of a sudden stiffening of the strong arm where her own hand rested. For even as the gentle voice of that young prince if he were angry, so now in his countenance, pale as ashes, and in his eyes, was something, a tang, a menace, a half-raised mask, that even a brave man might sicken at, as if in the apprehended waiting presence of the damnablest of all Furies found in hell.

When Amaury, after a minute, had mastered his senses to look again, Derxis, and his lords with him, was gone from the hall.

Above measured beats, plucked, throbbing slow, from the strings of the bass viols, came now the melody of the pavane, like the unrolling of the pageant of dawn when vast clouds, bodied forth from the windy canopy of night, ride by in smouldering splendours; and the splendours take fire, and in the glimpses qf the sky, rainwashed, purer than dew or awakening airs upon the hill-tops, comes the opal morn; even as that, was this music of the pavane. Lessingham, treading its rhythm with the Queen's hand in his, beheld, as a man folded ever deeper in contemplation, Anthea's face, and after a while Campaspe's, as they passed in the dance: the one cameo-like in its setting of sun-bright hair; the other the face of some little fieldish thing with features gathered to a strange charm, not beautiful but akin to beauty, by beady and coal-black eyes. In both faces he noted an air as if they, knowing somewhat, took a secret delicate delight both in it and in him and his unknowingness.

He looked at the Queen. On her face no such mystery sat. Only she smiled at him with her eyes. He bethought him of that Lady Fiorinda, Barganax's lover: in no woman's eyes save hers had he met, and now in Antiope's, that look of friendship familiar, mere, unalloyed, unconscious, fancy-free, as of his own inward self companioning him from withoutward.

Then, while their eyes rested in that untroubled regard, as adrift together upon some surgeless sea of quiet rest, suddenly he, for the first time, was ware of that music. Like a spate roaring down from some water-spout among hills it thundered upon his inner sense, blinded him, drowned him under. Well he remembered now this music, with its deep-plucked throbbing beats, above which the melody walked singing, and the thing desirable beyond all the stars of heaven trailing in its train. He looked at Antiope as he had looked, in Ambremerine, at that night-piece, of Fiorinda with glow-worms in her hair. For a moment it was again as it then had been: her face was to him unseeable: nought save the outshowering of spears of many lights and hues of fires. A chill-cold shivering took him. But then, in memory he heard, as it had been in very presence, the lazy caress of that voice that had seemed to play with time and the world and love and change and eternity as with a toy: *I think you will find there that which you seek: north, in Rialmar*; and with that, as with the sudden opening of a window in heaven, he saw the Queen truly, as in that dream in Acrozayana he had first seen her, and, for a second time, when he walked like a sleep-walker onto Barganax's swordpoint. Almost, it may be, as a God sees her, he saw her now; with eyes refined to look on the world new born. He knew her. The web of memories which, with his first coming up to Rialmar, had been torn up and scattered, was on the sudden whole again, so that, remembering, he recognized beyond peradventure too her voice: that voice which had spoken on that May night in Mornagay, unknown, yet beyond peradventure his: his beyond all familiar things, speaking, closer than blood or sinew, out of the abysses within his mind, while, with the meditation of bubbles mounting for ever through golden wine, his thought had hung like a kestrel stilled against the wind: *Be content. I have promised and I will perform.*

In this climacteric moment a sudden quiet seized him: such a kind of quiet as Gods know, riding betwixt the worlds: iron knees clamped against flanks of lightning: all opposites whirling to one centre, where the extremity and sightlessness of down-eddying flight stoops to awful stillness. And in that stillness, he considered now circumstance, and this Queen of his, in the spring-time and morning of her life, grey eyes where delicate morning's self sat ignorant and free. And, for the look in those eyes as they met his, he clamped tighter yet the grip of his knees; so that, if the Queen felt indeed the grasp tighten of the hand that held hers, the regard that she encountered in his eye was enough to have laid to sleep in her mind any half-wakening question ere it could come near to waking. And yet behind that unnoticed pressure of hand, given without his will and that he cursed himself inwardly for the giving of, was the whole weight of his iron spirit upon the reins to check

the stoop of the winged courser he bestrode, and make it bear
him still on the way he chose, superb and perilous between gulf
and gulf.

The melody of the pavane, which had returned, upon its last
variation, to walk in a glitter of all stars and in a hum of bees
and in wafts of honey-sweet fragrance sent out by flowering lime-
trees, paused now and, upon two soft pizzicato throbs, entered
the doors of silence. Lessingham, making his obeisance to the
Queen, handed her towards her chair. On the way to it he, looking
down at her as they talked, noted her glance range over the
assembled company: noted the dimple hover like a hummingbird
near her mouth's corner. 'Cousin,' she said, holding out her free
hand to Zenianthe as they met: 'praise my invention. It has
succeeded past belief: our enemy fled to mew, and durst no more
appear. What reward, Captain-General, will you ask for your share
in't? For truly, till tonight, ne'er was there prince in Rialmar so
yoked as I.'

'Some heights there are,' replied Lessingham, 'that a man may
but descend from. If I may yet be honoured, I'll choose the next
lower height, and ask this: that your serenity will graciously be
my advocate with my Lady Zenianthe for the honour of a dance.'

'Well, cousin?' said the Queen; 'shall I?'

''Tis a request,' answered she, 'which I think your highness may
pleasantly accept. And for this next dance following.'

Lessingham carried himself, through the remaining pleasures of
that evening, with open face, and as a man that gives him wholly
to the immediate matter: his discourse full of lively and bright
sparkles and, when need was, serious opinion. So that neither to
the Queen nor to Zenianthe, nor to any that was there, was aught
seen in it but of example and use: so masterfully he rode that
hippogriff steed within him, and upon so delicate a curb.

Night wore, and the high festival drew to a close. And now,
for an ending of ceremonies, the ladies of presence and they of
her council stood below stairs in waiting, while she went up in
state, alone save for her train-bearers, between the sea-horses.

Lessingham, watching, bethought him that not far otherwise might the foam-born Goddess Herself ascend azured spaces of Her eternal sea, between sunset and the moon's rising. And then he bethought him as if all time's treasure-house should have been distilled, from eternity to eternity, into one frail pearl, and in that superlative should pass, under his eyes, beneath cliffs of night.

XIV

DORIAN MODE: FULL CLOSE

LESSINGHAM'S 'I WILL HAVE BUT UPON NO CONDITIONS.'

QUEEN Antiope, upon that good-night, went up to her rest. But Lessingham, being come at length to his bedchamber, came and went betwixt window and bed and candle and hearth in an inward strife, as if right hand should grapple against left hand to peril of tearing in pieces the body that owns them.

'I will have nothing upon conditions,' he said at length, aloud. He stood now, looking in the glass until, with that staring, the reflection dimmed, and only his eyes, sharpened to steel with a veiling and confounding of all else, stood forth against him. 'Conditions!' he said; and, turning about, drew from the breast of his doublet a little withered leaf; the same which Anthea, for better convenience, had given him in Laimak. Upon this he looked for a while, musing; then opened the door: went out. The corridors were as ante-chambers of sleep and oblivion: night-watchmen stood to a drowsed salute upon his passage, down the stairs, through empty halls, to the outer doors. At that leaf's touch doors opened. He came so to the privy garden. On noiseless hinges, under that leaf of virtue, the gate swung wide. And he began to say in himself, walking now in the night-light under stars, and with slower tread, and with an equanimity now of breath and heart-beat whereon his riding thoughts seemed to mount into the starred sublimities of the unceilinged night: 'Nothing upon conditions. Condition of wedlock, kingdom, and be answerable: no. Betrayal so of his commission: no, by my soul! Throwing over of freedom: lean on this, 'stead of ride him as I have ridden aforetime: ha! No. Or, glutton-like: smircher of—' He checked; overtaken, as a man smitten on the nape of the neck with a stick, with a blindness of thought and sense. Then he quickened his pace for a dozen steps, then swung round and, rigid as a statue, stood facing Aphrodite's statue there: of Aphrodite, white between stars and paler stars reflected in the water, and water-lilies that floated asleep about Her feet. And he thought with himself, as thought stood up again: 'You are other. Even He that made You—' the night-wind moved for a moment in that sleeping garden, and in a moment was fallen again to sleep: 'Your power forced Him, making of You, make the one thing desirable.'

A breath from the lilies fainted from under Lessingham's nostrils. His mind stopped and stood still. So a man cloudbound upon the backbone of some high mountain stands clean lost, for the opening and shutting again of a window in the mists that has revealed, far below, a glimpse not of familiar country but of strange and unremembered: and yet embraced, upon some unseized persuasive contrariety of argument addressed to blind certitudes secure and asleep within him, for a country familiar and his own. And now, with a like alien outwardness that the inward touch denied, words which, for all their curiosity of outmoded idiom, he seemed to know for his own words drifted across his thought:

And we, madonna, are we not exiles still?
When first we met
Some shadowy door swung wide,
Some faint voice cried,
—Not heeded then
For clack of drawing-room chit-chat, fiddles, glittering lights,
Waltzes, dim stairs, scents, smiles of other women – yet,
'Twas so: that night of nights,
Behind the hill

Some light that does not set
Had stirr'd, bringing again
New earth, new morning-tide.

As a man awakening would turn back into his dream, yet with that very striving awakes; or as eyes search for a star, picked up out but now, but vanished again in the suffusing of the sky with light of approaching day; so Lessingham seized at, yet in the twinkling lost, the occasion of those lines, the thin seeming memory blown with them as if from some former forgotten life. Out of which passivity of dream, waiting on flight where no air is to bear up wings; waiting on some face but there is no seeing where all is darkness; some voice or hand-touch where all is deaf and bodiless; out of this his senses began to look abroad again only when he was come back at last now to his own chamber, and stood, where an hour ago he had stood, looking into his own eyes. And now, as the lineaments of earth are bodied to a gradual clearness under the grey of dawn, he began to see again his own face, as mountain should so at dawn look across to mountain through heights of air.

'I will have—' he said and was silent. 'But upon no bargains,' he said. 'Conditions is blasphemy.'

Shred by shred he tore up now his leaf of sferra cavallo, sprinkling it shred by shred upon the whitening embers in the fireplace; and so, with a half mocking half regretful look, stood watching till the last shred shrivelled, and burnt up, and disappeared.

XV

RIALMAR VINDEMIATRIX

CURBING OF THE HIPPOGRIFF • A QUEEN FANCY-FREE •
RIDE IN THE FOREST: SUDDEN LIGHT • VANDERMAST'S
WAYSIDE GARDEN • THE HOUSE OF PEACE • NAIAD AND
DRYAD AND OREAD • 'SPARKLING-THRONÉD HEAVENLY
APHRODITE' • SPRING-SCENTS OF AMBREMERINE •
WHIRLPOOL AND A NEW STILLNESS • '. . . WITH AN
IMMORTAL GODDESS: NOT CLEARLY KNOWING' •
SWIFT-FLYING DOVES TO DRAW YOU' • MEDITATION
AMONG NYMPHS BY FIRELIGHT • THE ROSE AND THE
ADAMANT • SUMMER NIGHT: ANTIOPE • AUTUMN
DUSK: THE STORING AND THE BROODING.

QUEEN Antiope proclaimed for Michaelmas day a day's delight
and pleasure, to ride a-hawking. That was a brisk sweet autumn
morning. Lessingham, booted and ready at his window, sniffed
the air. Amaury came in: bade him good morrow. 'Well,' said
Lessingham to that reproving eye: 'what now?' Amaury took a
looking-glass from the wall and held it for him.

'Is there a smudge on my nose? Is my beard awry?' He leaned
to survey himself with a mock solicitudeness.

Amaury set down the glass. 'O think not I care a flea, though old
Bodenay and a dozen more of 'em shall be killed right out, with your
denying them all respite and very sleep. But, for your own self—'

'Will you count how many shirts I have sweat at tennis this week?'

Tennis! Six weeks now, and the last three I think you're stark mad,' said Amaury. 'A half-year's business thrust into twenty days: the whole engine and governance of the Queen's strength in the north here picked in pieces and put together good and new: a great new body of intelligencers thrown abroad for a watch on Akkama, till now so ill neglected: the town in act to be stocked 'gainst a twelve months' siege if need were: works set in hand to make sure all defences: all things viewed, all put upon examination: the Constable and half the officers here cashiered: three or four heads ta'en off: every man else, by your own sole doing, manned and tamed to your fist—'

'Well,' said Lessingham, 'we should think the soul was never put into the body to stand still.' He took his hat. 'He that could dine with the smoke of roast meat, Amaury, should he not soon be rich? When I've set all in order: a week or two now: then off with my commission, throw it by and we'll begone overseas.'

Amaury followed him through the door.

Bright sun shone on Rialmar fair and beautifully as they rode down through the market-place. By the Quiren Way they rode, and so to the old town gate, and so out, and so, winding steeply down the shoulder of that great hill, south-about into the levels of Revarm. Orvald and Tyarchus led, with the guard of honour; then the Queen in her close-bodied green riding-habit trimmed with pearls: Anamnestra, Zenianthe, Paphirrhoë: Amaury: the Lord Bosra, new taken for Constable in Rialmar: accipitraries, seven or eight, with spaniels and red setting-dogs; and, to bring up the rear, with a tartaret haggard hooded on his fist, Lessingham upon Maddalena, deep in counsel with the old knight marshal.

The morning they spent in the open river-meads, flying at wildfowl. The river, meandering in mighty curves a mile and more this way and that way, ran shallow upon great widths of shingle; ever now and again they forded it with a plashing and a clank of hooves among shifting stones. The dogs must swim oft at these crossings, but nowhere was it deeper than wet the horses' bellies.

Out of the north-east the wind blew sharp from the mountains,
making sport difficult. The sun in a blue sky shone on rough blue
waves of the river and on pale swifter waves of wind-swept grass.
An hour past midday they rode up through lava, picking a way
among bosses and ridges of it as among stooks in a cornfield
before harvest home, and so by wide sloping stretches of black
sand, a country that seemed made of coal-dust, to a grassy saddle
between two smooth cratered hills. Here, sheltered from the wind
by the breast of the hill above them, they halted to eat a little
and take their ease.

'What means your highness to do this afternoon?' asked
Tyarchus. 'Turn back? Or on over the hause and ride races on the
flats there?'

'My Lord Tyarchus,' said Zenianthe, 'blindfold we'd know you!
Your highness were best let him have his way. His eyas flew ill
this morning, so the sport's suddenly out of fashion.'

'Be kind to him,' said the Queen. ''Twas so God made him.'

'And that's why there's nought he hateth worse in the world,'
said the princess, 'than dance, for instance.'

'Now I think on't,' said the Queen: 'danced not one single
measure upon my birthday.'

'Truth is,' said Tyarchus, 'I am somewhat nice in matter of
whom I shall dance withal.'

Zenianthe laughed. 'True. For you came first to me. Showed
knowledge, if not judgement.'

'O Zenianthe, and would you not dance with him?' said the
Queen.

'Bade him try Myrilla first. So as, if he trod not upon her dress,
as 'pon yours, cousin, a year ago—'

'That's unfair,' said Tyarchus. 'Her highness had forgot and
forgiven.'

Antiope seemed to have settled with this talk to a yet sweeter
companionship with the green earth where she sat; and not now
in her eyes only, but most subtly in all her frame and pose as she
rested there, was a footing it as of little mocking faunish things,
round and round, in a gaiety too smooth and too swift for eye to

follow. 'Most unfair,' she said. 'To make amends, ought I dance with you myself tonight?'

'Madam, I take that most kindly.'

'But in a dress,' said she, 'without a train.' They laughed. 'But I was but thinking. No; may be, all for all, better it were you, cousin, danced with him.'

'That,' said Zenianthe, 'I take most unkindly.'

'A penance for you,' replied the Queen, 'for your unkindness to him.'

'A penance?' Tyarchus turned to the princess. 'Shall's make friends then, as both offended?'

'I know the sure way to content him,' said Lessingham. 'Do him that favour as to let him try this new jennet of his 'gainst your grace's Tessa.'

'And to take down his pride 'pon the same motion,' said Zenianthe.

'Tessa?' said Tyarchus; 'was not she bred in the great horse-lands beyond the Zenner, of that race and stock your highness's father (upon whom be peace) so cherished and increased there, stablished since generations in that good land, and 'longeth now to Duke Barganax? Well, if I win, shall I have her?'

'No,' said the Queen, laughing at him across her fingers that played bob together. 'If you win, you shall have leave not to dance: neither me nor Zenianthe.'

'A pretty forfeit! There you stand both to gain.'

'You too; for do you not hate to dance? What could be fairer?'

'If your grace must be answered – thus then: choice to dance with neither or with both.'

'My Lord Lessingham,' the Queen said, rising, and all rose with her; 'have you not your mare of that same breed? And shall she rest attemptless?'

Lessingham laughed with his eyes. 'So your serene highness rode not in the race, though mine be seven year old, I doubt not mounted on her to outride any that treads on four pasterns. But let me remember that those who will eat cherries with great princes shall have their eyes dasht out with the stones. We low subjects—'

'No excuses,' said the Queen. 'I'll stake a jewel upon it. Come, cousin,' to Zenianthe: 'you and I; Lessingham, Orvald, Amaury, Tyarchus: that's six, upon well-breathed horses.'

With that, they took saddle again and rode on north, over the hause and so down into woodlands of silver birch with open turfy stretches, and among the grass pallid drifts of the autumn crocus. Where the glade ran wide before them near on a mile without bend, those six took station. After some justling and curvetting, Paphirrhoë with a wave of a white handkercher gave them the start. As they galloped, now in broad sunshine, now through airs dappled with lights and shadows, wet earth-scents flew. Rabbits that washed their faces or nibbled among the grass fled left and right to the shelter of bramble or hazel-coppice or birch-wood. Grey silver in the sun were the trunks and branches, and the twigs red as it had been copper glowing against the blue. At a mile the Queen led, outgalloping Tyarchus for all his spurring. The forest ride swung west now, and after a while south-westwards, into the sun, and began to fall gently away towards a bottom of green grass. Lessingham, for the sun's glory in his eyes, scarce could see. He leaned forward, whispered Maddalena, touched her neck: in a burst of speed she carried him past Tyarchus. As by conduct of some star he rode now: a timeless chase, wherein he lost at length all wareness save of his own riding that seemed now to outswift the wind; and of Antiope ahead, on her black mare.

At a three lanes' end she drew rein. The black mare stood with head down and with heaving and smoking flanks. Lessingham too drew rein. Maddalena herself was breathed and weary: she had carried the heavier load. On either hand were wide billowing tracts of whinbushes in full flower, yellow, of a sharp, stinging scent. On either hand upon the edges, of the wood, silver birches in their livery of autumn swayed in the bright air.

'We have outridden them all,' Antiope said, a little breathless yet with hard riding, as she turned in the saddle to Lessingham who was halted now within hand-reach. "Las, and I have ridden my hair loose. Will you hold my reins while I see to it?'

She dropped reins: pulled off her gloves: began gathering with

her fingers the coil of hair which, heavy, pythonlike, of the sheen
of palest mountain gold, was fallen at her neck. Lessingham made no
answer, neither moved. This that he looked on was become suddenly
a thing to darken sight and shake the stability of nature. The wind
was on that sudden fallen, and no breath stirred. On the stillness
came a flutter of wings, of a wood-pigeon flapping down unseen
among tree-tops. The Queen looked round into Lessingham's face.
The stillness laid its finger upon her too, even to the holding in
of breath. Like a lute-string strained in an air too thin to carry
sound, the silence trembled. The Queen parted her lips, but no
voice came.

At a grating of hinges upon the left, Lessingham swung round in
his saddle to behold, with eyes startled as out of sleep and dreams,
a wicket gate that opened in a low red brick wall smothered all
over with dark red climbing roses. A garden close was within that
gate, sweet with a hundred smells and colours of flowers, and
beyond the garden a low-built old timbered house in measurable
good reparations, straw-thatched, and with slender chimneys of
brickwork and long low windows. A vine hung the porch with
green leaves and pendulous black clusters. The wall on either hand
betwixt porch and window, besides all the length betwixt the
windows of the ground-floor and of the bedchambers above these,
was a ripening-place for apricocks and pears and peaches trained
orderly against the wall; and the slant rays of the sun turned the
hanging fruits to gold, sending long shadows of them sideways
on the wall, deep purple shadows against the warm and ruddy
hues of the brickwork. The decline of postmeridian brought coolness to the autumn air. Homing doves rested pink feet on the
roof-ridge. A smell of wood-smoke came from the house. And,
cap in hand upon the top step of three that led down from that
wicket gate, there stood to greet them, as bidding welcome to
expected guests, that same logical doctor, last seen by Lessingham
in the far southlands of Zayana. Well past all mistaking Lessingham
knew him: knew besides the little cat, white as new snow, that
rubbed head against the skirt of that old man's gaberdine and

looked ever with blue eyes upon Antiope. The sun's splendour
swung at mid-evening's height above great oak-woods. These, and
a high upland training across the north behind the house, shut
out all distances; not a birch was to be seen; no whins flaunted
yellow flowers; no galloping hoof drew near. Only Tessa and
Maddalena munched the wayside grass: from the roof came the
turtle dove's soft complaint: from the woodside a lowing of
cattle sounded, and nearer at hand a babble of running water.
Upon the left, to the right of the sun, a holm-oak upreared its
statuesque magnificence of bough and foliage, nearly black, but
with a stir of radiance upon it like a scattering of star-dust. Doctor
Vandermast was saying to Antiope, watching her face the while
with most searching gaze, 'I hope, madam, that in these particularities I have nothing forgot. I hope you shall find all perfect even
as your ladyship gave in charge at my depart.'

'Ladyship? Give in charge?' she said, looking on him and on
this new scene with the look of one whose senses, fresh wakened
out of sleep, stand doubtful amid things of waking knowledge and
things of dream. 'Nay, you mistake, sir. And yet—'

Vandermast came down the steps: put into her hands that little
cat. It purred and snuggled its face into the warm between arm
and bosom. 'I have been here before,' she said, still in a slow
wonder. 'That is most certain. And this learned man I have known.
But when, and where—'

The eyes of that Vandermast, watching her gaze about her and
turn in the end, with a lovely lost abandoning of the riddle, to
Lessingham, were of a lynx-like awareness. And there stirred in
them a queer, half humorous look, as of a mind that pleasantly
chews the cud of its knowledge while it beholds the sweet comedy
of others led in a maze. 'If I might humbly counsel your noble
grace and excellent highness,' said he, 'vex not your mind with
unentangling of perplexities, nor with no back-reckonings. Please
to dismount you and come now in to your summer-house, on
purpose trimmed up for you. And you, my Lord Lessingham, to
decide all doubts be ruled by me. For I say unto you, it is a short
ride hither from Rialmar but, tonight, a far ride back. So as not

tonight, no not in ten nights' riding could you come to Rialmar on your swift mare. Wherefore, settle your heart, my lord, and be patient. Pray you come in.'

Lessingham looked at Antiope. Her eyes said yes. He leaped from the saddle: gave her his hand. Her hand in his was an imponderable thing: a cool flame, a delicious-ness of mellifluous flowers; her coming down, a motion to convince the sea-swallow of too dull a grace, outpara-goned by hers. Vandermast swung back the gate: Lessingham looked round: 'What of the horses?'

Vandermast smiled and answered, 'They will not stray: no horse strayeth here.'

'Lip-wisdom,' said Lessingham, and set about taking off of saddles and bridles. 'It is my way, on the road, to see her watered and fed ere I feed myself, not leave her to horse-boys. And I'll the same for her grace's.'

'Here,' answered that old man, 'is water. And, for the grass of this wayside, 'tis of a singular virtue. Pastures of earth renew but the blood and animal spirits: but this of mine being grazed upon turneth in the vitals not to blood but ichor.'

As one expressed with sleep, Lessingham stared upon him. But Vandermast, with that close smile, turned to Antiope. 'As your ladyship hath cited to me ere this, the Poetess's words: κοθαρὸς γὰρ ὁ χρῦσος ἴω. – "Gold is pure of rust".'

Quite lost, yet too deeply taken with the sweetness of the place to seek answers, she shook her head. Without more words, they entered; and before them went that learn'd philosopher between lupins, blue and yellow, and flaming lychnis, roses and speckled lilies and lavender and rosemary and sweet thyme and pink and white anemones, up the paven walk.

Dim was the low-ceilinged hall that now they entered from that bright garden: to the left a table of pale oak shining with age ran long and narrow under the southern windows, and places laid there for supper, and chairs with cushions of dark velvet, and at the near end an armful of white roses in a bowl of crystal. Beams, smoked black with age, ribbed the ceiling: a fire burned of logs under a great open chimney over against the door with a settle before it and deep chairs for ease. In the western end of that hall a window opened, and another, lesser, to the left of the fire. In the corner between was some instrument of music, a spinet or clavichord, and a stool to sit and play. There were pictures hung on the walls, and thick brocaded curtains drawn back between the windows. A bare oaken staircase to the right of the fire led to the upper chambers.

'If your ladyship would shift your riding-clothes before supper?' said the doctor. 'And you, my lord? For for you besides there is a chamber I have prepared you, looking west, but your ladyship's south and east.' Lessingham heard, when the Queen was gone up, little cries of wonderment from above-stairs: past all mistaking, Zenianthe's voice laughing and joying with Antiope. He reached out a hand towards the fire: felt its warmth; then walked to the clavichord, opened the laburnum-wood lid and let his finger wander on the keys. The thin blade-like sweetness of the strings sprang on the air and there lay stretched, as if the first hueless streaks of a dawn which comes up seaward without wind should lie listening to their own grey stillness. He turned and was face to face with Vandermast. They looked each in the other's eye for a little without speaking. Then Lessingham said with a tartness on his tongue, 'And you, signior, with your so much outward submissiveness but (or I sadly misjudge), without that inward awfulness 't should in honesty proceed from: What in truth are you?'

'I am,' answered he, 'even as your excellence: a two-legged living creature, gressible, unfeathered. Will you that I conduct you to your chamber?'

Lessingham watched him for a moment through his eyelashes; then, with a slow smile, 'If you please,' he said. 'And what house is this?' he said, when they were come up, and he beheld the fair chamber and, in a bedazzlement, his own clothes and gear laid out ready upon chest and bed.

'By your leave,' said the learned doctor, fetching a bootjack; 'not to weight our presence with servants for the while, suffer me help your excellence off with your boots.' Lessingham sat down:

voluptuous deep cushions of sunset-coloured silk boiled up about him like swelling water-waves. He gave a leg to Vandermast. 'Well, it is, as I conceit it, the house of peace,' said that old man. 'And some would think this strange, that to this house should your lordship choose to come, that have the renown of a very thunder-smith and a carver in the wake of armipotent Ares.'

'It is part of your wisdom, I see,' said Lessingham: 'for a hot man cool drink.'

When they were come down again and, by invitation of their host, sat at board for supper, it was with strange company and strange household folk to change the plates. The sun had set. All down the supper-table candles were burning, and on tables and chests besides and on sconces of silver on the walls. Antiope had her place in the table's midst, facing the room and the firelight; over against her sat the other ladies: upon her right hand, Doctor Vandermast; upon her left, one whose face was hard to see, but his eyes seemed large past nature and Lessingham noted of his ears that they were sharp-pricked and hairy. Of extreme litheness and soft grace was every movement he made: pricking of ears, turning of the head or shoulders, reaching hands slender and fieldish as Campaspe's own to plate or winecup. And that was seen of his hands that they were furred or hairy, and the nails on the delicate fingers dark like tortoise-shell. Still would he be speaking whisper-talk in the Queen's ear, and ever, as she gave ear to that whispering, would a thoughtful cast overtake her counten-ance, as if with the swoop of some winged thing that checked and hung hovering in the sun-path of her thought; and ever, as this befell, would her glance meet Lessingham's.

Lessingham asked, 'What guest is that?'

The doctor followed his eye. 'That,' he replied, 'is a disciple of mine.'

Lessingham said, 'I had guessed as much.'

Sitting at the table's end whence he could see all faces in the candlelight, and see, past them in the western window, the feet of day disappear under night as ankles under a skirt dropped by some lovely hand as the wearer walks by, Lessingham felt himself sink into a great peace and rest. Strange and monstrous shapes, beginning now to throng that room, astonished no more his mind. Hedgehogs in little coats he beheld as household servants busy to bear the dishes; leopards, foxes, lynxes, spider-monkeys, badgers, water-mice, walked and conversed or served the guests that sat at supper; seals, mild-eyed, mustachioed, erect on their hind flippers and robed in silken gowns, brought upon silver chargers all kind of candied conserves, macaroons, fig-dates, sweet condiments, and delicate confections of spiceries; and here were butterfly ladies seen, stag-headed men, winged lions of Sumer, hamadryads and all the nymphish kindred of beck and marsh and woodland and frosty mountain solitude and the blue caves of ocean: naiad and dryad and oread, and Amphitrite's brood with green hair sea-garlanded and combs in their hands fashioned from drowned treasure of gold. When a sphinx with dragonfly wings sat down between the lights beyond Zenianthe and looked on Lessingham out of lustreless stone eyes, he scarce noted her: when a siren opened her sea-green cloak and laid it aside, to sit bare to the waist and thence downward decently clothed in fish-scales, it seemed a thing of course: when a wyvern poured wine for him he acknowledged it with that unreflective ease that a man of nice breeding gives to his thanks to an ordinary cup-bearer. He drank; and the wine, remembering in its vintage much gold molten to redness in the grape's inward parts, under the uprising, circling, and down-setting pomp of processional suns, drew itself, velvet-flanked, hot-mouthed with such memories, smoothly across his mind. And, so drawing, it crooned its lullaby to all doubts and double-facing thoughts: a lullaby which turned, as they dropped asleep, first to their passing-bell, then to their threnody, and at length, with their sinking into oblivion, to a new incongruency of pure music.

'But is this power, then?' he heard Campaspe say. 'To be bitten, taken in jaws, swallowed up?'

'Suppose he should kill her indeed,' said Anthea: ''tis but an act bestial. There is no form in it: no grace, no verity. It addeth not: taketh but away. Why, I can kill. I should know.' Her teeth flashed.

'It is well said,' said the doctor, as if answering Lessingham's
look. 'In this school she is my graduate. I have nought to teach
her.'

Lessingham's eyes met Anthea's. It was as if, in the slits between
the yellows, a light flared and was gone. 'I had it,' he said: 'but
lost again ere I could—' he saw that the room was suddenly empty
of all save those seven that sat at table. But, as if with the coming
and going of tiny wings, little draughts of air touched here an
eyelash, there a throat, and all the candleflames were a-waver. 'She
is form,' he said, and his eyes turned to Antiope. 'She draws us.
We who do, Gods be we or men, in Her is our doing. And if in
this, in action, we have our only being (and by heaven, I think
'tis so), then in Her our being. She draws our actions to a shape:
shapes them so, into a kind of beauty.'

Campaspe, with the shadow as of moth-like wings shedding a
furry and a shy and an elusive sweetness across her elfin features,
said softly, '"As the sheath is to the knife"?'

'It is good,' said Vandermast; 'but not enough. For the sheath
is but an image of receptivity *simpliciter*, and of that which is of
none effect of itself.'

'Goblet to wine were nearer,' said Lessingham, looking still on
Antiope.

'Or eyes to the inner fire,' Anthea said, leaning forward on her
two elbows. Lessingham turned at her voice: faced the slits that
burned and reverberated with green and yellow heat. The warm
sleek redness of the wine smoothed itself against him like a lover
betwixt dream and dream in the failing hour of night.

'Or,' Campaspe said at his side, 'weakness for strength to rest
upon?' He felt the touch of her gloved fingers on his forearm:
fluttering feathered bird-breast that a harsh breath might harm it.

'Goblet to wine were nearer,' said that learned doctor. Lessingham
turned to him: the countenance of Vandermast was mute like the
irradiation of the sun behind northern mountains at night in
summer on the confines of the Boreal pole.

Then Lessingham looked once more at Antiope. And slowly,
as the transmutations in nature of sunset or sunrise are without

the catastrophe of lesser changes, it was, as he looked, that three
were subsumed to one. Not subsumed bodily, for they sat three
as before, she on the left, they on the right facing her across
the table; and yet now, in Antiope the lambent eyes of his oread
lady, teeth of ice, clean fierce lips, breasts of snow; in Antiope,
the strengthless faëry presence of his Campaspe, a rose-leaf
hanging in the last near broken thread of a spider's web where
the dawn-dew glitters; and in Antiope, something not these, but
more than these: herself: easy to look on, fancy-free, ignorant,
with a shadow like laughter's in the allurance of her lips. Her
eyes, resting in his, seemed to wait betwixt believe and make-
believe, then turn to hyaline gulfs where sunbeams wade trembling
upon treasure inexhaustible of precious riches. 'Strange talk,' he
heard her say. 'And I remember,' he heard her say, 'but when, I
cannot tell; nor where: but goes it not hand in hand with your
saying, my Lord Lessingham?—

'Strength is not mine. Only I AM: a twilight,
Heard between the darts of the blazing noonday;
Seen beyond loud surges: a lull: a vision:
   Peace in the spear-din.
Granite leans earthward, as a mace impending.
Butterfly wings quivering abide the shadow:
Music bitter-sweet of the Gods:
   Their night-song,
      Older than all worlds.

'Is She not somewhat so?'
Silence shut behind the falling wonder of her spoken words.
Lessingham beheld the doctor's prick-eared disciple lift her white
hand in his, that was so slender and feral in its tawny hairiness,
and press it, as in a dumb worship, to his bowed forehead. This
he beheld as an act beautiful and apt, and that the beholding of
pleased him much as her little cat's love for her should please,
issuing in some such simplicity. Only the strangeness of it, and the
strangeness on her lips of words that he remembered, as if with

her memory, out of some fair expired season, and that he seemed to know for his own words (though when framed, when spoken, he could not tell): these things gathered now, as a rain-drop gathers and hangs round and perfect on the point of a leaf, into the memory of that streaming up of golden bubbles through golden wine last spring in Mornagay, and of her remembered voice.

Doctor Vandermast stood up from his chair. 'The night draweth in cold. Will it please you, madam, we suppose 'twere Yule-tide, and sit about the yule-log? And indeed I remember me, old customs have still pleased you from of old.'

Passing by the table's end, as Vandermast and Lessingham bowed and made her way, Antiope reached a hand to Campaspe: 'And you, dear, sing to us?'

'Yes, sing, dear chorister of the sleeping sallows, your May-night song,' said Lessingham, 'of Ambremerine. It told me more than you knew,' he said, speaking to her but looking on Antiope, and so saw not the deriding 'More than I knew!' in those beady eyes.

Campaspe, with swift naiad grace, was at the clavichord. She opened the lid. 'May I choose my song?'

She had taken her answer, from eyes where everlastingness seemed to look, half awake, out of infinities to skyey infinities, ere the Queen's lips could frame it: 'Choose: my choice is yours.'

Campaspe preluded on the keys. The silence, divided with the passing of those blades of sweetness, fell together again. 'My Lady Fiorinda's song?' she said: '*The nightingale my father is?*' Vandermast turned in his chair, to rest his gaze, with that veiled, wine-tasting smile of his, upon Antiope. Lessingham too watched her across the hearth from his deep chair: her face, shone upon by two candles in a sconce beside her, was lovely fair, pictured against warm darkness. Surely in the peace of her his own spirit settled, as the day settles in the west.

Campaspe sang: a bird-voice, so small and bodiless that through its faëry texture even those frail chords gleamed clear:

'Li rosignox est mon père,
Qui chante sor la ramée
El plus haut boscage.
La séraine ele est ma mère,
Qui chante en la mère salée
El plus haut rivage.'

Now there hung upon the wall, upon Lessingham's left where he sat, a looking-glass framed in tortoise-shell; and so it was that midway through her singing, with a kindling in his veins again, from that name, and from that song, of memories of Ambremerine, he chanced to look in the looking-glass. For a count of seven he stared, whether in the body, whether out of the body, he could not tell: a face, not Lessingham's but the Duke's, stared back. With the sweeping of terrible harp-strings through his blood, he sat blind.

As his blood beat steadier it seemed to him as if out of that tumult a new figure took clear shape at last of counterpoint and descant. And yet for a minute he dared not lift his eyes to where she sat beyond the hearth listening to the song. For a doubt was on him, lest he should see not the thing he would but the thing he would not: so breathing clear was his memory of what he had seemed to look on but now, when that song began that but now drew to its ending: not her, but another sitting there: a second time (as once in Acrozayana), with too near bodement of the mutability he so much affected and transience of things, as that the levin-bolt might fall not afar to gaze upon, but very here, to thunder his eyes out that gazed. He drew hand over his chin, as to sure himself of it, shaven and hard: looked in the glass: looked at last cautiously across the carpet. This was her foot: no changeling could have stole that: he knew it better than his own. 'Pew!' he said in himself, 'slip not the reins,' and let his eyes run upward. There she sat, under the weak candles, a star between flying darknesses in a night of thunder. Side-face towards him, her chin lifted a little sideways as if, mindful of her own beautifulness, to feed his eyes a little with the silver splendour of her throat and its lovely strength, she stared in the fire through black half-closed lashes. Her head moved lazily, almost imperceptibly, as to the familiar cadence of Campaspe's song. For all else, she sat motionless: all save this, and, with each lightly taken breath, her breasts' fall and swell.

The Duke, so sitting and watching, felt sails fill and his spirit move out once more on that uncharted dangerous ever undiscovered main.

He rose: took a dish of fruit from the sideboard. Vandermast was half risen to have taken it from him, as scandalled that his great master should do handmaid-service, but the Duke prevented him with his eye, and came with the dish to where she sat. 'If your ladyship will have any conceits after supper, as medlars, nuts, lady-pears?'

Very daintily she examined them, took one, and, looking at him not with eyes but with the snake-black gleams of her black hair and with the curve of white neck and shoulder, held it up for him to take and peel for her. He peeled it in silence: gave it back: her eating of it was with an air of creative awareness, as of one who carves or models: of conscious art, rather than the plain business of eating. The Duke watched her for a minute; then, behind her chair, leaned over the back and said in a low voice, 'What crinkum-crankum was this?'

She leaned back her head till he could look straight down into her eyes as he bent over her, facing him as it were upside down. He looked in them; then in her mouth's corner where that thing sat at alert; then over all the imperial pitiless face of her, where a dozen warring imperfections were by some secret fire transmuted to that which is beyond flattery and beyond alchemy; then to the warm interspace where, with her leaning back, the bosom of her crimson dress strained closer; then into her eyes again. 'I wonder,' he said: 'can the Devil outsubtle you, madonna?'

'How can I tell?' she said, with great innocence, and the thing there covered its face. 'Why? Would you engage his help against me?'

'Yes. Save that I think somewhat scorn to bribe your servant.'

'Is he my servant?' she asked, as who might ask an indifferent matter for information's sake: Is Vandermast your secretary? Is Campaspe a naiad?

'Or I have long been misinformed,' answered the Duke. 'Come, what wages do you pay him? Though I fear all the wealth I have shall scarce avail me to bid against you.'

'As for me, I pay not,' said that lady. 'Neither am paid. Still, I have servants: perhaps him we spoke on: could at least have him if I would. And still, I am your mistress. Is not that singular?' She put up a jewelled hand, took his that rested on her chair-back, drew it secretly against her neck, then swiftly put it away again.

The oaths you sware me,' he said, close in her ear, 'after that night last May, never to do it again. And yet, worse this time. By my soul, I dreamed, and I was – Lessingham.'

Fiorinda said, 'I have heard tell of stranger dreams than that.'

'And she? That other?' he said, still lower. 'Who is she?'

Fiorinda sat up and smoothed her gown. Barganax moved a couple of paces round towards the fire so as to see her face again. 'O, this large-eyed innocence,' he said, 'becomes your ladyship badly, who have all these things in your purse. What, is she a dress of yours?'

'I had thought you had learnt by now,' she said, with a swan-like smooth motion of her hands settling the combs in her hair, 'that everything that is is a dress of mine. Ever and since the world began,' she said, so low as he should hear not that: but that little white cat, gazing up at her, seemed to hear it.

The Duke looked about. Campaspe at the clavichord fingered out some little lilting canon. Zenianthe had drawn her chair up beside her, and watched her as some sweet oak-tree might watch the mouse-like darts and pauses of the tree-creeper along her steadfast dream-fast limbs. The old man talked low with Anthea: that strange disciple of his was curled up on the carpet as if asleep, one arm about the little white cat that with slow blinking eyes still studied Fiorinda from a distance. 'You shall know this,' said the Duke: 'I loved her as my life.'

250 *Mistress of Mistresses*

With that scarce perceptible little upward scoffing backward movement of her head, she laughed. 'O sweetly pathetical. You mouth it, my lord, like a common play-actor.'

'And would a let you, madam, go hang.'

'Who would not be so lovered?' she said; and, with a flower-like grace which had yet the quality in it as of the outpeeking from flowers of a deadly poisoned adder, she stood up. 'I am indeed,' she said delicately, 'of a most lambish patience; but I much fear, my lord, you grow tedious. Zenianthe, my cloak.'

'Stay,' said the Duke. 'My tongue can run on patterns as well as your ladyship's. And men that be in love can ill away to have lovers appointed them by others. It was a dream.'

'It was true,' she replied, and her green and slanting and unfathomable eyes held him while he took a stab from every sensuous movement of her putting on her cloak. 'The first (as for loving) was true, but not the second: the second was but said in a bravado to plague me. Think, and you will remember, my friend, that I say true.'

He made no reply.

'Moreover,' she said, 'you would not, no not even this moment, let even her go hang. No, fling not off, my lord: think. You shall find I say true.'

The Duke faced that lady's eyes in an arrested stillness. 'Think,' she said again; and he, looking now steadfastly on her lips that seemed to rest upon the antique secret memory of some condition, primal and abiding, where the being of these things is altogether at once, which is the peculiar property of everlastingness, slowly after a pause answered and said, 'Yes: but that is not to say love. For no man can love and worship his own self.'

'This that you have said,' said that lady, and her slow voice was like honey of roses, 'I have strangely heard before. Yet not heard,' she said, her eyebrows lifting with their look of permanent soft surprise as she looked down, drawing on her gloves; 'for 'twas but thought, not spoken: seen, in eyes: his eyes, not yours, in Acrozayana.'

'In his eyes?' said the Duke. The silence opened quivering wings above them like the wings that shadow the dream-stone.

'There have been, to say, brothers and sisters,' she said. It was as if, under the ironic lazy seductive voice of her, the wings were upstrained to that ultimate throbbing tension that must dissolve the next instant in some self-consuming cataclysm of its own extremity. Then, whether upon the mere whim and fantasy: whether of her most divine discerning bounty, *bis dat quae tarde*: whether but of her April mood (now lovely sunshining, now hail from a louring sky, suddenly again those stones melting at a gleam to jewelled drops on the yellow daffodils and celandines: half-fledged leaves of sallow and birch and thorn turning to green tiny flames against the sunlight: the heavens all soft and blue, and the blackthorn and wild cherry starry above new lambs): whether for all or for none of these reasons, she loosed hold. 'Reverend sir, are my horses ready?'

'Truly,' said the Duke, as if awake again, 'I ne'er saw my—' and suddenly his eyes became veiled. 'Unless—'

Vandermast came back from the door: 'Madam, they are ready at the gate.'

Barganax started. 'What is this place? Madam, I pray you go not yet. 'Least, I'll go with you.' But, out by the door that aged man held open for her, she was gone. Barganax, like a man that would pursue in a dream, but his legs, held in the woolly fetters of sleep, will not obey, stood rooted. Then the door shut.

He saw Anthea's eyes levelled upon him in a sphinxian expressionless stare. Letting that go unregarded, he stood now, back to the fire, in a study, erect, feet wide apart, one hand thrust in his jewelled girdle, the other twirling and smoothing up his mustachios. The dark fires slept and woke, glowed and slept and glowed again, in his half-closed eyes. He said in himself, 'But no, dear Lady of Sakes, beguiler of guiles, O you, beyond soundings: there's something there beyond that. That he hath in him something of yours, I'll not think it past credit, that am inured to marvels. Nay, I believe it: it is a lamp: shows me much was dark till now. But you are more. O you! not with the help of all the devils could I, at this day, be bobbed with such an insufficient answer.'

Doctor Vandermast followed that lady through the garden: bare beds rough with hoar-frost, and over all, hanging high in a frost-clear heaven, the winter moon. 'While you are in a condition, madam,' said he, 'to understand and teach me: lest I fall out, may I know if my part is so far justly enacted, and agreeably to your ladyship's desires?'

'Desires?' she said. 'Have I desires?'

'Nay,' said he, 'I speak but as men speak. For I am not ignorant that *Dea expers est passionum, nec ullo laetitiae aut tristitiae affectu afficitur*: that She Who dwelleth on high is with no affect affected, be it of sorrow or of joy.'

'How sweet a thing,' said she, 'is divine philosophy! And with how taking a simplicity it speaketh, so out of your mouth, most wise doctor, flat nays and yeas of these which were, as I had supposed, opinable matters and disputable!'

'Oh You, Who albeit You change, change not,' said that old man: 'I speak as men speak. Tell me, was there aught left undone?'

She took the reins and let Her beauty shine out for an instant, as a blaze of fire, now bright, and now away. His eyes took light in the light of it. 'There was nought undone,' She answered. 'All is perfect.' And they that were harnessed took wing and, thickening the crisp fine air with a thunder of countless wing-beats, sped with Her in an instant high below stars through the down-shedding radiance of the frozen silvery-moon. And the learned doctor, straining eyes and ears towards heaven, followed their flight, their mounting, circling, descending; and at length beheld them at his eastern upper window hovering, that their driver might alight; and there like a dream he beheld Her enter by that balcony, or like a pale moonbeam. For he saw that not as Our Lady of Sakes She entered now, but once more Our Lady of Peace.

So now he himself turned again, came in, shut the door, and came to the fireside again and his company.

The clock at his so coming in (as if She in that dove-drawn flight betwixt earth and stars had swept the hours, bound to Her chariot, to a speed beyond their customed measure), struck the last hour before midnight. That old man came to Lessingham where he stood yet, in a study, his back to the fire. 'Sleep, my Lord Lessingham, is a surceasing of all the senses from travel. Her ladyship that came hither with you hath this hour since ta'en her chamber. Suffer me to conduct you now to yours.'

Pausing for good-night at his chamber door, Lessingham at last spoke. 'Tell me again,' he said: 'what house is this?'

Vandermast answered, saying, 'I have told your excellence, it is the house of peace.'

'And,' he said, speaking, as old men speak, to himself, when he was come downstairs again and stood at the open door, scenting the April air that blew now from that garden and the scents of spring: 'it is the house of heart's desire.'

May be for the very deepness of the peace that folded that sleeping house, so that even his own breathing and quickened heart-beats had power to keep him waking, Lessingham might not sleep. An hour past midnight he arose and dressed and softly opened his chamber door. At the head of the stair he paused, seeing lights yet in the hall both of candles and the flickering firelight. Noiselessly he came down a step or two, and stood still. On the great cushioned settle drawn up before the fire sat Doctor Vandermast. Anthea, upon the same settle, lay full length, a sleeping danger, very lovely in her sleep, her head upon the lap of that learned doctor. Zenianthe sat upon the floor, her back against his knees, staring in the fire. Campaspe knelt, sitting on her heels, her back to the fire, facing the others; Lessingham saw that she played some little game with cards on the floor, very intently, yet listening through her game to the doctor's words as he talked on in his contemplation.

'Be it but perceived and understood,' said Vandermast, '*sub specie aeternitatis*, it can never be too sensual: it can never be too spiritual.'

Zenianthe, smiling in the fire, slowly shook her head. 'Multiplication of matterless words,' said she.

'Nay, you, dear lady, should know this *per experientiam*, as from withinward. For what will a hamadryad do if her tree be cut down? What but die?'

'Can anything die?' she said. 'Least of all, we, that are not of mortal race?'

'I speak,' said he, 'as men speak. And indeed I have thought may be there is in very deed a kind of death, as of foolish bodies who say, Tush, there is no spirit: or others, Tush, there is no sense. And have not old men ere this become dead before their time, with forgetting that this winter of their years is but a limbeck of Hers for trying of their truth and allegiance, as silver and gold are fined and tried in the fire? But, even as 'twas always that the cat winked when her eye was out, so they: 'stead of hold fast and trust in Her to bind up and bring back and give again hereafter.'

'Are you, to say, old?' said Campaspe, marrying queen of spades and king of hearts.

Vandermast smiled. 'I am, at least, no more fit for past youth-tricks.'

'No more?'

'I speak,' said he, 'as of here and now.'

'What else is there?' said she.

Vandermast stroked his white beard. 'It may be, nothing.'

'But you spoke but now,' said Zenianthe, putting very gently a fresh log on the fire so that the flames crackled up, and that oread lady, with the doctor's knees for her pillow, turned in her sleep: 'you spoke of "hereafter".'

'It may be,' said Vandermast, 'that "hereafter" (and, by like process of logic, "heretofore") is here and now.'

Campaspe turned up the seven of diamonds. 'What is old age?'

'What is youth, my little siren of the oozy quagmires and wood anemones in spring and sallow catkins where the puss-moth feeds at dusk of night?'

'Well, it is us,' she said.

'As for old age,' said Zenianthe, 'the poet hath it—

'My grief lies onward and my joy behind.

'That for age. And for youth I would but turn the saying, and say—

'My joy lies onward.'

'Who taught you that?' said the learned doctor.

'My oak-woods,' answered she.

He mused for a while in silence. Then, 'It is of divine philosophy,' he said, 'to search lower into the most darkness and inspissation of these antinomies which are in the roots of things. I am old;' and his eyes overran the sleeping beauty of Anthea, stretched feline at her length. Scarcely to touch it, his finger followed her hair where it was pressed upwards in aureate waves from under her left brow and cheek where her head lay on his knee in the innocence of slumber. 'I am old; and yet, as the Poetess—

ἐγὼ δὲ
φίλημ' ἁβροσύναν, καί μσι τὸ λάμπρον
ἔρος ἀελιω και τὸ κάλον λέλογχεν

'I love delicacy, and for me love hath
the sun's splendour and beauty.'

Zenianthe said, 'We know, sir, who taught you that.'

Still Lessingham, upon the stairs, stood and listened. Their backs were towards him. Vandermast replied: 'Yes: She, ingenerable and incorruptible. Are youth and age toys of Hers? How else? Seeing She plays with all things. And age, I have thought ere now, is also a part of Her wiles and guiles, to trick us into that folly which scorneth and dispraiseth the goods we can no more enjoy. Then, after leading of us as marsh-fires lead, through so many turn-agains, unveil the grace in Her eyes: laugh at us in the end.'

'Love were too serious else,' said Campaspe. She fetched for the queen of hearts the king of clubs: 'Antiope: Lessingham.'

'What is Lessingham?' Zenianthe asked the fibre. 'What is Barganax?'

'What am I?' asked Vandermast. 'Tell me, dreamer and huntress of the ancient oak-woods, is it outside the scheme that there should be, of young men, an old age wise, unrepentant, undisillusioned? I mean not some supposititious mathematical *esse formale*, as some fantastics dream, but bodied, here and now? For truly and in sadness, searching inward in myself I have not once but often times—' He fell silent.

'What is here and now?' Zenianthe said, gazing into the heart of the fire with brown dreaming eyes.

Vandermast was leaned back, his head against a cushion, his lean hands slack, palms downwards, on the seat on either side of him. He too gazed in the fire, and, may be for the hotness of it, may be for the lateness of the hour, the gleam of his eyes was softened. 'As part of Her peace?' he said. 'As part of Her pleasure? – O gay Goddess lustring, You Who do make all things stoop to Your lure – Seeing all the pleasures of the world are only sparkles and parcels sent out from God? And seeing it is for Her that all things, *omnia quae existunt*, are kept and preserved, *a sola vi Dei*, by the sole power of God alone?'

Zenianthe spoke: 'And of lovers? Will you not think a lover has power?'

'Love,' said that aged man, 'is *vis Dei*. There is no other power.'

'And to serve Her,' said Campaspe, still sitting on her heels, still playing on the floor, '(I have heard you say it): no other wisdom.'

'To shine as stars into everlastingness,' said that hamadryad princess, still looking in the fire.

For a few minutes none spoke, none stirred, save only for Campaspe's playing her little game. Lessingham, upon the stairs, noted how the learned doctor, as old men will, was fallen asleep where he sat. Campaspe, noting it too, softly swept up her cards.

She stood for a moment looking at him so sleeping, then on tiptoe came and bent over him and, very prettily and sweetly, kissed his forehead. Anthea, turning in her sleep, put up a hand and touched his face. Lessingham very quietly came down the stairs behind them and so from the stair-foot to the door. Only Zenianthe, sitting quite still, turned her head to watch him as he passed.

Lessingham went out and shut the door behind him and stood alone with that garden and the summer night. Under stars of June he stood now, in an awareness like to that which once before he had known, upon that night of feasting in her Rialmar: as then before the pavane, a hardening of sensual reality and a blowing away of dreams. Only no hardness was in this lily-scented night: only some perfection; wherein house and slumbering garden and starry sky and the bower of radiance south-eastward where the moon, unseen, was barely risen behind Zenianthe's oak-woods, seemed now to flower into a beauty given them before all ever-lastingness. Slowly between sleeping flower-beds he walked to the eastern end of that garden and stood watching the top leaves of the oak-trees fill with the moon-rise. In the peace of it he remembered him of someone, not Campaspe, that had sat so a-nights upon heels before the fire, playing and talking and listening all at once: a strange accomplishment he thought now, and had thought so then: but as to speak of when, or who, the gentle night, as if it knew well but would not say the answer, held its peace in a slumbrousness of moon-dimmed stars.

He looked again at her windows. There, which had a minute before been empty, and no light within, he beheld her upon the balcony: facing the moon. From his place in the deep shade of a yew-tree, he watched her: Antiope: all in white. It was as if she stood upon no firm substance but on some water-wave, the most adored beauty that ever struck amazement in the world. Almost in disbelief, as if night had spoken, he heard her speak: 'You, my lord? Standing there?'

Slowly he came towards her. As spread out upon some deepening of the stillness and the blessedness, the long churr of a nightjar sounded near. It ended, purring down like the distant winding of a clock, into silence. 'I could not sleep,' he answered, under her window.

'Nor I,' said she. All being seemed now to draw to her, as lodestones to the lode-star, or to a whirlpool's placid centre the waters which swirl round it and their floating freight, both of the quick and of the dead.

'Nor you?' said Lessingham. 'What is here, to inquiet your mind?'

Her answer came as upon a catch in her breath: 'Deep waters, I think.'

The wistaria blossoms hung like heavy grape-bunches below her balcony: the limbs of the tree, lapped about and crushed in the grip of their own younger growths, showed gnarled and tortuous under the moon. 'I think,' Lessingham said, 'I am broken with the fall of such as climb too high.'

Again the nightjar trilled. Upon his left, sudden and silent it slipped from the branch where it had lain. He felt it circle about his head: heard the strange wild cry, Pht! Pht! saw it swoop and circle, its body upright as it flew, its wings, as it flew, uplifted like a great moth's that alights or like a bat's: heard the clap of its wings: heard Antiope's voice as in a dream, or as the summer night stirring in the wistaria's pendent blooms: 'There is a remedy: to climb higher.'

He took one step and stood quivering like a dagger struck into a table. 'Ha!' he said. 'If master but now, yet now am I waterweak.' Then in a sudden alteration, 'Tempt me not, madonna. In action I was ever a badger: where I do bite I will make my teeth meet.'

He heard her say, as a star should lean to the sea, 'What boots it me to be Queen? O think too,' her voice faded: '– howsoever they may seem chanceful – are yet by God.'

The swinging heavy blossoms, brushing his face and beard, blinded him as he came up. Standing before her in that balcony, looking down into her eyes that were unreadable in the warm and star-inwoven darkness, 'Who are you?' he said in a breath without voice. 'Sometimes I hardly know,' she said, leaning back as if in a giddiness against the window-frame, her hands holding her breast. 'Except there was a word,' she said, 'written inside a ring, HMETEPA – 'Las,' she said, 'I remembered; but it is gone.'

'And I remember,' said Lessingham. 'To say, *ours*: λμετέρα' you, ours: ημετέρα' of all things, ours: of you and me, beyond all chanceableness of fortune.' Sometimes so in deep summer will a sudden air from a lime-tree in flower lift the false changing curtain, and show again, for a brief moment, in unalterable present, some mountain top, some lamp-lighted porch, some lakeside mooring-place, some love-bed, where time, transubstantiate, towers to the eternities. ''Tis gone!' he said. 'But you' – her body in his arms was as the little crimple-petalled early-flowering iris that a rough breath can crush. He felt her hands behind his head: heard her say, in breaks, into his very lips, 'I cannot give you myself: I think I have no self. I can give you All.'

Through the wide-flung casements of Antiope's bedchamber in that wayside house came the golden-sandalled dawn: the sky gold, and without cloud, and the sun more golden than gold in the midst of it. The Queen said, at Lessingham's side, 'Thanks, my lord, I'll take my reins again.' As she gathered them, the thud of galloping hooves came down the whinflower-scented air behind them, and Tyarchus and Zenianthe, knee to knee, with Amaury thundering close upon their heels, swept round the turn from behind the screening birch-woods.

They were nearing Rialmar when Lessingham found means of speaking with her in private. It had been late afternoon when they turned homewards, and now, the autumn day closing in early, the sun was setting. On their right, two-horned Rialmar was lifted up dark and unassaultable against clouds that drifted down the west. The air was full of the crying of sea-mews. Southward, the wash of the sea answered from bay to bay. The blue smoke of houses and their twinking lamps showed about Rialmar town. Far as the eye could see from the eastern highlands round to Rialmar, the clouds were split level with the horizon. The dark lower layer was topped as if with breaking waves of a slate-dark purple, and in

the split the sky showed pink, golden, crimson, apple-green.
Above the clouds, a rosy flush thrilled the air of the western
heavens, even to the zenith, where the overarching beginnings of
night mixed it with dusk. The turf beneath them as they rode was
a dull grey green: the whinbushes and thornbushes black and
blurred. Lessingham looked at the Queen where she rode beside
him: the cast of her side-bended eye: the side of her face, Greek,
grave, unconscious of its own beautifulness. He said: 'I had a
dream.'

But she, with a kind of daybreak in her eyes very soberly looking
into his: 'I am not learned to understand these matters; but 'twas
not dreaming,' she said. 'I was there, my friend.'

XVI

THE VICAR AND BARGANAX

'THE DIVELLS QUILTED ANVELL' • APPREHENSIONS IN
KESSAREY • STORMS IN THE AIR • A FIEF FOR COUNT
MANDRICARD • 'BULL TREAD PANTHER'.

THE Vicar meanwhile, sitting in his closet alone with his cursed
dogs, upon the very morrow of Lessingham's setting out for
Rialmar, sent for Gabriel Flores. 'Take ink and pen: write.' Word
by word he gave it him, and, when it was written, scanned the
letters; signed them: certified them with his seal vicarial. The same
hour, he took a secret person, commanding him go with these to
the High Admiral, that lay with the fleet in Peraz Firth, and to the
Chancellor in Zayana. Another he sent to Kutarmish, to Earl Roder.
That done, he summoned Count Mandricard from Argyanna, and
Daiman, Thrasiline, and Rossilion from outparts of Rerek, and had
with them Arcastus besides, that was already at hand. With these
men, all five being creatures and instruments of his, and with
Gabriel, he for a full day till supper-time held talk in secret, showing
them of his mind so much as he deemed convenient.

Now came answers again from those three great commissionaries, not concerted, for they had had no time to confer together
upon them, yet as showing one common mind; which, plainly
stripped, was readiness indeed to meet with him, but not as cattle
with the lion in the lion's lair: not in Owldale. Upon this, having

considered with himself awhile, he despatched more letters, and first to Jeronimy in quality of regent of Outer Meszria, to the intent that he did, as earnest of his friendship and as not unfitting to the Admiral's charge and estate, give over and assign to him Kessarey castle and the township and lands thereof and all the roadstead harbour and sea-works of Kessarey, which, albeit within the March of Ulba, yet by its situation threw far into Meszria the shadow of its power; and now there let their conference be, in Kessarey instead of Owldale. And, for example of friendship, he would thither come with no more but a bodyguard; and upon such open and undoubtable terms of faith let them take counsel for the realm's good and their own.

To Kessarey then, about middle August, came these four: Beroald, Jeronimy, and Roder, with the Vicar. There was nought given out, that folk might have known what manner of fowl were hatched in these layings of heads together. The Chancellor, after a day or two, betook him home to Zayana: the Earl to Kutarmish: the Admiral settled him down in Kessarey with the fleet, and had good strength of men both for land and sea. They parted all with manifestations of affiance and regard, the Vicar proceeding now upon a progress through the March and Outer Meszria to take oaths of allegiance from towns and strongholds in those parts subject to the regent Jeronimy, like as he had taken them from the regent's self in Kessarey, for the acknowledging and receiving him as Vicar and Lord Protector, and owner of their fealty in peace and war. It went not unremarked that, whereas in the great King's day had forms and salutations upon like occasion been as unto the King's highness, and if through viceroys, commissionaries, or other, then but through them as middlers, and so expressed; yet now in this progress was all taken by the Vicar in person as unto himself, without all mention made of the Queen, principal and sovereign and fount of his authority. Which, furnishing with mischief such as will still be tale-bearers in matter capable of reward, came, upon such tongues, to the regent's ear in Kessarey. To such kind of talk Jeronimy listened open-eared but close-mouthed.

The Vicar, returning now to Laimak, caused Gabriel to write him a letter to Duke Barganax as sweetly and amiably as could be devised. To this, after not many days of waiting, the Duke answered as pleasantly again, excusing himself from bidding the Vicar to guest with him in Zayana (which, had it been offered, the Vicar would, for jealousy of his own safety, have upon no conditions been minded to accept), and proposing instead a meeting in the Salimat. There, being that it was the border betwixt Outer and South Meszria, he would about October ceremonially receive the Vicar and do homage to him, as vicegerent of the Queen, for the regency of South Meszria, by the Concordat of Ilkis upon such terms of suzerainty conferred upon the Duke.

Now autumn wore, and all quiet.

In the first days of November the Chancellor came north again. Upon an afternoon he with the Admiral walked the poop of the Admiral's ship royal, at anchor in Kessarey haven. It was a tempestuous and cloudy sky, with gulls hanging in the wind, and circling intercrossing flights of sea-swallows, and sometimes the passing of a line of gannets, strong-winged, keeping their line like ships, high through that windy grey tumult of wintry weather which swept in eastwards from the high seas without. Elbow to elbow those two lords paced, cloaked and hatted against the weather and in great sea-boots, keeping to the lee side for the wind sake and spindrift.

'In Owldale,' said the Admiral: 'Owldale. I said, you did not carry your friendship so far as accept that inviting to go to him in Owldale.'

'No. And yet that showed a certain nobility, to trust us here in Kessarey.'

'The measure of his trust is but the measure of his contempt.'

'For my part,' said Beroald, 'I will trust no man these days. Saving present company.'

They took another turn or two. Then said the Admiral: 'Truth is, I have it by kind to see clear and feel my power in a manner thus, with the tar smelling in my nostrils and with good oak planks

and salt water a-wash beneath my feet; never so ashore. Remember,'
he said, after a pause, "tis alway stab i' the dark with him. Attempt
'gainst Ercles in September, miscarried but by accident, even as
that 'gainst yourself last spring in Zayana.'

Beroald said, 'O I take my precautions.'

Jeronimy shot a sidelong look at him. 'And he is a layer of
baits.'

'Well?'

'Well: Sail Aninma.'

The Chancellor's lip curled. 'So your lordship knew of that? It
was propounded to me upon terms of secrecy, and indeed I urged
him keep it so. Yet in a ten days' time I found my lady sister knew
it, and had inspired the Duke and his mind incensed to have made
it matter of open quarrel with the Vicar. But he was not to be
moved: laughed at it: said I would never take it.'

'And I doubt said rightly so?'

'Such horses,' said the Chancellor, 'are not to be looked too
near in the mouth.'

'Perilous counsel. Consider Kessarey: it is good, but I am not
deceived. My lord, these things are writ big, in a manner, for our
instruction: that he, yes, as long since as August, I say, hath said
in his heart, "'Tis time now: all lets removed: now, in the happy
absence of this Lessingham, *divide et impera*." Why, the action
walketh apparent, smelleth so rank a perfume of supposed seduction the gorge clean sickens at it: holding out of himself to me
with such crude blandishments as disinterested noble guardian of
her highness' rights: blackening the Duke to me with such palpable
lies and wrestings of plain honest – Faugh!' he said, checking in
his walk; 'design is, gull and flatter us to the top of our bent: crush
the Duke: that done, crush us. The wind setteth where last May
it set; and 'tis that voyage over again: same lee shore, same weather,
same tide-race 'twixt skerry and skerry. With the Duke of our side,
and with right of our side – well; but, fail either condition – good
night! My lord Chancellor, forget not that.'

'I forget nothing,' said Beroald. 'I know the Duke. More, know
my sister.'

'And did your lordship foresee,' said the Admiral, 'upon that knowledge (as, by my soul, I think few else did), that patience and loyalty whereby he did last month do homage, meeting of him in the Salimat? 'Fore all the folk assembled acknowledging him and swearing fealty? Even to taking in that ceremony the Vicar's horse by the rein and humbly, while that other sat in the saddle puffed in his insolence, leading it north to south over the beck in token of submission? Did not that argue, in this loose age, a wonderful exampleless example of noble truth and word-keeping? But I say 'tis the blood determines it. Royal blood: and that will out.'

'It was the act,' answered the Lord Beroald, 'of a disciplined and law-abiding person.'

'Ha, and, for law-abiding, what of those late proceedings in my own vicariate, a month or so ere that? and of the Queen's highness no more mention made than had the vile murderer, by will deputed overseer of our estate, been crowned King and all?'

'That too,' said the Chancellor, 'is not to be forgot.'

'I wish,' the Admiral said, after a silence, 'your lordship would, in a manner, throw back flat this offer of Sail Aninma: might give him pause, where all till now hath swum too easy.'

'It handsomely becomes you, my lord Admiral, with Kessarey and the half of Meszria into your hand, to lesson me in self-sacrifice.'

'O take me not so thwart. You do know I mean not thus. More power to your hand, the better for us all. But this, a fief in South Meszria: 'tis stamp on Barganax's sore toe: 'tis wrongful, too, clean 'gainst the Concordat—'

'Not so fast,' said the Chancellor. 'Hath been matter of legal controversy these three generations and more, of the right status of Sail Aninma, whether of Meszria, whether a demesne apart and of itself. Do me so much right as not imagine I'd trespass one iota beyond the law.'

'Then let only policy determine, and effect upon the Duke, already tried near patience' ending. You have your own man holdeth Argyanna as governor, and that is key of south Rerek, like as Kutarmish is and Kessarey of the Meszrian Marches. So, and with

Roder in Kutarmish, and me in Kessarey – albeit Roder, I am
sometimes apt to doubt, useth a little too much security in feeding
on these morsels from the table of Laimak—'

'My good lord Admiral,' said the Chancellor, 'I do fear your
eye so vigilant bent on Laimak importeth your too much negligence
toward Zayana.'

They came to a stand. The High Admiral, leaning with his
elbows on the bulwark, clasping and unclasping his hands, gazed
landwards. 'Your lordship is known,' he said, 'for the flower of
legists in these days. And I applaud your politics. But remember,
my lord, neither to you is it given to see all and err never.'

The tide was running. Like white horses ridden at barriers, now
here now there all the sea-length of the mole, breakers plunged
and tossed mast-high in the wind manes of spray. The castle, built
of mighty blocks of sandstone mottled with lichen and sea-scurf,
stood bare and square upon the seaward point of the low long
shattered headland from which the mole, built of the like stone,
takes a sweep, first west and then south-about to the line of sker-
ries, giving so a sea-mile and more of sheltered water with good
anchorage and safe riding in all weathers. The ships of the fleet,
a score of them besides lesser craft and a few great carracks laden
with costly treasure of merchandise, lay outward from the Admiral's
that was anchored scarce three hundred paces from the land. And
now those two lords, looking shorewards so through that flurry
of wind, saw where an eight-oarer put out from the quay under
the seawall of the castle and began to row towards them. Swiftly
she rowed, as upon some urgency. 'Why,' said Jeronimy at length,
as she drew near, ''tis his grace's friend, young Barrian;' and made
ready to welcome him aboard.

When greetings were done and they three alone upon the poop,
'My lord Admiral,' said Barrian, 'I was directed to your excellence
upon matter runneth to danger. And 'tis more than common fortune
I should also a found your lordship,' (to the Chancellor); 'Medor
was sent to you, and some question where to find you. But, for
the business, 'tis shortest peruse this letter, that my lord the Duke
had but on Saturday evening from him we know on, out of Rerek.

No forgery: the signet is knowable; and trusty for bad, if less for good. And for what his grace accounteth of it, let its plight acquaint you: ripped up the middle like a pair of breeches.'

'Let's read it,' said the Admiral, fumbling for his perspective-glass. He and Beroald, holding it down upon the binnacle, read it together. 'Openeth very sweetly: the hand I know too (too well by now), that Gabriel Flores': unctuous sweet beginnings wont to steam up in the end into assafoetida. Ha, and there's the true whiff on't,' he said, scoring it with his thumb-nail: '"*Mandricard to be of Alzulma enfeoffed in fee simple.*" But, Alzulma? 'Tis in South Meszria, broad as barn doors: in by a dozen miles. Were I his grace, I'd answer: Good; and to pay back the courtesy, I've gi'en to my Lord Barrian here Mornagay, Storby, or Anguring itself. Nay, in sadness, 'twere fair comparison: he that sits in Alzulma can say who shall pass and who pass not by the Ruyar road from Rumala to Zayana; and his saying hath currency not in weak words, but in power and deed.'

They read to the end: '*And so, wishing God the Father glorious bee your conduct, given by vertue of al powres and liabilities enabling me thereunto both for mine owne Selfe and vicarially as Lord Protectoure for the Quens Highnes, HORIUS PARRY. In Laimac, thys VII daie of Novembre anno z.c. 777.*' And then the superscription: '*Unto hys Grace and Excellent Lordshipp Barganax, cawld Duke of Zayana, regent under Me Meszriae Australis. So obey and perform it. H.P.*'

The Chancellor, when he had read it, stood yet for a minute looking down on it, his brow a little clouded, the proud lineaments of his face a little colder drawn than of custom, with a tightening now and again about the lips especially and the wings of his nostrils. The Admiral smiled: a mirthless smile: then blew out his cheeks. 'This is bull tread panther, in a manner. Are we too late?'

'His grace,' answered Barrian, 'hath in this bay borne himself beyond example – not nobly: when was he less than noble? – but beyond example calm. And not for lack of egging on, neither; for I and his most friends think it better that men envy him than that he should stand at reward of their pity. But was in a most happy and merry vein when this news found him; and, the first rage over and past, sent thus to you, and to you, my lord Chancellor, to call upon you both in person now to mediate his peace with the Vicar; who if he give not back from this last proud mock, the whole realm must shortly squelter with bloody wars; for this thing his grace will not swallow but thrust it down the Vicar's throat again.'

The Admiral said, 'Pray him for all sakes use yet a little this noble patience. Tell him I'll come to him.'

'He bade me offer you this: a meeting-place halfway, in Peraz.'

'Five days from tomorrow,' replied the Admiral, 'that's on Wednesday, expect me in Peraz, there to confer with his grace upon best means to use.'

'Can I assure him,' asked Barrian, 'of your friendship? You will easily suppose, my lords, upon what an edge is all now poised in Zayana, and how much lieth on what I must report. "Tell them," he bade me (last words at parting), "tell them I'll play fair: but tell them, by the Gods in heaven, I'll not be played with."'

Jeronimy's eye waited on the Chancellor. The Chancellor said, 'The thing is flatly against the Concordat of Ilkis. I stand upon the law, upon that Concordat. Tell the Duke so, my lord, from me.'

The Admiral said, 'And the like from me, Lord Barrian.'

'Your excellences are to be thanked, then. But, being thus agreed, were't not fittest act? A little slacking may all our purposes let. Sudden, and we may end it.'

The Chancellor smiled. 'We offer him first the law,' he said; 'and not till that fail use open violence.'

'Ay. I have fallen down, ere this,' said the Admiral, 'in these civil broils; and that was always upon unripe heady action.' In the dog-like open honesty of his regard there came a twinkle as it rested on Barrian. 'And say to him, too, if he with his high-horsed frenzies o'erset the pot before we be met in Peraz, then am I free of my bond, to do as shall seem me fit.'

Barrian, a little damped, looked from one to the other, then gripped them by the hand in turn. 'I will begone back this very hour. Sleep in Ulba, thence by the Salimat: I can be in Zayana by Sunday evening. I pray you, my lord Admiral, fail not tryst.'

He being gone, 'When mean you to set forth for Peraz?' asked the Lord Beroald.

'Why, tomorrow, and leisurely by land, not to hazard delays in this rageous wind. Will not you come too? For 'twill need seamanship, in a manner, to handle him safely, under full sail as he is and with such young hare-brained counsellors as this, to blow him on the rocks.'

The Chancellor drew up his lips and smiled. 'If, with my own flesh and blood, my word could weigh as much as for my years it should,' said he, 'I'd instead through to Zayana. For there will she bewitch him with her beauty and dainty seductive talk till he is as wrought up as if to storm heaven, let pass Laimak, with the whirlwind inside him and flinging fiend of hell.'

XVII

THE RIDE TO KUTARMISH

PERAZ, AND FAIR SUNSHINING • A BLOODY ENCOUNTER •
THE ROSE-LEAF GALLERY IN ZAYANA • MEDOR AND
VANDERMAST • HER LADYSHIP SITS • FIRE-SHADOWS FROM
AN UNSEEN MOUTH • MEMISON MIDNIGHTS • 'WHEN SUCH
A MUTUAL PAIR' • PAPHIAN STILLNESS • OUR LADY OF
SAKES • BIS DAT QUAE TARDE • THE DUKE, ANVIL NO
MORE • THE VICAR WITHOUT AN ALLY.

DULY upon the set day was that meeting held in Peraz, of the
Duke, the Admiral, and the Chancellor. There all was accorded
as among sworn brethren; and so next day, farewell and they
parted, the Duke riding home by easy stages, the long way, by
Memison; Medor with him and a dozen of his gentlemen. In a
gay security he rode, all doubts removed now, seeing they had
sided in his behalf, Jeronimy and Beroald both, in face of this
last highblown overweening of the Vicar, in giving, thus wrong-
fully and within the Duke's dominions, of land and licence to
Count Mandricard.

The second day, about three of the afternoon, coming by the
highway round the slack of a hill where the road drops to the ford
a little beside the out-fields and muir-ground of Alzulma, they saw
where men on horseback came up from the river, and a big man
in red in the midst of them. Barganax drew rein. They were not

near enough to see faces. 'Were this Mandricard,' he said, 'come to take delivery, that were a jest.'

'Let us ride round,' said Medor, 'by the upper road. Your grace will not wish at this time to bandy words with them.'

'They are more than we,' the Duke replied. 'Whoever they be, I desire no speech of them, but by God, I will not turn out of the road for them.'

'This upper road is better going,' said Medor.

'You should a thought on that a minute sooner. If we turn now, and if here be Mandricard indeed, they will say we were afeared to meet with them.'

As they rode down, Medor said, 'I pray you yet remember but my lord Chancellor's words at parting, that your grace should wait well that you take not the law into your own hand: that, that provided, all should in a few weeks be carried to a conclusion conducible unto your most contentment and honour.'

The Duke laughed. 'Very well: 'tis commanded, no biting of thumbs. Untie your swords, but 'pon pain of outlawry, no man speak till I speak. We will let them go by and they will.'

So now they began to ride down to the ford; which when those others beheld, as though having seen it was the Duke and being willing to avoid a meeting, they turned out of the road and bare away northwards at a walking-pace towards Alzulma. But Barganax, knowing now the man in red for Mandricard, must needs, against all protestations, send a gentleman to ride after them and pray the Count turn back that they might have speech together apart from their folk. They waited now, watching the messenger overtake the other party, doff hat to Mandricard; then their talking, pointing, Mandricard as if refusing, the other pressing, Mandricard at length consenting, seeming to give command, turning his horse's head, and now riding with Barganax's man and a man of his own back towards the road. 'This is to tempt the fates,' said Medor. The Duke said, as merry as a magpie, ''Tis the most fortunate good hap: a heaven-sent chance to show him I know he is here within my borders, nosing about Alzulma: that I know he hath no right to be here: that I am so good and sober a prince as will, even being dared with such an insolency as this, proceed all by law and in nought by violence. Last, to show him I count him not worth a pease, neither him nor his master.'

'Stand ready, gentlemen,' said Medor, as the Duke rode away. 'When his heart is set thus upon a merry pin, no staying him. But stand ready, see what they will do.'

The Duke when they were met bade him good morrow. 'I had not heard your lordship was doing us this honour to be our guest in the south here.'

Mandricard answered and said, 'This meeting, my lord Duke, may save us both some pains. His highness, I am informed, hath acquainted you of his intentions as touching me. I have here,' and he drew out a parchment, 'licence to have and hold this manor of Alzulma by grand sergeanty. See it, and you like: "letters of legitimation made to the said Mandricard": 'tis sure and no question. Brief, I am here to overlook the place, and 'tis for you to give order the keys be now made over to me.'

'We are indeed well met,' said the Duke; 'and I can save your pains. The thing you hold in your hand, my lord, you may tear up: it is not worth the parchment 'tis writ upon. The manor is mine, fiefed in the tail, and I'm sorry I have no mind to give it you.'

'That will help never a dell,' replied he. 'The Vicar gave it me, and bade me take it up too.' He spat on the ground and glowered in a dull insolency at Barganax.

'I am nowise bounden,' said Barganax coldly, 'to reason with his highness' servants on things that concern but me and him, well agreed as we are together, and our agreement resteth upon law. Yet, to end the matter, know that, in refusing of Alzulma to your lordship, I stand upon the law, and as read by my lord High Chancellor.'

Mandricard gave him a sour look and sat there spitting and spawling. 'Well, fare you well,' said the Duke. 'And since your lordship is not a particular friend of mine and hath besides no business here, save which is alleged by us not loisible by the treaty, I will desire you to begone north again as soon as may be.'

'May be I shall find a mean to stay i' the south here.'

'You stay then at your peril. Bethink you that you are now in Meszria: trust not here in the shadow of Laimak.'

'I know my liripoop without coming here to learn it,' said Mandricard as the Duke began to move off.

Barganax turned in his saddle and drew rein. 'And learn,' he said, 'to do after another fashion than to be thus malapertly cocking and billing with me that am your better.'

Mandricard gave him a buggish word. Barganax's sword leapt from the scabbard, his face dark as blood. 'Fief in the tail?' said Mandricard as he drew. 'That's bungerly law, damn me else: to the bastard of Zayana!'

'Dismount and to it,' said the Duke. 'You are renowned to me as profoundly seen in all arts of sword-play, else would I scorn to measure swords with such a buzzardly beast.'

They dismounted and went to it, *stoccata, mandritta, imbroccata*. The Duke's foot, sliding upon a stone, let Mandricard through his guard: a flesh-wound in the muscles of his sword-arm above the elbow. They stopped to bind it and stay the bleeding. His gentlemen prayed him give over now, but, as if the hurt did but exasperate his wildness and fierceness, the Duke stood forth again, his sword in his left hand.

'Have, here it is then,' said Mandricard, feeling his enemy's mettle in his sword as the blades engaged, controlled one another, ground together: 'it were alms you were dead. I'll spitchcock you.' At the third venue Barganax with his unforeseen sudden deadly *montanto* ended the passage, sending his sword through Mandricard's throat-bole.

Upon a Thursday of mid-December, five weeks after these things, Count Medor, with letters in his hand, waited in the long gallery under the west tower of Acrozayana, expecting in a hot impatience audience with the Duke. The southern sealand Meszrian air, that even at Yule-time has not laid by all its summer burden, came and went through deep-mullioned sashed windows, twelve upon either hand, the length of that gallery. Rosalura, in a window-seat midway down the western side, reading her book, laid it again in her lap at whiles to look out upon the prospect: bare tree-tops of the gardens below, and beyond these Zayana lake, its face altering always between glassy expanse and patches where the wind flawed it, and beyond it the woods and ridges folded about Memison. All was white in that gallery, walls and floor and ceiling and marble frieze. Under the western windows the sun began to make patterns on the floor; through the eastern windows all was of a cold grey quietness, of the storeyed pillars of the inner court, stone balconies, and long roof-line level against the sky. 'And yet best of all in summer,' she said, touching hands with Medor as he paused beside her seat: 'when we have rose-leaves scattered in drifts over the floor, and cool airs to stir them even in sultriest weather.'

To and fro from door to door, Doctor Vandermast walked under the windows, passing at every third footpace from sun to shadow and so to sun again. 'Four o'clock?' said Medor; 'and it is now but two?'

'It was upon strictest command.'

'If you knew but the urgency! Will you not go through the ante-room, knock at the door? For indeed, the fury of his grace when he shall know we let it wait may jeopard us worse than should we, as upon necessity, brave him in pure loyalty to disobey him.'

'Is it matter of life and death? Or if not, shall two hours make it so? Or if, can two hours, so taken by anticipation and well plied, unmake it?'

Medor snapped his fingers.

'My Lady Fiorinda,' said the learned doctor, 'is but yesterday come to court. 'Tis his grace's pleasure this whole morning and till four of the afternoon to have her to himself several, painting of her likeness. Your lordship well knows that, upon such orders given, it is lawful neither for us nor no man else to prescribe or measure them in his behalf.'

'Well,' said Medor, taking impatiently a turn or two, 'it is greatness in him: under such red and louring skies, while he waits on action, to be able to lay all by, recreate himself with swimming, tennis, painting; not sit melancholy watching for levin-bolts that, fall they or fall not, 'tis no longer in his dispensation.

'Well?' after a minute. 'Are you not impatient for my news? It is at least news, when he shall hear it, to rouse and raise him from out this lethal security.'

'Impatience,' replied Vandermast, 'is a toy of great men, but in men of mean estate a distemper. For my particular, considering how now my age draweth to its latter term, I have long eschewed impatience. And for news of so much import, not to my safe ear even could I with conscience receive or you with conscience tell it, till it be told to the Duke.'

Medor looked at him. 'Signior Vandermast, wholesomely have you lessoned me. Were all his mouth-friends of like temper – fie on turntippets that turn with the world and will keep their office still! Yes, you are wise: haste is our mischief. Had he but ridden somewhat slowlier home from Peraz, 'pon the morrow of that good meeting a month ago, when all was fair weather—'

Vandermast smiled, standing in the window and surveying thence, with hands clasped behind his back, chin raised, eyes half closed, the sunny vault of the sky, the lake spreading to shimmering distances. 'Yet was this Mandricard,' said he, 'a bob which should in time have been a beetle, had the Duke not set heel on him. And yet, when destiny calleth on the event; tread down one such creeping instrument as this was, what is it but to suffer, by that very deed, another to go by that shall ascend up in due time to implement the purpose? These advertisements you have now in your mouth to speak to his grace, are they not an exemplification to approve it? No, Medor, it is a demonstrable conclusion that in haste is not our mischief, but in the commixtion rather and the opposition of divers attempts and policies, working all according to that law whereby *unaquoeque res, quantum in se est, in suo esse perseverare conatur*: everything which is, in as much as it hath being, striveth still to continue in its own proper being and so persist. "That excellent correspondence" (saith the philosopher) "which is between God's revealed will and His secret will, is not legible to the natural man." I concede, had you ridden leisurely from Peraz, Mandricard belike had been gone when you came below Alzulma. But had you, contrariwise, galloped, a league or so ere your coming down, then had you been past and away ere he came thither. Had the Vicar been honest – Why, I can unwind you hypothetical probabilities and conjectures till your brain spin round, but to what purpose? For always the event is thus and not (as might have been) thus.'

Medor laughed. Then, serious again, 'Ah,' said he, 'howe'er you wind it, mischief is that bloody fact, when by forbearance we should a stood in the right with all men. Might you but know the tangle now—'

'To pass away the time,' said the doctor, drawing chairs to a table between windows, 'I'll to chess with you. And, to inspire a fine peril in the gambit, we'll drink old wine.' Medor set out the ivory men, while Doctor Vandermast from an old Athenian amphora poured out into goblets of cut crystal. He filled them but to the half, the better to let him that should drink of it savour the fragrancy of that wine, clinging to the goblets' sides. The first cup the doctor brought to the Countess, but she gently refused it. 'This wine,' said he, sitting now to the chessboard and pledging Medor, 'may, as I have sometimes conceited, be somewhat in kind with that which is caroused away upon high marriage nights among the Gods, when the bride is laid and the epithalamion sung, and the blessed wedding-guests, going upon the golden floor, eat and drink and renew their hearts and minds with wine not all unlike to this.'

'And while they walk,' said Medor, breathing in the heady perfume from his cup, 'imagining some portentous birth?'

'Yes,' said that aged man, touching the wine with his lips, then lifting it to gaze through against the sunlight:

> 'The prophetic soul
> Of the wide world dreaming on things to come.'

Within, beyond the ante-chamber and beyond inner doors which, even were it against him their captain, Medor's own guardsmen barred, Duke Barganax now laid down his brush. Wrapped, as in a toga with right arm and shoulder bare, in a voluminous flowing gown of silk brocade of a creamy dun colour and edged with black fur, he sat back now in a deep chair. Before him, on the easel, was the beginnings of his picture: from it to her, from her to it, and so back again, his eye swung restlessly and as if unsatisfied.

'γλυκύπικρον ἀμάχανον ὄρπετον – You,' he said. '*Bitter-sweet*. You are that.'

She, bare from the waist upwards, lying on her face upon cushions of a white silken couch under the cool light of the north window, rested on folded arms, her back and shoulders flowering so, in a sleek-petalled warm paleness as of old ivory, from the dark calyx of her skirt of black silk spangled lace. From armpit to elbow her right arm, folded upon itself, swept its immaculate line. Above the lazy weight of it, midway of the upper curve, about the biceps, her nose rested daintily ruminant. From beneath the armpit, as four serpents from some vine-shadowed lair of darkness should lay out their necks to feel the day, the fingers showed of her left hand bearing the soft lustre, starred about with a circle of little emeralds, of a honey-coloured cat's-eye cymophane. Her mouth was hidden. Only her eyes, showing their whites, looked out at him sideways. 'Yes,' she said. 'I am that.'

'γλυκύπικρον,' he said, under his breath: then suddenly scowled, as if upon the motion to destroy his work.

'"*Post*"—' she said: 'in what musty book was that written? —"*omne animal triste*".'

'It was written,' replied he, 'in the book of lies.'

As in the quivering of a dragonfly's sapphired flight across the tail of a man's vision, under the down-weighing intolerable heat of a cloudless summer noonday, hither and back betwixt them the halcyon glance leapt, overtaking all befores and afters. The Duke rose, went to the table in the window upon his left, opened drawers, took out needles and a copper plate: came back to his seat.

'You have resolved then against chryselephantine work? Each hair?' she said, out of that unseen mouth. 'Wisely so, I should say.'

He pushed aside the easel. 'Why do I make away at last every picture I paint of you?'

'How can I tell? Easier destroy than finish, may be? A harder question: why paint them? Having the original.' Lights moved in her green eyes like the moving lights on a river.

'Can you be still – so, a minute? Perhaps,' he said, after a silence, 'perhaps I try to know the original.' Chin in hand, elbow on knee, in the tenseness of a panther crouched, he watched her.

'To know?' said she, out of the long stillness. 'Is it possible (if you will credit Doctor Vandermast) to know, save that which is dead?'

Barganax, as if body and mind were enslaved to that sole faculty of vision, did not stir. After a while, his face relaxed: 'Vandermast? Pah! He spoke but of dead knowledge. Not my way of knowing.'

'And you will know me, when, in your way of knowing? Today? In a week? Next hawthorn time?'

'Never.'

'O, it seems then, this knowing of me is as your painting of me: as Tom o' Bedlam, would warm a slab of ice with his candle to make him a hot plate to hold his supper?'

'That which can be done, 'twas never worth the doing.'

'Attempt is all,' she said.

With the overtones of a new music that cast firefly gleams across the darkness of her voice, 'You have much changed your former carriage: become strangely a harper of one string,' she said, 'this last year or two. Before, they tell me, there might not one of our sect come here to court that, unless she were a very owl or an urchin for ill favour—'

'Tittle-tattle,' said the Duke.

'O, some of their private, lavish, and bold discourses. That you bearded at fifteen: is that true?'

He lifted an eyebrow: 'It pricketh betimes that will be a good thorn.'

'Let me but fantasy myself,' said she, 'in your skin. Nay then, 'tis certain. I should say to myself, "Well, she is very well, high-witted Fiorinda. But – there be others." And yet? And why? It is a mystery: I cannot attain to it. See but Rosalura, left in your way as harmless as a might lodge his wife in some seminary. Though, to give you your due,' she said, caressing delicately with the tip of her nose the smooth skin of her arm and returning so to her just pose again, 'you were never a hunter in other men's preserves. Save but once, indeed,' she said, browsing again in that lily-field. 'And indeed I count not that, being that it was neither preserve there, nor—' She fell silent.

Barganax caught her eye and smiled. 'Set a candle in the sunshine,' he said.

'A courtly instance, but not new. Nay, I will have you tell me, why?'

'Pew!' he said: 'a thing so plain as it needs no proof.' He took up the plate as though to begin drawing, then slowly laid it down again. 'Let me fantasy myself in your skin,' he said, his eyes still picture-finding. '"This Duke," I should say, "is one who, as in that song of mine, desireth,

> 'por la bele étoile avoir
> k'il voit haut et cler seoir.

'"And, to show I have that same star, if I chose to give it, while others kiss with lip I'll give the cheek."'

'To say, which is what I do? Ungrateful!'

'May be my ingratitude and your ladyship's parsimony—'

'O monstrous! And today, of all days!'

After a pause, 'And I too,' she said, 'have strangely changed my fashions, since you eased me of that: cut off my train and all. Pity, since the Devil's servants must serve now without their casualties. Singular in me, that herebefore was almost a generalist in that regard. And yet,' she said disdainishly, 'not so singular; if to be given in wedlock, young, twice, to so and so, through policy. To spit in the mouth of a dog is not indecorous for a lady, and grateful too to the dog.'

Like the shimmer of the sun on water, some reflection of her talk played about Barganax's eyes the while they studied her from under his faun-like eyebrows, as if he would burn first into his perception the elusive simplicities of that wherein the changing

stings and perfumes and unseizable shapes and colours of her mind
had their roots and being.

'Your royal father, too,' she said, '(upon whom be peace), was
a picker of ladies. Was it not his eye chose out my late lord for
the lieutenancy of Reisma? And, that done, enforced the Duchess
your mother, 'gainst all good argument she found to the contrary
(for I was never in her books), receive me as one of her ladies of
the bedchamber in Memison? Without which chance, I and you,
may be, ne'er had met. Three years since. I was nineteen; you, I
suppose, two and twenty.'

'These things,' said the Duke, 'wait not upon chance.'

There was a long silence. Then, 'You took little liking for me,
I think, at first meeting,' said she: 'upon the out-terraces of her
grace's summer palace: midsummer night between the last dances,
after midnight: I on his arm: you with Melates, walking the terrace
by moonlight and meeting us at each return. And I but the tenth
week married then.' She fell silent. 'And his breaking away (you
looked round and saw it), and running to the parapet as if to
vault over it into the moat? And your saying to him, jesting, as
we met at the next return, you were glad he had thought better
of it, not drowned himself after all? And his laughing and saying,
"If you did but know, my lord Duke, what I was a-thinking on
in that moment!" You remember?'

'And I will tell you a thing,' said Barganax: 'that when we were
gone by, I told Melates what, as I had ne'er a doubt, the man had
in truth been thinking on.'

'Well, and I,' said she, 'will tell you: that I read that easy guess
in your grace's eyes. But this you did not guess: what I was
a-thinking on. For besides,' she said, 'my eyes are my servants:
train-bearers but no talebearers.'

All the time the Duke's gaze was busied upon that unravelling
quest amid many threads of knowledge and outward seeming. As
if the memory of the words had risen like a slow bubble out of
the marish waters of his meditation, his lips, while his eyes were
busy, played now with that old sonnet which carries, even to the
written page, the note of the lyre that shook Mitylene:

'Fra bank to bank, fra wood to wood I rin,
    Ourhailit with my feeble fantasie;
    Like til a leaf that fallis from a tree,
Or til a reed ourblawin with the win.

Twa Gods guides me: the ane of tham is blin,
    Yea and a bairn brocht up in vanitie;
    The next a Wife ingenrit of the sea,
And lichter nor a dauphin with her fin.

Unhappy is the man for evermair
That tills the sand and sawis in the air;
    But twice unhappier is he, I lairn,
That feidis in his hairt a mad desire,
And follows on a woman throw the fire,
    Led by a blind and teachit by a bairn.'

Their eyes met, a merry, humorous, feasting look. 'You are
forgetting the good there is in change, I think,' she said after a
silence. 'For my own part, I incline much to fair hair in women.
Anthea, for instance.'

The Duke winced.

'I am resolved: good: dye my hair yellow.'

'If you dared but even do your hair any way else but my ways—'
he spoke slowly, as lost in a contemplation, his mind on drawing,
not on his words.

'So, then I'll cut it off,' said she.

His feeding gaze seemed to grow keener. He said on his breath,
'I'd kill you.'

'I should make you some sport ere that,' said the lady, her
mouth still hidden behind the lily smoothness of that indolent
arm. 'Have you forgot our first assay, laying aside of ceremonies,
a month after that first meeting, three years ago next summer? I
showed you then, my friend: bit a piece of flesh off your bones.'

'Two minutes, my heart-dear!' He suddenly fell to drawing, line
by line in swift and firm decision. There was a stillness upon that

lady, while line after line traced, true and aware, its predestined furrow on the polished copper, like the stillness of a sunshine evening upon some lake in which mountain and wood and sky hang mirrored in reverse, and nothing moves save (may be with the settlings of little winged creatures) the dancing gleams, one here, one there, seven or eight at a time, of liquid golden stars coming and going upon that glassy water.

The Duke sprang up: went to the table to rub lampblack into the lines. When he turned again, she had put on again her bodice, as it were a sleeved mail-coat made of thousands of tiny orient pearls, close fitting like a glove, and sat with her back towards him, upright on the couch. He stood for a minute looking at his drawing, then came and sat down behind her, holding the plate for both to see it. The clock struck three.

'As for painting, that was a true word you said that night to Lessingham.'

'To Lessingham?' she said.

'For a lover: hard to paint the thing which is.'

'O I remember: by the dream-stone.'

'The One, that I still was a-hunting of in the Many, till your day; and now the Many in you.' Her face was sideways towards him, looking at the dry-point. Her eyes were become Medusaean and, in its repose, her mouth snakish and cruel. 'Paintings,' he said: 'all trash. They give me but a barren One out of your Many, and never your One that breeds those Many, as the sun breeds colours.'

'But this is better, you think?'

'It is beyond comparison better; and my best.'

'Of that which changeth ever, and yet, changeth not?'

That lady's voice took on yet another quality of wonder, as if into the sun-warmed, cud-chewing, indolence of it were distilled all the warring elements of her divinity: fanged peril couched amid blood-red peonies: green of seawater, still and deep, above a bottom of white shell sand, or the lights in lionesses' eyes: the waved blackness of the Stygian flood in the ferrying across of some soul of sweetness untimely dead: coal, snow, moonlight, the light of burning cities, eclipse, prodigious comets, the benediction of the evening star; and behind these things, a presence as of some darkness that waited, awake, shawled, and still: gravid with things past and half remembered, and things present yet not apprehended well, and with things to come: or, may be, not to come, swaying betwixt birth and the unbeing of the void.

'Of manifoldness: yes,' said he, after a minute. 'But of your Oneness, a shadow only: Persephone beneath the sod.'

She considered the picture again. 'You have my mouth there, I see?'

'Ah, you can see that? Though your arm hides it?'

'You have it in the eyes, and in the fingers.'

'I am glad,' said he: 'for I meant it so.'

'It came of itself I should say. I set much by mouths: especially my own.'

He stood up, laid the plate on the table, turned and stood looking at her. '*Omne animal triste?*' she said, the devil of provocation viperine in her mouth's corner.

'I told you that was a lie,' Barganax said, his eyes on hers. She settled back a little, sitting there facing him, and her eyes seemed to grow darker and larger. 'It were not for every man's comfort,' he said: 'mate with you: a swan swimming with her wings expansed, then, whip, in a moment mew that white outward skin, soar against the sun, bring out your pounces, fly at fools and kill too. Nor for every man's capacity.'

'And yet you will still be picture-making.'

'O it is well,' he said: 'well that eagles do mate together: other else—'

'Other else,' said she, 'must Fiorinda have led apes in hell? Or, worse, lived housewife in Reisma? Well, I like that a man should high himself even thus insufferably, so he have the pith to maintain it.'

The Duke came a step towards her. 'There is no middle way with you,' he said: 'you are all night and day: dazzling night and intolerable day.'

'And roses.' It was as if not she but the very stillness of her mouth had spoken. 'Some red, some pink-colour.'

'And eyes that are the sea. I drown in them,' he said upon a sudden intake of the breath. 'When I kiss you, it is as if a lioness sucked my tongue.'

She leaned back with hands clasped behind her head, Valkyrie breasts breathing under that pearl-woven byrny, and above it her throat's lithe splendour and strength. 'Seas are for who can swim,' she said, and a sweeping of lyres was in the lazy voice of her. 'White noon is for the eagle to kindle his eyes upon: the sweetness of the red rose is to be weighed down upon, to be crushed, to be scented: the wonder of darkness is lest you should despair and, numbering perfections, say, It is the sum: it is all. For am not I all, my friend? I am more than all. And when all is told and numbered and multiplied and told over again, I say to you, In my darknesses I have more. Come. Prove it again. Come.'

Upon the chimes of four Doctor Vandermast knocked at the topaz-studded cedar doors of the painting-room and entered to the Duke's 'Come in.' The Duke, wearing no more that brocaded fur-purfled gown, but fully dressed in doublet, ruff, and hose, apprised of Medor's importunities for audience, went out to him in the gallery. The Lady Fiorinda, yet in some disarray and with her hair unbound, reclined upon the couch fanning herself with a fan of white peacock feathers twined with silver wires and set with apple-green chrysoprases in the ribs.

'Small advance, it is to be feared,' she said as Vandermast surveyed the picture on the easel. 'But what will you have, if two hours must be expended but in settling of my pose?' There stirred in the accents of her speech a self-mocking, self-preening, sleepy grace which, to the attentive and philosophic ear, carried some note of that silver laughter that the ageless remembering waters yet dream of, foaming disconsolate in Paphian sea-shallows.

The doctor smiled, looking on the painting but half begun; then, seeing the dry-point on the table, took it up and considered it awhile in silence. 'I judge from this,' he said at last, 'that your ladyship has been teaching some lessons in philosophy. It is better.

Nay, confine it but within its limit of purpose defined and propounded for it, there is no more to do: it is perfect.'

'You will say "Othello's occupation's gone", then? A melancholy conclusion.'

'I will not say that, save after your ladyship,' answered that learned man.

'Well, you must do maid-service first (these ill-appointed ways we live in): bring me the looking-glass to do my hair. Thanks, reverend sir;' she sat up, putting off in an instant her grace of languorous ease for a grace of wakefulness and speed of action, with deft sure fingers pinning into a formal court elegance her hair's braided lovelinesses, night-black, smooth-waved, with blue gleams where the light struck, like the steel-blue gleaming of certain stars, as of Vega in a moonless night in autumn. Her hands yet busied upon a last pranking of her ruff, she turned to meet Barganax's face as he strode into that room like a man that contains within his breast the whirlwind. Medor, with flushed countenance, followed at his heel.

'Here's news, and hell's fires in the tail of it,' said the Duke, making with great strides towards the window and flinging himself down in his chair. 'The hennardly knaves: yes, I mean your strutting stately brother, madam, with's prims and provisoes,' he said, rocking from side to side: 'he hath accepted Sail Aninma bestowed of him by the thundering tyrant, slick as was Mandricard to take Alzulma 'pon like offer. And Jeronimy with's cringing in the hams, licking the hand of the king-killer: if there be a badder man than that Beroald 'tis this back-starting Admiral with his thin wispy beard, ever eats with the jackals and weeps with the shepherd: now sworn new entire allegiance and obedience: given out all's o'er 'twixt them and me, our late confirmed league, 'cause of slaying of Mandricard. Damn them! After a month's digesting of it, now the meat bolketh up again. Damn them!' he said, springing up and stalking, like a beast caged, about the room: 'they're all habs and nabs, foul means or fair: hearts in their hose when they catch a breath from Rerek. I almost enrage!' He caught Fiorinda's eye. 'Well, will not your ladyship go join your brother in Sail Aninma?

Will you not be i' the fashion, all of you, and down with me now
I'm going?'

Fiorinda, in a statuesque immobility, followed him with her
gaze. 'What means your grace to do now?' she asked. 'Paint, and
let the wide world wind?'

The Duke checked and swung round upon her as if bitten. Little
comfort there was in that lady's eye or in the stony curve of her
lip. Yet as he looked upon her, meeting stare with outfacing stare,
it was as if, like fiery molten metal in a furnace, his rage ran into
some mould and cooling took shape and purpose. His jaw set.
His eyes, leaving their flashes, burned steady into hers. Then there
came upon all his pose and carriage that easy magnificence which
best became him; and in his voice that was right antiphone for
hers, bantering, careless, proud, 'I'll tell you,' he said: 'secret, within
these walls,' and he looked round upon Medor and Vandermast.
'Within three days I'll be man or mouse.'

With a feline elegance the Lady Fiorinda rose, gathering with
one white hand, not to trail them on the floor, the black shimmering flounces of her skirt, and walked to the window. There
she stood, one knee upon the window-seat, her back to the room;
but the Duke's eyes, as the mariner's on the cynosure amid flying
cloud-rack, were fixed on her.

'Medor,' he said, 'you are both a count of Meszria and captain
of my bodyguard. You must now for a while be my lieutenant and
commissioner of my dukedom in the south here, to do all in my
name: what, I shall speedily command you. Write out the commission, Vandermast: I'll sign it. For you, Medor, you are to muster
up an army suddenly: Melates, Zapheles, every lord i' the south
here. High master in Meszria I yet will be. But it must be suddener
than move an army: take the prey with a jolly quickness, before,
like water cut with a sword, they have time to join together again.
Roder holds Kutarmish: by the carriage away of that, all the
defenced places of Outer Meszria, and may be o' the March too,
will without resistance be yielded. This then sooner of my own self
than by any other middlers. I'll take with me Dioneo, Bernabo,
Ansaldo, him o' the wall-eye – Friscobaldo, Fontinell: choose me

out the rest: twenty-five of the most outrageousest beseen and likely men we have in the guard. I'll ride tomorrow.'

'Twenty-five men?' said Medor. 'Are you out of your princely wits?'

'If the gear cotton, I need no more men for this dust. If not, more were useless.'

Medor laughed bitterly. 'Falleth not for me to question your grace's orders. But if you are thus resolute to cast your life away, let mine be in the cast too; for indeed I care not for it a pudding-prick if you miscarry.'

'No, Medor. If I must be had by the back, you shall avenge me. But I know at my fingers' ends what kind of men are in that city. I do esteem this a sport.' His eyes met Vandermast's. Surely the eyes of that old man were become as the thin pure radiance that suffuses the starless heavens eastward before the sun-spring of a windless dawn. Fiorinda turned. She held her head high, like a leopardess that scents the wind. 'I have been anvil long enough,' said the Duke: 'I will now be hammer. Let all be made ready; for I've bethought me, I'll not stay for tomorrow: I'll ride tonight. 'And now, give us leave.'

When they were alone there fell a stillness. At last Barganax spoke: 'So runneth the hare then. Well? And if it be farewell?' She reached out a jewelled hand: he took it in his, bowed over it, raised it to his lips, then, as with a sudden flaming of the blood, began to run with hungry kisses from palm to wrist, from wrist upwards, pushing back the sleeve till he reached the tender inner bend of the elbow, then with a stride forward seized her to him. 'No,' she said, withholding her mouth. 'When you come back.'

'That may be never.' He mastered her, but her lips were lifeless under his kisses: all her body stiff and hard and unkind. 'Was there ever such a venomous tyrant?' he said, letting her go at last. 'All ice. And you have turned me to ice too.'

'You are rightly served,' replied she, 'for being a glutton. The fuller fed, the greedier. This livelong morning: then more this afternoon. Well, marry Myrrha, then, or Pantasilea: some obedient commodity to all your bidding. Me you shall not have o' these terms.' Leaning against the door-jamb, her hand upon the crystal knob, she watched him from under a drooped curtain of long black eyelashes while, like summer lightnings, there played about the dear beauties of hand and neck and cheek, and about the sweep of frills and ruffles and many-pleated gauzinesses of her skirt, glints of fang or claw. 'Indeed,' she said, 'I know not why my girdle should still be at your command. Unless if it be that in you too,' she said, 'for all your idle plaguy ways, there is no sit still, no rest, nothing predicable. And because of that:' she suddenly paused upon a miraculous softening of every line and contour; a breath, like the sudden filling of a sail, lifting the Grecian curve of her breasts; a slowing, as if it were honey with the bee's sting lost in it, of her voice; a quivering of eyelids; an exhalation of intoxicating sweets, zephyr-like, like dark roses, in all the air about her: 'because of that – I love you.'

Upon which most heavenly farewell, eluding a kiss or any touch or caress, she was gone.

Barganax rode that same night. He sent up word to his mother in Memison castle as he passed next day that he intended a week's hunting of oryx and bears in the Huruns. So fast he rode that by Saturday midnight he was come up to Rumala. Here he rested horses and men till late evening of Sunday, and so at dusk came down the Curtain. They rode all night, avoiding the highway, and a mile or so south of Kutarmish, in a beech-wood of the spreading hills, waited for dawn. Twenty men, by driblets of twos and threes, he sent ahead to be ready outside the gates. At dawn the gates were opened, and there began to be coming and going of the day's traffic. The Duke with his five rode up openly; they had blue osset cloaks and common country bonnets to dissemble their warlike gear and quality. As they drew near the gates, those twenty joined them. In a moment they killed the guards and rode briskly into the town to Roder's house. Roder was upon coming forth with some men, and had but at the very instant swung himself into the saddle. Few folk were abroad, it being thus early, and the Duke and his fared swiftlier than the hue and cry at their heels. He took

Roder by the hand: 'How fares it this morning with your excellence?' In his left hand he held a dagger, well placed, to let Roder's bare skin feel the prick of it through his doublet, while the Duke might feel through the pommel in his hand the leaping of Roder's heart. The face of Roder turned dark as blood, then grey like well-thumbed parchment. His jaw fell, and he sat still as a mouse, with dull blood-shotten bull's eyes staring at the Duke. About the two of them the Duke's men, swiftly casting off their cloaks, had made a circle, facing outwards with drawn swords. People now ran together from the houses, these in the street screeching out to those within who burst forth in heaps. 'If you love your heal, be sudden,' said the Duke, 'and proclaim me. Here is your argument: hath a sharp point and a tart. If 'tis die and go to hell now, be certain you, my lord, shall in the entrance of this massacre be murdered: I'll send you first, show me the path. If not, sudden, while you may.'

'I am your grace's man,' said the Earl then out of a dry throat, 'whatsoe'er my mouth have jangled. Aware, fellows,' he shouted, 'and stand a-room: blow up your trumpets that every man of good will shall stand 'pon his allegiance to the lord Duke of Zayana, for whose behalf I have hold this city and do him right so.'

The Duke commanded him, 'Proclaim me Vicar of the Queen in Meszria.' They blew up the trumpets and so proclaimed him.

By evening was all quiet in the town, and the Duke's power well seated. For they of his faction, that had fared this while with hidden head while Roder held it for the Vicar, came forth upon his proclamation and set upon those of the other party. These turmoils the Duke put down with a heavy hand without fear or favour, using the soldiers, to the number of four or five hundred, that Roder held the town with: not of his own private following, but of the royal army established in the south these many years, from whom the Duke took oath of allegiance now in the Queen's name, they accepting him sooner than accept the Vicar, after this autumn's doings, as upholder of the house of Fingiswold. But the Vicar was proclaimed by trumpet up and down the town as traitor, usurper, and king-killer, that every loyal subject should refuse and reject him and receive instead, as Lord Protector and Vicegerent for the Queen, the Duke of Zayana. And now as the day wore, and men grew bolder, they of the town began to come with whole cart-loads of complaints and grievances against Roder, petitioning the Duke to deliver him up, either else punish him himself. Barganax, finding that Roder could not bungle up but a very poor answer to these complaints; finding besides, upon seizure of the Earl's papers, plain proofs of wicked devices devised by him with the Vicar, upon price of Kutarmish, for invasion of Meszria contrary to the Concordat, and a plot drawn to murder the Duke; considering too how (and that by proof of documents) they had hatched up such bloody practices since October even and that meeting in the Salimat; accordingly next morning let lead out Roder into the market-place and there, with these proofs exposed and a man to cry them, take off his head. By which example of severity, as well as by his yesterday's insulting wild fierce and unaffrighted quick seizing of the town with so little a band of high-resolved men, men's minds were wonderfully sobered, to beware how they should make themselves as of a faction or party against him, or think to play bobfool with him.

He sent now, by chosen safe hands of men that rode with him from Zayana, to the princes in the north, Ercles and Aramond, requiring them of aid and upholding. Letters he likewise sent to Jeronimy and Beroald, in measured terms blaming them for friends unfast, and counselling them now repent and back him, rather than, for one high act by him upon bitter provocation done, forswear themselves and, to such scorned purpose, be tools for the Vicar.

And now was he within a little, while he hoped to catch a gudgeon, to have drawn up a pike. For upon the twentieth of December, being but the second day after that thunder-bounce in Kutarmish, the Vicar himself chanced to come down thither with two companies of horse, having there his secret war-chest and much treasure and muniments both of weapons and horses and other things necessary for his design of Zayana; and was come well nigh within hail of the town, having, as was oft his manner because men should not have notice of his coming, fared across country to shun highways and haunts of men. But here, as the Gods would have it, was word brought him of rebellion afoot and Kutarmish lost, into which he had else entered all unknowing: wolf into trap. Nor was there given him bare five minutes law betwixt safety and undoing, for Barganax, understanding who was here, galloped out with a hundred horse to fetch him in and chased him twenty mile to the very gates of Argyanna where, in the nick of time, he went to earth, with his horses nigh foundered and himself nigh bursten with rage and furious riding. The next day, not willing, belike, to be closed within a fortress whereof, in the windings of his policy, he had lately appointed governor a creature of Beroald's, since now and amid these stounds himself and Beroald might begin, belike, to stand in very doubtful terms, he betook himself north again to Owldale. It began to be seen how, with this sudden attempt of war, the Duke was likely to make a shrewd adventure to have taken Outer Meszria from him and the March besides; for they of the Queen's upholding in the March of Ulba who had some months since begun to doubt the Vicar as the more dangerous usurper, began now openly to affect Barganax.

In a week came Melates and Barrian through the Ruyar pass with near a thousand men, to join hand with the Duke. Neither from the Admiral nor from the Chancellor had the Duke any reply as yet. But a little past the turn of the year came tidings that the Chancellor was moved eastwards in strength and sat down in Argyanna; where, because the place is both impregnable and over-hangs the road that leads north from Meszria, he like a waiting hawk might cower those partridges of the march-lands and quiet their flutterings, giving Barganax besides reason of prudence not lightly to advance far out of his bridgehead beyond Kutarmish. The Duke indeed stood shortly between this and a new danger, when the regent Jeronimy, marching with an army through the Meszrian borders from the west along the Zenner, seemed to offer him battle, or if not, to menace his communications southwards. But it was as if Jeronimy, with the plain choice at last before him,

yea or nay, this coming day-dawn before Kutarmish, could not
find it in his heart to draw sword against a prince of King
Mezentius's blood. He sent in word to the Duke, and they made
peace together.

So, while the Vicar gathered force in Rerek, and while all Meszria
(even such as Zapheles, who had in a discontent been used to lean
towards the Vicar) rallied to Barganax as to their native lord, only
Beroald waited inscrutable in Argyanna. Most men thought that
he saw in this fresh war-rush of the Duke's the old danger come
again that he had feared aforetime. They thought, too, that this,
may be, held his hand: the opinion (that he had from the first
inclined to) that in law the Vicar's claims were hardly to be assailed.

XVIII

RIALMAR IN STARLIGHT

THE MANTICHORE GALLERY • DESIGN AGAINST AKKAMA •
STIFF NEWS FROM REREK • THAT 'MORE PRIVATER
COUNCIL-CHAMBER' • ANTIOPE: THE GODDESS STIRS •
TWO WAYS OF LOVE • WASTDALE DISTILLED IN
ZIMIAMVIA • CHOOSING UNDER STARS •
TERROR ANTIQUUS • PARTING AT MORNING.

QUEEN Antiope decreed a high banquet in her royal palace of
Teremne, upon the night of the equinox, for the turn of spring.
In the Mantichore gallery was the banquet set: in the ancientest
part of that palace, built when the old kings first raised walls upon
two-horned Rialmar to make it a nursery of their tyranny and a
place of strength: hundreds of years gone, before ever they issued
from their watered valleys betwixt twin desolations of desert
southward and eagle-baffling frozen mountains on the north, or
turned eyes towards the southlands of Rerek and Meszria. Lofty
was that gallery, built all of a warm grey stone having a dusky
sheen like marble and beset with black spots or strikes. The long
tables and the chairs besides were of the like stone, with silken
cushions, for feasters to sit and feast. Forty-and-four lamps wrought
in silver and copper and orichalc, and hanging by chains from the
vaulted roof, went in two rows endlong of that great gallery.
Beneath, upon the tables, candles of green wax burned in

candlesticks of gold, a candle to every feaster. To the careless eye, roof and wall alike seemed plain and without all ornament; but looked to near, they were seen to be drawn upon with narrow channelled lines as of burin or chisel. Employing which property of shining superficies and elusive graven outline, he that in former days made that gallery had by curious art brought it about so as whosoever should remain there awhile should, little by little with the altering aspects of those drawings upon the walls, seem to be ware of shadowy presences of the beast called mantichora: here a leonine paw or leonine shaggy mane, there a porcupine's quilly rump, a scorpion's tail, a manlike horrible face fanged and with goggling great eyes: and that is a kind of monstrous beast reputed anciently found in sandy places and gravelled in the borders of the Wold, next against the hills hitherward of Akkama.

The Queen, in a dress netted and laced with gold upon a groundwork of silk, sombre orange-scarlet of bog-asphodel in seeding time, and in her hair a high comb of tortoise-shell edged with balls of yellow sapphire, and about her throat a delicate cream-white ruff with setting-sticks of silver, sat in the high-seat: Lessingham upon her right as representing the Lord Protector and upon her left the old knight marshal. Beyond Lessingham the Princess Zenianthe had place, and beyond Bodenay the Countess of Tasmar: these and a few more only in place of honour upon the cross-bench and the rest of the company at the long tables, facing inwards with their backs to the walls. All the space between tables was kept clear for service of the banquet.

'Two weeks' time or three, then, Captain-General,' said the Queen, 'and you mean to fare south?'

'Two weeks come tomorrow, with your serene highness' leave,' answered Lessingham. 'My Lord Bodenay and I,' he said, leaning a little forward to include the knight marshal and speaking low, not to reach the general ear, 'have baked so well as we shall ask you, madam, summon a meeting tomorrow of your inner council upon the whole matter to condescend.'

'And what within the pie, then, when we shall cut it?'

'A journey for me south and then, say in a three months' time, north again, upon your highness's business.' He glanced carelessly about him to make sure of no eavesdropping. 'In a word, madam, we shall advise you that he whose insolencies you so wittily and wisely bore with last summer is rope-ripe: so—'

'O if little cur-dogs must be whipped,' said the Queen, 'I whipped him last September.'

Bodenay shook his head. 'Ah, madam, not the boy only, but that land and folk he standeth for. There is danger thence. And my Lord Lessingham will tell your serenity 'tis a maxim of great captains and men of charge: best defence is strike first.'

'We will take your highness' pleasure tomorrow,' said Lessingham. 'I hope you will let the thing go forward. A people that have so soon forgot their lesson, and of an old enmity towards us, kinged by a scorpion, unquiet as locusts: 'tis but plain prudence, outwar and subdue them this summer and lay them to your dominion. And my mission now to raise and bring you great armies from the south, and the Lord Protector's self (that were good if I can compass it) to command them.'

'That giveth you your date, Myrilla,' said the Countess Heterasmene, holding out her fingers above a golden bowl for a waiting-man to pour over them water of roses. 'If my Lord Lessingham will take his lieutenant into Rerek, you will have even just ten days to become weary of your new-wedded lord.'

'Yes, and you see in this, madam,' said Amaury, 'how well the fates have devised for my good. For indeed I have kept me in with a lady ere this for a month may be; and, as modest as I am, I dare think I shall not be out with my Lady Myrilla within ten days, albeit a week longer might strain things.'

'I'll stop your mouth: no, not as you'd have it, but thus,' said Myrilla, sitting next him, and made a dab at it with a piece of marchpane. They laughed, and Lessingham said apart to the Queen: 'Your highness was well advised to make this marriage up. The Admiral is a man of safe anchorage. Ties of affinity 'twixt him and Amaury will do much to settle friendships.'

'Lieutenant,' said the Queen, 'we will set forward your wedding a day or two: see if two days more may do it.'

Amaury, a little outmatched and put to silence with so many
eyes upon him, laughed as for courtesy sake, turned red, and
stroked his mustachios. From this abashment he was delivered by
a beck from Lessingham: stood up with a by-your-leave to his
lady, and went to him. The Queen's sergeant of arms was behind
Lessingham's chair: '—waiteth without, and craveth instant speech
with your excellence to deliver it.' 'What's the fool's secret news?'
said Lessingham: 'well, if it will not wait, go to him, Amaury. Be
eye, ear, conscience, for me: bid him confide in you.'

In a few minutes Amaury came back. 'My lord, the key fits not.
Will say nought to me save that 'tis matter of fieriest urgency, and
but for your particular ear. Hath letters too, as I suppose from
the Vicar, but these too only to be given up into your very hand.'

'From Laimak?' said the Queen. 'But shall we not make room
for him?'

'With respect no,' Lessingham said. 'I know the man: a domestic
of my noble cousin's much used by him upon matters of weight
and exact import: one Gabriel Flores. If it please your serenity he
be given supper in the buttery, I'll despatch his business anon.'

'See to it,' said she. And the banquet proceeded.

When it was now mid-part done, and cups began to be borne
round of Rian wine, and upon golden dishes macaroons, sallets of
violet petals, and the conserve that is made of the flowers of mari-
golds confectioned with curious cookery, Lessingham upon leave
given him by the Queen went from table and forth into a certain
upper room, having sent word before to Gabriel to attend him there
if he desired his conference. 'Marked you that strange trick of the
lights, cousin?' said the Queen, 'how, as the Captain-General walked
'twixt table and wall, the things upon the wall seemed to wave their
paws as he passed, and grin as they would have eat him?'

'It is a trick of the lights,' answered that hamadryad Princess;
'and your highness has seen it before.'

The Queen turned now, in merry talk as before, to the old
knight marshal upon her left, and to Tyarchus and Heterasmene
and old Madam Tasmar.

*   *   *

'In what estate left you his highness?' said Lessingham, taking from Gabriel the despatch and sitting in a great oak chair with a lamp beside it while he undid the seal. Gabriel stood before him with an anxious pinched look upon his face. 'I pray you read first,' he said.

Lessingham read it swiftly, then turned again to the beginning and read it again, slowly, as if to confer and weigh each word; then with a delicate deliberation folded it again: with a sudden movement tossed it to lie beside him on the table, and so sat motionless for a minute, leaning forward, right hand on hip, left elbow on knee, his finger-nails drumming a marching lilt on his front teeth. In the side-shining of the lamp across Lessingham's face Gabriel could see the eyes of him in that stillness: unrevealing eyes, as if the mind behind them had sounded deep to meditate with itself. Then suddenly in those speckled grey eyes of Lessingham there danced something as if in a round of dancing girls should be glittered forth in advance some triumph.

He sat up, erect. In all his presence there dwelt that sense of abidingness, which is in the steady glitter and conflict, shining still stones and shining ever-churning ever-fleeting waves and eddies, of some watersmeet where two rivers run between green shades of oak and ash and alder, and the banks of water-worn boulders and pebbly granite shingle lie white about that murmur under the power of the sun. 'Well, good pug,' said he, 'you are acquainted with all this?'

'It is took down from his highness' mouth, and in my own character which I think is known to your lordship.'

'How comes it I am told nought of this before? Despatches two a month, good as clock-work, as if all's well, sailing fair with wind and tide: then sudden this turn: the whole boat upset; Meszria lost us and the March too: says great men hath late assembled from all the land over, offering 'pon some lying rumour of her highness' death (pray Gods forfend the omen!) the throne to her brother Barganax: Laimak close invested, and like to be smoked out of it as boys take a wasps' nest. Who heard the like? And screameth now for me to pick him out of this pot of treacle the Devil only

and he know why a hath fallen in't. By my soul, I am well minded
let him stay there.'

"'Tis his great pride, said Gabriel. 'Would not ask your help till
need drove him to it. Fed you, it is true, with figments and fittons
and leasings to keep you here in Fingiswold. You will belie your
greatness if now in his sore need you will upon such pretexts
refuse him.'

'Flatter not yourself, and your master, to suppose,' said
Lessingham, 'that I am a child, with no more means of intelligence but such advertisements as he shall think good to send
me. It is true, my news is three weeks, or may be a month,
behind yours: I much fear a messenger hath miscarried this last
journey, fallen into Prince Ercles' claws, like enough, under Eldir.
Howe'er it be, I am six weeks away, so tell me. And forget not
this, my pug,' said he, as Gabriel cast a sheep's eye at him, 'if I
shall take you lying to me or hiding aught, not you alone will
smart for it.'

'Well, this your excellence knows, as I judge,' said Gabriel: 'the
bloody inrush into Kutarmish of the accursed bastard—'

'When you speak to me of great men,' said Lessingham, 'speak
with respect, be it friend or unfriend, and with just titles of honour.
I'll have you flogged else.'

'The bloody inrush of his grace of Zayana,' Gabriel said with
a snarling look, the teeth gabbing out of his mouth. 'And sweet
doings there. Lord Roder ta'en and strapped in a big chair, open
in the market-place, and a lad with a sword ground to a good
edge: swash and away, head him like a pig, and all the sight-gazers
to see it; and justly rewarded so, or why did a not hold better
watch on the gates and all the treasure and goods his highness
lost there? and himself too might a miscarried, intending for
Kutarmish—'

'Leave particularities. I know all this.'

'And the Admiral gone over, heard you that (mid-January, that
was), hand and glove to the Duke's allegiance?'

'That I knew not till I read this letter,' said Lessingham. 'Nor,
till then, of the Chancellor: last news was he yet wavered.'

'Your lordship's intelligence was eight weeks stale 'pon the one, and three weeks 'pon t'other. As for my lord Chancellor, seemeth that when a had lodged himself safe in Argyanna, a sent for his learned books out of Zayana, whistled to him from all the three kingdoms a dozen doctorable men, legists, sophisters, whate'er to call 'em, and set 'em down to ferret him out colourable reasons for what, you may make no doubt, if you know a fox by's furred tail, a was all the time resolved to do. You may wager their reasons had taken water: rotten ere they might come to shore. Howso, found him the thing he asked for. Cometh out then, smooth-tongued as a dancing-madam, with item this, item that, as pretty as you could wish: conclusion, Barganax rightly called King as in male descent, and – to make all sure, if this false report of the Queen's decease, hatched up, as 'tis thought, by that Barganax' – ('Have I not warned you?' said Lessingham) – 'by that Duke, to give colour to his usurping: to make all sure, if this report be shown without contradiction false – some reputed law dug up out o' the dust-heaps of two centuries past to say females shall not hold kingdom in Fingiswold: thus even so securing him in's usurpation, and prefer his bastard blood before her birth noble.'

Lessingham rose from his chair: took a turn or two about the room, stroking his beard. Gabriel with little swinish eyes watched him eagerly. 'I was hard put to it to a come through to your excellence,' he said after a while: 'what with their armies set down before Laimak, and then those princes in the north that this Duke feedeth with his gold to countermand his highness' will and check his friends: do gather a power of men too. Arcastus durst not trust his nose outside Megra walls. I know not, my lord, if you have such force as that you can keep such curs in awe, to come through them?'

Lessingham stopped by the table, took up the Vicar's letter, perused it again, laid it by, then stood looking down upon Gabriel with a disturbing smile. 'Your chickens, my little Gabriel, are not yet hatched. And for my intents in this pass your lord hath brought himself unto, you might more easily guess their drift if the ability were given you to look men in the eye.'

'Nay,' said he looking and looking away: 'your worship hath an eye to shine down basilisks. I can't abear it.'

Lessingham laughed. It was as if from a waiting-place above the watersmeet a sea-eagle had stooped: feinted: resumed his waiting.

Gabriel thrust out his chin and came a step nearer, looking down and tracing with one finger, while he spoke, rings and crosses on the corner of the table. 'I would your noble excellence could a seen what I have seen,' he said: 'these six weeks. No more o' this lukewarmth then, I dare wager my head. Great men 'gainst great odds in my day have I seen, but never as this. The undutiful and traitorous affection borne against him by these lords, the more it drew men from him, made shrink his armies, disappoint his designs, the more would he give 'em still lill for loll. It is a world to see him. With but a thousand men, made a great stroke in the western Marches and then, when that Chancellor thought to a closed him in between Fiveways and the Zenner, marched sudden round his flank, then north-about by night, catched Melates 'pon a foray into Rerek, made him eat lamb-pie. And later, shut up in Laimak with the leavings of his army, and six times his numbers barking like midden tykes at's doors but e'en so durst not come at grips: scarce a day but out he cometh with a sally, ever himself i' the front to lead it: does 'em some hurt, fetch in provisions, slay some men, what not.' He ceased, his finger still fiddling on the table's corner. Suddenly he looked up, met Lessingham's eye, avoided it: with a gowked movement grabbed at Lessingham's hand and kissed it. Lessingham, as if strangely touched and ill at ease with such a homage from such a suppliant, took away his hand. 'You shall have your answer tomorrow,' he said; and so dismissing him returned to the banquet-chamber.

And now as Lessingham walked between table and wall, beholding the Artemisian loveliness of her where she sat sweetly talking, it was as if in the tail of his eye he saw monstrous paws brandished, and mouths of beastly great murdering teeth ready to come nigh to her.

He and she looked at one another as he resumed his seat. Amid the general talk none noted, unless it were Zenianthe and Amaury, that for a minute neither Lessingham spoke nor the Queen. Nor none guessed (unless it were these) that she and Lessingham, while they seemed for that minute but to sit silent and thoughtful at that banquet-table, had in truth retired themselves to a more privater council-chamber; where, in that which is to outward sense but the twinkling of an eye, days, weeks, and months and the changing seasons can act their slowed passage like the opening of a white rose; and thither many a time since that first night last Michaelmas had Lessingham and the Queen retired them, to pursue their noble wishes, and dwelt there in love together.

The learned doctor, standing with Zenianthe in a grassy hollow of the hill where her oak-woods upon their furthest limits face the afternoon, shaded his eyes. The sun was so far declined as barely ride clear of a fir-wood which followed the shoulder of the hill where it rose beyond the pond a stone's throw from the doctor's feet. Black against the sky was that wood, but upon the hither side of it and its cast shadow the edge of the green hill was in brilliant light. Below that band of brilliance, hillside and pond were as a curtain of obfuscate golden obscurity which yet, with a hand to shade the eyes of him that looked, became penetrable to sight, revealing detail and contour and varied growth of herbage, and the pond's surface below, smooth and still. The figures of Lessingham and Antiope coming down out of the fir-trees' shadow into the band of sunshine were outlined about their edges with a smouldering golden light, so that they seemed to burn against their background of the black wood. The sound of their talk, as it became audible, seemed the translation into music of that smouldering light and of the sun and the shadows within shadows and water and green hillside about them: not into words, for words were not yet to be distinguished; nor laughter, for they did not laugh: rather the notes and rhythms that noble voices borrow from that inner vein of laughter, which enriches the easy talk of minds so well mated that each being true to the other cannot but so be true to itself.

They were come down now. Lessingham with a nod acknowledged the doctor's salutation, sat himself down upon an outcrop
of stone, and there seemed fallen into a study. Anthea, erect, statuesque, with hands clasped behind her back, stared at the sun.
Campaspe, in a soft clinging dress of watered chamblet coloured,
like certain toadstools that grow on dead thorn-trees, of delicatest
pale rose-enewed madder brown, and wearing a white lace hood,
from beneath which dark curls of her hair escaping shadowed
throat and cheek, and on the left her bosom, busied herself with
finding flat stones to play ducks and drakes. Ever now and then
the pond's still surface was broken with the scuttle and skim of
her stones. Swift and dainty and mouse-like were all her movements, as a little dunlin's tripping the sky-reflecting mud-flats of
tidal creeks on a sunny evening in autumn when the sea is out.

Antiope stood with the doctor and Zenianthe. Their eyes were
on Lessingham, where he sat looking into the sun-path. Vandermast
spoke: 'You have debated all fully, then, and determined of
somewhat?'

Antiope answered, 'We have nothing debated, and determined
all.'

'That is better still,' said that ancient man.

For a while, they kept silence. Vandermast saw that her gaze
rested still upon Lessingham. It was as if she slept where she stood.
Vandermast said, in a voice still and warm as the innermost
unpierced shades of those oak-woods behind her, which outwardly
the sun bathed with so lovely a splendour of golden green: 'I have
opined to your ladyship ere this, that there is but one wisdom.
And but one power.'

Antiope stood listening as if for more. 'I wonder?' she said at last.

Vandermast said: 'It is your own doing, this: a dress of Yours.
You choose this. He chooses it with You, whether he know or
not, willing it for Your sake. That loftiest of all Your roses, to
pluck it for You.'

She said: 'I know.'

Vandermast said: 'For my part, I had sooner die with your
ladyship than be made immortal with—'

She said, 'Well? Who is my rival?'

Vandermast said, 'You have none: not one: with Your starry beauties to make paragon.'

She waited. The Knidian mystery lay shadowy about Her lips. '*Before the day was*,' She said.

The silence trembled.

Vandermast said: 'Yours is not as our choosing, who out of many things choose this thing and not those others, because we judge this to be good. But Your choice maketh good: higheth the thing You choose, were it very nought before, to outsoar all praises.'

She said: 'And yet every time I pay for it. The mere condition of being, this of he and she: did I not choose it? Should not He, as easily, had I so chosen instead, have created and made Me of His omnipotence self-subsisting and self-sufficing? But this I chose rather: to be but upon terms to be loved, served, made, recreated, by that which is My servant. How were love serious else?'

Vandermast said: 'Death: a lie: fairy-babes to fright children. From within, *sub specie aeternitatis*, what is it but *vox inanis*, a vain word, nothing?'

She said: 'And yet, how were it possible to love entirely except some living being which liveth under the terror of those wings? Else, what needed it of love?'

Vandermast said: 'And time: what evil was there ever but time sowed it, and in time it hath root and flourisheth?'

She said: 'And yet, without time what were there? The crack-brained ecstatic's blindation of undiscerning eyes upon me: the music of the spheres condensed to a caterwaul. Or how else should beauty round her day? How else should he tell my lip from my eyebrow, but in time?'

Vandermast said: 'The passing and the vanishing: what else beareth witness to the eternal?'

She said: 'This will-o'-the-wisp of power: that other, scorning of certainties which abide safe and endure—' Her voice vanished as, out to sea, a questing tern vanishes as the sun leaves it.

Zenianthe, with oak-leaves set round her lovely hair, said, laying a hand on the doctor's arm: 'Are you part of Her? as I am?'

Vandermast said: 'No, dear lady of leaves and squirrel-haunted silences. I am of that other kind.'

Zenianthe said: 'But if the house be part of who dwells therein? If my woods be part?'

Vandermast shook his head: made no answer.

Antiope said, startling as a sleeper wakes: 'What is it, cousin? What have I spoken? You can witness, I never walked in my sleep till now?' Her eyes were troubled. She said, and her words came slowly as if with night-groping: 'A black lady. I have never seen her.'

Vandermast said: 'Shall Self see Self?'

Antiope said: 'You may better answer that: you that are a philosopher.'

Vandermast said: 'I can ask questions, but some I cannot answer.'

Antiope said: 'Has she seen me?'

Vandermast said: 'I have been told so.'

Antiope said: 'Who told you?'

He answered: 'My art.'

Antiope said: 'Does that speak sooth?'

Vandermast said: 'How can I tell? It flares a light. I follow that, a step at a time, and so watch and wait: remembering still that, in this supermundal science concerning the Gods, determination of what Is proceedeth inconfutably and only by argument from what Ought to be. Thus far I have not been bogued.'

Antiope said: 'How then should she see me, if I may not see her?'

Vandermast held his peace. The words of her speech were like shadows falling. Her eyes, like a dove's, now sought Lessingham, but his face was turned from her sunwards.

Anthea said:

> 'I am love:
> Loving my lover,
> Love mine own self:
> For that he loveth it,
> Make it my paramour,

Laugh in the pride of it,
Beat in his veins:
So, by such sharing,
Loving prevail
Unto self-seeing.
—Such-like is love.'

Campaspe said:

'I am love:
Loving my lover,
Love but his love:
Love that arrayeth me,
Beddeth me, wardeth me—
Sunn'd in his noon,
Safe under hand of him,
Open my wild-rose
Petals to him:
Dance in his music.
—Such-like is love.'

Lessingham said: 'You sit there, silent: I at the table's head, you, Señorita Maria, at the side, as fits a guest of honour; but on my left, as fits you. For on that side my heart is. There is no more haste now. Peace now: *requiescat in pace*: the peace of the Gods that passeth all understanding. Some note or flavour of it I caught now and then even there, because of you, *madonna mia*. Do you remember?

Mistress of my delights; and Mistress of Peace:
O ever changing, never changing, You—

'Do you remember? But the dream clouded it, and the illusion of change and—'

'Hush!' Mary said, and trembled. 'Lastingest blessednesses are subject to end. Is this a dream? We may wake.'

Lessingham said: 'That was the dream. No waking again to that. For what was it but the marred reflection, prophetic or memorial, of this present? a wind-marred image of all these things: of you and me here alone, of those peaches, the dark wine and the golden, the Venetian finger-bowls: a simulacrum only but half apprehended of that Gloire de Dijon over the window, and of its perfume which is your breath, *O reine des adorées*, perfume of love. These, and the summer's evening leaning, with long cool shadows on the lawn, as I towards you; and this sapphire, warm to my fingers where it sits softly here, in this place which is of itself benediction and promise of awakening night, and of the unveiling and the blinding and the lotus that floats on Lethe: in this dear valley of your breast.'

'Wait,' she said, scarce to be heard. 'Wait. It is not time.'

He sat back again in his chair. So sitting, he rested his eyes upon her in silence. Then: 'Do you remember the Poetess, madonna?

> Ἕσπερε, πάντα φέρων, ὅσα φαινόλις ἐσκέδασ'αὔως,
> φέρεις ὄϊν, φέρες αἴγα, φέρεις ἀπύ μάτερι παδα.'

As if spell-bound, she listened, very still. Very still, and dreamily, and with so soft an intonation that the words seemed but to take voiceless shape on her ambrosial breath, she answered, like an echo:

> 'Evening Star – gath'rer of all that the bright daybreak parted:
> You gather the sheep, the goat; you gather the child safe to the mother.'

The low sunbeams touched their goblets, and the beaded streams of bubbles became as upstreaming fires.

'It is things we counted most of substance,' he said, after a minute, 'it is those have fallen away. Those that, where all else was good, spoiled all.'

'All,' she said. 'Even I,' she said: 'spoilt at last.'

Lessingham started: sat rigid as if struck to stone. Then he laid out a hand palm upwards on the table: hers came, daintily under its shimmer of rings as a tame white egret to a proffered delicacy, touched with its middle finger the centre of his open palm, and escaped before it could be caught.

'Well, it was a dream,' she said. 'And, for my part in it, I felt nothing. No pain. No time to be frighted. It was less than a dream. For of a dream we say, It was. But this, It was not nor it is not.'

'A dream,' said Lessingham. 'Who dreamed it?'

'I suppose, a fool.'

A trick of the low sunlight in that panelled room seemed to darken the red gold of her hair even to blackness. A Medusaean glint, diamond-hard, came and went at her mouth's corner.

'Ah,' he said, 'we talk dream and truth till each swallow other, like as the two pythons, and nothing left. But as for that old world: it was you, Mary, said it to me in the old time, that it was as if One should have sat down alone with the chessmen and said to them, "Live: and now see whether they can teach themselves the game." And so wait, and watch. Time enough, in eternity. But needeth patience. More patience than for manning of a haggard, madonna. More patience than mine, by heavens!'

'The patience of the Gods,' said she.

'An experiment of Hers? for the mere pleasure of it, will you think? to while away a morning, as fly at the heron?' He sat silent a minute, gazing at her. Then, 'I think,' he said: 'another painting.'

'Painting? A barrenness of One? Or dry-point, that shall give you, as you say, a bodiless thin Many?' They waited, as if each had heard or seen somewhat that was here and was gone. The alexandrite stone was upon her finger, water green in this light of evening, yet with a stir as of embers below the green ready to flare red when lamps should be lit.

'An experiment,' said Lessingham, taking up his thread. 'A breath: then no more to touch: no more but sit down and see if the meanest rude nothingness, once it be raised to being, shall not of itself in the end become the thing She chooseth. Infinite patience

of the Gods. Slow perfection. The refining and refining of the
Vision. – You said it, Mary. Do you remember?'

'Why will you say "of Hers"?'

Lessingham smiled. 'Why will you, "His"?'

'Well, if it pleases me?'

They looked at one another, each with that scarcely perceptible
half-mocking challenge of the head: a grace of the antlered deer.
'A very good answer,' said Lessingham. 'I cannot better it. Unless,'
he said suddenly, and his voice died away as he leaned nearer, his
right elbow on the table, his left arm resting, but not to touch her,
on the back of her chair. It was as if from without-doors a distant
music, as once upon Ambremerine, made a thin obbligato to the
accents of his speech that came like the roll of muffled thunder:
'unless indeed it has been with me, from the beginning, as with
Anchises it was: a mortal man: not once, but many times: but
many times:

’ἀθανάτη παρέλεκτο θεᾷ βροτός, οὐ σάφα εἰδώς’

'—with an immortal Goddess: not clearly knowing.'

The deep tones of Lessingham's voice, so speaking, were hushed
to the quivering superfices of silence, beneath which the darkness
stirred as with a rushing of arpeggios upon muted strings. Mary
nodded twice, thrice, very gently, looking down. The line of her
throat and chin seen sideways was of a purity passing all purity
of flowers or wind-sculptured mountain snows. 'Not clearly
knowing,' she said; and in the corner of her mouth the minor
dia-bolus, dainty and seductive, seemed to turn and stretch in its
sleep. They sat silent. By some trick of the light, the colour of her
hair seemed to change: to a gold-drained pale glory of moonlight,
instead of, as her dress, red of the bog-asphodel in seed. And her
eyes that had been green seemed grey now, like far sea horizons.
Lessingham felt the peace of her mind enfold him like the peace
of great flats of tidal bird-haunted marsh-land in a June morning
looked on with the sun behind the looker: no shadows: the sky
grey of the dove's breast, toning to soft blues with faint clouds

blurred and indefinite: the landscape all greens and warm greys, as if it held within it a twilight which, under the growing splendour of the sun, dilutes that splendour and tames it to its own gentleness: here and there a slice of blue where the water in the creeks between wide mud-banks mirrors the sky: mirrors also boats, which, corn-yellow, white, chocolate-brown, show (and their masts) clear against sky in those reflections but less clear, against land, in nature: so, and all the air filled, as with delicate thoughts, with the voices of larks and the brilliant white and black of martins skimming, and white butterflies: drifts of horses and sheep and cattle, littler and littler in the distance, peopling the richer pastures on the right where buttercups turn the green to gold: all in a brooding loveliness, as if it could hurt nothing, and as if it scarce dared breathe for fear of waking something that sleeps and should be left to sleep because it is kind and good and deserves to be left so.

Campaspe said, at the clavichord: 'You will have more?' The bodiless tinkle of the preluding blades of sound drew like streaked clouds across the face of the stillness: then, 'What shall I sing to you?' she said: 'another of my Lady Fiorinda's songs?' And her naiad voice, effortless, passionless, bodiless, perfect on the note, began to sing:

> 'Se j'avoie ameit un jor,
>   je diroie a tons:
>   bones sont amors.'

Lessingham leaned forward on the table, his fists to his temples. He raised his head suddenly, staring. 'I have forgotten,' he said. 'What is this I have forgotten?'

After a minute, he sprang up. 'Let us go into the garden,' he said to Antiope: 'settle it there. I must south. I would have you return no more to Rialmar until this tempest be overblown. You can be safe here, and my mind at ease so.'

Anthea exchanged glances with Campaspe, and laughed a laugh like the crash of spears.

Lessingham followed the Queen to the door which that unnamed disciple now opened for them. They stepped out, not into that wayside garden of Vandermast's, but now, strangely, into an appearance of that Teremnene garden: the statue gracious above floating lily-leaves: terraced granite walks and steps going up from the pond: flowers asleep in the borders: the path where Derxis had thrown his stone: over all the star-dim spring night. The door shut behind them, shutting them out from the glow and the candlebeams. Antiope put a hand in his.

'Why do you tremble?' said Lessingham. 'Be safe, you are now free from him.'

Antiope said: 'There is nought to bind you in your choice. But neither is there to bind me. Different ways you and I cannot choose. If yours to walk through dangerous and high places and to approach near steep downfalls, so mine. Or if you the safe way, so then I. And so, if you will abide by your saying and go south, then must I queen it out in Rialmar.'

They looked each at other. Lessingham took a great breath. He turned to Aphrodite's statua in its cold high beauty, netted and held in the loneliness of starlight. 'Let Her,' he said, 'choose for us.'

'Be it so,' said Antiope. 'There is no other way of wise choosing.'

'Let me look at your face,' he said. She raised it to his under the stars.

After a while, he spoke in a whisper. 'What mystery was this? Looking but now in your face, I have been my own love: seen myself: loved myself, being myself you for that instant, madonna: chosen for you, and for me, with your love as from withinwards. Been your love. Been—' he caught his breath: 'Was that the threshold? Upon Ambremerine, with glow-worms in her hair?'

'I do not know,' Antiope said, her face hidden now against his shoulder. 'But what you have seen I have seen too: I too have chosen: been you for that instant, loving me. For a pang, and away.'

For a minute they abode so, as one, motionless: then stood back and joined hands as might two brothers before battle. 'Then, this being our choice,' he said, 'better it is, madonna, that you remain in Rialmar rather than come south with me. For all Rerek and Meszria are up in war now, and my going is to put all in hazard that must us save or spill. And well as I can answer for my cousin while I sit in the saddle, I would not, were I to fall, leave him executor of my trusts toward you; nor with the means to come at you. I leave you a great army here, and the lord knight marshal: a general expert and to trust. I take but my own eight hundred horse, and may be three hundred more. And Rialmar is by nature inexpugnable. By heavens, they shall see lightning out of Fingiswold, and the thunder of it shall shake Meszria and Rerek ere they shall have reckoned with me.'

Antiope said, as he kissed her hand under starlight: 'We have chosen, my friend – ἴομεν.'

He raised his head again, her hand still in his. 'ὦ πέπον, εἰ μὲν γάρ—' It was as if the stars and the huge darknesses without remembered again for their own that saying of the Lycian king to his loved kinsman, standing forth under windly Ilios:

Ah, lad, and were't but so: and, from this war fleeing,
We twain, thou and I, for ever ageless and deathless
Might endure: not then would I in the van do battle.
Neither send forth thee to battle which maketh glorious.
—But now, – since thus serried the fates of death come
    nigh us:
Thousands, nor is't in mortal to flee such, neither elude
    them –
On! be it praise we become for another, or, haply, reap it.

Lessingham's nostrils were like a war-horse's that hears the trumpets. Then on the sudden, in that questionable garden under stars, he seemed to see how a change, as with eclipse or deep clouding of the moon, overcame the beautiful face of this Queen of his, as if night should suddenly have clothed her with the mantle, inexorable, stony, archaic, of Astarte or if there be any crueller dethroned divinity of ages outworn: Terror Antiquus, treading the dead mouldered faces and unfleshed skeletons of nameless forgotten men. Then, as the silver moon with the passing of that red shadow, her beauty shone fair.

The awe of that sight darkened his voice as he spoke: 'Who are you?'

Antiope trembled. 'Sometimes, in such places as this,' she said, 'I scarcely know.'

It was morning now in Doctor Vandermast's wayside house. Lessingham, booted and spurred ready for setting forth, stood beside her pillow, as debating whether to wake her or let this, awake and asleep, be the last before their returning again to action and that banquet-table. Antiope lay asleep on her side, back towards him where he stood, so that he saw, partly from behind, the line of her cheek and brow and the rose of sleep that warmed it. Lessingham said in himself: 'Forgetfulness. What does it matter? Belike the old man spoke aright: that it is a precious gift of Her lap, this forgetting; in order that She may give all again, morning-new. Every momentary glimpse: every half-heard overtone in her voice: the sheet drawn so, as it always is, nicely across that mouth of mine: eyelid, virginal quiet line and long drooped lashes, closed asleep: pale dawn-like gold of that hair of mine tied back with those ribbons: I have forgotten, and even these shall be forgotten. Well: so She give it anew. Well: so that She have said: "They are Mine: I keep them: I store them up. In time they are gone for ever, but they are Mine unto all eternity."'

He tucked the sheet gently in behind her shoulders. She turned at the touch with a contented inarticulate little murmur and, between half-opened eyelids, as only half waking, looked up at him. 'Those two songs,' she said after a moment, her voice soft with the down of sleep.

'Did the little water-swallow say hers for you?' said Lessingham.

Antiope said, 'Say it for me again.'

Lessingham said:

'I am love:
Loving my lover,
Love but his love:
Love that arrayeth me,

Beddeth me, wardeth me—
Sunn'd in his noon,
Safe under hand of him,
Open my wild-rose
Petals to him:
Dance in his music.
—Such-like is love.'

Antiope said, 'I like it better than that other. Say you like it better too.'

'I like it best.'

'Why?'

His mustachios stirred with the flicker of a smile. He paused, thoughtful, stroking his black beard. 'As not my way,' he said, 'could I by some magic be turned to a— As not known from within. I am not Barganax.'

'My brother,' she said. 'I have never seen him. Have you seen: that lady?'

'So far as any but he may see,' answered Lessingham, 'I have seen her.'

'How far was that?'

He said, as if searching for words, 'May be, so far as— But no: you have never seen him. What are brothers and sisters? In the main, so. But once, until I beheld nothing. Then once, until I beheld you.'

'Say it again, that you like Campaspe's best.'

Lessingham said again, 'I like it best.'

'I am glad.' It was as if on her breath two shadows crossed, of laughter and tears. 'I cannot, that other way.'

'Because it is your way, I like it,' he said. 'I love you,' he said, 'beyond time and circumstance.'

She put out an arm, and with that about his neck drew his face down to hers, warm with sleep, upon the pillow.

XIX

LIGHTNING OUT OF FINGISWOLD

THE FIRST FLASH • QUELLING OF THE FREE TOWNS •
LESSINGHAM BETWEEN PINCERS • BATTLE BEFORE LEVERINGAY
• MARCH OF THE LORD JERONIMY • BATTLE OF RIDINGHEAD
• PEACE GIVEN TO THE ADMIRAL • STORM AND TEMPEST
AT RIVERSHAWS • THE SECOND FLASH •
ECLIPSE AND DARKNESS.

LESSINGHAM came south over the Wold by great journeys and on
the fifth day of April passed by the land-march into Rerek. He had
with him barely a thousand horse, but not a man of them that was
not proven in war, headstrong, bloody, and violent, and of long
custom bound to his obedience, not as water-spaniels but as the
hand is stirred to obey the mind: of his own following, the most of
them, six and seven years gone, when the great King warred down
Akkama. Of like temper were his captains of troops: Brandremart,
Gayllard, Hortensius, Bezardes: all, like as the Captain-General's self,
in the lusty flower of their youth, and such as would set no more
by the life of a man, nor have no more pity thereof, than of the lives
of partridges or quails which be taken in season to eat. Amaury he
left in Rialmar, to be eye, ear, and hand for him in those northern
parts. Gabriel Flores had set forth alone (supposed for Laimak) in
advance, the very morrow of that banquet. So now Lessingham
halted in the fortress of Megra, and held counsel of war.

And first because the free towns in these outlaid parts should learn to fear him, nor trust too securely in the princes of the north, Ercles and Aramond, that still cloaked them underneath their wings, and because he would secure his rear and left flank a little ere adventure far south with an army that was all head and very little body, he rode in a sudden foray south to Abaraima. Here had Ercles last summer put down the captal and other great men that held the city in the Vicar's interest, and in their rooms placed other his own creatures. But the more part of the townsfolk, who passed nothing on Prince Ercles and much less passed they on the Vicar, but desired nothing better than be let live at ease with their pleasant houses and gardens and fishponds and wives and children and delicate dogs and beasts tamed to the hand which they have *in deliciis*, beholding this army suddenly at their gates, and knowing their defences weak, and hearing now the word of Lessingham that if they were taken by force they should all die and the town burnt and spoiled without mercy, upon that present terror threw open their gates to him. Lessingham, that was well served by intelligencers here as otherwhere these many months past, and judged, both from these and from his own seeing and hearing, the temper and inclination of the people, sternly withheld his soldiers from all cruelty against them so as not a man should suffer harm whether of body or goods. Only some few towers he flatted to the ground, and seized those principal persons, unquiet, busy, and high-climbing spirits, who had sided themselves and sworn to Ercles. These, to the number of seven, he caused to be brought before him in the great paven square before the courthouse, where he, armed from heel to throat in black armour and with all his soldiers arrayed under weapons about him, sat in state. Whereupon, after proclamation at large of their fault, these seven were by his command thrown down and unheaded with axes and so hanged along the wall in that place, for a warning to who would be warned. Which being done, and a baily and officers brought in and sworn in name of the Lord Horius Parry to the Queen's allegiance, Lessingham wore no more these dreadful looks but showed himself so cheerfully that within a few days' time every man in that city was joyful to behold him. Well nigh a hundred horse were added to him now, gathered of their own free will from Abaraima and the townships thereabout.

But barely seven days tarried Lessingham in Abaraima: then, for a knock of the iron gauntlet upon Aramond's door to let him know the Queen's Captain-General was afoot now and to be reckoned withal, he turned upon the sudden eastwards and in a day's hard riding came through the hills of the Mortelf down upon the rich open city of Bagort. This is the quiet heart of Aramond's country: a mediterrane or inland secret valley where not in twenty years till that day had an enemy's foot trodden; so that they listened secure to all rumours of unpeace without; and here had Prince Aramond his delicate lodge beside the salt lakes of Methmarsk. And here, in his unprepared idleness and with but a very small force at hand, the prince had but time to take boat and escape down the lake ere Lessingham's black riders were in the city. Lessingham took great store of minted money and precious stones and costly treasure besides, and took away too all weapons and armour he might come by, but the town he spared, and seeing they made no defence against him there was no man lost his life there. In Bagort he stayed three nights and refreshed his army, and upon Wednesday the eighteenth of April departed again by the same way west to Abaraima.

Upon Saturday night he stood with his army before Veiring gates. Here was Roquez nigh a twelvemonth set in power by Ercles after much strife and blood-letting: his wife a Meszrian, cousin german to the Lord Melates: she was a cruel lady, and had of late so wrought with Roquez and, through him, with them of the prince's party as that they were in purpose shortly to do somewhat against such as they loved not, that the streets should run again with blood. Lessingham sent in a herald under safe conduct to speak with them at the barriers, straitly enjoining them, on pain of their lives and goods and to be reputed enemies of the Queen's highness, that they should deliver up the town to him as Captain-General, and that within the space of one hour after the morrow's sunrise. Which Roquez denying, and speaking great words against him, there began to be a tumult in the town all night, and they of the Vicar's upholding rose up and made head against Roquez; in so much that a little before sunrise, while the issue stood yet in doubt, some suddenly surprising a gatehouse opened the gates to Lessingham. But when Lessingham and his were come in to help them, then almost nothing held against them. In that battle fell Roquez, and when they of his following knew this, in despair of speed they gave back till they were come to the keep and there shut themselves in and shot from the walls and loop-holes. Lessingham let fetch wood and firing to burn them up; so, when the fire began to take and they saw there was nought to do but surrender themselves, they came down and surrendered to his discretion.

In those days was Veiring a strong town as for walls, being by nature well postured too in a bend of the river, whereby it is from three sides hard to come at. But in length and breadth within the walls and in number of folk that dwell therein it is but as a platter to a table-top as beside Telia or Abaraima. Lessingham made but short work, after the taking of the keep, of quieting the town. With the late ruling party he had little trouble: ready enough were they to go each to his own house and fare with hidden head, not to draw eyes which might single him out for retribution. But they that had been for the Vicar, seeing good harvest now beyond hope or dreams, and the readier because of that to make haste to cut it down and in it, began like jack sauces to jet the Streets, quick to beat or kill any that should displease them or withsay anything that they would do. Even in the eye of the Captain-General's self or his own men-at-arms, as at great dogs little tykes should snar, would these flaunt their roynish fashions, their bawdry, and their insolences. To end it, Lessingham proclaimed upon trumpets through and about the town that whoso, save only soldiers of his, should after the third hour before noon be found in the streets with weapon upon him, were it but a hand-dagger, that should be his death. By noon had a score been hanged in the streets for this offence: 'twixt noon and mid-even, two more. That ended it. Of general turmoil indeed, there was none later than breakfast-time, when there gathered a band together before Roquez's house supposing to have had out his lady, who with some of her household there sought safety, and quite her for those things they thought she had devised against them. But Lessingham, riding to and about with a troop of horse, so that while yet any spark smouldered of disorder he might with his own eye see it to tread it out, came thither, as God would have it, in the nick of time when they had beat in the door and were upon dragging her forth. He, upon sight of such a beastish act against a lady, was as if taken in berserk-gang: with bloody rage suddenly surprised them as he had been a wolf or a lion, and in such good coin paid them, that seven men shortly lay dead or bleeding under his feet as with one arm he bore off that lady, harmless but swooning, while in his other hand the reddened sword boded ill to any man that would nigh him near. Next morning Lessingham sent her with a conduct over land to Megra, for safety until means should offer for her faring south to Meszria to her kith and kin. He set Meron in Roquez's stead, captain of Veiring, and, because of the fury of their factions there, left him fifty horse to his bodyguard and to cow them. Three-and-thirty citizens of Ercles' faction Lessingham condemned to exile perpetual with loss of all their belongings: two hundred more to like banishment, but with leave to carry away their goods and chattels. Five he sent to be hewn of their heads in the public market-place; two of whom suffered that punishment not as traitors to the Vicar, but for divers outrages and cruelties acted by them out of private malice upon Lessingham's entry into Veiring and under cover of their espousing of his cause. It was the talk of men that Lessingham had shown by his dealings in Veiring that he was a lord both just and fearless, and wise besides and merciful, and terrible besides in season. And now was good settled peace in Veiring as had not been for many a year.

It being now near the fourth week ended since he came down from the Wold, and news of these doings flown before him about the countryside, he made haste to depart out of Veiring by the highway southward. The second of May he came to Lailma which opened gates to him: and here came word to him that Ercles

himself was come down from Eldir and held the Swaleback passage
by the shore of Arrowfirth. Next day Lessingham moved south,
going gingerly with espials before him to feel the way, and pitched
for the night a little beside Memmering, where steep and stony
hills, covered all with thick-grown trackless forest, begin to close
in westwards toward the sea shore. Here in the morning he had
sure tidings that the prince was fallen back southwards. But while
he waited to satisfy himself of this, came Daiman, ridden in huge
haste from Telia upon word brought thither of Lessingham's march
south, with this news now: that the lord Admiral was come round
about by sea from Kessarey up to Kaima and was there disem-
barked the week before with a great army of as some said three
thousand, others four thousand, men. Lessingham upon these
tidings resolved, now that the passages of Swaleback were opened
to him, swiftly and at all hazards to come through; seeing that if
with so great forces they should once be closed against him he
were as good pack home again to Rialmar. Upon which resolution,
he struck camp and came, without sight or rumour of an enemy,
through the highway past the head of the firth and pitched in
strong ground rising amid open fields apt to the use of horse-
soldiers some five miles west of Eldir.

He stood now in this case. Ercles, not with a handful of horse,
as had at first been bruited, but with an army more than two
thousand strong, was retired not to his hill fortress of Eldir but
to Leveringay, seven leagues or more to the south, where, astride
of the main high road southwards, he awaited Lessingham, and
in the meantime burned and harried that countryside where folk
yet held firm for the Vicar. Upon the other part, west-away, the
Admiral was reported moving leisurely up the wide lowland vales
of Fitheryside. Between these forces, each by much outnumbering
his own, was Lessingham now in danger to be taken as the nut
in the crackers; or if, eluding Ercles, he should escape away southwards, then to be shut in betwixt their united power and the
Chancellor's that maintained siege before Laimak. All weighed, he
chose to fight both; and Ercles first, the rather for two respects:
the one, for that Ercles lay the nigher at hand, the other, because

they that dwelt about Leveringay and Mornagay were of a tried loyalty, and, a victory once had there, they were like to take heart and flock to the Queen's banner. But now, going about to fight Ercles, he was resolved that the time and ground and manner of their fighting should be not Ercles's but his.

Lessingham struck camp in the misty early dawn of Friday, marched by the road south a mile or so, then turning suddenly north-eastward behind Proud Eldir, the little black crag that stands on the last spur of the ridge that runs south-west for two leagues or more from Eldir itself, took to the rocky upland valley of Nivararnadale and so came with his army up into the bare wild hill-country that goes up to the watershed of Swaleback. The spring was late, and there were still snowdrifts where the gills look northwards, and ice sometimes in the passes. A wind sprang up out of the north-east, bringing hail and sleet in swirls. Breath of man and horse blew misty on the ice-cold air, and the beards and mustachios of Lessingham and his men were stiffened with hoar-frost. Their march was due east among the heights till past noon, then in a sweep south-east, south, and so down south-westward from Stoopland Brink. In the failing light they rode down to the fir-wood's edge that fringes the open pasture-lands of Leveringay. The wood and the gathering darkness covered their presence: cold they supped and ill, and cold they laid them down.

Ercles's pickets came in to report no enemy this side of Eldir. None the less, as night wore, Ercles began to be ware of somewhat afoot. About the third hour after midnight he summoned his captains and upon counsel taken bade make all ready and so be in posture to join battle, if need be, at point of day. Lessingham waked all night maintaining a kind of fretting skirmishes all night long against Ercles's outposts, as if he feared nothing so much as that Ercles should carry away his army westwards ere battle could be joined, and so touch hands with Jeronimy; for, call it a fine rashness against so great odds to fight with either, Ercles or Jeronimy, to have fought with both at once had been plain madness. But Ercles and his held good espial north-westward along the high road, mindful too of these threatenings from the wood upon their right north-eastward, which yet they supposed belike (since, when the sun is set, all beasts are in the shade) sheltered but some country levies gathered to harry the prince's march and take any stragglers they might hap upon. No man was so fantastical as look that way for Lessingham, last seen at Arrowfirth head, or imagine he and his army could cross, like a flight of battle-cranes, with such suddenness and in such weather and thus early in the year, so wild a tract of mountain and surprise the prince's army upon the flank.

At spring of day Lessingham drew up his men before the wood and let blow up the war-blast. Ercles disposed his battle hastily as best he might, his main battle in the centre, the levies from the free towns upon the wings. His main battle, that had in it his own bodyguard of two hundred chosen men and was all of old tried soldiers, alone outwent in numbers the whole vicarial army under Lessingham which, like a mighty storm thundering from out of the north-east, now fiercely assaulted them. Under that onslaught, this main battle alone of Ercles's held ground: the levies, beginning to be cut down in heaps, presently broke. In an hour, the field was won. Lessingham carried the pursuit to the out-fields of Mornagay and about by Shottenshaw and Hangwater and the Riddering valley. Some fled east to the fell with Brandremart at their heels: some scattered westwards: some fled into the tower of Leveringay. The prince himself escaped to Eldir. There were, by estimation, slain in that battle, and in the rout, seven or eight hundred of his army: scarce had it been more had every soldier of Lessingham's slain his man. Of Lessingham's side but three lost their lives: but one of these was Hortensius, to the Queen a servant of price.

Twelve days Lessingham rested his army after that battle. Men drew to him from the countryside, and he was now fourteen or fifteen hundred strong. Last news of the Admiral was that he had, of all arms, somewhat less than three thousand men, and lay this night, the eighteenth of May, but ten miles off, at Rangby. The next morning Lessingham said to his men, 'You have come south with me upon an enterprise to throw down them that would

o'erset the ancient governance of this land of Rerek, and to bring
again the Queen's peace upon all this land, like as it was when
we fared north last summer to Rialmar. Them that followed and
obeyed Prince Ercles, when he would poll pill and shave the Queen's
subjects in these parts about Leveringay and Mornagay, we have
bloodily overthrown. Now there be many a hundred men here
that follow me in war who have their belongings 'twixt these parts
and the coastlands. For sake of these that have served me truly
in every tide, loth should I be to bid 'em fare south now and leave
their homes and families to the Admiral and his hired fighters out
of Fingiswold or Meszria, that are not friends nor well willers of
yours. Nor I like it not we should turn our back on these pick-
purses: leave 'em so, when they have gotten our money, then to
strike us in the brain from behind. If it be odds against us, I care
not, seeing that which was seen o' Saturday two weeks. But now
is no time to play the litherby now, or lazy lubber. We must on,
and we must in, and we must in deep: huddle blow upon blow.
And now, if there be a man had rather turn back now 'stead of
follow me against the Admiral, let him stand forth. I will bid him
go in peace.' But the whole army roared with a great shouting
that they would follow him and drive the Admiral back into the
sea.

The Lord Jeronimy, considering with himself that he had force
of men sufficient to crush Lessingham: that Lessingham even so
was eager for battle, and moved now upon Rangby to engage him:
that a patient outlengthing of delays is of good effect to wear
down such rash hasty spirits: that westward the landfolk bore
slacker allegiance to the house of Parry than they of these more
inner parts: that being enticed westward Lessingham would be the
less likely to draw to any dangerous head, and that the face of
the land there, standing much in mud and ooze and much cut
about with streams, was less fit for horsemen, wherein was the
main power of Lessingham but the Admiral's weakness: weighing
these things, the Lord Jeronimy wisely refused battle and fell back
north-westwards, drawing Lessingham after him towards Telia. A
little beyond Arminy he changed his course leftward and lay that

night at Bank. Lessingham, willing to force battle ere the Admiral should win to Kaima, came by swift marching across to the coast-road at Minearness, three or four leagues east of Kaima castle and betwixt it and Jeronimy; but Jeronimy, still holding his enemy off, swung now south-eastward into Fitheryside again and the open marish lakelands and streamlands. Lessingham, thus drawn in a circle into this little habited and little friendly countryside, could gather little sure tidings now, save by his own men's eyes and tongues. He came at evening of the twenty-second of May to the farm at Ridinghead, that sits on a rise between the low lands of Westerwater and the Fithery. It was a dank unseasonable misty evening. The farm was deserted and no intelligence to be had. With the fall of darkness the rain began in a heavy downpour, and so settled in for the night. Lessingham supposed the Admiral heading now for Streamsteads, whither next morning he was minded to follow him. But not to be caught by any means at unawares in so thick and water-curtained a night of darkness, he threw out his sentinels and outposts far afield upon every hand with command to maintain an alert through every hour till morning.

The lord Admiral with his forward passed a bridge into Eastering Side and there lay. But as evening fell and the weather thickened, he called a council of his chief officers, whether it were not now the moment to dislodge and to draw westwards again toward Lessingham, happily to surprise him in the night and in these unhandy water-soggen ways destroy him. Which thing being by all applauded as good and forthwith put in ure, they came short of their suppose so far that Lessingham's out-sentinels brought him word of the enemy's approach in time for him to array his army to receive them.

Day broke up, grey and wet, while Lessingham posted his men for battle. The foot, between five and six hundred strong, he posted upon the right where the high ground runs down south and east beyond the steadings. Of these was Brandremart in command, and Lessingham bade him bear forth there the Queen's banner of Fingiswold, so as the enemy should think that here was the

Captain-General and his main battle, and should that way throw the main weight of their assault accordingly. The steadings and outbuildings along the ridge in the middle he held lightly with but a handful of men, bidding them still make great show and din as if of numbers so as the Admiral should imagine a strength of men there and Lessingham's whole force more than the little it was. The whole main body of horse Lessingham held on purpose out of sight upon his left, behind the crest of the little hill, north or leftwards of the farmstead. Towards Fitheryside the ground falls gently to a bottom of moss and bog with a little syke running along beyond it, may be a half mile's distance from the farm. Below the steadings eastwards it is rough muirland, overrun with heather and sweet gale and here and there a dwarfed birch straggling among the blaeberry bushes and tussocks of coarse grass.

The lord Admiral drew up his battle east of the syke, and they advanced now, the main body of foot in the centre little short of three thousand strong, and upon either wing two hundred and fifty horse. But Brandremart, beholding the enemy before him cumbered (and most of all, their horse) in soft ground where they must cross the syke, forgot in that fever the orders laid down for him by Lessingham, and forgot the vantage of his position on the hill and the odds of seven to one they bare in men against him, and suddenly, unable to abide this waiting for them to attack him up the slope, came down with his five hundred, point and edge upon them. Gayllard and Bezardes stood with Lessingham at the corner of a wall north of the northernmost cow-byre whence they could overlook the whole unfolding of the battle: the fury of Brandremart's onset: the bloody brunt in the low wet bog-land: and now the weight of numbers thrusting him back south and west towards the upper ground: and great man-slaying they saw was befallen now. Both in a breath, they willed Lessingham take pity of Brandremart and his: bid the horse charge and succour them.

Lessingham stood there stiff and erect, like an arrow new-fastened in the ground from a far shot. His nostrils quivered: his eyes like wind-troubled stars stared down into the hurly-burly. 'Not yet, on your life,' answered he. They, knowing that look, durst not for a minute speak to him again.

'My lord,' said Gayllard at length: 'flesh and blood can no more. Let us in to help them. See, they are thrust backward up to the pigstyes and the hay-garths. Shall your men die like sheep? Shall my own brother Brandremart? And half of 'em butchered belike already! O 'tis past bearing!'

Lessingham, never shifting his gaze, shut his hand upon Gayllard's strong wrist like hasps of iron. 'Will you lose me this battle?' he said: 'you and Brandremart?' He watched the field in silence a minute: then, 'He at least is about man's work – ha! see the heads fly off: cabbages under his drawing swash-blows! But hath outjumped the time: so, as he brews so must he bake. But you,' he said after a while, through gritted teeth, 'you and Bezardes, be still, you were best. Show me by your quietness you be men, and fit to govern an army – ha! well done, by heavens! – govern an army. Aspy the time. Then strike. Not to stand quittering like quails when the event walketh on razors' edges—' In a sudden witched stillness, his voice faded to silence: a stillness and a silence that had in that rush and tumult of outward things no proper being, save as it were of shadows thrown by the sudden stiffening of Lessingham's eye and mind to a yet tenser strain of inward readiness, while he stared across into the unequal battle, as a great beast's sinews should gather and stiffen before the spring.

'Now!' he said, letting go Gayllard's wrist. The word came as a trumpet's blare, and the face of him, suddenly facing them, as the thunder-smoke of dawn.

The lord Admiral Jeronimy, well assured now of a most complete victory, looked on the battle from a knoll upon the other side to the eastward, beholding (not without some discomfort, as at a sight his very flesh rebelled against) how the royal banner of Fingiswold staggered still backwards, with swayings and swoopings and sudden backward rushes, towards the steadings. From which contemplation he was suddenly shaken by the trumpets and shout and thundering hooves of Lessingham's horse that swept now round and down from the shoulder of the low hill on the west, and came upon his right flank like a rock-fall. The Admiral's two hundred and fifty horse were swept like a herd of goats before that onset, and the flank of his main army of footsoldiery left bare. These, taken at open shields with so well knit a body of fresh horsemen, and in the moment when they had supposed the work done, all save the slaying of Lessingham's remnant among the pigstyes, found for a time in that reeling confusion no respite and no rallying-point. Brandremart, in this breathing-while, gathered his weary and bebloodied companies where the Queen's banner still stood aloft before the steadings, and against all odds struck again. This, as the last axe-stroke when the tree creaks and totters, brought down all in havoc. The Admiral's great army was turned to a rout, which spread many miles over Fitheryside. Belike six hundred perished. Peropeutes, that fought in the centre against Brandremart, was slain, and every man that followed him. Lessingham himself was wounded, charging the Admiral's flank at the head of his men; but of his army the losses, save in Brandremart's battle, were few. Of those five hundred indeed that with Brandremart had withstood the first brunt, more than a hundred fell, and scarce a man of the four hundred that remained but took some hurt or other.

The lord Admiral, seeing this overthrow, and thinking scorn to flee when the day was lost, abode quietly in his place with sword drawn and a few about him who were of the mind to die first ere he should. Lessingham, when the flying rout began, stayed not for so much as to bind up his hurts but galloped across with his bodyguard to the Admiral to bid him peace. The Admiral, when he understood, rode down to meet Lessingham and in a noble silence offered his sword hilt foremost.

'What night-dog howled you this bad counsel, my lord Admiral,' said Lessingham, 'to a come and held side with her grace's enemies? Or hath God closed up the eyes of you, that you knew not the banner of the Queen's most excellent highness of Fingiswold, your lady and mistress? Upon whose commands when I fared south now, intending from Rialmar to Laimak, I looked not to find your lordship here to bar my way with an army; for in truth I was yet to learn you were a truce-breaker and a reneguer of your written word.'

The Admiral reddened and said, 'You do foully, my Lord Lessingham, to abraid me with either. And I will answer you in a manner thus: that I do use to look lower than banners, which be things outward and extern, but I will pry more inward. And against the Queen's highness (whom pray Gods tender and preserve) I ne'er drew sword; nor ne'er broke I word, much less broke solemn indenture. Only against your lordship's usurping cousin, that minister of mischief and sergeant of Sathanas, nuzzled in all evil, against him, 'cause of a hundred forepast proofs, I drew that sword; and against you, 'cause you sustain and aid him. And so will I do again, liability and means presented. Wherefore, if my life must answer for this, so be it. For indeed I was bred up young in King Mezentius' house and his royal father's before him (upon whom be peace), and I am over old, in a manner, to learn new tricks.'

Lessingham beheld him in silence for a while, then answered and said, 'Of the Concordat of Ilkis have not I taken upon me to be warranty for his highness's performance? Thus far, I one of all other, party to that concordat, have not failed of my undertaking. By God, I think I have cause against your excellency, to a sought to foin me in the belly when I go my ways south for to right things.'

Jeronimy, facing him with unwavering gaze, made no reply.

'Take back your sword, my good lord Admiral,' said Lessingham suddenly then, giving it again hilt foremost. 'Ill it is if, within the Queen's highness's dominions in these slippery times, her faithful servants cannot agree. I pray go with me not as prisoner, but upon this only bond between us of word of honour. Bezardes, stay the pursuit: spread it abroad there's peace given and taken 'twixt me and the lord High Admiral. For the army, lie tonight at Rivershaws. And as for particulars,' he said to Jeronimy, 'we'll talk on 'em tonight.'

'Your excellency is very pale,' said the Admiral, as they took hands.

'Pah, a little too much blood-letting. I had forgot. Some, go send a leech,' Lessingham swayed in the saddle: 'nay, 'tis but a fleshing: 'twill mend.' He steadied himself and would not dismount. Two or three galloped away: the Admiral, from a flask at his saddle-bow, poured out cordial drink. 'Too much haste,' he said. Lessingham, quaffing it down while they unbuckled his gorget and stopped the blood, might read in the Admiral's dog-like eyes matter that can be profoundlier discovered by such eyes as those than by noblest tongues with their traffic of words.

Lessingham made his quarters for that Wednesday night of the twenty-third of May in the old moated grange of Rivershaws, a league or more eastwards of Ridinghead in the water-meadows of the Fithery. Weary they were after that battle. Lessingham and Jeronimy supped private in an upper room in the south-western corner of the house, and after supper talked, as well as they could to speak or to be heard for the great noise of the wind which awoke now to strange fury after that rain-soaked day. Lessingham, in buff leather doublet and with Meszrian brocaded slippers to ease his feet, lay at his length on a settle drawn up near the table to the right of the fire. The Admiral sat yet at his wine, at the table, facing the fire and Lessingham.

'No,' Lessingham said between the gusts: 'he must first renounce the crown: no treating till then. That done, let my head redeem the promise but I will secure him all that should be his by the Concordat, and payment too for all misdone against his rights there: Sail Aninma and so forth. But today he standeth plain usurper, and as such I'll not treat with him save at length of weapon.'

'I doubt your lordship will persuade my lord Chancellor so far,' said the Admiral, 'e'en and though I should second you. Many will say, mischief is that here be two usurpers, and choosing Barganax we but choose the less hurtful.'

'They that will say so,' replied Lessingham, 'would spend their eyes to find hair upon an egg. 'Twixt the Vicar and him there's no such likeness; and were it so indeed, you shall see I shall shortly amend it.'

'It was a pity,' the Admiral said, 'that your lordship abode not here to see to it, 'stead of go north to Rialmar.'

The wind roared in the chimney, and sent with a down-blow a great smother of smoke into the room. Lessingham smiled, lifting his goblet against the lamplight. 'You think so?' he said, and drank slowly, as tasting some private memory. But the wine was red. And no bubbles quickened its inward parts.

He stood up and went to the western window behind his seat and, with hands for blinkers to shut out the reflections and the lamplight, peered through the glass into the darkness. The wind came in gusts that lasted two or three minutes at a time, striking the house till the solid masonry quivered: clatter of casements, squealing under the eaves and behind the wainscots, lifting of the arras, lampflames ducking and upflaring; without, trees bent and grass laid flat: a shaking, a leaping, a stamping over the hillside: then sudden silence and calm.

Lessingham, in this din, had not heard the door open behind him; and now, turning from the window, he saw stand in the threshold a man of his guard that said, upon the salute, 'Lord, there attendeth your commands one that nameth himself the Lord Romyrus out of Fingiswold, new ridden from the north, and prays you admit him. And bade me say, 'tis evil tidings, as he were liever not be bearer of unto your lordship.'

Lessingham bade admit him: 'Nay, go not, my lord Admiral. This is our late cashiered Constable: whatso he will say, can say it as well to both of us. I trust him but little, nor his news neither.'

'I like not tidings that come upon a storm,' said Jeronimy.

Lessingham stroked his beard and smiled. 'Omens were ever right, my lord. Let but the event answer the bodement, we say, Behold it was foretold us! If not, say, Such omens work by contraries.' The windows rattled, and the door in a loud gust of wind blew open. Lessingham, standing with folded arms and unruffled brow and in a posture of idle elegance with his shoulders against the pillar of the fireplace, waited at ease, stirring not at all when Romyrus entered, save for a gracious word and movement of the head to bid him welcome.

Romyrus came in: behind him the door shut to: they regarded one another in silence a minute, Jeronimy, Lessingham, and he.

Romyrus was all spattered with mud from spurs to chest. He was like a man that has gone many nights without closing eyelid. There was ten days' growth of beard on his cheek: his face had a yellowed withered look, like a corpse's dug out of some recent grave; and he had the fear in his eyes like a hunted fox's. Lessingham took him by the hand, made him sit, poured out a great bumper of wine, and made him drink it down. 'Whence come you?'

He answered, 'From Rialmar.'

'How then? Did her highness send you?'

He shook his head. His eyes, ringed round like an owl's, seemed now like a dead fish's eyes, goggling and charged with blood, as they looked into Lessingham's. 'What then?'

Without, the wind went whining down Fitherywater like a wounded beast.

'Speak, man,' said Lessingham.

Romyrus said, 'Derxis holds Rialmar.' With a kind of moan he pitched forward on the table, his face buried in his hands.

The silence congealed like blood. Out of it Lessingham said, 'What of the Queen?'

He answered, yet grinding his face against the table, 'She is dead.'

Jeronimy, that had missed these words, saw Lessingham stagger where he stood against the fireplace and turn ghastly. 'Your excellence's wound,' he said, starting up. But Lessingham, seeming to gather himself like a serpent coiled, as the wind again hit the house, caught out a dagger and leapt at Romyrus, shouting terribly, 'A lie! And here's your death for it!' The Admiral, swift as had been praised in a man of half his years, sprang to Lessingham's armed hand, so turning the stroke, which yet ripped from the man's shoulder down to the hucklebone. Lessingham threw him off and, dropping the dagger, sank upon the settle. Romyrus slid from chair to floor with a blubbering noise. The Admiral went to him, raised him, looked to the wound. Lessingham caught the bell-rope, gave it a tang: soldiers ran in: bade them see to Romyrus, bear him out, call a chirurgeon: so sank upon the couch again and there sat bolt upright, staring as a man should stare into horror of darkness.

The wind, in its alternating fits of raging and dying, came again: first a soughing of it far off in the south-west and whistlings far away; then the return, as if some troll or evil wight should run with intermittent bursts and pauses, nearer and nearer, until with a howl of wind and huge flappings as of wings and the lashing of rain, it once more smote the house, vaulting, leading the wild round about and about as of violent waterquakes, riding the roof-tree till it was as if the roof must founder: then, in a gasp, quiet again.

Late that night Amaury, spent with long riding from the north and his horse near foundered, rode in to Rivershaws.

All night Lessingham lay upon his bed, open-eyed.

And the darkness within said: I have consumed and eat up that which was within. Forehead, indeed; but no mind inhabits behind it. Eyes, but there dwells no more anything within that might receive their message. Outward ears, servants of deafness. This throat, since I swallowed all below, is become but the shudder only, above this pit that is me within you.

And the darkness at his left hand said: Hands: fit for all noble uses. Ay, grip the bedside: is that sweet? Hands entertained for your soul's liege ambassadors, so often, into such courts: but now never again for ever.

And the darkness at his right hand laughed like a skull and said: Noble uses, as tonight! aim blade against him that ran to you, a wounded snipe to a stoat, to bring you true tidings, but you lay bloody hands upon.

And the darkness that was within said again: I strive. I will burst this shell that was you. I, that am not, will swell up like a blue poisoned corpse and burst and deflower all being.

And the darkness that was above and beneath said: I am heavy: I am fallen: I draw you: the weight and the woe for ever in your vitals of a misbegotten and never to be delivered birth.

And the darkness that was at his feet said: For then Amaury came (Lessingham looked in the darkness towards the other bed where Amaury lay unsleeping): Amaury, that would have died a hundred deaths in Rialmar to have saved her; but when she had drunk the cup—

The darkness within, and the darkness above, and the darkness beneath, sank, until the drag-hooks became an agony beyond mortal agonies.

The waning moon, in the grey latter hours, said: I wax and I wane: the sickle, the plenilune, the folding darkness. I change, and I change not. You have said it: Beyond time and circumstance. You have said: Upon no conditions.

And as the waning moon to the full, so was now the radiance as of a lunar rainbow that suffused that bedchamber upon memories, a year old that night, of Ambremerine: Vandermast's 'An old fool that is yet wise enough to serve your ladyship:' Vandermast's 'There is no other wisdom;' and again, 'No other power.' And that lady's 'Does that need wisdom?' as she looked at the moon.

XX

THUNDER OVER REREK

THE BAYING TO RAGNAROK • LESSINGHAM FORCES PEACE •
BEROALD'S FORE-JUDGEMENT • THE VICAR WILL STILL PLAY
MACHIAVEL • YET IS SEEMINGLY PERSUADED • COMING OF
THE PARRY TO ARGYANNA • HOMAGE DONE BY HIM TO
BARGANAX • THE DUKE AND HIS VICAR • STRANGE
BROTHERHOOD • BARGANAX TO FIORINDA.

LESSINGHAM upon that night's morrow took his way westwards
with his army slowly towards Mornagay, sending word before
so that all the bruit should run in all Rerek, and so through
Meszria to Zayana, of this back-winter, and of need come upon
all that stood now in civil strife to lay that by, and think on an
enemy indeed. He had it now fully from Amaury: how Derxis,
by the employment of spies, by traitors whom he had greased
well in their hands, or by some other advisoes, had obtained
entry for himself and some few of his men into Rialmar; where,
with the chancing together of several matters which fell out well
to his hand and he used them better, he had contrived his purpose
so close as procure the murder, at one chop, of Bodenay and a
dozen more. Which done, the Queen's power, made headless,
might no longer but sever and dissolve, leaving this Derxis to
be his own carver: a beast unmerciless.

Lessingham, now for two days, scarce took bite nor sup. Whether

he slept none knew: only that not an hour in the night but
somewhere was he to be seen about the camp, armed and in his
riding-coat. Save to give orders, not a word had he for any man,
neither durst any speak with him. It was, through these days, as
if there rode there a man abiding indeed in his bodiness, but lapped
in lead: in all else deceased, but his great heart carried him. And
now began to be heard in a susurration about men's ears, the
thing that in all those months past in Rialmar had not been spoke
nor imagined except by Derxis, with so wise a discretion had
Lessingham and the Queen refrained themselves: but now it was
said, What grief was this that should so benumb a man, for but
loss of his Queen? And it was answered, Past question, she loved
him paramour and no other. Which coming to Amaury's ears, he
was highly displeased: said to him that let fall the word, 'I should
slit thy tongue for chattering so wide,' and by all discreet means
wrought to scotch this prittle-prattle. But the rumour, once sown,
ran like quitch-grass in a garden, much underground; and yet to
no bad effect, knitting their hearts the closer in his service as
to a man not great only, but great and unhappy. For of such kind
were most that followed Lessingham, that their loves grew up as
the watercresses, slowly, but with a deep root: not so ready to
praise the sun at his uprising as worship him at his downgate.

The third afternoon they came to Mornagay. Lessingham would
not lie here, but press on by Killary and so by the Tivots and
Scorradale Heath to be in Bardardale before nightfall. Amaury rode
with him, and, after the carriage beasts were well through the ford,
they two drew ahead. On the great open mile-wide ridge of the
heath Lessingham reined in Maddalena and, turning in the saddle,
looked back northwards. The sun was set in a clear sky: the heath
was become a darkness made up of all shades of blackish greens:
the sky a pallour of all greys akin to blue: tarns and standing
waters gleamed lighter than the sky itself, as if lit from under.

From the east, little white wisps of mist came like feelers
drifting from right to left over the dark heathland.

Lessingham spoke: "You were with me that night thirteen
months ago, in Mornagay.'

'Yes'

'Never name it again. Never name to me again aught that came of it.'

'No, my lord.'

'What think you, Amaury? Is it true that all things have their life, their limits, their diseases, and their death?'

'All things?'

'Yes, all.'

'Not all, my lord.'

'What then? What hath not?'

'You have bid me never name it.'

'I say, all things, Amaury. Dispute it not, else God knows I might murder you. I am in these days become a wild beast, first made fierce with tying, and then let loose. And not I alone: so is all become.'

'I hope, not murder me, that loved you 'bove the world.'

'Yes, you and all. Then gallop apace to my ruin.'

'O, this is madness.'

'No,' said Lessingham, and his voice was like the muttering of distant thunder: 'it is like the Twilight of the Gods: the baying of the hell-dog before Gnipa's cave: the crowing of the cocks in the three worlds: will you call that nightingales? –

'Geyr nú Garmr mjök fyrir Gnípuhelli:
Festr mun slitna, enn Freki renna!'

'Yes, Amaury: "The fast must be loos'd, and the Wolf run free."'

Amaury sat silent, his jaw set. Those feelers had by now drawn a coverlet of mist over all the heath, hiding the ground. On the hummock where Lessingham and Amaury waited, their horses' feet were in the mist but their own heads in clear air, and the stars clear and bright above them.

Lessingham laughed. 'Say over to me again, those words he used. For God knows I have dreamed and waked and dreamed till I know not well which is dream and which true.'

'I dare not say it.'

'Say it,' said Lessingham terribly.

Amaury obeyed: 'He said, "If not to be my Queen, then you shall at least be no longer the strumpet of a soldier of fortune."'

A full minute Lessingham neither spoke nor moved. His face, seen sideways, proud and unreadable against the May night, showed like stone or iron. There came the ring of bridles up from the Scorradale side, of the vanward nearing the brow. Lessingham shook rein, turned and rode away down before them into Bardardale. Amaury, following beside Maddalena's off hind quarter, heard him say in his teeth, 'I have shut my mind against these things.' Then suddenly drawing rein and staring into Amaury's eyes through the darkness: 'Remember that,' he said. 'But remember, too, not winged horses shall prevail him to outskip my vengeance. And so, Amaury, to work.'

There went messengers now, while Lessingham and the Admiral lay in Bardardale, betwixt them and the Chancellor before Laimak. By this, in a few days it was brought to a meeting betwixt them, and a charter of peace sealed with Lessingham upon provisoes and a truce to endure until the fourteenth day of June, and in the mean season counsel to be had for that matter with the Duke, late come up to Argyanna after sojourning at home awhile in Zayana. Upon the tenth of June came these lords, Lessingham, Beroald, and Jeronimy, with Amaury, to Argyanna. Here with the Duke was Count Zapheles, and the Lords Melates and Barrian and a dozen besides, men of mark. Medor, wielding by procuration the ducal power, abode yet in Zayana.

Lessingham was greatly feasted and nobly received, nor, when they fell to their business, seeking of agreement, were they slow to find sured ground: at first, common cause against Derxis, to destroy him and revenge his abomination in Rialmar: secondly, King Mezentius's lawful issue being by two murders in this short while miserably dead, there remained no colourable pretender to the throne but the Duke, whose claim thus stood waterfast. But when it was to speak of the Lord Horius Parry, and upon what terms the Duke and his would take him into their peace again, straight they lost (as for agreeing) more in a minute than they got in a day: Lessingham of the one side, all they of the other against him. The Duke required surrender without all conditions: 'Which, come what will, he cannot choose but be forced unto, in a month or less. By God, I discommend your wit, my Lord Lessingham, if you think I know not a fox by his bush now, or think, now I hold him earthed in Laimak, I'll let this one wend free at your asking, to play me such another touch as last winter he did.'

'He will never surrender without conditions,' said Lessingham. 'Why should he? Would you or I?'

'Well,' said the Duke, 'no more blind reckonings. This is the one sure card: soon as ever I have him, to cut off his head.'

Lessingham answered, 'We be all agreed that it is time we began to destroy our enemies, and first let us begin at Derxis that hath done villanies not to be spoken and threateneth our mere being. For this, we must give over even rightful quarrels amongst ourselves, else can we never achieve it. And the Vicar is a great captain not easily to be spared in the manage of so great a war as this. Besides, our folk of Rerek are stubborn and hard and can not easily digest the government of a stranger.'

'They have by many a hundred rebelled against him now,' said Barganax.

'That,' replied Lessingham, 'was when I was not by.'

'They will obey you sooner than him. Let him go.'

Lessingham stroked his beard. 'No. If your grace take that way, I sit out.'

Two days they argued it. The second, the Chancellor took Lessingham apart: said, 'My Lord Lessingham, you have gotten the right ear of his grace; but in this you will not move him. This ill weed of yours, maugre your warming and watering, hath now been parched up. Only bethink you: upon what consideration, but of this man alone, should the Duke have seized power in Rerek and, by implication, in Fingiswold? 'Gainst his sister he'd ne'er a stood usurper, but 'gainst this man only that under her name cloaked his large ambitions. Your lordship hath heard how myself did in aid of that enterprise allege a law which barreth women from kingdom to the end the realm fall not into the hands of a strange prince or nation. 'Tis of questionable authority: I lent it mine, not for any quarrel with the Queen's highness (on whom be peace), but because I would not trust this man. You and he sort very ill together. If conscience will not suffer you to oppose his interest, then get you gone for a season: leave him to us. We shall speedily deal with him.'

'The things,' replied Lessingham, 'which be main counts against his highness my cousin were done when I was beyond the Wold upon the Queen's business. For all that was then misdone I have, upon his behalf, offered atonement.'

'I see your lordship will not hear reason,' said Beroald. 'Well, you are like to pay dear upon your bond.'

'That the Gods must rule,' answered he. 'But remember, I am upon safe conduct here in Argyanna, and with right upon safe conduct to return to that army I have afoot, and with that, be it little in numbers, I have ere this done somewhat. And remember the lord Admiral is upon parole to go back with me if this peace be not concluded. And if his grace will have no peace (and a hard peace for the other is this I offer you, and good for his grace), but will, as is now said, slay the Vicar, then I will promise you this: it shall be so countervenged that it shall be spoken of a hundred years hereafter.'

Beroald said, 'We will not talk on thunder.'

'Lessingham,' said the Duke, coming upon them in this: 'the man is not by a noble heart such as yours in any way to be avouched or defended. Must our friendship fly in pieces for sake of such a villain?'

'If our friendship, my lord Duke (which the Gods forfend) must fly in pieces, 'tis because, to end his heroical great defence that hath so long time held you off and your armies, you will in cold blood use this same cruelty I have so oft checked in himself, of the beheading-block. But if my friendship be aught, then prove it: for I have told your grace I will, so you give him

but to me, be answerable upon my honour and upon my life
that he shall all repay and no more disease you.'

'But to what wild purpose—?' Barganax paused silent for a
minute, looking in Lessingham's eyes. There sat in them a
bantering mocking look that he knew, but as belonging to other
eyes: not to these speckled grey eyes of Lessingham, but to green
eyes, beaconing as from every unrest and from every incertitude
and peril, which things, taking on those eyes' allurance, burned
high and desirable beyond all lusts and fires.

'Each to his taste,' Lessingham said. 'I have given you reasons
enough in policy. And if you will have more, say he is a dangerous
horse: say I taste a pleasure in such riding.'

'Say you will break your neck, my Lord Lessingham,' said
the Chancellor.

But Barganax and Lessingham, like as formerly at the council-
board in Ilkis, now faced one another as if, for all their company
about them, they stood alone, and a third presiding: a third,
perceived but by them alone; and scarcely, indeed, to be named
a third, as being present strangely to the Duke in the person of
Lessingham, and to Lessingham in the Duke.

Two days later, a little before noon, Lessingham rode into
Laimak. It was a day of close, hazy weather, boiling up for
thunder-storms. The Chancellor's armies still held siege before
the castle, for the allies had no mind that the Vicar should
use this truce for getting in of provision, then defy them anew
and so drag on. Lessingham and his they let through with no
delays, for he bare letters of credence under seal of Zayana. All
the valley for a mile about the castle was wasted with fire and
eaten up. The Vicar greeted Lessingham as a man might greet
a son long given up for lost. He carried him to his closet in
the keep, and hither was dinner brought them, poor campaigning
fare indeed: bacon pies, black rye bread, cheese, and smoked
fish, with a runlet of muscadine to wash it down and a little
joy the heart withal.

'Are you come with a treaty in your wallet?' said the Vicar

when the waiting-men had set all in order and, upon his command, left them to dine private.

Lessingham smiled. 'No more treaties, cousin, of my making. I have somewhat here: but you shall sign for yourself, if it like you; and no room for cavil afterward.'

'It will keep till after dinner.'

'Yes. It will keep so long: not much longer.'

The Vicar looked swiftly up. Lessingham's face, careless and with eyes averted, was not to be read. 'You're come none too soon,' said the Vicar then, and took in a great mouthful. 'Rations left for seven days. Starving men make best fighters; but 'tis not a discipline fit to hold 'em to too long: though it be good to savage 'em, yet in this other 'tis as bad, that drawn out beyond a day or two it sloweth and feebleth the animal spirits. And so ninth day from this had I set for the grand carousal, warm meat and blood puddings i' the field below there, and the leavings for the crows to pick on.'

'Rant it not to me as if I were a woman,' said Lessingham. 'You have not sufficiency to withstand their forces: not one hour, in the open.'

'Well: end so, then.' He watched Lessingham through half-shut lids. 'Better so than swallow another treaty like the last you crammed down my throat, cousin.'

'Your highness is a great soldier,' said Lessingham; 'but politician, not so good. How should you now look for so good a treaty as that? which was just and equal, but you did break every article and published your every breach too from the house-tops. Be thankful if I have saved you your life, and some few false beams of your supposed honour.'

'So!'

For a long while, eyeing each other, they ate and drank in silence. The Vicar's neck swelled like a puff-adder's. At length, 'You've been a weary while,' he said, 'dallying on the door-step: more than a fortnight. Talking with those devils (the sweat and swink they've cost me!) Might a talked to me ere this, I'd have thought?'

Lessingham said nothing, only with a delicate air raised his cup and drank, regarding his cousin the while with level and thoughtful eyes. The Vicar took a gobbet of bacon-rind out of his mouth: leaned sideways to give it to Pyewacket. The play of the light revealed, as might some great master's brush, the singularity that belonged, but seldom so lively seen as now, to his strangely-sorted countenance: heavy eyelids, wide-winged jutting nose, lean lips like a snake's, delicate ears, ruffianly reddish-be-bristled jowl, serene smooth forehead, small swift-darting eyes: a singularity of brutish violence joined with some nobler element in a marriage wherein neither was ever all subdued to other, nor yet ever all distinct; so that divorce must needs have crippled a little both, as well the good as the bad. And upon Lessingham, while he so watched this renewing of a pageant he knew well, a mantle seemed to fall, enduing limb and sinew and poise of neck and head with a grander and yet more pantherine grace. And the Grecian lineaments of Lessingham, and the eyes of him thus savouring his cousin, seemed not so much to be informed now with a swift beast's majesty or an eagle's, but rather as if strength and mastery should take to itself the airy loveliness of a hummingbird, and so hang hovering on viewless wings, as the bird quivers bodiless upon air beside a flower, uncertain into which honeyed fold amid petals it shall aim its long and slender beak.

'You were ever at your best,' he said after a little, 'back to the wall. Trouble is, set you at your ease, you fall athinking. And that is bad for you.'

'I know not, cousin, what you account good for a man. My belt's half a foot the shorter since Yule-tide.'

'What dispossessed your wits,' Lessingham said, 'soon as my back was turned, treat this Duke as you would some poor-spirited slow boy? And did I not tell you what he is? And could you not use him accordingly?'

'That which is, is,' said the Vicar, and drank and spat 'That which was, was. That which shall be, 'tis that concerneth me and you. This new turn in Rialmar,' fleet as a viper's his eyebeam flashed upon Lessingham's face and away, 'hath upsy-versied all, ha? Or how think you on't? Look you,' he said, after a silence, and leaned forward, elbows on the table: 'I will tell you a thought of mine: may be good, may be naught, howsome'er hath come me oft in mind since Kutarmish set all afire here. That Derxis. Could a been used, ha? Matter of marriage, had't been nicely handled.' He paused, studying through red eyelashes Lessingham's face, inscrutable and set now as a God's likeness done in marble. 'And so, using Akkama to put down Zayana, afterward – well, there be ways and means.'

Lessingham toyed with his wine-cup. 'Ways and means!' He tossed off the wine, sprang up, walked to the window, and there stood looking down on him as in a high displeasure. 'Pray talk to me of your soldiering, for there I can but admire, and even love you. But these twisting policies, I can but laugh at 'em.'

'Nay, but hangeth together. My wardship's lost: so. Well, shift weight to the well-lodged foot then.' He paused, sat back in his chair. Their eyes met. 'I know not what this paper may say which you have in your purse, cousin; but would you'd a talked to me first ere talk to Zayana. You had not thought on this other way, ha? and yet opened fair before you: to use Derxis, I mean, as our instrument? And not too late now, neither, if rightly handled.'

'What are you,' said Lessingham, 'but a bloody fool? Have I not told you long ago there's no way but the straight cut? the Mezentian way, not these viperine crawlings: weld all fast under Barganax now, and crush this vermin, this of Akkama. Sweet Gods in heaven, cousin, is't not your own kith and kin (in a distant way, I grant)? And as for use Derxis, I'd as soon the putrid skull of some invenomed serpent, and use't for my wine-cup.'

'Go,' said the Vicar, and there was the look in his eyes as of one that weigheth *pro* and *contra* as he gazed on Lessingham: 'here's a talker.'

Lessingham took two parchments from his doublet: tossed them before the Vicar among the dishes. 'Take it or no, 'tis you to choose, cousin: but if yes, today's the last day: sign it or say good-bye. You may thank the kind Gods and me, that have hooked you out of this quagmire you have by your own curst mulish obstinacy rushed and stuck fast in. May be, since indeed I think you're mad now, you'll liefer choose your feast of tripes in Laimak home-mead a week hence; or t'other choice: that the Duke will give you, and please him best. Three livelong days I wrought for you, and little thanks I see for it, ere I won him to offer you this good bargain, 'stead as he would a had it: and that was, get you dead or alive, as in a month's time or less no power on earth could a letted it: head you and side you, and nail the meat up so for crows to eat on Laimak walls.'

But the Vicar had snatched the parchment and was by now half-way through it, his great stubbed finger following the words as he read. When he came to the end, he read all again, this time the duplicate copy: then, without word spoken, reached pen and ink from the sideboard and signed and sealed. He then stood up: came to Lessingham beside the window, took him by both hands. 'Think not I forget it, cousin, that this is by the great wit and prowess that is in you, the which I mind me well hath stood me in good stead many a time and yet shall do again.'

'Good, then we're friends,' said Lessingham. 'You have ta'en it well, cousin, as a wise prince should do. And the sixth day from today, as there writ down, your highness will come to him in Argyanna, enact that ceremony, your allegiance full and perfect?'

'Ay, as a cat laps milk.'

'You do well, cousin.' He took up one copy of the concordat, scanning the hands and seals: the Duke's, Beroald's, Jeronimy's, and now the Vicar's. 'This raiseth the siege today. I'll begone with it, and we meet 'pon Wednesday in Argyanna. But remember, cousin,' he said upon departing: 'I look for deeds from you upon this: no more false closes designed to shun a final end.'

'Go, you have read me a fair lecture,' answered he. 'Think not I'll stumble at a straw now that I've leapt over a block. Fare you well.'

The twentieth day of June was appointed a great festival and holiday for ratifying of this peace whereby, Barganax being now in both Rerek and Meszria taken for King, the lords of those countries should in his service fare shortly with great armies north across the Wold, win back Rialmar, and so carrying the war through Akkama ravish and ruinate all the cities and people thereof and lay them under subjection, seizing above all King Derxis whom they meant to punish and kill not as befits a noble person.

Betimes that morning was the main army of the Chancellor, come down on purpose from Hornmere side and Ristby and those parts, besides the Duke's two thousand that he how held in Argyanna and thereabouts, marched under banners and with singing of war-songs and music of trumpets and drums three times round the bluff without the moat. The Duke, with fifty red-bearded men of his bodyguard bearing their great two-handed swords, had place of honour before the drawbridge. He rode upon a fierce white stallion with sweeping mane and tail and with harness all black and trappings and saddlecloth of black sendaline. Of like sad hue were the Duke's cloak and bonnet with black estridge-feathers and all his armour: black gloves upon his hands: the very ruff about his throat black, that should have been white: all this in formal sign of mourning and lamentation. The Lords Beroald and Jeronimy wore plumes of mournings in their hats and black mourning cloaks: the like tokens wore every one, high or low, man or woman, soldiers, townsfolk, that day; but the Duke alone, both for his royal estate and near kinship, that extremity of blackness.

And now, well upon the hour appointed, marching from the north down the granite-paven causeway that in a ten-mile span, laid on a foundation of thousands upon thousands of strong oaken piles, bridges the quaking-bogs in the midst of which is Argyanna, came the Vicar and his following. Twenty trumpeters on horseback headed the march: great was the flashing of their helms and trumpets, all of silver: their kirtles and hose were dyed with saffron: they had black mourning saddle-cloths and black cloaks: at every twenty paces they sounded upon their trumpets the owl-call of the house of Parry. Behind them, guarded by two score of Lessingham's black riders, went the royal banner of Fingiswold, by him brought victorious from the northland through many deadly chances and the bloody battles at Ridinghead and Leveringay. The owl of Laimak, sable, armed and beaked gules upon a field or, followed after: its motto, *Noctu noxiis noceo*, 'Nightly I prey upon vermin.' There went a company of veteran spearmen of Rerek four by four behind it, helmed and byrnied and with great oblong shields. The Vicar himself rode with Lessingham a score of paces behind these footsoldiery, and a score of paces before the rest of their following: Amaury, Brandremart, Bezardes, Thrasiline, Daiman, and so horse and foot to the number of five hundred or more bringing up the rear.

Now when they were come close under Argyanna before the gates and the drawbridge, the Count Rossilion bearing the Vicar's banner rode forth with two trumpeters that blew a fanfare. And Rossilion, doffing cap to the Duke and reading from a writing in his hand, cried out with a loud voice that all might hear: 'For behalf of his most excellent lordship Horius Parry I do salute the Lord Barganax, Duke of Zayana, and do receive and acknowledge him the said Duke to be great King of Fingiswold and of all states and dominions appertaining thereto, and in particular of all Meszria and the Marches and of all this territory or land of Rerek and places situate therewithin, being especially the fortresses or strong holds of Laimak, Kessarey, Megra, Kaima, and Argyanna, and of this March of Ulba. And thus saith the Lord Horius Parry: I hereby give, O King, into the hands of your princely highness all those estates and powers whatsoever which, whether as private-vassal and subject, whether as Vicar of the Queen, whether as Lord Protector, I herebefore have held under kingdom of Queen Antiope of glorious memory (upon whom be peace), hoping that your serenity may adjudge them to have been truly and diligently by me administrated and used, in the behoof of the weal public and the great glory of the crown of the three kingdoms. Humbled on my knee I now kiss your grace's hand, tendering my love and service true and perfect, and fearfully expecting your royal commands.'

The Vicar meanwhile, being dismounted from his horse, and standing ten paces or so behind Rossilion, looked on and listened with no outward sign save the great puffing out and great redness of his neck. He was all armed, with a byrny of polished iron edged at throat and wrists and skirt with links of gold; thigh-pieces and greaves and toe-pieces and golden spurs. No weapon he bore, only in his right hand his staff vicarial. Two boys, dressed in the russet and purple livery of his bodyguard, bare up behind him the train of his great black cloak.

'But look upon him,' said Zapheles in the Chancellor's ear. 'What charter of peace can you contrive, my lord, but this great devil will break it?'

Beroald shrugged his shoulders.

'Well, now a hath put his head in the lion's mouth,' said Melates, as Rossilion ended, 'cannot some contrive to set the King in a fume against him? Bite it off, and all were well.'

''Tis but yonder Lessingham standeth 'twixt this and that,' said Barrian. 'A thing past man's understanding.'

'That he so stands? Or that his grace should heed him?'

'Both,' said the Chancellor with a tart smile.

Lessingham said in the Vicar's ear, 'Your highness would be well advised, put off your bonnet: he did the like for you, if I am told aright, in the Salimat last autumn. Besides there is about your bonnet the diadem, which you must assume again but at his bidding.'

'Let be. I'm afeared of this sun. Shall not fry my brains, concordat or no concordat.'

Men noted that in the very act of homage the Parry wore still his crown vice-royal with rich stones and orient pearl beset. Some murmured at it: the Duke, whose eye no littlest thing might ever escape, could not but note it, but yet let it go unremarked. Upon kissing of hands, the trumpets of either side blew a fanfare. The Vicar upon that, taking from off his head the coronal, presented it to the Duke, who straightway raised it on high that all should see, then set it again upon the head of the Vicar, saying, for all to hear: 'Be witness whom it may concern, and the blessed Gods Who keep the wide heaven, that, upon homage thus made to me in my estate as high master of these kingdoms and agreeably to articles of peace late sealed and made betwixt us, I do hereby assign unto you, Horius Parry, the strong holds and demesnes of Laimak, Kaima, and Kessarey, and all the country and principality of old Rerek, but not Megra nor the lands north of Swaleback, and not Argyanna nor the Ulba March, to hold as my vicar or vicegerent, answerable to no man save to me, but to me to be answerable with your head. In witness whereof, receive this coronal and name of Vicar of Rerek.'

This done, amid great noise of trumpets and drums and shouting of all the soldiers and people there assembled, this solemnity had its end. But first the Duke let proclaim silence, and bade the Lord Beroald say forth on his behalf this, in a great voice, that all might know: 'Thus saith the most renowned and most mighty prince and lord, Barganax, great Duke of Zayana, our sovereign master and King: that it is his pleasure, even as he will change not these mourning colours till he shall have beat the outborn usurper from the land and with the Gods' help punished him with death, so will he think it scorn, and not suitable with his princely dignity, to take yet the King's name, but will first, like as all other Kings of Fingiswold, be crowned in Rialmar. At his command publish it so accordingly. God save his serene and most excellent highness, Barganax, Duke of Zayana, of the three kingdoms our sovereign lord.'

They rode now in a progress once about the hold with their bodyguards, the Vicar and Barganax riding in the midst somewhat apart, jointly taking the salute from those on the walls and those in the field and all the army drawn up beside the way in double line, so as men should perceive with their eyes this new condition of peace and friendship, and the conclusion of the war and hate there had been so long betwixt them.

'This is a great pride in you, my lord Duke,' the Vicar said, 'not to take the style of King.'

Barganax smiled. 'I had thought it a great modesty.'

'It was to shame me,' said the Vicar. 'Not clip the wings only of my vicariate, a thing I honourably endured, but make me do homage but to a ducal cap.'

''Las,' said the Duke: 'I fear I was thinking of my own affair, and not at all of you, my lord.'

'I was gulled in it,' said the Vicar. There shone in his eyes, the Duke's head being for the moment turned away to acknowledge acclamations upon his right, a most cruel, mortal, and inexorable hatred.

'Give credit, the thing ne'er entered my head,' said the Duke. 'But indeed,' he said, 'now I think on't, I can but praise your courteous carriage and affability; for indeed, God knoweth well enough without remembrancer, myself did bow as low, and to a like necessity, not a year since, i' the Salimat.'

''Tis of no moment,' said the Vicar. 'Only for this I thought fit to speak on't to your grace, considering we shall wisely avoid now whatsoever might diminish my estimation and authority, and so tie me shorter when we should work together for common ends.'

The Duke said, 'I'll not forget it. I have bespoke a banquet about noon, which I hope your highness and whom you will of your following will honour me to share with us. After that, hold council of war. Midsummer already, and much to do ere we may march in full force. And it were folly think to lead a great army over the Wold once it be turned September.'

The same night, when save for the sentinels upon the walls and at the gates none was astir, Barganax and Lessingham went forth alone together to take the air and so came slowly a mile or more down the causeway from Argyanna southwards, walking and talking. The leavings of sunset, dusky orange-tawny on the horizon, crept slowly round towards the north. Bats skimmed overhead.

'A month today, then,' said Lessingham: 'that's the twentieth. In Mornagay.'

'In Mornagay,' said the Duke. 'What shall we be? Seven thousand?'

'That's not to count the princes and the free towns.' 'We shall be too many.'

'A stroke that shall not miss,' Lessingham said, and they fell silent.

After half an hour they came to a stand. Barganax picked up a stone and tossed it in a reed-bed to wake the reed warblers that forthwith began their chattering. He said, 'What make you of that light, there in the darkest bit among the moss-hags? A pool? A broken goblet throwing back the sky? A broken sword? A whole nation of glow-worms gone astray? A chink in the saucepan lid to let us see 'tis here they brew the marsh-fires?'

'I think you shall find it but stagnant water if you go to it,' said Lessingham. 'Here, it might be all those things.'

'A light asleep in the dark,' said the Duke. 'I should like to paint this night,' he said, after a little. 'The past: all gone. The thing to come, crouching in those obscurities of ooze and reed-bed, ready to spring. The thing present: you and me. And that is strangest of all: unpaintable, too, like as are most things worth painting.'

Lessingham was silent.

'Were you a tenderer of your own safety, you'd now leave me,' said the Duke. 'Espousing my cause thus wholly, and enforcing this last settlement of peace upo'n him, you now go naked to his claws. No argument remains of self-interest, as before most strongly served, why he should not destroy you.'

'I have now a kind of freedom,' said Lessingham. 'I'll not give up you; nor I'll not give up him.'

'Pity that savage mare of yours, who biteth and striketh all men else, will not content you.'

'Would she content your grace, and you stood where I stand?'

They began to walk slowly, in their companionship of silence, back again towards Argyanna that stood squat, square, and black, against the sky to the north. They were half-way home when the Duke began to say, under his breath, as if the words had been not words but echoes only, answering the measured tread of his musing footsteps along the causeway.

'Earth I will have, and the deep sky's ornament:
    Lordship, and hardship, and peril by land and sea—
And still, about cock-shut time, to pay for my banishment,
    Safe in the lowe of the firelight I will have Thee.'

Lessingham, who had listened with breath held back lest a
word should be lost, suddenly, when the stave was ended, checked
in his stride. They halted and faced one another in the stillness.
'Who are you?' Lessingham said at last, staring through the soft
darkness into Barganax's face: so like to his sister's, save for the
varying characters of he and she, that Lessingham's very being
was, for that likeness, confounded within him. Barganax made
no answer. The silence was full of bird-voices afar on marshes
that never go quite to sleep: now a redshank's cry, now some
little plover. Lessingham said, 'Who made that stave?'

'That? I made it.'

'You?' In the stillness a curlew whistled far away, awake in
the night.

'I like it,' Barganax said, 'if for its very vanity.'

'Its vanity!' said Lessingham, and they stood silent.

'Why did you bid me,' he said then, 'to your love-feast upon
Ambremerine? Why that night did she draw me through doors?
What changed then in your throne-room? Why did she send me
to Rialmar? Who is she?' he said, last of all.

Barganax shook his head. ''Las,' he said, 'I can answer none
of these riddles.' He met Lessingham's eyes through the dark.
Inch for inch he and Lessingham stood of a height. It was as if
he could not easily resolve to let loose that which was upon his
tongue. At last he spoke: 'Lessingham, I can, as I said, answer
none of your riddles. But I will tell you this: upon Michaelmas
night, taking my ease in a certain house of Vandermast's, I looked
in a mirror and I beheld there not my own face, but yours.'

Lessingham neither spoke nor moved.

'Well,' Barganax said. 'What was it? Know you such a house?'

'And I beheld,' said Lessingham, stare for stare, 'your face,
not mine. In that house. Upon Michaelmas night.'

He swung round: began walking again homeward. Barganax, at his elbow, heard the gritting of his teeth upon a smothered groan, as a man might grit them with the turning of the blade in a wound. But in time, as they walked on in that commerce of mind with mind in which speech were but a troubling of the stream that else runs crystal clear, Lessingham tasted again, as upon Ambremerine, the leaning of Barganax's spirit towards that seeming woman of his; and strangely in the tasting took balm to his own mortal hurt, until his own spirit within him was borne up on high like a great violent flame of fire, as for the grand last act indeed.

The Duke wrote that night, and sent it south by safe hand betimes the next morning:

'*Righte Expectable and Noble Lady, these to kiss your hands and informe you that matters occurent must hold me in the north now well till autumne. I would be sured therefore that your Ladyship will keep my private lodging as your own upon Akrozayana till these inconveniences be over past. I have todaye with the Parry sealed againe the infringible band of faith, but fear I shall never love him, nor would you, not for the honesty of his conversation neither nice in bodie but grossly sett and thick. And kinde will creep where it may not go, hee is enemy I think to all men save to such as will subject themselves to him. As for L. I doo think your Ladyship knoweth more than I of his affair, I mean not my Sisters parte which was with so much wisedome kept close as never a whisper went on it, I mean things deeper farre than that. My thoughts growe busy that some way there bee IV of us but some way II only. O beguiler of guiles, opening of your garments, sudden flashing of your Beauty, what webs are these. But no more, it is coriander in swete wine. I shall never have done when I am once in, and never settle my self for want of lipwork in stead of penwork. O Blacke Lily one and onemost, disdainer, and hallower, of all things, blinder of sight, bedde of the dragon and the dove, robe state and crowne imperiall of my desire, in daylight acte my Cynosura, wanting you here, in my dreames I taste you, and wanting wordes to endear you, call you but Mine, me, Yours.'*

XXI

ENN FREKI RENNA

PACK'D CARDS WITH DERXIS • THE THING LAID BARE TO
LESSINGHAM • LAST CLASH OF THE ADAMANTS • INSULTANS
TYRANNUS • THE WOLF RUNS • ANTIOPE IN MORNAGAY.

LESSINGHAM, being by the Duke confirmed now in his office of
Captain-General, departed next day out of Argyanna about taking
order, against the trysting-time set for Mornagay, for yet more
forces and muniments of war. Upon which great business was he now
for weeks journeying without delays or respite through Rerek and
the Marches and Outer Meszria, cementing alliances, pacifying
squabbles. The High Admiral was rode back to take the water again
at Kessarey and so move to Kaima; Zapheles and Melates fared
south into Meszria; the Lord Horius Parry home to Laimak. Barrian
the Duke sent in embassage to those Princes Ercles and Aramond,
to salve their wounds with estates and signiories in the north there,
carved out of that great slice which had by the peace of Argyanna
been trimmed off from the vicariate. The Duke himself, with the
Chancellor, and with Lessingham's thousand horse, lay yet in
Argyanna, meaning in time to move north in great strength; and
command was that all with their armies should come together the
twentieth of July at Mornagay, thence to march north to the Wold,
whence tidings now began to be had of Derxis's advance southwards,
as upon a design for invasion of Rerek ere summer be too far worn.

But the Vicar, soon as he was come again to Laimak, retired himself to his private chamber; took from the iron chest, where he kept such matters, the new concordat; sat thinking with himself an hour or two; then sent for Gabriel Flores. 'Come hither, good pug, let's closely to our business. You must north again, "to Megra", as we'll call it: "to Arcastus", we'll say.'

Gabriel waited obedient.

'I'll set down nought in writing, no more than I would before. This,' the Vicar flicked the edge of the parchment with a finger, ''gins smell too much of the inkhorn already. Get yonder ragman's-roll by rote ere you go: tell it him word by word. Then tell him this pointeth north to his destruction ere he shall be ready to come conquering down hitherward: that, the Queen being dead by some misfortune – how, I know not: miss not that – and the royal line of Fingiswold come so to an end, this Zayana entirely hath now the love of all nobles, princes, and all other in the realm save mine only, to back his usurpation; and mine but in show and policy. Speak to him so: show him what stark folly 'twere in him to enterprise to seize kingdom here without some bolsterer or comforter in his deed: and for such, he may take me, whose help is worth ten armies; and so on. Speak earnestly, even till his teeth run a water. Let him understand by all means that you are sent to practise my good and his. Then let him know my easy condition: letters patent under his royal hand and seal confirming me in perpetuity, as for him and his heirs and successors, his Vicar for all Meszria and all Rerek; 'pon receipt of which by your hand, I will, in token of faith and as his loyal obedienciary, shortly send him the heads or other proofs of the taking off of the persons here most disaffected, and these the principal: Barganax, Beroald, Jeronimy. Which I shall find good opportunity to perform ere it be well onward in summer, having lulled 'em into so lethargic a sleep with this,' and he flicked the parchment again, 'and preparing me an occasion.'

'Your highness hath forgot to name one name,' said Gabriel, 'will, for the king's jealous hate and spleen, weigh with him 'gainst these as gold against feathers.'

'And whose is that, my pigsnye?'

'Your highness will not wish I should name it.'

The Vicar's eyes narrowed upon him. 'No, or may be I'd tear your tongue out.' With such a sudden fury he hurled the inkpot, that Gabriel was barely in time to save his teeth, or may be an eye, by swift raising of his arm.

'Meddle not beyond your commission,' said the Vicar, while Gabriel mopped the ink-splashes with his handkercher and looked to his bruised arm. 'Sit down. Study your part. I'll hear it over ere you go.'

Gabriel was ready to set forth that evening. The rather not to be remarked, he made himself like a peddling chapman; took a spare horse and some huckstering wares, put on coarse blue country-garb, trimmed his hair shorter, and dyed that and his beard and eyebrows with henna. Ere he took horse, he was sent for again to the Vicar's chamber. 'Well, scab, are you busked and ready?'

'So please your highness.'

'Come, you shall drink some malmsey for stirrup-cup:' he poured it out, gave it him with his own hand. He put, when Gabriel set down the cup, a great arm about his neck, drawing him to him, and so looked down into the weasel eyes of him: 'I did wrong to strike at you. There,' he said, holding him off at arm's length: 'when, until now, said I ever to you or any man that I was sorry for aught I'd done? But truth is, you were right in reason, my pug. And truth is, I cannot well digest reason in this particular, for truly I cannot root out of me the liking I have for the man; having both already made my profit by him and wishing still so to do; and yet, little commodity I see in't, as things sort. And yet,' he said, 'I have a kind of love for the man.'

Gabriel stood awkward, listening to these words, that seemed as the rumour of some fight conduced in the very soul of his great master.

'Fare you well, then,' said the Vicar.

'Highness, farewell,' said Gabriel. 'And as for loving,' he said, as upon a sudden bursting of the doors of speech, 'be certain of this: your highness cannot now afford to bear love or liking to any: no, not even to me.'

It was now upon mid-July. The Vicar, with some thousand heavy-armed troops of Rerek, was come up to Mornagay. Here Gabriel, back from his mission, was two days closeted with his lord. None knew, nor none guessed nor sought to know, what might be there a-hatching between them; for in all things, in peace as in war, it was the Vicar's custom so to deal closely with this man or with Lessingham if he were at hand, but with others seldom or never.

Upon the thirteenth, Gabriel rode north again, now in a new disguise and with beard and mustachios shaved clean off. That same day, as the Gods would have it, came Lessingham riding post from Bardardale. He took day-meal; would not tarry, spite of the Vicar's wish to stay him, but saddle up again and on north-ward; being by appointment to meet with Barrian and Prince Ercles beyond Swaleback, for concerting of certain movements against next week's beginning of the great march north. This the pretext: but the true necessity was upon word from Barrian that this should do great good now, if Lessingham might but with the sunbeams of his countenance be finally his own peacemaker for all back-reckonings those princes yet held noted against him, as for plunder of Bagort that spring and the bad entreaty Ercles had had at Leveringay.

Lessingham rode with but five-and-twenty and Amaury. About the fifteenth mile, midway on from Leveringay to Eldir, they happed upon Gabriel, pricking fast, two or three hundred paces ahead. He, when he saw them, turned out of the road and made down towards that boggy bottom where a bridle-path, going among fields and then among woods, cuts off a large loop of the main north road. That, if the waters had not been up, had been the best way: but not so now. All saw him, but through that disguise Lessingham only knew him. Lessingham said apart to Amaury, 'This jackal hath seen us: it is plain he would be glad to avoid me. I like not that.' He bade the others wait while he alone galloped after Gabriel. Gabriel, when he saw he was followed and could not escape, drew rein and waited.

'If I could know you under these mumming weeds, and beardless as a pig,' Lessingham said, 'you sure knew me? Why run away then? What hath so uncivil'd you?'

'Nay, by the Gods I knew not your worship.'

Lessingham's glance seemed like that winter wind that will go clean through a man, clothes and body and all. 'So you begin with a lie, my Gabriel? We'll talk further, then: see wherefore truth's so coy today.' At first Gabriel's answers came pert and pat: then he began to trip amid the threads of his own invention: at last, tied up in a knot of plain contradictions, could no more, but stood ridiculous with all the tangle of his lies made manifest. Then, to cap ill with worse, he upon a swift chance struck spurs into his horse to flee. In a moment Lessingham had ridden him down: caught him by the collar. 'I smell a pad in the straw: come, we'll search you.' Gabriel, while this went forward, by a swift sleight crammed a crumpled paper in his mouth. Lessingham forced open his mouth: made him spit it out like a dog: took him such a cuff across the head as knocked him half-stunned from the saddle: sprang to earth, secured the paper, spread it and read it. Gabriel, standing up quakingly and gathering his senses, shrank under Lessingham's look; for there was in the countenance of Lessingham as he laid up the half-chewed paper like some jewel in his bosom, that blazing of eyes, that same deathly white paleness of terrible anger, which Gabriel had once before beheld; and that was when Lessingham, chained and under the strength of six men's hands, had been, in that helplessness, shamefully by the Vicar stricken across the face with the Concordat of Ilkis.

'This is private,' said Lessingham, ''twixt your lord and me. No living soul else shall know on't. So much for your ease of mind.' So saying, he caught him by the throat: shook him thrice and again until the eyes of Gabriel began to bulge from his blood-boiled choking face, then threw him cruelly on the ground. 'When I break my rod,' he said, 'it shall be on a bigger back than yours.'

Gabriel, may be as conceiving it safest to feign death, did not move till Lessingham was mounted again.

Lessingham rode but a score of paces to have sight again of his folk, where they waited some quarter of a mile away: made sign to Amaury he should come alone; then leisurely returned to where Gabriel stood afeared. Amaury galloped up to them: halted, looked obedient at Lessingham, then fierce at Gabriel. 'Tell them, Amaury, this was but a messenger sent to seek me and had missed us in the way, so luckily overtaken, with word from my lord Chancellor upon which I must myself return for a night. You and the rest, ride forward; bring my excuses to Prince Ercles. Expect me in two days at most in Memmering.' Amaury read notice, in his lord's mask of careless ease, of some great matter toward: read notice, too, not but at his peril to be called in question, that in this thing his part should be but to hear exactly and exactly to obey. Lessingham with a light word farewelled him, and turned south again at a walking-pace alone. When they were out of sight, he touched rein, whispered Maddalena: she carried him south like the wind.

In the long meadow-close below the northerner of the out-farms of Mornagay, as Lessingham rode in, were Rossilion, Thrasiline, and others, casting at the mark with javelins for their sport. 'Why, 'tis like a masque,' said Rossilion: 'one fresh pageant after another. First, but an hour since, message to say the Duke and all his great army, seven days afore the day appointed, is come up now and shall be before sunset here in Mornagay; and now, back cometh the Captain-General.'

'The eagles gather,' said Thrasiline. 'Sure, now shall be do somewhat.'

The Vicar came by as Lessingham dismounted before the hostelry. In Lessingham's look he might read no danger, nor (knowing of old these sudden swift turns and changes of settled order) need he marvel if, set forth but three hours since for the north upon urgency and in company, Lessingham were now in great haste come south again. 'Cousin, there is a business I must utter to you. Will your highness give me private audience?' The Vicar consenting with a shrug, they retired themselves to that same upper room where, more than a year ago, Lessingham and Amaury had supped that night when news came of King Styllis dead, and all the balance of affairs tipped above new deeps of peradventure: a room of beginnings and of memories.

Three of the Vicar's great dogs lay there in the rushes. There was wine upon the table, and drinking-cups: on the settle, the Vicar's armour: goose-feather pens, ink, papers, parchments, all Gabriel's writing-tackle, in a hodge-podge upon the sideboard. Lessingham said, 'Who will write you your so many letters, cousin, whiles your secretary maketh up secret treaties betwixt you and Derxis?'

There was not a tremor in the Vicar's great hand, reaching the wine-jug, pouring a cupful. 'Nimble and quicksilvered brains such as yours need this to settle 'em: quiddling upon such moonshine.'

Lessingham struck the cup from his hand. 'Did you not hear something cry thump?' he said upon the crash, as the Vicar, eyes aflame, leapt to his feet. 'Come, I'll read it you: here 'tis, under your hand and seal.' He watched the Vicar, at the pulling out of the paper, change colour. 'Ay, spittly and slimy too from the beast's mouth I plucked it out on. But legible.'

'Go, you are a fool. Counterfeit letters. My fine device to draw him out.'

'Prettily thought on,' said Lessingham. 'Tell me the crow is white.'

The Vicar, with the table between himself and Lessingham, and eyeing him from beneath bent forehead, began to move with a sidelong motion leftwards towards the door. But Lessingham, swift as a leopard, was there before him, hand upon sword-hilt. His left hand shot home the bolt behind him. 'Had you been drunk so long you'd a done your estate better service. Plot treason? Is't come to this? And with this princox, voice like a woman, this filth of filths, this murderer of—'

'O leave your cackling,' said the Vicar, hand upon sword-hilt, head down, like a bull about to charge. 'Thought you, while you played your games at put-pin, I'd sit idle for ever? I'll tell you, here's been small leisure for kissing and haking in Owldale this five month past, by the Gods!'

Lessingham's sword flamed out: the Vicar's too. 'Loo! Loo! Tear him! Pyewacket! Peck-i'-the-crown! Tear his lights out!' As the dogs rushed in from the side, Pyewacket, as moved by a friendship strangely struck in that dungeon under Laimak, fastened her teeth in the backside of one, so that, missing of his spring, with a howl of pain he turned to fight her. Another, Lessingham stabbed dead with a dagger snatched left-handed from his belt; but, since a man's eyes look but one way, the Vicar, foining at Lessingham's middle, passed under his guard; but, by good hap, no more than a skin-wound beside the thigh. Amid the rage of the dogs yet worrying and snarling, and the charging against the door by soldiers without, whom the Vicar now in a voice of brass shouted for again and again to come and aid him, Lessingham, free now, albeit hurt, to use his swordsmanship, in a few passes sent the Vicar's weapon flying.

The Vicar, crouching like a cat-a-mountain, seemed for the instant as if he would have leapt onto Lessingham's sword-point. But the hinges began to yield under that thunder of blows, and, as lord of his mind once more, he reared himself up and, stone still and with arms folded, faced Lessingham, who, regarding him again in a high and cool carelessness that was yet alert for all mischiefs, now sheathed his sword. The door gave and fell. A dozen men armed leapt in with it. In the sudden hush of that obstreperous noise the Vicar commanded them, pointing with his finger: 'Arrest me that man.'

For two breaths they stood doubtful. Then, one by one as their glances met Lessingham's, so one by one they were gathered by him and held. 'You have won the wager, cousin,' he said, throwing with a laugh his purse of gold on the table. 'And truth to tell, I feared you would. Not your own men, at your own bidding, will so far forget your highness's edict as lay hand upon the King's Captain-General.'

With swift comprehension, the Vicar, bursting into a great boisterous laugh, clapped him on the back, took the purse, tossed it up ringing in the air, caught it, and thrust it away in his bosom.

When they were alone again, 'Well, fanged adder?' said Lessingham, speaking low; 'so you dare try masteries with me? So you set your dogs on me, ha?' Pyewacket, looking up at him, fawned and wagged her tail; 'set your men on me?'

The Vicar, sitting at the table sideways, left hand akimbo on his hip, right elbow crooked far forward on the table top, the hand a rest for his mighty jowl, looked steadily up at Lessingham. 'You have forgot your part,' he said, and his voice, low and quiet, came like the dank air from some grave. 'And your hand is out.'

To Lessingham, thus looking down into the eyes of his cousin, it was as if their hard and adamantine lustre and wicked fires should have been but the image upon a still water, in depths whereof, were no image there to veil them, deadlier matters should have been beheld. And now, as upon that surface, memories stirred like a flaw of wintry air, blurring the image: memories of a voice which, a year ago, borne up loud and hoarse over water, had unsphered a summer night and withered fair flesh to a mountain-lynx's pelt and sinew and claw.

The Vicar seemed to wait. There seemed a contentment in his waiting, as of one that had weighed all and all determined. But to questioning eyes his countenance showed no answer. As well might a man, looking from the fields across to Laimak, have hoped to divine, only with such looking, the prison-houses that lay quarried in the rock's bowels: the prisoners, their names, qualities, aspects, and conditions, who rotted in those prisons: the deaths some died there.

'By God, then, I will teach you,' Lessingham said. 'By God, I will tread you under feet. Come, you shall be my secretary. Write,' he said, thrusting from Gabriel's table the means before him, and taking out, to read from it, the damning document: ''tis well enough worded, do it out fair. "Unto the most high king" – foh! The words foul my mouth. On then: your own invention: out with it: all the sweet persuasive points, the special trust and affiance he hath in

you, as fitted by nature for rapes and treasons and all villany: let
not the filth be in doubt, you are his good jade, hate us all, too,
'cause of your quondamship: let him but trap you in gold, quid
pro quo, vicariate and so forth, as here set down, and you'll have
us all murdered with bodkins pat o' the eve of his coming south
hither: and now, time that for Mornagay, night o' the first new
moon in August. Write,' he said, and it was as if the rehearsing
only of the thing had blown his cooling rage to great flames again
within him. 'We shall be ready. O this is double treason! Lure him
like a polecat to the gin.'

The Vicar in all this moved not at all. Only across his eyes,
adder-like, resting on Lessingham, it was as if a film had been
drawn, veiling the unfoldings of his thought; and along the lips
of him something, the scales whereof glinted colours of mockery,
gaiety, and disdain, seemed to draw its subtle length. At last, taking
up the pen, he with awkward slow unclerkly fingers began to write
under Lessingham's eye. When it was done he pushed it towards
Lessingham, who took and read it. 'Is it fit?'

Lessingham read. 'It will serve.'

'Reach me the wax,' said the Vicar. 'A candle: so.' He sealed it.
'What safe hand now have you to bear it? There's heading business in this were't wrongly handled. Where's Gabriel?'

'Give it to me,' Lessingham said. 'I'll be bearer of both.' The Vicar
gave it in silence. In silence their eyes engaged. Then first this paper,
then that (which Gabriel had disgorged), Lessingham held in the
candleflame: scornfully beheld them catch fire, curl up, flare, burn
down, fall in black ashes. 'Ah, cousin, am I yet to teach you,' he said,
'that I do that I will do, not upon condition of this and that, as use
your bungerly foul plots, but in my own way, and with clean hands?'

He turned and went. The Vicar, watching his passage to the
door, the sweep of his cloak, the carriage of his head, the swing
of his gait to the clanking of golden spurs, narrowed his lids to
a gaze serpently shrewd. So, left alone, in a sullen grandeur of
storm-tormented sea-cliff against which every great wave that rides
crashes and falls broken, he sat, and waited.

*   *   *

In the same hour came Gabriel Flores. The Vicar sat yet in his chamber. Gabriel came tiptoe to the table. 'Highness, spake my Lord Lessingham aught to you of the letter I bare? Upon my soul, I would a died sooner—' Here, upon his knees he blubbered out the story.

'Well,' said the Vicar when it was done: 'give you your due, you did all you might. This but shows I'd better a holden to my resolve, spite of all, to put nought in writing.'

'There's this,' Gabriel said: 'not a soul hath knowledge of the thing except you and me and his lordship. Not Amaury, I know: they spake not together but in my presence, I swear to you, and then one rode north, t'other south to you. Hath your highness the paper?'

'I have both had it and burnt it.'

'Good so far,' said Gabriel; then paused. His furtive gaze came again under his master's eye. 'Lord, I pray you, 'tis but my love and service speaketh: be not angry. But must your highness not fear lest he will not thus leave you, nor your part in this, undiscovered?'

The Vicar looked down upon him. 'The Duke,' he said, 'with five thousand men, will be here afore sunset.' He paused. Gabriel met his eye and trembled. 'And so, my nobs and cony sweet, infix your mind to virtue and prudence: employment in a work shall please your disposition, and upon a very small warning. Look you, the skies do thunder. My cousin Lessingham: let not the Duke nor any of these come at him, on your life.'

Gabriel bared his teeth like a stoat. 'What means shall I use?'

'All means, so nor you nor I be not seen in it. Give me notice in some secret sort when you have prepared the thing.'

Gabriel gave a little laugh. There was a fell and ugly look on the face of him.

'How now?' said the Vicar, 'are you afeared?'

'Of your highness somewhat. Not of aught else.'

'The deed is meritorious.'

'Ay. I trow it should not much go to my heart so that another did it. But would your highness would give a name to the deed. I durst not go by guess.'

'Will you play bodger with me, you scurvy scrub? Is not your life mine? Standeth there aught but my might and my name 'twixt you and a hundred men that have no dearer wish than your heart were leaping in their hand? Will you traffic with me, filth?'

'Your highness knoweth my inward mind,' replied he. 'I would but be sure you know your own: will not repent and tear me in pieces, who did you this service, when 'tis done.'

'Go, I'll tell you,' said the Vicar. 'There is i' the camp here, and walked from this chamber not ten minutes since, one that hath today with so many and vile injuries abused me and borne me such derision as, not were he set upon the inflexible purpose to destroy himself might he a done more. I will use him no longer. Choose your instrument: let him think this is done i' the Duke's service; that there have been promises he caused to be performed in these late peace-makings to the feeblishment of the duchy; that the Duke will reward it if the person be made away.'

Gabriel looked at him: ran his tongue along his lips. 'I have a lad for the work, manful of mind, but as wise as a woodcock. How likes your highness this pleasantness, to do it in sight of the Duke before they may come to speech together? And I being by, soon as the stroke is struck, will, in a seeming indignation to revenge it, stab the striker, and so, sith dead men tell no tales—?'

'Enough. Away and to it. And the Devil and the whirlwind be your helpers.'

Gabriel went. The Vicar, sitting awhile in his melancholy with the westering sun beginning now through the window to shine into his eyes, yielded his hand to Pyewacket's nuzzling cold nose and restfully with his fingers searched her jowl and behind her ear. 'Ay, my brach,' he said in himself: 'I'll not blame you to a ta'en his part, all and it had been easier otherways. Dead men, quotha?' he said in himself after a minute, and the wings of his nostrils hardened suddenly. 'May be, poor pug, you counselled me more wholesomely than you bargained for.'

The day was near spent when the Duke with the forward of his army began their winding ascent by the Killary road towards

Mornagay. The Vicar, with Lessingham and a dozen other of his gentlemen about him, came a little upon the road to bring him in with honour. Before the hostelry where they lodged, a score of trumpeters took their stand, and bagpipers wearing the Parry's livery of russet and purple, and drummers, and fifty spearmen to be a guard of honour, and bearers of the banners of Fingiswold and Rerek: all in a golden magnificence of the declining sun, and in a windless summer stillness. The Vicar was in his robes of state, and bare-headed, save for his circlet of gold: Lessingham, upon his right, went armed to the throat, but without his helm. Gabriel Flores, like a shadow, kept step with his lord, a little behind, and betwixt the two of them.

'You look merry, cousin,' said the Vicar as they walked.

'Not merry,' Lessingham answered: 'contented.'

'With that you have? or with that you look to?'

'Contented,' answered Lessingham, 'that all sorteth now to wished effect: power where, were it mine to give, I would give it; and our sword, not now to be escaped neither eluded, lifted up against our enemy.' Upon that word, there seemed a triumph to clothe him, such as stars wear riding between clouds in a gale at sea, when all perils of night and shipwreck are become but a carpet unrolled for those flaming feet to walk on. His eye, as from that pinnacled certitude, met the Vicar's, that till now had avoided the encounter.

They halted. The Duke on his white pawing stallion, with the Chancellor upon his right and the Meszrian lords in great splendour about him, was approached now within twenty paces and still came on. Trumpeters sounded the royal salute. In Gabriel's secret ear the Vicar flung a sudden word: 'I have changed my mind. Prevent it.' In this, at ten paces' distance, Barganax and Lessingham met eye to eye. And even as Barganax a year ago in Acrozayana had, upon such an eye-glance, seemed to behold very incarnate in Lessingham the masculine of his own dark lady and queen of his desires, so Lessingham now, in a slow astonishment to master body and soul, beheld in Barganax the like marvel; and then, in a moment, as night is opened for a flash with lightning, not that masculine, but, as to carry perfection beyond perfection, her, very Antiope: given back, for that flash, in this world-without-end sunset hour of Mornagay, this place of beginnings and of endings.

Gabriel was too late. The murderer, shouting, 'This from the great Duke of Zayana!' sent it down a foot deep into Lessingham between neck and gorget. In the same instant Gabriel, swift upon his cue, had despatched the doer of the deed beyond justification, repentance, or confession. The Vicar, amid the sudden huge turmoil, smiting left and right with his hand-mace, struck with the one stroke his kinsman's slayer, that reeled butchered already by Gabriel's sword, and with the other his last imaginable danger extant and repository of his secret treason: Gabriel Flores. Whose brains, as serviceable unto this extremity, but now no further, to the master he had so faithfully nursed and obeyed, were thus, for last warranty of that master's safety, spattered unregarded upon the grass.

But the Vicar, that had for this safety so much adventured and so much cast away, looking up, swift from these strokes, into Barganax's face, stood as a man at whose feet suddenly opens the abyss. For there glared upon him out of that face not Barganax's eyes, but eyes speckled and grey: the eyes of Lessingham.

And Barganax, in a voice like a great crack of thunder, commanded them, 'Take the Vicar!'

XXII

ZIMIAMVIAN NIGHT

ANTIPHONE TO DAWN • HER INFINITE VARIETY •
'MORE THAN WAS PROMISED OR WAS DUE' •
MOONSET BETWEEN THE WORLDS.

FIORINDA, in the Duke's private lodging that looks from the citadel over Zayana lake, set down her crystal, having beheld that end. The eye of day stared red now from a split in the clouds that shrouded up the evening, west over Ambremerine; in which glare of settle-gang, all the element was become as a flame: tongues of it licking the folds and falls of the damask table-cloth: sparks of it in momentary death and birth upon every shining surface of knife or fork, goblet, platter, or smooth-skinned fruit: smoke of it invading the dimness of Barganax's bedchamber which, within part-opened folding doors, stood void and dream-fast as upon memories of so many sunsets, and of lamplight times, and pleasure, and sleep, and dawn, and the long interludes of clear daylight emptiness which is, for beds, their night-time and time of reposing. And in the proud pallour of that lady's brow and cheek, and in the exaltation of her carriage, the glory sat throned, gleaming again from her jet-black seat-waved hair; and of it some touch or savour was in the terrible and unfathomable eyes of her, as she stood so, and upon such tidings, gazing from that high western window into the conflagration of the west.

So she stood, while night gathered. Colour began to fail before
the shades, both here in the room with its so many rarities of
gold-broidered curious hangings, rich and costly treasures of
furniture, and lilied golden chapiters of pillars and gold-wrought
ceiling; and, without, in the lake stretching dim, and in the mountains companying with clouds and frozen immensities of night,
and in the flowers of Barganax's gardens folding their petals for
sleep. 'So falls a thundered tower,' she said. From some pine-branch
in the garden beneath, a nightjar thrilled. 'No self – but All,' she
said.

She took a taper: lighted it where the fire was dying on the
hearth: lighted the candles. Wine was on the table, and crystal
beakers. She filled one and held it up, crowned with foam, between
her eye and the candles, watching the beads mount upwards:
through a golden element, atomies of golden fire. She quaffed it
down and turned to the looking-glass. And now, with movements
swift, yet of an easy staid nobility of sequence as when the leafage
of a wood sways to the wind in summer, loosing of girdle and
brooch and pin, she put off her ruby-spangled red silken dress
and all raiment else, and so, in that mixed light of candles and
afterglow, fronted in a stillness her own image in the glass. With
a strange look she beheld it, like as a year ago last May, in that
other great mirror within, at dawn she had beheld it, upon the
morrow of his twenty-fifth birthday: a distant, appraising look.
With such an eye might her lover himself have considered not
her, but one of those many portraitures he painted of her and
had smudged then or slashed to oblivion, as being not her, or at
least not her enough. But not with such lips. For that which,
sleeping or waking, held licence of the lips of that lady, inhabiting
the corners of her mouth: a thing once bottled by him in paint
but straight let out again: this woke and viewed in the glass now
its own superlative, which thence, with a sidelong look, acknowledged her.

'Fiorinda,' she said. 'Mary,' she said. 'Antiope.' The names
remained on the silence like ripples on still water. She took out
the pins one by one, and let down in floods of blackness her

hair; and so, yet gazing in the glass, settled upon a couch that faced it, her feet along the couch, her right hand making a rest for her cheek. So in the mirror she regarded for another while with flickering eyelids that which was of itself mirror of all wonders; her beauty-clad naked body, awful as mountains in the dawn, and completing and making up in its Greek perfection quintessences of night and of scented gardens and of glory of sun and moon, and, in eyes, the sea. With hands clasped behind her head, she leaned back now upon the cushions of honey-coloured silk, watching in the glass her image, which now began to change. And so watching, she named the changes by names whereof but the spoken sound is a train of fire, beauty across darkness: Pentheseleia, Lydian Omphale, Hypermnestra, Semiramis, Roxana, Berenice; spotless and unparagoned Zenobia, Queen of Palmyra, Queen of the East, for so long time matched against the overmastering odds of imperial Rome, and in the end triumphed on yet not dishonoured; Gudrun of Laxriverdale; Petrarch's Laura; Boccaccio's Fiammetta; Giulia Farnese, Vittoria Corombona, and the white and deadly blossom of the house of Borgia. Even, passing all these, her for whom Trojans and well-greaved Achaians so long time suffered sorrows; and (mother of her), that Argive Queen, lovely-ankled Leda, and other earth-born paramours of Olympian Zeus. And with every change, it was as if the likeness in the mirror was yet her own, or, at least, part of her.

Her left hand, lazily fallen behind the milk-white somnolent supple grandeur of her thigh, chanced between couch and cushion upon a book there, slipped down and forgotten. Drawing it forth, she opened it and knew the writing: Greek upon the left, Barganax's Englishing of it upon the right:

ποικιλόθρον᾽ ἀθἀνατ᾽ Ἀφροδιτα,
παῖ Διος, δολόπλοκε, λισσομαι σε

So far she read, softly, aloud, in a voice that took on, with the Poetess's words, a more diviner grace, as with a letting

through, by some momentary rift between time and eternity,
of some far-off cadence of the honey-sweet imperishable
laughter:

'Sparkling-thronéd heavenly Aphrodite,
Child of God, beguilder of guiles, – beseech You,
Not with sating, neither with ache and anguish,
            Lady, my heart quell.

Nay, but come down, if it be true indeed that
Once to cry of mine from a far place list'ning
You did hark and, leaving Your Father's golden
            House, did come down with

Chariot yok'd and harness'd, and so in beauty
O'er the black earth swift-flying doves did draw You,
Filling high heav'n full of the rush of wing-beats
            Down the mid ether.

Swift, and they were vanisht. But You, most blessed,
Smil'd with eyes and heavenly mouth immortal,
Asking me what suffer'd I then, or why then
            Call'd I on You, and

What, all else beyond, I desir'd befall me,
In my wild heart: "Who shall, at My sweet suasion,
Even thee lead into her love? Who is't,
            O Sappho, hath wrong'd thee?

For, though she fly, presently she shall seek thee;
Ay, though gifts she'll none of, yet she shall give then;
Ay, and kiss not, presently she shall kiss thee,
            All and unwilling."

Very now come so, and, from cares that tangle,
Loose; and whatsoever to bring to pass my

Heart hath thirsted, bring it to pass; and be Your-
Self my great ally.'

She stood up, saying again, in Her beauty-blushing orient, those
last words again:

'Σὺ δ'αὐτα
σύμμαχος έσσο'

'Yes; for so will I be petitioned,' said She. 'Yes; and by such great
mettled and self wild hawks, which fall and perish in their height.
I promise: do I not perform? O more than either was promised
or was due.'

Upon a table by the couch, in a golden bowl, were roses, withered and dead. She took one and held it, like Cleopatra's aspick,
to the flower of Her own breast. And, as if to show upon experiment that in that place nothing but death can die and corruption
self-corrupted fall like a foul garment to leave perfection bare, all
the starved petals of the rose, shrivelled and brown, opened into
life again, taking on again the smoothness and softness of the flesh
of a living flower: a deep red rose, velvet-dark that the sense should
ache at it, with a blueness in its darkest darknesses, as if the heavy
perfume clung as a mist to dull the red.

As the wind whispers cool through apple-boughs, and sleep
streams from their trembling leaves, She spoke again: 'One day of
Zimiamvia, my Lord Lessingham; one day, my lord Duke. And
what is one, in My sight? Did not you say it: *Still about cock-shut
time? – Safe in the lowe of the firelight*: Have not I promised it?
And now is time for that.

'For now Night,' She said, scarce to be heard, 'rises on
Zimiamvia. And after that, Tomorrow, and Tomorrow, and
Tomorrow, of Zimiamvia. And all of Me. What you will. For ever.
And if it were possible for more than for ever, for ever more.'

Upon the sudden, She put on Her full beauty, intolerable, that
no eye can bear, but the heart of Her doves turns cold, and they
drop their wings. So the eternal moment contemplates itself anew

beside the eternal sea that sleeps about the heavenly Paphos. Only
She was: She, and the hueless waiting wonder of the sea at
daybreak, and Her zephyrs, and Her roses, and Her hours with
their frontlets of gold.

In that high western room in Acrozayana, the transfiguring
glory passed. So shuts darkness behind a meteor that, sliding out
of darkness silently between star and star in a splendour to outface
all the great lamps of heaven, slides beneath stars silently into the
darkness and is gone.

The Lady Fiorinda turned to the sideboard beyond the mirror.
Its polished surface was dulled under the dust of neglect. There
lay there a sword of Barganax's, a pair of her crimson gloves, a
palette of his with the colours dried up on it, and a brush or
two, uncleaned, with the paint clogged stiff in their bristles; and
among these toys, two or three pear-shaped drops of coloured
glass, one blue, another red, another purple of the nightshade,
no bigger than sloes and with long thin tadpole tails, such as
are called Rupert's drops. She, upon a remembrance, took one
daintily and between jewelled fingers snapped off the end of its
tail, and saw the drop crash instantly into dust. So she dealt with
another and beheld it shatter: another, and beheld that: so, till
all were ruined; and so stood for a while, looking upon their
ruin, as if remembered of the saying of that old man. At last,
she went to the window and stood, and so after a time sat down
there in the window, upon cushions of cloth of gold. Her face,
turned side-face to the room and the warmth, was outlined against
night that rolled up now filthy and black. When, after a long
time, She spoke as if in a dream, it might have been Her own
Poetess herself speaking out of the darkness in the high between
the worlds:

> ʻΔέδυκε μέν ἁ σελαννα
> καὶ Πλμιαδες, μέσαι δέ
> νύκτες, παρὰ δ' ἔρχετ᾽ ὤρα,
> ἔγω δέ μόνα κατεύδω.

The moon is set, and set are
The Pleiades; and midnight
Soon; so, and the hour departing:
And I, on my bed – alone.

Motionless She sat: Her gaze downward: upper lids level and still: eyes still and wide. There was no sound now save in change-less ceaseless rhythm, through the open window of the Duke's great bedchamber and the open door that led there, the land-wash of the sea.

Seeing that Her thoughts are higher than our thoughts, it were the part of a fool to think to comprehend them, or set them down. And yet, very because that they are higher, it sorts not to man to let them go by: rather note such looks and such casts which, upon such nights, have ere this shadowed the outward seeming of Her divinity; as if that impossible were possible, and His hand had failed wherein Her weak perfections lie trembling; or as if the thunder of His power were turned an insensate thing, and His eyes seeled up, and love found but a school-name, and She (for all that nought else is of worth or of verity) found not worth much at last. And as if, under the imagination of such thoughts in Her – Who of Her vernal mere unquestioned I AM recreates and sets Him on high, the patent of Whose omnipotency is but to tender and serve Her – the very heart of the world should be closed with anguish.

As the glory, so now this agony passed, resumed so, with that glory, into Her pavilion of Night.

Χαῖρ' ἑλικοβλέφαρε, γλυκυμείλιχε· δός δ' ἐν ἀῶνι
νίκην τῷδε φέρεσθαι, ἐμὴν δ' ἔντυνον ἀοιδήν.
αὐτὰρ ἐγὼ καὶ Σεῖο καὶ ἄλλης μνήσομ' ἀοιδῆς.
                    HYMN TO APHRODITE

NOTE

In Vandermast's aphorisms students of Spinoza will recognize that master's words, charged, no doubt, with implications which go beyond his meaning. Readers who have a holiday place, as in some isle of Ambremerine, among the rare surviving pages of Sappho, will note that, quite apart from quotations, I have not scrupled to enrich my story with echoes of her: this for the sufficient reason that she, above all others, is the poet not of 'that obscure Venus of the hollow hill' but of 'awful, gold-crowned, beautiful Aphrodite.'

As for the verses, all originals, except as noted below, are mine, as also, except as noted, are all translations. Baudelaire's *Le Balcon*, which appears on a fly-leaf as a kind of motto, is so apt (even in details) to fulfil that function that it is well to note that I never read it until after this book was written. Lessingham's reference to it ('reine des adorées' in *Rialmar in Starlight*), was added on final revision.

With one exception, the references for the *Sappho* quotations are to H. T. Wharton's edition (John Lane, 1898). In the corrupt third line of the fifth stanza of the *Ode to Aphrodite* (Ch. 22) I have taken the amended text adopted by the *Loeb Classical Library*.

Three friends of mine I can never thank as I would: Keith Henderson, for enriching this book with decorations which in an almost magical way have caught its moods and spirit: George Rostrevor Hamilton, for reading and re-reading it in manuscript and giving me the benefit of his delicate judgement and constructive criticism on a hundred points of importance: Gerald Ravenscourt Hayes for a like assistance, and also for his delightful maps which should help readers in picturing to themselves the country where the action takes place. Last I am much obliged for permission given me by Messrs Heinemann to quote (in the *Overture)* from Swinburne's *Ballad of Death;* by Mr Claude Colleer Abbott and his publishers to quote from his fascinating collection of *Early Mediaeval French Lyrics* (Constable, 1932); and by the Clarendon Press to use the text of Mark Alexander Boyd's 'Sonet', printed in *The Oxford Book of English Verse.* For the *Webster* quotations I follow the text of Mr F. L. Lucas's magnificent edition (Chatto & Windus, 4 vols., 1927).

OVERTURE	*A Ballad of Death*	Swinburne, *Poems and Ballads, First Series.*
	'Ici gît Clarimonde'	Théophile Gautier, *La Morte Amoureuse.*
CH. II	*'Bitter-sweet'*	Sappho, 40.
CH. X	*'In a dream I spake'*	Sappho, 87.
	'Thou, and My servant Love'	Sappho, 74.
	'Gondul and Skogul the Goths'-God sent'	Eyvind Skaldspiller (fl. circ. 970 AD) *Hákonarmál.*
CH. XII	*'O we curl'd-haird men'*	Webster, *Vittoria Corombona,* Act IV, sc. 2.
	'That Friend a Great mans ruine strongly checks'	Webster, *Duchess of Malfi,* Act III, sc. 1.
CH. XV	*'Gold is pure of rust'*	Sappho (Loeb Classical Library) *Lyra Graeca,* I, fr. 109 (conjectural).
	'Li rosignox est mon père'	Early French.
	'I love delicacy'	Sappho, 79: transl. Wharton.
CH. XVII	*'The prophetic soul of the wide world'*	Shakespeare, Sonnet CVII.
	'Bitter-sweet'	Sappho, 40.
	'Por la bele estoile'	Early French.
	'Fra bank to bank'	Mark Alexander Boyd (1563-1601).

CH. XVIII	'Evening Star, gath'rer of all'	Sappho, 95.
	'Not clearly knowing'	Homer, *Hymn to Aphrodite*, I. 167.
	'Se'j'avoie ameit un jor'	Early French.
	'Ah, lad, and were't but so'	Homer, *Iliad*, xii, 322-8.
CH. XX	'Enn Freki renna'	Völospá (in the *Elder Edda*).
CH. XXII	'Sparkling-throned heavenly Aphrodite'	Sappho, 1.
	'The moon is set'	Sappho, 52.

P.S. For two small errors in the maps I am responsible, viz. (1) the misspelling of 'Tabarey Sound', and (2) the omission of the route taken by the Admiral *east* of Ridinghead, and his attack on that position from the east.

E. R. E.

DRAMATIS PERSONAE

THE action in Chapter I begins on 22nd April, *Anno Zayanae Conditae* 777, about ten months after the death, in the 54th year of his age, in his island fortress of Sestola in Meszria, of the great King MEZENTIUS, tyrant of Fingiswold, Meszria, and Rerek.

In this list the number of the chapter where each person is *first* mentioned is given in brackets after his or her name.

BARGANAX	(I)	Duke of Zayana, bastard son to King Mezentius.
LESSINGHAM	(O.)	Cousin german to the Vicar.
ANTIOPE	(III)	Daughter to King Mezentius, sister to King Styllis, and half sister to Barganax.
FIORINDA	(II)	Sister to the Chancellor (her elder by some sixteen years), and a lady of honour at the ducal court of Zayana.
STYLLIS	(I)	King of Fingiswold, Meszria, and Rerek: son of King Mezentius.
DERXIS	(XII)	King of Akkama.
HORIUS PARRY	(I)	Lord of Laimak, and Vicar of the King in Rerek.

JERONIMY	(I)	High Admiral of Fingiswold.	Joint Commissioners for the King in Meszria.
BEROALD	(II)	Chancellor of Fingiswold.	
RODER	(III)	An Earl of Fingiswold.	

ERCLES	(I)	} Princes in northern Rerek
ARAMOND	(I)	
ARCASTUS	(IX)	
BEZARDES	(XIX)	
BRANDREMART	(IX)	
DAIMAN	(XVI)	
GAYLLARD	(XIX)	} Lords and gentlemen of Rerek.
MANDRICARD	(IX)	
MERON	(XIX)	
ROQUEZ	(XIX)	
ROSSILION	(XVI)	
THRASILINE	(XVI)	
BELINUS	(IX)	
BODENAY	(XIII)	Knight Marshal of Fingiswold.
BOSRA	(XV)	Constable in Rialmar after Romyrus.
HORTENSIUS	(IX)	} Lords and gentlemen of Fingiswold.
ORVALD	(XIII)	
PEROPEUTES	(IX)	
ROMYRUS	(XIII)	Constable in Rialmar.
TYARCHUS	(XIII)	
VENTON	(XIII)	
BARRIAN	(III)	
EGAN	(III)	
IBIAN	(IX)	
MEDOR	(II)	A Count in Meszria, captain of Barganax's bodyguard.
MELATES	(III)	} Lords and gentlemen of Meszria.
ZAPHELES	(III)	
ALQUEMEN	(XIII)	} Lords of Akkama.
ESPERVERIS	(XIII)	
KASMON	(XIII)	
ORYNXIS	(XIII)	

AMAURY	(I)	Lieutenant to Lessingham.
GABRIEL		
FLORES	(III)	Secretary to the Vicar.
VANDERMAST	(II)	A learned man, secretary to Barganax.
ZENIANTHE	(XIII)	A Princess of Fingiswold, niece to King Mezentius.
DUCHESS OF		
MEMISON	(II)	Mother to Barganax.

ANAMNESTRA	(XIII)		
HETERASMENE	(XIII)		
MYRILLA	(XIII)	Daughter to the High Admiral.	Ladies at the court of Rialmar.
PAPHIRRHOË	(XIII)		
RAVIAMNE	(XIII)		
COUNTESS OF	(XIII)		
TASMAR			
ZENOCHLIDE	(XIII)		

ANTHEA	(VII)		
BELLAFRONT	(VII)		
CAMPASPE	(VII)		Ladies at the
MYRRHA	(II)		court of
PANTASILEA	(VII)		Zayana.
ROSALURA	(II)	Daughter to Prince Ercles, and wife to Medor.	
VOILANTE	(II)		

LADY MARY LESSINGHAM (O.)

MAPS OF THE THREE KINGDOMS

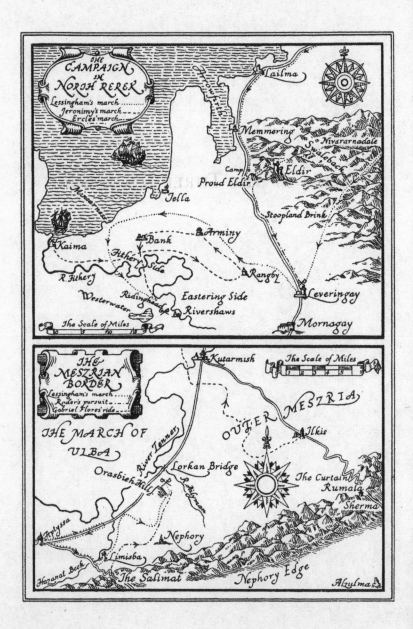

THE
CAMPAIGN
IN
NORTH REREK

Lessingham's march ....
Jeronimy's march ___
Ercles' march ....

The Firth

Tailma

Memmering

Nivararnadale

Swaleback

Campo

Eldir

Proud Eldir

Stoopland Brink

Jella

Mirrowmere

Kaima

Bank

Arminy

Fithery

Side

Rangby

R. Fithery

Ridinghead

Eastering Side

Leveringay

Westerwater

Rivershaws

Mornagay

The Scale of Miles

THE
MESZRIAN
BORDER

Lessingham's march ....
Roder's pursuit ....
Gabriel Flores' ride ....

Kutarmish

The Scale of Miles

THE MARCH OF
ULBA

OUTER MESZRIA

River Zenner

Ilkis

Orasbiek Hill

Lorkan Bridge

R. Rumon

The Curtain

Rumala

Argyssa

Sherma

Nephory

Limisba

Hazanat Beck

The Salimat

Nephory Edge

Alzulma

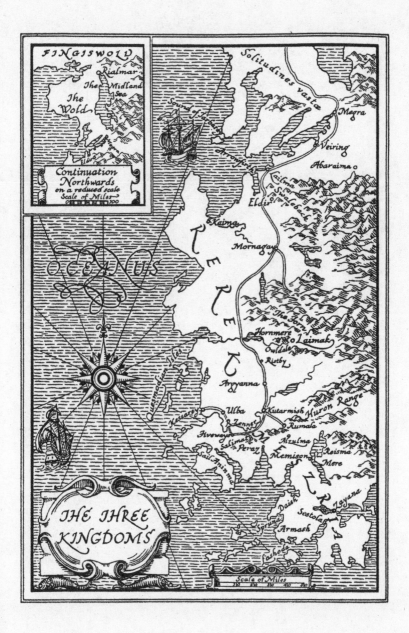

FINGISWOLD

Rialmar

The Midland Sea

The Wold

Continuation
Northwards
on a reduced scale
Scale of Miles
100

Solitudines vasta

Sound of Island

Arrowfirth

Megra

Veiring

Abaraima o

Ceilmar

Swalebak

Eldir

Kaima

Mornagay

OCEANUS

The Torn

Hornmere   o Laimak

Owldale

Ristby

Aryanna

Ulba   Kutarmish

o Zennr   Rumala

Sveaberg   Alzulma

Salim   Peraz   Reisma

Memison   Mere

KEREL

Huron Range

Z R

Teryana

Daish   Sestola

Sprava   Armash

Fashola

THE THREE
KINGDOMS

Scale of Miles

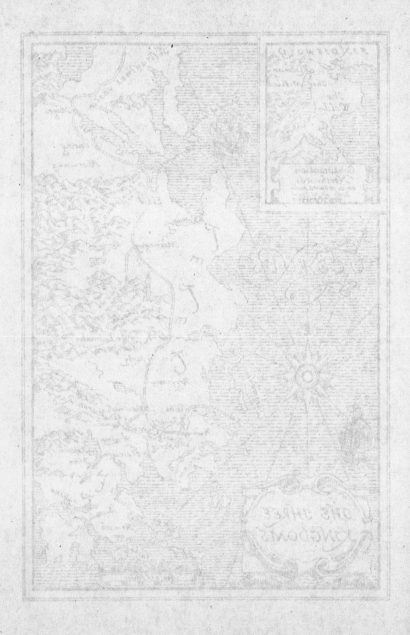